Absolved from Allegiance

Douglas F. Shupinski

BLACK ROSE writing™

The final approval for this literary material is granted by the author.

First printing

This is a work of historical fiction. Apart from the well known actual people, events, and locales that figure in the narrative, all names, characters, places, and incidents are the products of the author's imagination or are used fictitiously. Any resemblance to current events or locales, or to living persons, is entirely coincidental.

ISBN: 978-1-61296-290-0

PUBLISHED BY BLACK ROSE WRITING

www.blackrosewriting.com

Printed in the United States of America

Absolved from Allegiance is printed in Traditional Arabic

Photo Credits: Wendy Shupinski

Map Credits: Wendy Shupinski

Acknowledgments

I would like to sincerely thank the following people for their assistance and support. Ray Iram spent countless hours, reading, editing, and discussing my book with me. His suggested changes to both the content and style were invaluable. Dawn Iram also provided insightful comments in her review of the book. As always, my Mother read my manuscript and pronounced it perfect – that's what mothers do. My three children – Matt, Alex, and Nick – exhibited constant encouragement and interest throughout the writing process. And last, but never, ever least: my beautiful wife, Wendy. For nearly 30 years you have been my source of strength and motivation.

This book is dedicated to the memory of my best friend, Jackson. Even though I know you would have rather been chasing squirrels or eating food off of the table, you sat with me night after night keeping me company. You were truly a man's best friend, and I will always miss you.

Absolved from Allegiance

Uncle Joe,

Thank you for always being my Father's
best friend — and for being an example
to our family of what's possible from
humble beginnings!

I hope you enjoy the book....
Your Favorite Nephew

"...That these United Colonies are, and of Right ought to be Free and Independent States;

that they are **Absolved from all Allegiance** to the British Crown,

and that all political connection between them and the State of Great Britain, is and ought to be totally dissolved..."

The Declaration of Independence

Part One

Boston Area

Captain Thomas Preston

29th Regiment of Foot, British Army

Boston Customs House

10:45 P.M. March 5, 1770

It was obvious that things were quickly getting out of hand.

A furious crowd of between three and four hundred shouting men and boys had quickly surrounded Captain Thomas Preston and his eight British soldiers who were now stranded on the steps of the Customs House in the center of Boston. Preston and seven others had arrived at these steps just a few minutes earlier in relief of Private Hugh White, who had been the lone sentry in this part of the city until just a few minutes ago. White had sent a frantic message to the barracks of the Twenty-Ninth Regiment, pleading for reinforcements. Captain Preston, knowing that Private White was a solid soldier not prone to overreaction, immediately responded by organizing the small relief party that now faced its current situation.

Thomas Preston was himself, by all measures, a man of experience and composure. At the age of forty-eight, he had served for many years in the King's Service, and had seen his share of dangerous situations. However, this was a situation for which he was not prepared. The enemy he was facing was not really the enemy and, therefore, the typical rules of engagement were both precarious and ambiguous.

The crowd had become increasingly vocal and violent in just the last few minutes, as one act of aggression led to another of greater magnitude. Whereas, the mob had initially been satisfied with hurling insults at the British soldiers, this had quickly escalated to snowballs and sticks, and now rocks and other large objects were getting thrown in their direction. At least one of the British soldiers had been struck by these heavy objects, and the situation was becoming more and more dangerous by the moment as his men began to fear for their lives.

Preston briefly tore his eyes away from the menacing crowd and looked down the row of British soldiers who had literally placed their young lives in his hands. The men were trying to remain stoic – after all, to do otherwise would be unbecoming a soldier of the Crown. But the fear was there, just below the surface. It was visible only in their eyes, the place where most men betrayed their true emotions.

"Stay close together, men," Preston shouted above the noise. "Maintain your positions, and stay calm. We shall be receiving reinforcements shortly."

Preston could almost feel the shiver of hope that rippled through his men at the mention of reinforcements, and he briefly felt guilty for having lied to them. The truth was he had no idea if, or when any help would arrive.

The ringing of church bells had continued for several minutes now, their ringing initiated by some unknown party clearly intent on further escalating the riot. This signal usually meant a fire had broken out and was threatening to burn down the city. Hundreds of people had responded to the bells, and the resulting crowds soon jammed the streets around the Customs House, making movement into or out of the area extremely difficult. Captain Preston and his men had been forced to level their bayonets as they moved through the crowd in order to reach the beleaguered Private White standing alone and rattled on the steps of the public building.

But now it was Preston's entire tiny command that was alone and threatened, as the taunts were becoming daring and dangerous.

"C'mon, you cowards, fire!" shouted one man just a few feet away

Douglas F. Shupinski

from the muzzles of the soldiers' muskets.

"Fire, why don't you fire, damn you? You can't kill us," shouted another man, shaking a large club at the soldiers.

In fact, many of the men in the crowd were armed, not with firearms, but with clubs, sticks and, in some cases, cutlasses. As the mob continued to tighten its ring around the soldiers, there was no doubt in the minds of Captain Preston and his men that, given the opportunity, these people would use their primitive weapons.

**

The roots of this unfortunate confrontation had started as far back as a year and a half ago, when British troops had first arrived in Boston for the ostensible purpose of providing order and protection throughout the city. The problem with this was twofold.

First, the addition of two thousand soldiers in a city of less than twenty thousand citizens meant a serious strain on the resources of the population. To make matters worse, the initial plan was for these soldiers to be quartered in the houses of the citizenry. When the outcry against this imposition became so boisterous, the plan was quickly abandoned in favor of placing the troops in public buildings. Still, it did little to placate the men and women of Boston who saw these soldiers as an affront to their independence and ability to manage themselves.

Second, virtually everyone knew that the real reason troops had been brought into Boston was to smother the efforts of the Sons of Liberty, a group of radical colonists whom the British government viewed as potentially hostile, and a threat to its control of the American Colonies. Not surprisingly, these Sons of Liberty had done everything in their power to subvert the authority of this military presence, even going so far as to stir up several minor physical altercations between the townspeople and the soldiers.

But lately, these actions on the part of the Sons of Liberty had become bolder and better coordinated. Just a few weeks earlier on February 22nd, these radicals had planned a demonstration outside the shop of Theophilus Lillie, a man who had remained staunchly loyal to the British government. This demonstration, either by design or mistake, had resulted in a violent clash. Ebenezer Richardson, a neighbor of Lillie's and also a British Loyalist himself, had fired into the crowd of protestors, wounding eleven-year old Christian Seider in the chest and stomach. Carried from the scene back to his house and mother, Christian Seider died at nine o'clock that night.

The effect was both predictable and electrifying. Many people, content to remain neutral up to that point, began taking sides, and many of these forced allegiances were with the radicals. As a result, the coordination of a larger, more violent event by the Sons of Liberty for the fifth of March had been the very essence of ease and simplicity.

***

A man stepped forward out of the crowd in the direction of the soldiers, and got close enough to calmly place his hand on Preston's shoulder. Preston vaguely recognized him as the young man who worked at a local bookshop that he had visited on a number of occasions. Knox was his name, Preston recalled almost absentmindedly; Henry Knox.

"For God's sake take care of your men," Knox begged the captain, "for if they fire your life must be answerable."

"I am well aware of that," Preston replied, unable to keep the agitation out of his voice. He knew that the young man was simply trying to interject some sense of logic into the situation, but right now Preston was in no mood to be lectured.

At that moment a large piece of wood came flying through the air from the back of the crowd, striking Private Montgomery and knocking him to the ground. As he attempted to regain his footing, a dark-skinned man reached out and grabbed at his bayonet, trying to wrench the musket from the Private's hands. Making it to his feet, Montgomery fired his weapon at the man's chest, just as the soldier standing directly to his right did the same.

The effects of these two shots were horrific, as they tore into the chest of their intended target, knocking him backward into the crowd.

Douglas J. Shupinski

One of the musket balls exited the back of the dark skinned man and struck another person standing behind him in the head. The ball had enough remaining velocity to shatter the second man's skull, splattering the people around him with blood and bits of brain.

Both bodies collapsed onto the cold ground, dead before anyone even had the opportunity to come to their aid.

Captain Preston, momentarily shocked at the speed and brutality of the last few seconds, shouted furiously at his men.

"Why did you fire?" Preston yelled at the top of his lungs, but most of his question was lost in the roar of the crowd now brought to its full, deadly potential. All that the soldiers heard was the final word of Preston's outburst.

Several soldiers fired their muskets into the now frenzied crowd, wreaking additional destruction. Across the street from the Customs House, a man was moving away from the scene when one of the musket balls struck him squarely in the back. Collapsing to the ground, he was quickly attended to by several people who attempted to stem the tide of the blood pouring from the gaping wound. But their efforts were worthless, and within minutes the man's lifeless body was surrounded by a ring of deep crimson mixing with the stark white snow.

Still being threatened by the mob, those soldiers that had discharged their weapons had reloaded, and several of them had fired a second round into the crowd. More people were wounded, some quite seriously, and it appeared as if the scene might spin completely out of control into an all-out battle.

At that moment, Thomas Hutchinson, the Lieutenant Governor of Massachusetts, appeared out of the crowd. A young boy had been sent to alert Hutchinson several minutes before the shooting had begun, begging him to come and exercise some form of authority on the situation. While his arrival was too late to avoid the events that had already occurred, at least he could stop any further bloodshed.

"Who is in command here?" Hutchinson demanded as he reached the front of the crowd just a few feet from the soldiers. The crowd continued to roil in the street, but the arrival of someone who clearly had authority had a slight calming effect, and the gap between the people and the soldiers widened by a few yards.

Preston stepped forward and addressed the Lieutenant Governor, whom he knew from previous interactions.

"Captain Preston, sir, of His Majesty's Twenty-Ninth Regiment of Foot," he replied formally, coming to sharp attention.

"Why did you open fire on the crowd without the proper orders?" Hutchinson demanded. What Hutchinson was referring to was that no officer could order his men to open fire in a civil situation without first requesting and receiving permission from the appropriate legal authority. Based on the speed with which events had unfolded that evening, Captain Preston viewed the question as being more than a little ridiculous.

"I did what I felt needed to be done in order to save my sentry," Preston replied defensively, referring to the embattled Private White.

Hutchinson eyed Preston carefully, realizing that at this point he had no understanding of what had actually occurred. Hutchinson knew that jumping to any conclusions, one way or another, could only make a bad situation worse.

Lowering his voice and moving closer to the officer, Hutchinson stated quietly, "You had better be sure, Captain."

Gradually, people began to grudgingly disperse, and when the soldiers departed the steps of the Customs House and returned to their barracks, the focus of the crowd's anger ceased to exist. Like a fire running out of fuel, the crowd sparked and sputtered for a short time longer, eventually melting away into the night.

***

The night may have ended along with the fire of the mob, but it was an event that would smolder in the hearts and minds of people throughout the American Colonies for years to come. The Sons of Liberty, having achieved the fodder for propaganda they had so carefully cultivated, claimed it was absolute proof that the British had nothing but the worst of intentions toward the colonists.

Douglas J. Shupinski

The British, desperately engaging in damage control, claimed that the officers and soldiers involved had acted in self-defense, and could not be blamed for the terrible result. In fact, this proved to be the case, at least from a legal perspective, as all but two of the British officers and soldiers were acquitted of the charges lobbied against them.

Ironically, these accused British soldiers were represented in court by none other than John Adams, one of the most radical members of the Sons of Liberty. When challenged by his colleagues as to why he would do such a thing, Adams replied simply: "If we can prove that a British soldier can receive a fair trial in these Colonies, we have proven that *any* man can receive the same."

A pamphlet claiming to accurately recount the events of the fateful evening was published in England entitled, "A Fair Account of the Late Unhappy Disturbance at Boston in New England." The pamphlet attempted to downplay the role of the British soldiers, and focused on the buildup of tensions throughout the city brought on by the coordinated actions of the Sons of Liberty.

While widely accepted as being balanced and accurate in England, the pamphlet was roundly rejected by the Colonists. To them, the events of March 5, 1770, would forever represent the ultimate in tyrannical behavior, and many individuals previously content to remain passive observers suddenly became active participants in the rebellious atmosphere of New England.

Despite the best efforts of the British government, the event would not be remembered as an "Unhappy Disturbance". For everyone in Boston and throughout the American Colonies; for all of history; this night would forever be known as, "The Boston Massacre".

Private Robert Boyle had his pleasant slumber rudely interrupted by being roughly shaken awake. Choosing to ignore this rather insistent action was the first mistake of what was to be a long and arduous day.

"Wake up, you slimy whore," a voice hissed into his ear, which was followed immediately by a knee being driven violently into his side. Now fully awake, Boyle sat upright on his cot and came face to face with the sneering face of Sergeant Hawkins, his platoon sergeant. The stench of foul breath and rotting teeth just inches away made Boyle gag, and he leaped from his cot onto the wooden floor of the barracks building which had served as his home away from home for several months now.

***

Robert Boyle had been a private in the British army for almost a year and a half, and he couldn't imagine a more miserable existence.

The living conditions were Spartan to say the least, the food was barely edible, and the nature of his daily duties was generally monotonous and mindless. He was supposed to be paid the rather paltry sum of one pound six pence a month, but a significant portion of that was routinely deducted from his pay to cover the cost of uniform accessories and other basic items necessary for daily survival.

Other than the fact that Robert hated virtually every aspect of his life, things seemed to be going fairly well for the twenty year old young man from the heart of London.

Prior to enlisting in the army, Robert Boyle had harbored dreams of becoming an artist. At a very early age he had demonstrated an uncanny ability to draw almost anything he laid his eyes on with such accuracy and detail that people were amazed by his talent. At the age of twelve he had sold his first drawing of a church, which hung in a local clothing shop to this very day. Soon after, he had developed a modest but consistent business, selling sketches of anything people asked him to draw. Boyle had progressed from simple inanimate objects to drawings of people, animals, and landscapes. By the time he was eighteen he was making enough money from his efforts to nicely supplement the family income mostly generated by his father, a stableman for a wealthy London businessman.

It was during a routine visit into one of London's busy marketplaces that the world had changed dramatically for Robert. Carrying five or six of his sketches under his arm carefully wrapped in butcher paper, he had come across an army recruiting party lounging outside a tavern.

"You there!" one of the soldiers had called out to him, "come here a second, boy." Robert had stopped walking down the street and meandered suspiciously in the direction of the tavern.

"Me, sir?" Robert had inquired of the rather grizzled looking man in the scarlet uniform he now faced.

"Yes, you boy. What 'ave you there in that paper, eh? Something illegal, I'll bet!" The man chuckled heartily, and the other soldiers joined in the laughter.

"Oh no, sir, nothing illegal I assure you. These here," Robert explained, as he unwrapped his drawings, "are me pride and joy. You see, I'm an artist."

Robert proudly displayed his sketches to the soldiers, who had suddenly begun to show an increasing interest in the situation. Several of them moved forward and began pointing and commenting to one another, and Robert soon found himself surrounded by the men.

"Why, you're quite the talented lad, ain't ya?" commented the grizzled soldier, and his assessment was met with a chorus of agreements from the other men. "But, I ask you now, do you get bored drawing the same things here in dreary old London?"

Robert, confused by the question, furrowed his brow and responded, "What d'you mean?"

"Why, I would think a man of your abilities shouldn't be confined to drawing what he sees right 'ere in his hometown. Imagine the chance to draw pictures of things all around the world! Imagine the chance to draw the great palaces of Europe and India, or of wild animals and landscapes in America. Why, a man of your talents could become famous by bringing the rest of the world back home to the people unfortunate enough to be stuck 'ere for the rest of their miserable lives!"

The hook had been set and there was no turning back. Before Robert had been able to sharpen another lead on one of his many pencils, he found himself enlisted in the British army, the point of his pencil replaced with the point of a bayonet.

***

Robert's introduction into the army had been a shocking experience. He quickly realized that, while many of the men had willingly enlisted for a variety of personal reasons, many others had been threatened, duped, or simply physically forced to join the British military. It was a game of numbers, and no one seemed to care where the bodies came from, or how they had arrived.

The training was conducted by men who had decades of military experience, and these men never missed an opportunity to share that experience with the new recruits. As one aging sergeant put it to them,

Douglas J. Shupinski

"I best prepare ye for whatever you'll be facing. After all, I'll never know when one of you sorry bastards may save my rotten life!" It was a hardened, pragmatic view of the world.

Surprisingly, Robert adapted quickly to the environment. He appreciated the fact that there were clear rules and structures, but understood that each situation had the potential to require a different approach. This perspective and maturity had made him somewhat of a natural leader among his peers, but he had been hesitant to accept any formal responsibilities, as yet unsure of his true capabilities as a soldier.

Despite the fact that Robert and the other members of his regiment were generally from widely divergent backgrounds, the men quickly became close as the rigorous training forced them to depend on one another. Within a few months, Robert had developed relationships stronger than any he had experienced during his twenty years of civilian life, with the possible exception of his immediate family. These were men into whose hands he would willingly place his life, and would accept them placing their lives into his.

When news had arrived that his regiment would be sent to America, Robert had initially been dismayed, natural tendencies of a young man leaving his home for the first time. But as the day got closer, he realized that he was anxious for the opportunity to see another part of the world. He was anxious to do some "real" soldiering. Ultimately, he was anxious to prove himself as a man.

***

Private Boyle and the other members of his company were quietly but insistently instructed to get into full uniform and prepare themselves and their equipment for an immediate march. When anyone so much as whispered something to a nearby comrade, they were quickly ordered to keep quiet and continue making ready to move out. The word was passed from man to man that they had fifteen minutes to be combat ready.

After that exact period of time had elapsed, the sergeants began moving the men out of the barracks in small groups, being careful to avoid any large scale movement at any one time. Each group was marched in total silence to an isolated beach located on the northern edge of Boston's Back Bay, and orders were given to stand down until further notice. In the near total darkness, the men could just barely make out the shapes of countless small boats bobbing in the gentle current of the river.

By half past ten, the entire company had been assembled on the beach, still groggy from their recent slumber, and everyone began the time-honored game of the soldier: waiting, wondering and worrying about what the army had in store for them. And as was almost always the case in these situations, that game of waiting would stretch out for an inordinately long period of time.

Gradually, other units began to appear out of the darkness, taking up positions on either side of Boyle's unit until the beach was filled with British soldiers. Although Robert was unable to see very far in any direction, he sensed that there were at least five hundred men gathered around him, maybe more.

More time passed, and the men began to think that perhaps this was just another drill to test their readiness. A quiet murmur passed along the beach, men hoping against hope that they would soon be allowed to return to their recently vacated beds. But these hopes were soon dashed with the arrival on the scene of Major John Pitcairn of His Majesty's Marine Forces. Every soldier knew that when the Marines were involved in something – and even more certainly when those Marines were commanded by Major Pitcairn – things were about to happen.

Immediately, the various company commanders left their respective units and headed to where Major Pitcairn was standing. A brief conference of perhaps two minutes was held, after which the commanders nearly sprinted back to their men and issued hushed, insistent orders to the other junior officers and senior enlisted men. At that point, groups of men began moving in the direction of the small boats and boarding them, once again in virtual total silence.

Private Boyle's unit was one of the first companies to embark on the boats, and they were rowed quietly out into the river approximately twenty or thirty yards from the shoreline. At that point they came to a halt, allowing time for the other soldiers to engage in the same evolution. However, even after all of the boats had been filled to capacity and rowed a short distance off shore, the men continued to bob aimlessly in the water. The unspoken question raged in every man's mind: what in the Devil's name were they waiting for?

The answer to the mystery was soon revealed. Nearly a full hour after the men had rowed into the darkness of the river, Lieutenant Colonel Smith arrived. Smith was the commanding officer of the Tenth Regiment of Foot, and the man who had been placed in charge of the expedition at hand.

Lieutenant Colonel Francis Smith had been an officer in the British army since his commissioning in April of 1741. In many respects, Smith was a capable officer. He understood military tactics, he appreciated the role of logistics, and he had seen and done many things during his nearly thirty-five years of service. But in one respect, he was woefully inadequate: Francis Smith simply didn't know the meaning of the word "speed".

Despite the fact that Lieutenant Colonel Smith himself had given the orders to be prepared to cross the Charles River by ten o'clock, he had failed to arrive until nearly midnight. It was at this point that Smith realized that there weren't enough boats to get his approximately seven hundred men across the river in one trip. Much to the chagrin of all parties involved, two trips would be required.

***

Finally, the men had been ferried across the river and delivered to the opposite shore. There they waited for almost an additional two hours until everything was in order to march. At long last, the order was given to move out and head north away from Boston. It was after two o'clock in the morning – over four hours since their rude awakening - and the British troops had moved a total distance of approximately four hundred yards from their starting point.

The Rider

Boston

11:00 P.M. April 18, 1775

The Rider's horse had become restless for the last hour or so, no doubt sensing the mood of its owner. He, along with several other men tasked with the same mission, had been waiting somewhat impatiently for what seemed like an eternity. That mission, were they ever allowed to complete it, was to alert the countryside just outside of Boston of the approach of British troops – who were tasked with accomplishing their own objectives.

***

The city of Boston had become a virtual prison to its occupants since the British government had enacted the rather severe Port Act on June 1, 1774. This Act made it illegal for any boat to carry cargo into or out of the city of Boston, unless it was arriving from or departing to England. The effects had been immediate and drastic, as the people of the city nearly starved from lack of provisions. In addition, a majority of Boston's working men became idle and desperate, as so much of the city's prosperity relied on the very traffic which had come to a screeching halt.

Douglas J. Shupinski

The city might have starved, in fact, had it not been for the generosity of many of the other American colonies. Some sent livestock of various kinds; others sent wheat, rice, flour, and fish. Many others sent the purest gift of all: money. These things, along with that which could be smuggled into the city through various means, allowed the people to continue to live a surprisingly normal life, much to the disappointment of the British government who had anticipated that their actions would bring this hotbed of rebellion to its knees.

The rebellious actions of the Bostonians had taken many forms, some of which were quite overt while others were considerably more subtle. The most infamous had involved a "Tea Party" organized and carried out by a group of men known as the Sons of Liberty in December of the previous year. This "party" had been in response to the British government enacting a tax on tea, a commodity that was nearly as ubiquitous to the culture of New Englanders as the air they breathed. A group of men dressed rather unconvincingly as American Indians had boarded a British merchant ship, and dumped crates of tea valued at 15,000 pounds into the waters of Boston harbor.

Meanwhile, General Thomas Gage, the Commanding General of the British troops stationed in the American Colonies, had taken advantage of a law which allowed his soldiers to be quartered in the private residences throughout the city. In addition to these living arrangements which accommodated only a portion of his army, he had ordered the construction of numerous barracks designed to provide his men with living conditions far superior to their current situation of tents exposed to the elements.

Not surprisingly, both actions were met with an undercurrent of revolt. The owners of the houses in which troops were quartered did everything in their power to make life miserable for their unwelcome British boarders. Meanwhile, it was nearly impossible to find any skilled craftsmen in the city willing to be employed for the purpose of constructing the desired barracks. Gage was forced to search far and wide outside of Boston to eventually procure the required workforce, and it was well into the season of cold weather before he was able to move his men into their new accommodations.

The British government had been somewhat surprised by the degree to which the colonists had taken offense to the existence of the British army in Boston. After all, the main purpose for these soldiers being in America was to provide protection to the colonists. Was it so ridiculous as to expect these same colonists to pay for at least part of the cost of their presence? It was for this express purpose, the British government had explained time and again, that certain taxes had been levied on the colonies.

In the opinion of many of the colonists, these taxes had little to do with paying for protection, and much more to do with refilling the British Treasury which had become seriously depleted as a result of numerous recent wars fought by the British both in America as well as elsewhere around the globe. The British government, so reasoned many colonists, had spent money well beyond their means, and now expected the prosperous colonies to make things right from their own pockets.

***

That had been several months ago, and since that time the situation had continued to escalate to its current state. The Sons of Liberty were no longer a group of extremists with a relatively narrow agenda and a selective membership. Instead, they were now advocating for the expulsion of the British army not only from Boston, but from all of the American colonies, and they had become very much a popular movement. The result was their ability to exert a certain level of control over a group of individuals known as Minutemen.

The Minutemen had existed for many years in the colonies, dating back to the days when every town needed to have a local militia capable of turning out and defending their territory in the event of an attack by marauding Indians. Even after much of New England had ceased to be a frontier, these militias had remained in existence and provided a certain degree of protection and law enforcement, albeit sparingly utilized.

While many of these militia units had fallen into habits of lethargy, still others had remained active, drilling with surprising frequency by officers who possessed fairly significant combat experience. This experience had been gained through brush wars with Indians, and time spent serving with the British army during the French and Indian War which had ended just a few years earlier. That war, a battle for control of much of the eastern and northern portions of North America between the British and the French, had ended with the French being forced north into Canada and westward toward the new frontier.

To their credit, the British had utilized a rather extensive network of informants that lived in and around Boston to ascertain as much information as they could regarding the intentions of the Sons of Liberty, and their increasing ability to mobilize and control these local militias. This network had recently yielded two critical pieces of intelligence. First, John Hancock and Samuel Adams, two key leaders of the Sons of Liberty, were reported to be staying in Lexington, a small town approximately twelve miles from Boston. Second, the Minutemen had succeeded in accumulating a significant amount of gunpowder, ammunition, and arms in the town of Concord, approximately five miles further out past Lexington.

General Gage had reasoned that a lack of gunpowder and munitions would seriously impair the ability of these Minutemen to pose any serious threat to his army. And while the capture of Hancock and Adams would certainly be a pleasant bonus, it was the capture of these arms that he was truly looking to achieve. To that end, Gage had ordered an expeditionary force under the command of Lieutenant Colonel Francis Smith to conduct a raid on the outlying towns of Lexington and Concord in order to capture the heretofore elusive Hancock and Adams, and then proceed on to Concord where they would either confiscate or destroy any munitions and supplies they might find there.

This expedition, at least in theory, was intended to be kept in extreme secrecy. No one was told the true objective of the raid, and even Colonel Smith was given sealed orders with instructions to not open them until he and his troops had embarked on the road leading north out of Boston.

However, there were two inherent flaws to Gage's plan to maintain secrecy. First, while he made every effort to keep secret the *destination* of his raid, he made feeble attempts to hide the fact that there was to actually *be* a raid. As a result, throughout the day of April 18th there was a virtual buzz throughout the city regarding the fact that the British army would be on the move very shortly. The second flaw was that anyone capable of putting two and two together could quickly ascertain that Lexington and Concord were the most likely objectives of any move made by the British. In fact, the only real variable in this whole equation was the route that would be taken by the British toward their intended objectives.

The result was the Sons of Liberty being able to quickly mobilize a group of approximately thirty riders that stood at the ready to head out into the neighboring countryside to rouse the local populace into some form of action. Of course, the big mystery in all of this was what sort of response would take place on the part of the colonists. Would these Minutemen simply rattle their proverbial sabers and disappear into the surrounding woods when confronted with a major force of the enemy? Or would they, in fact, stand their ground and offer anything that even remotely resembled organized resistance? Only time, and the appearance of British soldiers, would tell.

***

At long last, the Rider received word that the British were on the move. A code had been worked out with other members of the Sons of Liberty to provide information regarding the route of the enemy. Across the Charles River from Boston was the small town of Charlestown. If the British were planning to take the overland route north toward Lexington and Concord, a single lantern would be hung in the steeple of the North Church in Charlestown to indicate as such. However, if the British opted to take the somewhat shorter route of moving their troops across the Charles River by boat and then march north, two lanterns would be displayed in the steeple.

As the Rider watched intently atop his horse, a single lantern appeared in the steeple across the river, followed shortly by a second. The route was to be by water first, and then north. He had received his orders.

Moving north, the Rider traveled along the Cambridge Road, his objective to reach Lexington and warn Hancock and Adams. At the same time, other riders headed in all directions to spread the word that the British were on the move and had intentions of threatening their homes with search and seizure. It would turn out to be an easy proposition to sell.

As the Rider continued north, he suddenly noticed two men on horseback just ahead of him. Just in time, he was able to identify them as British officers, their side arms visible in the moonlight. General Gage had previously issued orders to his officers and men strictly forbidding them to carry arms when venturing out into the area surrounding Boston. Gage was adamant on insuring that any presence of his troops was seen as purely recreational in nature, with no aggression intended. The fact that these officers were armed, coupled with the fact that no one would be out on a joy ride in the middle of the night, alerted the Rider that these men were engaged in the active role of military scouting.

The Rider pulled his horse to a halt, then turned and galloped back toward an intersection that he had just passed. The British officers immediately gave chase in a clear attempt to intercept him. Arriving at the intersection, the Rider quickly rode up the Medford Road, followed closely by the officers. Fortunately, the horse that the Rider had commandeered from a local deacon proved too fast for his pursuers, and the British soon abandoned their chase.

The Rider continued on his mission, now made somewhat longer by the need to take a looping direction around Cambridge, toward Lexington. Along the way, he made stops at the houses of other Minutemen, spreading the word of invasion. The result was a growing alarm throughout the various small towns, with men rushing to organize themselves in anticipation of the coming onslaught.

Arriving in Lexington, the Rider made his appearance at the home of Jonas Clarke, the religious leader of the small town, and a noted revolutionary in his own right. The reason for the Rider's visit was his knowledge that both Hancock and Adams had elected to make the Clarke residence their base of operations over the last few days. Knocking insistently on the front door, the Rider demanded to see the Reverend Clarke, as well as his somewhat infamous guests.

"Gentlemen," the rider exclaimed, having gained an audience with the two wanted patriots, "might I suggest you consider it a good time to move on to other accommodations. It is quite likely that the British are but a short distance behind me, and have indicated a keen interest in making your acquaintance."

Despite a brief time in which Hancock and Adams hesitated to believe the man, they were eventually convinced that discretion might, in fact, be the better part of valor. They quickly gathered the few things they had brought with them, and made a hasty exit from the reverend's dwelling. Thanks in large part to the Rider, these two men would avoid coming face to face with British soldiers on this day.

***

Continuing on, the Rider soon met up with two other men also tasked with the responsibility of alerting the surrounding countryside of the approach of the British. They quickly determined that they would ride together to warn the town of Concord, the rationale being that there was inherent safety in numbers. This rationale soon proved to be borne of folly.

They had traveled a short distance when they spotted two British officers ahead on the road. Almost immediately, a larger group of British soldiers made their appearance, making it nearly impossible for the three riders to escape. All three broke in different directions, and for two of them, they would escape to continue their mission.

But not the Rider. Surrounded by no fewer than nine British officers, he found himself being interrogated as to the nature of his midnight ride.

"Tell me, sir," said the senior British officer, "what brings you out to these parts at such a late hour? And I assure you," he added rather ominously while cocking a pistol and pointing it directly at the head of the Rider, "that if you fail to tell me the truth, I shall have no problem with blowing your brains out!"

The Rider may have had many faults, but dishonesty was not one of them.

"I know what you are all here to do," said the Rider. "You have crossed the Charles River with no less than five hundred soldiers, and your aim is to capture Mr. Hancock and Mr. Adams in Lexington, and then continue on to Concord. I know this — and because I know this, I have made it my mission to alert this countryside of your objectives."

The senior officer, along with his fellow officers, appeared somewhat shocked by the accuracy of the Rider's statement.

"Well, then," the officer replied, "we shall be compelled to take your horse from you to prevent you from issuing any additional warnings. Not that it would really matter. You see, the King has seen fit to send over *fifteen hundred* troops to address your little insubordination, not a mere five hundred. And besides," he added, nodding in the direction of the heavily breathing horse upon which the Rider was sitting, "it appears your mount is near its death. And I assure you, my misguided friend, that should any of your — patriots — indicate a willingness to stand up to the King's finest, they will find themselves a great deal closer to death than this nag!"

The Rider was forced off of his horse and unceremoniously booted in the hindquarters by the senior officer, forcing him in the direction from which he had come.

"Go back to your bed," shouted the officer, "and consider yourself fortunate that you will be spared the circumstances just down that road!"

Maintaining his dignity to the degree possible, The Rider walked off casually into the evening, content in the knowledge that he had fulfilled at least a significant part of his mission. However, he couldn't shake the ripple of fear he had experienced at the words of the British officer; fifteen hundred soldiers? If that was, in fact, a true statement, then the situation faced by the Minutemen was a dire one indeed.

***

So ended the rather fateful evening of a man who had helped to awaken an entire nation to the monumental events that were just ahead. So ended the evening of the Rider.

Douglas J. Shupinski

Captain John Parker

Commanding Officer, Lexington Militia Company

Lexington Common

4:30 A.M. April 19, 1775

John Parker was a farmer by trade, and had lived nearly his entire forty-five years in the small town of Lexington. He was content with the modest success he enjoyed through his vocation, and had provided a stable life for him and his wife, along with their seven young children. John was considered an educated man, in that he was not only *capable* of reading, but often took the time to actual *engage* in reading. Finally, John Parker was known for his common sense, his sense of fairness, and his cool-headedness under pressure. It was partly for this last reason that Parker had been elected by his peers to be the commander of the town's militia.

But there was another side of John Parker that few people in Lexington really knew about, and it was also a major reason that he had been elected militia commander. John Parker was a veteran of combat.

During the French and Indian War which had ended several years earlier, Parker had fought with Rogers' Rangers, an American unit well known for its bravery under fire, and its ability to fight the Indians on their own terms. Specifically, Rogers' Rangers had been skilled in the arts of ambush, cover and concealment, and marksmanship. As a result, John Parker was well versed in these arts as well.

***

"Mr. Diamond, if you please," Captain Parker called out to his young drummer boy. William Diamond, with the enthusiasm that can only be displayed by a sixteen year old, dashed the short distance across the Lexington Common and came to a rough approximation of attention in front of his captain.

"Yes, sir," William replied smartly, "at your service, sir!"

"Mr. Diamond, beat the call to arms, if you please. I believe our town is about to be invaded by some red-coated visitors. A welcoming party would be appropriate, don't you think?"

William smiled broadly at Captain Parker's remark.

"Indeed, sir, a welcoming party indeed! I shall see to it immediately!"

The young drummer boy proceeded to sprint to the center of the Common, unsling his drum, and begin beating the traditional staccato of a call to arms.

The Lexington Common was a small patch of land that was no more than two acres in size and roughly triangular in shape. The Common had been purchased collectively by the townspeople of Lexington back in 1711, and stood at the intersection of the Boston, Lexington, and Concord roads. Several buildings surrounded the Common including a meetinghouse, a schoolhouse, Buckman's Tavern, and several houses.

This was the second time that the young drummer had followed these orders. Having received word several hours earlier regarding the approach of the British, Captain Parker had ordered the militia of Lexington to assemble on the town Common. At that point, Parker counted approximately one hundred and thirty men who had responded to the call. However, this previous report regarding the approach of the British had proven to be premature, as several riders sent out by Parker had reported no such sighting. As a result, the men had been allowed to disburse, some returning to their nearby homes, while others waited in nearby Buckman's Tavern located just off of the Common.

Now at 4:30 AM, word had arrived that not only were the British on their way, but they were less than a half mile down the road from Lexington! Time was of the essence, and men began to tumble out of nearby houses as well as the tavern. Unfortunately, many of the men had no ammunition for their muskets, and that fact – which had previously been a minor detail when called out to drill – suddenly took on a much greater level of significance. Some men returned to their houses in search of ammunition, while others crowded toward the meetinghouse where a small amount of powder and musket balls had been stashed.

Those that had been prepared with weapons and ammunition at the outset quickly gathered on the Common under the discerning eye of Captain Parker, who was clearly dissatisfied with, but not overly surprised by, the lack of military discipline. After all, most of these men weren't soldiers, but rather farmers like him. In fact, of the seventy men that ultimately organized themselves in two ragged lines parallel to the marching route of the British, many of them were actually related to Parker. All three of his commissioned officers were relatives, as were approximately one third of the soldiers. Were it not for the loaded muskets and nearly audible tramping boots of the approaching British, this might have been more akin to a family reunion than a military operation.

Despite his military background, Parker was experiencing an uncomfortable fluttering in his stomach. He knew that the men marching towards them not only greatly outnumbered them, but they were obviously much more experienced than the rather motley crew gathered around him. But his intentions were set: He would face the British.

Parker's trepidation was somewhat eased by the nearby presence of two solid, albeit elderly, Lexington citizens. Ensign Robert Munroe was third in command on the field, joined by two of his sons and two of his sons-in-law. At the ripe old age of sixty-three, he was well known for the bravery he had displayed during the previous war against the French. In addition, Captain Parker's much older cousin, Jonas Parker, stood calmly in the front line next to his son, Jonas, Jr. The older Jonas immediately made it clear that he meant to stay right where he stood, as he carefully placed his hat on the ground in front of him and placed a number of musket balls inside of it for easy access.

Captain Parker now turned and faced the men under his command. Allowing his eyes to sweep over their ragged ranks, he addressed them.

"Gentlemen," he began, "we all know what's coming down that road. It is quite possible that we will be outnumbered to a great degree. But let us not forget that this is our home, and these men coming at us are threatening everything we have worked to create. They are threatening our *future*."

Parker's gaze rested briefly on Prince Estabrook, one of the few slaves still remaining in Massachusetts, and the only one in Lexington. He was pleased to see that Estabrook's eyes betrayed no sign of fear or confusion. It was clear that despite his humble status within the community, Estabrook saw his own future being threatened as well.

"We will not fire upon the British but for one circumstance: should they fire upon us first, we will fight," Parker continued.

Noting the shuffling of feet on the part of several of the men, Parker's face hardened suddenly into that of a man who had already faced Death and had lived to tell about it.

"And any man who turns and runs will be shot down."

With that chilling comment, Captain Parker faced about, and prepared to meet whatever might arrive on the road from Boston.

Douglas F. Shupinski

Major John Pitcairn

Commanding Officer, His Majesty's Marine Forces

Lexington Common

4:30 A.M. April 19, 1775

The dawn was still a short time away as the five companies of British light infantry moved down the Boston Road. In the distance, the head of the column was gradually able to make out a small grouping of houses clustered around a plot of open ground. Despite the earlier attempts at secrecy, by this time all of the soldiers of the expedition had been made aware of their objective. They knew that their first stop would be in the town of Lexington to capture several Rebel conspirators who were known to be hiding out there. The view in the distance matched what they had been told about Lexington – their first objective lie just ahead!

This advance unit of 238 soldiers was under the command of Major John Pitcairn of His Majesty's Marine Forces, who was second in command of the overall expedition. Pitcairn had been selected by General Gage for two reasons: first, there had been some sensitivity as to which of the company commanders of the light infantry should be selected to be second in command to Lieutenant Colonel Smith.

Selecting Pitcairn, a Marine officer, deftly sidestepped this potential political landmine. And second, Pitcairn was one of the most respected British officers serving in America. Even more significantly, this respect extended not only to the British and its Loyalists, but to the Rebels as well. Many of the most influential members of the Sons of Liberty knew John Pitcairn personally, and while their political views were clearly divergent, they had learned to trust and respect his intelligence and common sense as an officer and a gentleman. One famous Rebel preacher had described him as, "a good man in a bad cause."

***

John Pitcairn had been born on December 28, 1722. At the age of twenty-three, he was commissioned as a lieutenant in the Marines. Promotions in that branch of the military were very different from those in the British army. In the army, one advanced in rank by purchasing an available promotion that resulted from a death, retirement, etc. However, in the Marines such promotions were earned due to performance and experience. As a result, it had taken John Pitcairn twenty-five years to advance to the rank of Major.

John and his wife Elizabeth had sired ten children including six boys and four girls. It was the quintessential military family, with three of the sons entering military service, and all four daughters marrying navy or army officers. Two of John's sons were currently serving in the British military in America; Thomas was a lieutenant in the Royal Artillery, and William was one of Major Pitcairn's own junior officers in the Marines.

***

"Well, we should be seeing something soon," Pitcairn stated to one of the company commanders, Captain Rhodes. "We've been marching for over two hours, which means it should only be bloody midnight, not dawn. Damn it, Rhodes, you'd think after this long in His Majesty's service I'd stop being surprised by the bloody delays."

Despite the fact that Pitcairn attended Sunday services unfailingly and considered himself to be a religious man, the curses seemed to roll off of his tongue like the sermons delivered by his ministers.

"Aye, sir, it took a bit of time to get going. I would guess the General's plan to surprise the Rebels before they could organize might have been put in jeopardy," observed Captain Rhodes.

"*Might* have been put in jeopardy?" Pitcairn responded, looking incredulously at the captain. "Damn it, man, you know how I feel about these Rebels. The only thing they lack is the necessary ammunition and an opportunity to use it. They've been organized for years now, and quite a few of these 'Minutemen' as they're called have combat experience. No, my young captain, they'll be waiting for us — you can be assured of that."

Almost on cue, a rider galloped up to Major Pitcairn and Captain Rhodes.

"Sir, I beg to report that the town of Lexington is located just ahead," the man stated breathlessly. "I regret that I cannot provide details, sir — I chose not to ride too close to the town for fear of alerting anyone there of our presence."

"No apology necessary, corporal, your actions were appropriate. I shall observe the situation for myself."

Riding to the head of the column, Major Pitcairn took in the sight of the town of Lexington. His experienced eye quickly noted the disposition of the walls and wooded areas leading up to the town, as well as the arrangement of the buildings that lined both the road and the Common. These were all possible hiding spots for Rebels intent on taking potshots at his men as he approached the town. Pitcairn had been informed that he would most likely be facing between five hundred and a thousand armed insurgents gathered at the Lexington Common; as a result, Pitcairn ordered the movement of the column to take on a much slower, and more deliberate pace.

As the distance to the town decreased, Pitcairn was eventually able to see the outline of a group of people gathered on the Common, as well as a number of other individuals milling about the edges of the open ground. It took no time to realize that this group was nowhere near the size that he had been prepared to face, but was perhaps no more than two hundred or so including those both on the Common as well as its surroundings.

"Company commanders," Pitcairn shouted into the chill morning air, "form your companies into line of battle and prepare to advance!"

With a precision honed by hundreds of hours of drill, the men quickly went from their column formation into three lines that stretched perpendicular to their original direction of march. Orders were given to fix bayonets, and the men prepared to move out at the orders of their officers. There was a certain level of energy – almost enthusiasm – in the soldiers' movements. Even the experienced men among them felt a sudden rush at the prospect of going into battle. They had been cooped up in Boston for almost a year with virtually nothing to do but drill and stand guard duty. This situation finally offered them the chance to display their skills as soldiers, and they would be damned before they would be denied that opportunity.

The people in and around the Common began to form into two distinct groups; one group was clearly made up of townspeople gathered out of a sense of curiosity brought on by the situation. The other group had arranged themselves into two lines at the center of the Common, one in front of the other. This second group had more on their minds than curiosity – but exactly what was on their minds was still a mystery to Pitcairn and his men.

Captain Rhodes, who had remained at Pitcairn's side during the deployment into a line of battle, nodded toward the men lined up on the Common.

"It looks like no more than a hundred men, sir. But they appear to have aggressive intentions, don't you think?"

"Aggressive intentions, Captain?" Pitcairn observed. "Perhaps so. But there are not nearly a hundred men as you suggest, but I think somewhat less. And let us remember that these are the King's subjects, not an opposing army. While I don't particularly appreciate their actions, we will treat this situation with the greatest of both caution and rationality. Do you understand?"

"I believe so, sir," replied Rhodes, with a hesitation that clearly indicated that he did not.

"What I am saying, Captain, is that we will not fire on those men unless placed in a situation in which we have no choice. Our objective here is not to engage in a fight; in fact, we will not even attempt to capture these men. Our objective is to diffuse the situation by compelling them to lay down their weapons and retire from that field."

Rhodes looked quickly at Pitcairn, a bit surprised by the apparent lack of boldness in the direction he was being given.

"We will surround the Rebels," continued Pitcairn, "and I will issue the necessary demands to these men. Once they have complied, we will gather their weapons and continue on with our mission. Now, if you please, communicate my orders clearly to the other commanders."

Rhodes immediately moved off to pass on Pitcairn's orders to the other company commanders. When Major John Pitcairn gave an order, there was no need for discussion, comment, or acknowledgement – merely compliance.

As the company commanders bellowed the necessary commands, the British battle line began moving forward slowly in the direction of the Rebels. Pitcairn was dismayed to see that this display of power failed to have the desired effect of causing the Rebel formation to break and run, a reaction that would have solved everyone's problem. Instead, they stood firmly in their ragged lines, one man who was clearly their commander standing resolutely out in front.

Approaching to within fifty yards of the men on the Common, Pitcairn issued the order to halt, and the British lines stopped, facing their adversary. Pitcairn and several of his staff officers rode to a position off to the side and between the British and Rebels. This location allowed his orders to be clearly heard by both groups, decreasing the possibility of any miscommunication.

The quiet of the spring morning was broken only by the sounds of nature, along with a gentle breeze stirring the surroundings. The townspeople had retreated into the nearby buildings, and watched in complete silence from the windows and doorways. An occasional clank of metal coming from the equipment of the armed men facing one another was the only sound that betrayed the scene as being anything other than peaceful.

Major Pitcairn drew himself up to his full height atop his mount and addressed the Rebels.

"I am Major John Pitcairn of His Majesty's Marine Forces. I am hereby ordering you, in the name of the King to lay down your arms and disperse immediately! You are in violation of the laws against bearing arms against the British government, and your actions are treasonous!"

Several of the Rebels looked uncomfortably at Pitcairn, but most of them continued to stare at their British adversaries standing directly in front of them. Slowly, several of the Minutemen began to move out of their ranks and away from the British soldiers opposing them. However, they failed to comply with the order to lay down their arms.

"Companies!" shouted Pitcairn, "move forward on my orders! March!"

On that order, all 238 British soldiers moved forward with a shout, as was the tradition when advancing on an enemy. This display of aggression seemed to fluster the Rebels, and several more broke ranks and began moving away.

As Pitcairn contemplated his next order, a shot rang out, perhaps to his right, perhaps to his left – perhaps even from the direction of the buildings directly in front of him. The scene suddenly changed from being one of calm intensity to complete confusion, as several of the British company commanders began issuing orders of engagement to their men. At the same time, many of the Rebels remaining in their ranks raised their muskets and pointed them directly at the British troops.

"Hold your fire, hold your fire!" Pitcairn shouted repeatedly, but his voice was quickly lost in the din of both sides giving orders to execute the exact opposite. Several British companies, who had continued to move forward, unleashed volleys at the Rebel formation, while the Rebels returned a ragged fire of their own. The quiet morning suddenly became a desperate battle between the two opposing forces.

Helplessly, Pitcairn watched his men advance on the Rebels, continuing to fire when possible, and lowering their bayonets in a fierce charge after they had discharged their weapons. He recklessly rode into the center of the melee, continuing to shout orders to cease fire and return to their battle lines.

But once Hell is unleashed, only the angels can still its violence. As much as any man, Major John Pitcairn had feared this result, for he sensed that this awful exchange between two small groups of men was only the beginning.

Captain John Parker

Commanding Officer, Lexington Militia Company

Lexington Common

4:35 AM April 19, 1775

Nothing in John Parker's past could have prepared him for the situation he was about to face. First, Parker immediately realized the obvious fact that he was outnumbered roughly four to one by a better armed, better trained force. And second, he knew that the lives of many of these men – his relatives and neighbors – depended on his actions in the next few minutes.

The British major commanding the approaching troops had done exactly what he would have done, had their positions been reversed. The major had brought his superior numbers immediately to bear, placing his men into a battle line and advancing on the Minutemen. Parker was a bit surprised, and very relieved to observe that the major apparently had no intention of firing upon the Rebels, but was rather attempting to compel them to retire.

The ensuing orders to lay down their arms and disperse confirmed his observation, and Parker briefly contemplated ordering his men to do exactly as they had been ordered. But Parker quickly recalled his earlier conversation just a few hours before with John Hancock and Samuel Adams. These two prominent members of the Sons of Liberty had impressed upon him the need to make a symbolic stand in the name of liberty, explaining that his actions that morning would send a resounding message to King George that the American colonists believed in their rights and in their personal freedom. To skulk away at the first sign of trouble would simply not do, they had said. The actions of John Parker and his pitifully small band of Minutemen would have far greater meaning and impact than the simple words that had been spoken by any of them up to this point.

With that thought firmly in his mind, John Parker determined that his men would also remain firmly in place − at least to the degree that he was able to control. And so, he issued his own orders.

"Stand in line men, and do not fire unless fired upon," he yelled. "But if they mean to have a war, then let it begin here!"

Parker was disappointed to see that while many of the men continued to maintain their positions, others began to melt away and make for the safety of the nearby buildings or the woods to their rear. Apparently, the fact that dozens of family members and neighbors were looking on simply wasn't sufficient to steel the resolve of all of these men.

The British major continued to demand that Parker's men leave their weapons and disperse, clearly angered by the fact that few of them were following his orders to retire, and those that did were taking their weapons with them in direct disobedience to his demands.

Parker turned to face the men gathered behind him. What he saw − with a few exceptions − was a group of confused and scared farmers who had suddenly begun to question their motivations for placing themselves where they now stood. Grossly outnumbered and outgunned, theirs was a gesture that if not for the potential disastrous consequences, might have seemed almost comical.

This reality became immediately obvious to Captain Parker, and he did what anyone with common sense and humanity would do − he gave the orders necessary to save their lives.

"All right, gentlemen, there is nothing more to be gained here. Retire from your positions − but *do not* abandon your weapons!" Parker ordered to those remaining in their ranks.

Just then, a shot from some direction Parker could not determine rang out, and the small semblance of control being orchestrated by he and the British major immediately evaporated.

The British troops were suddenly advancing with a vengeance, and they unleashed a brutal volley of fire directly into the dwindling ranks of the Minutemen. The first to fall was Ensign Robert Munroe, Parker's third in command and the hero of the war against the French. Struck by at least two musket balls, Munroe crumpled to the ground and died immediately.

Young Isaac Muzzy, standing next to his father, was likewise hit by multiple British bullets. His father caught him in his arms before he was able to fall to the ground, but Isaac died in seconds as his father looked on in despair, begging his son to continue breathing.

A few of the Minutemen instinctively returned the fire of the British without any orders from Parker, but most were so shocked by the sudden turn of events that they simply turned and fled. To their credit, almost no one dropped their weapon as they had been ordered by the British major, but it was a rout nonetheless. They had broken — but could anyone have reasonably expected them to stand up to the awesome onslaught that was now bearing down upon them?

But some did. Jonas Parker, Major Parker's elderly cousin had earlier made a display of preparing himself to fight it out with the British if need be. And so he made good on his unspoken promise, firing his musket at the enemy and then calmly bending over to grab another cartridge from his hat lying upside down on the ground. At that point, he was hit by a musket ball which toppled him over backwards onto the ground. Seemingly undaunted, he gathered himself together and reached back toward his hat to try and continue the fight. But by this time, the charging British troops were upon him, and he was run through by the bayonets of several frenzied enemy soldiers and died instantly.

Perhaps the saddest casualty of the day was Jonathon Harrington. Jonathon was a lifelong resident of Lexington, and had married the daughter of the local doctor. He and his wife had moved into one of the houses that lined the Common, and had been blessed with a son who was now eight years old.

Upon the appearance of the British troops on the road leading to the town, Harrington ordered his wife and son to return to their house and its relative safety, while he ran to the Common to do his duty as a Minuteman.

The second volley fired by the British wounded Jonathon rather badly, and he crawled slowly in the direction of his house. After several awful minutes of pain and determination, he made it to the doorstep of his house, bleeding tremendously from the gaping wound caused by the enemy projectile. He arrived just in time to die there, as his wife and son watched in disbelief from a window of the same house. They would never again know the love and companionship of their husband and father.

As the Minutemen scattered away from the Common, the British continued to fire at them. Four more Lexington men were struck and killed, and ten others were wounded as they fled the scene of what had become a nightmarish fiasco.

Lieutenant Colonel Francis Smith

Commanding Officer, 10th Regiment of Foot, British Army

Lexington Common

4:55 A.M. April 19, 1775

The sounds of combat just ahead on the road to Lexington had compelled the British column to dramatically increase the speed of their march. Commanded by Lieutenant Colonel Francis Smith, this column consisted of the remaining 400 or so British soldiers that made up the rest of the expeditionary force that had been sent from Boston several hours before.

To the degree that he was capable, the portly Smith moved with haste in the direction of the firing, intent on making it to the Common in advance of his troops. He succeeded in arriving at the same time as the head of the column, and was shocked by what he observed.

British soldiers, seemingly without a shred of organization or discipline, were running about an open field, indiscriminately firing at everyone and anything that caught their attention. Smith watched as several Minutemen, stampeding in great haste away from the Common, were shot in the back by the pursuing British soldiers. For an army that prided itself on its professionalism and restraint, it was a most disturbing display of barbaric behavior.

"Cease fire, you men!" shouted Smith as he rode onto the

Common. "Damn you all, cease fire I say!" he repeated. Smith saw that his second in command, Major Pitcairn, was attempting to control the men as well, but was clearly having little success.

"You there!" Smith shouted to a nearby man carrying a drum, "beat 'Assembly' loudly and immediately! Do it, man, before I shoot you down and bang that infernal drum myself!"

The drummer, momentarily surprised by the appearance of the Commanding Officer of the expedition, hesitated briefly upon the receipt of the initial order. But the threat of bodily harm at the hands of his commander quickly goaded him into action, and he began to beat the order to assemble the troops.

Slowly but surely, the firing began to slacken and eventually cease, as the British soldiers stopped their pursuit of the retreating Minutemen and returned to the center of the Common. Once there, the company officers organized their men by their units in order to gain control of the situation and assess the number of casualties. There were none, save for a soldier who had been grazed on the leg by a Yankee musket ball. The wound was so slight, in fact, that his company mates were already making fun of the fact that the removal of the bloodstain from his white pants would result in greater discomfort than the scratch he had suffered at the hands of the Rebels.

***

"Sir, I deeply apologize for the conduct of the men," Major Pitcairn said to Lieutenant Colonel Smith. "There is no excuse for my inability to appropriately manage the situation. Perhaps if I had been clearer in my orders – "

"Nonsense, Major," Smith interrupted. "You and I have both seen combat before. It is a bloody and confusing business that is, at it's very best, nothing more than a loosely controlled chaos. After all, if these Rebels had not been so foolish as to place themselves in an inherently dangerous situation, this whole mess would have been avoided."

As the two men spoke, the British officers and senior enlisted men were completing the reorganization of the full expeditionary force, now nearly seven hundred strong. Initially, many of the soldiers had made attempts to search the buildings on and near the Common in order to flush out any hiding Minutemen or discover any military supplies. But Lieutenant Colonel Smith had quickly given orders to cease any such searches and prepare to move out.

"Colonel, I assume you'll want an advance guard and flankers put out on either side of the column as we make our return march to Boston," Pitcairn stated to Smith. "Being that the entire countryside has now been alerted, we may find ourselves harassed by more of these self-proclaimed Minutemen."

Smith looked at Pitcairn with thinly veiled disdain on his face, and paused for several seconds before making his reply.

"You are very nearly correct in your assessment of the situation, Major," replied Smith, "with one exception. We will require an advance guard and flankers to guard against harassment as we continue on to Concord – not as we return to Boston."

Major Pitcairn, surprised by his commander's statement, replied with just a hint of alarm in his voice.

"But sir, as I have suggested, the entire countryside has been made aware of our presence here, as well as our ultimate destination! This expedition, sir, was predicated on the element of speed and surprise. We are clearly well behind our intended timeline, and surprise is no longer a reality."

Smith, intending to show his disinterest for the major's concerns, refused to even give Pitcairn the courtesy of eye contact as he replied.

"Major, we are nearly seven hundred soldiers of His Majesty's army. Should we choose to continue on in the fulfillment of our given objectives, we will not be deterred by such rabble as we have already faced today. And we will certainly not be stopped by the rather trivial concerns of a major in the Marines. Now, insure the men have been resupplied as necessary, and prepare to move on to Concord within fifteen minutes."

John Pitcairn's face burned red with anger at Smith's comments. Of all of the personal attributes that he believed he possessed as a man, courage was the most significant. It was this characteristic that allowed a man to maintain or change anything about himself, and therefore determined who he was at his very foundation. The fact that Smith was questioning that quality was nearly intolerable to Pitcairn, and it took every ounce of his considerable reserve of discipline to not lash back at his commanding officer.

"However," Colonel Smith continued in a tone that bordered on condescension, "your concerns are not completely without merit. In the unlikely event that these Rebels are capable of raising anything that even resembles an army, I will take the precaution of sending a messenger back to General Gage requesting reinforcements. Taking such an action will allow us to continue our mission, while also mitigating what slight risk may exist."

Smith finally turned and faced the major, looking at him with an almost bored expression on his face.

"Will that be satisfactory, Major?"

Pitcairn had to admit to himself that while the plan wasn't exactly what he would have done had he been in command, it did possess a certain level of military logic. Nevertheless, he was still uncomfortable marching further away from their base and, ultimately, their safety.

"Absolutely satisfactory, sir," replied Pitcairn. "I shall make the necessary arrangements immediately."

"Very well," Pitcairn said quietly to himself as Smith cantered awkwardly away, "I shall see to your orders – *sir*. And by the end of this day, we will see who was truly foolish!"

***

It was approximately eight o'clock in the morning when the lead elements of the British column arrived at the center of the small town of Concord, Massachusetts. Concord, which was nearly twice the size of Lexington in terms of population, had a topography which consisted of a number of ridges that dominated the surrounding terrain. It was upon these ridges that the British had observed the movement of Rebel soldiers as they had approached the center of Concord. While the presence of what appeared to be a sizable force of Yankees was a bit unsettling to the British soldiers, the fact that they were not fired upon made things considerably less threatening. Perhaps these Rebels were simply observing the movements of the British, with no intent to confront them. Perhaps they had learned their lesson at Lexington.

The soldiers wearily dropped their packs as they were given the order to fall out. These men had now been awake since nine o'clock the night before, and had been on the move for nearly ten straight hours. They had marched seventeen miles, and many of them had engaged in a firefight, albeit minor. Nevertheless, such engagements were stressful and exhausting, regardless of their magnitude. In a word, the men were getting close to exhaustion.

Lieutenant Colonel Smith and the now fully composed Major Pitcairn were conferring together as the men took their much needed and well deserved rest.

"There are at least two places here that require a presence of our troops," Smith explained, as he referenced a rough map he had of the local area. "There at the South Bridge," he gestured behind him in the general direction from which they had come, "and there at the North Bridge," he said as he pointed to the other side of the town.

"Colonel Smith, if I may?" asked Pitcairn.

"Of course – what are you thinking?"

"Sir, we have observed the presence of a fairly large group of Rebels that have been watching our approach for the last hour or so. Many of those Rebels now appear to be assembling across the North Bridge on the other side of the creek. As we have no knowledge of their intentions, perhaps it would be prudent for us to retain our full power by maintaining unit cohesion, sir."

In effect, Major Pitcairn was advocating for keeping the men together as one fighting unit, a rather wise suggestion considering the vagueness of their current situation. But Smith had different views.

"Major, I understand your point, and military doctrine would certainly suggest that I not divide my command," conceded Smith. "However, I believe in this particular scenario, such a division is exactly what is called for. By placing troops at both the North and South bridges, we will deny the enemy any opportunity to enter Concord in force."

Pitcairn's expression remained stoic, as he was unwilling to offer

Douglas F. Shupinski

additional counsel that suggested anything that even resembled caution. He had already endured an attack on his courage once today; there would not be a second.

"Very well, sir," Pitcairn replied coldly. "What are your specific orders, sir?"

Smith paused briefly, clearly considering what would be the most judicious use of his ten companies of light infantry.

"Place one of our companies at the South Bridge – I doubt there will be a significant threat from that direction. Place seven of the light infantry companies at the North Bridge. If there is to be any attempt at engaging us, I believe it will come across that avenue of approach."

"Yes, sir," replied Pitcairn. "I assume you'll be taking command of those seven companies, sir? I can remain here and oversee the search of the town for military supplies."

"No, I believe I'll stay here and oversee that operation. That is, after all, the main objective of this expedition," reasoned Smith.

"Understood, sir. May I request then that I take command of the force at the North Bridge? As you suggested, that will be the most likely location of any action."

"No, that won't be necessary, Major. Have Captain Parsons of the Tenth Regiment take command at the North Bridge. I'll need you to stay here in the town with the remaining two companies of light infantry and the remaining grenadiers and assist in our search," Smith concluded.

Major Pitcairn remained silent for several seconds without moving. Placing a rather inexperienced captain in charge of a bulk of the troops at the most volatile location – that was not what Pitcairn considered to be a sound decision. In a very cautious, level tone, he replied to Smith.

"Sir, I know that you have served with Captain Parsons for a considerable length of time. I have no doubt that in your judgment his capabilities are sound. However, I'm not sure – "

"Excellent," interrupted Smith before Pitcairn could complete his statement, "then we're in agreement. Not that I required your approval, of course. Now, if you please, Major, see to the disposition of our men as I have directed."

Colonel James Barrett

Commanding Officer, American Militia

North Bridge, Concord

10:45 A.M. April 19, 1775

For the last few hours, groups of men from throughout the Boston area had been streaming into Concord, having received news of the British advance from the dozens of scouts that had spread the alarm for miles in every direction. These men much like those that had faced the British just hours ago in Lexington, spanned a wide range of characteristics. Some were young, the youngest being Abner Hosmer, a mere lad in his very early teens assuming the somewhat appropriate role of drummer boy. The oldest was eighty year old Josiah Haynes who had just arrived from the nearby town of Sudbury. Most were farmers, as before, but a variety of tradesmen were present as well, including a strong willed gunsmith named Captain Isaac Davis. Some, like Davis, had a fair amount of experience in these sorts of situations, having either fought in the French and Indian War, or having fought off hostile Indians from their homes. However, while all of the men knew how to handle a musket, precious few had the distinction of having ever aimed one at another human being.

By late morning as the British entered the center of Concord,

Douglas J. Shupinski

nearly four hundred Minutemen had assembled on a ridge on the far side of the North Bridge. They consisted of six companies from Concord, Acton, Lincoln, Carlisle, and Bedford. Their position had been selected in that it allowed them to observe the British from a safe distance, while also placing them at a location where additional men arriving mainly from the west of Concord could join them. In ostensible command of this rather ragged group was Colonel James Barrett.

Barrett had been born in 1710, making him quite a bit older than Joseph Parker, his commanding officer counterpart from the Lexington skirmish. Barrett had served in the French and Indian War with the British, ultimately obtaining the rank of captain. Following that excursion, he returned to Concord where his common sense and leadership skills made him a well-respected member of that town, and he had served in any number of official political capacities in recent years.

Perhaps the true measure of his standing within the community was the fact that the decision had been made to store most of the cannon and ammunition acquired by the Sons of Liberty on his property, which was located just a few miles up the road from the current location of his command. Unfortunately, this fact was also well known by the approaching British.

***

As the Minutemen watched from their position on the ridge on the far side of the North Bridge, a column of British troops departed the center of town and began moving towards them.

Major John Buttrick, one of the company commanders of the two Concord companies, was standing beside Barrett as they watched the spectacle unfold before them.

"That's most of their men coming this way, don't you think?" Buttrick asked the colonel.

"Ay, I'd say about two hundred of those lads are coming this way," guessed Barrett. "I believe they might be thinking about paying a visit to my Missus back at the farm," he said, not a hint of concern in his voice. "She and my boys will know how to handle themselves. I told them to bury the cannon in the fields and make no trouble if the British arrived."

Buttrick shot a quick glance of concern at the colonel, wondering if the Barrett family might be tempted to give up their precious treasure too easily.

"Don't worry," the colonel continued, taking note of Buttrick's expression, "they'll keep their mouths shut. They're all Barrett's to the last one – they know how to manage a tough scrape."

Soon, the British arrived at their end of the North Bridge and began to deploy themselves. However, it quickly became obvious that many of these men had no intention of staying on their side of the bridge. As Barrett and the rest of the four hundred Minutemen watched, the British soldiers broke into two nearly equal groups. One group began to fan out on either side of the bridge, while the other group began to cross over in the direction of the Rebels.

"Just as you thought, Colonel," said Buttrick. "They're leaving half of their men to guard the bridge, and the other half are heading down the road toward your farm. Shall we prepare to engage the approaching column?"

Barrett carefully considered the question, weighing the understandable desire to protect his home and family against the more prudent tactical considerations.

"No," Barrett replied slowly, almost regrettably, "let them pass. We'll not be the ones to start this fight."

The column of British troops proceeded to march directly past the Minutemen on the ridge, no more than two hundred yards away. While a few of the Rebels appeared a bit anxious, most of the men were content to watch in silence as the parade passed them by.

***

After a short time, the British column had disappeared down the road, and the Rebels had returned to observing the activity going on in the town. While they were unable to see clearly from their location what was occurring, there was obviously a great deal of movement in and around the houses of Concord. Unbeknownst to the Rebels, the British were going about their assigned objective of searching the town for anything of a military nature. As many of the Minutemen had homes and families in Concord, a growing sense of unrest began to develop. The situation suddenly came to a head as smoke appeared over the center of town.

"Damn it, Colonel!" Major Buttrick nearly shouted in surprise and contempt, "will you let them burn the town down?"

Barrett turned sharply and looked hard at the man. While this group of men might not exactly be an organized army, they were still under his command, and the lack of military discipline angered him.

"No, *Major*," Barrett snapped, nearly spitting the rank at Buttrick, "I will not. But that is not a decision of yours to make, and I will not have you stirring these men into hasty action!"

Buttrick nearly shrank into the ground at the sharp rebuke, immediately realizing he had overstepped his bounds as a mere company commander in the presence of the overall commanding officer.

"Now," continued Barrett, "if you can keep your emotions in check, order the men to prepare to cross the bridge and enter the town. But we will *not* fire on the British unless we are fired upon first. Is that clear – *Major?*"

"Completely, sir," replied Buttrick, returning to his previous professionalism. "I shall see to it immediately."

Within minutes, Barrett's Minutemen were moving down the ridge, not with the greatest of order to be sure, but at least in control of themselves. In the lead was the gunsmith, Captain Isaac Davis, looking for all the world as a man on a mission. Directly beside him, dwarfed pathetically by the size of his drum, was young Abner Hosmer beating out the order to advance.

As the Rebels closed the distance between themselves and the soldiers guarding the bridge, Barrett noticed that the actions of the British appeared to be less than organized, even bordering on confusion. Barrett, as well as the other men around him, took confidence in the obvious disarray of their enemy, and they continued to move forward with determination.

At first, a few sporadic shots could be heard from the direction of the British. Then suddenly without warning, a sheet of flame erupted from the muskets of many of the British soldiers, the ensuing blast shocking the inexperienced Minutemen. Isaac Davis, striding confidently at the front of the attack, was killed instantly, getting knocked backwards by the force of at least two musket balls. The young drummer boy, Abner Hosmer, suffered a similar fate when a bullet struck him in the forehead. The men marching directly behind the boy were showered with an unspeakable mess, and several dropped to the ground retching at the sight of what remained of the youngster's head.

"Men, fire, for God's sake, fire!" shouted Major Buttrick, abandoning any pretense of proper military commands and protocol. The Rebels, incensed at the sight of two of their own being killed, let loose with a murderous volley that ripped into the compact ranks of the British. Several of the enemy toppled to the ground, either wounded or killed.

At that point, the attacking Rebels let out a loud, guttural shout as they immediately broke into a running charge. The British, their confidence already on thin ice and shaken by the casualties they had just taken, turned and sprinted for the safety of the town and the other British soldiers located there. Not a single additional shot was fired by them in their retreat, as they left a number of their dead and wounded comrades to the vengeance of their attackers.

***

But vengeance was no longer on the minds of the Rebels. Colonel Barrett gave no order to halt the charge, and none was needed. Surprised by the disorganized and speedy retreat of their enemy, the men simply stopped after they had progressed no more than sixty or seventy yards past the bridge. The reality of what had just occurred took hold in their minds, after having convinced themselves that they were doing nothing more than showing a unified front. The fact that they had actually attacked and routed a force of British regulars was beyond anything for which they had been prepared.

Most of the men began simply wandering back across the North Bridge, several of them stopping to pick up the lifeless bodies of Isaac Davis and Abner Hosmer. Others remained on the town side of the bridge, spreading out behind a nearby stone wall that allowed them to keep watch on the activities in the town.

Major Buttrick carefully approached Colonel Barrett, painfully aware that his order to fire had been yet another transgression of ignoring the chain of command.

"Colonel Barrett," he began, looking down at the ground, "I apologize, sir. I became overwhelmed by the sight of – "

"Major, calm yourself," replied Barrett quietly, suddenly exhausted and overcome by the enormity of what he had just seen. "None of us could have possibly been prepared for what just happened. The fact that you reacted the way you did makes you a man of flesh and blood – nothing more, nothing less."

Buttrick exhaled a deep sigh of relief at Barrett's words, and raised his head. "Thank you, sir. I assure you that it will never happen again."

Barrett turned his gaze toward Buttrick, a strange, sad expression on his face. "Ay, John," he replied, returning to his role of being just another farmer in their small community. "But I regretfully believe our future will hold ample opportunities for you to fulfill that promise."

Captain Walter Laurie

43rd Regiment, Light Infantry, British Army

North Bridge, Concord

11:00 AM April 19, 1775

There are certain times in a man's life when he finds himself in the middle of something for which he is totally unprepared. He suspects that, seemingly regardless of what he does, things will turn out poorly. And he realizes – with brutal clarity – that the world simply hates him.

Today was such a day for Walter Laurie.

While Captain Laurie had been an officer in the British army for several years, he had never had the opportunity to experience two things: first, he had never held an independent command of his own, but rather had always been a member of a larger unit, exercising authority by passing on orders he had received from a higher command. And second, he had never been in combat.

A short time ago, Laurie and his company had been detached from the main column of troops under the command of Lieutenant Colonel Smith. While Smith had remained in Concord with the majority of the troops, he had sent most of his light infantry, a total of seven companies in all, to the North Bridge to face a sizable force of Rebel militia which had gathered on a ridge just across the creek located there. This

Douglas F. Shupinski

detachment sent to the bridge was under the nominal command of Captain Parsons of the Tenth Regiment.

***

The detachment had arrived at the bridge just a few minutes earlier, and Captain Parsons had immediately called for a meeting between himself and the other six company commanders.

"Gentlemen," Parsons began, "we have been tasked with two specific objectives. The first is to set up a blocking position here at the bridge, in such a way that the Rebels located on that hill there cannot possibly cross over."

The other company commanders nodded confidently, their mission thus far clear to them.

"Second, we have been ordered to search the Barrett farm located approximately two miles up that road." Parsons gestured toward the road that crossed the bridge and disappeared into the distance. "A store of powder, shot, and cannon are reportedly located there, and we are to confiscate what we can carry, and destroy whatever remains."

Looks of alarm and confusion spread over the faces of the officers. One of the men articulated what was on the minds of the others.

"But Captain Parsons, how are we supposed to accomplish both of these assignments with just seven companies? We are clearly facing a hostile force that already outnumbers us by at least two to one, if not more! Surely, you don't intend to split us up!"

"I realize that we are outnumbered, Billings," Parsons addressed the man coldly, "but I have been given our orders and, by damned, we will do as we are told! So, unless any of you know of a way to both search the farm and guard the bridge without splitting our detachment into two forces, I am open to suggestion."

The ensuing silence indicated both a lack of ideas as well as a disgruntled resignation to what they were about to do.

"Very well, then. Captain Laurie, you will remain here at the bridge with your company as well as the companies of Billings and Peck. The remaining four companies will move down the road under my command to the Barrett farm to complete the search of that property."

Parsons looked around at the circle of officers, his gaze finally coming to rest on Laurie.

"Captain Laurie, do you fully understand your responsibilities here at the bridge?" Captain Parsons asked.

The true answer was, "Absolutely not. With virtually no experience in such matters, how could I have any idea of what my responsibilities might turn out to be?"

But Walter Laurie was an officer in the British army, and the facade of confidence always came first.

"Of course, Captain. I shall hold my position until your return from the Barrett farm."

"Excellent," Parsons concluded. "Those companies coming with me, we shall move out in five minutes. Captain Laurie, you may see to the disposition of your men here at the bridge as you see fit."

***

That meeting had occurred almost an hour ago, and Captain Laurie now found himself quite isolated with less than a hundred men looking nervously across a creek at what appeared to be a huge force of Rebels. The fact that these Minutemen had exhibited not even the slightest aggressive intentions; even when Parsons and his force had marched almost right by them; did little to ease the tension felt by Laurie and his men. If anything, the unsettled calmness that seemed to rest over the surrounding area was the most unnerving thing of all.

Laurie had decided to place two of his companies on the town side of the bridge, one to the left and one to the right. The third company, which consisted of approximately thirty men, he had posted on the other side of the bridge closer to the Rebels on the ridge. This assignment had been much to the chagrin of those thirty or so poor souls. This company now found themselves in the rather uncomfortable situation of being sandwiched between a creek and four hundred Rebels whose intentions were as yet unknown.

Captain Laurie was reviewing the situation with Captain Peck, one of the other company commanders with whom Laurie had been friends for several months now.

"It looks like they've started some bonfires back in the town," Laurie noted as the two officers gazed back almost longingly at the relative safety of Concord.

"Aye," replied Peck, "they must've found something of military value worth burning. The way I understand it, the Old Man is under strict orders not to do anything to upset the locals, so I don't believe it's any private property."

That much was true. General Gage, who had always been almost gentle with the colonials during his time as the Commanding General, had ordered Colonel Smith to only search for and destroy those items that could be used against the British in a military manner. Guns, cannon, gunpowder, etc. were on the list of items to destroy. Virtually everything else was off limits. Gage had even ordered his officers to insure that they paid full price for any food that they commandeered for themselves or their men.

Despite this fact, Captain Laurie was anything but comfortable with the current situation.

"Nathan, I hope you fully appreciate the precarious nature of our position," Laurie said to his friend, feeling no need to demonstrate the same false level of confidence he had displayed earlier. "If those men on that ridge choose to attack us, there is little we'll be able to do but retreat, regardless of their ragged nature!"

"Do you really believe those Rebels will attack us, Walter?" Peck asked. "They are a disorganized mob, and they would have to come at us in no greater dispersion than a double file. They may have us outnumbered by four or five to one, but *some* of them will have to take the lead as their formation narrows to cross the bridge. And those men will be shot down. No, Walter, the might of the British army, as undermanned as we are, will be enough to stop any – "

Captain Peck stopped in mid-sentence, as both officers turned and stared in disbelief at the sight of what was occurring across the bridge. As they watched, all four hundred or so Minutemen had moved off of the ridge, and were now descending as one body toward the North

Bridge. Despite the opinions of Captain Peck, apparently no one had informed these Rebels that their role was to sit quietly in awe of the British might in front of them.

"Quickly, Nathan," Laurie snapped to Captain Peck, "return to your company and prepare to face the enemy. I have no idea what their intentions may be, but they certainly look serious enough!"

Laurie, despite his relative lack of experience, quickly made two sound decisions on the spur of the moment.

"Lieutenant Sutherland, Sergeant Bryce!" shouted Laurie, and he was immediately in the company of these two men.

"Sergeant Bryce, cross the bridge and tell Lieutenant Kelly that he is to return his company to this side of the bridge and form alongside the two companies already posted there."

"Aye, sir!" replied Bryce curtly, and he hurried off to pass on the almost certainly welcome orders to the thirty odd men posted alone on the far side of the bridge.

"Lieutenant Sutherland," Laurie addressed the young officer, "I believe it would be prudent to inform Colonel Smith of our situation here, and request that reinforcements be sent with all possible speed."

Lieutenant Sutherland, a promising and capable young man, had already shown himself on several occasions to be up to whatever task he had been given. He recognized this most recent responsibility to be of an urgent and significant nature, and he quickly turned and mounted his horse without so much as a single word. He galloped off in the direction of Concord in a cloud of dust.

As Laurie turned his attention back to the bridge, he was pleased to see that the company across the bridge was almost completely back to his side, and was already deploying themselves for defense. This positive event was overshadowed, however, by the fact that the Rebel force was very nearly upon them, and had no apparent intentions of stopping.

It was at this point that Captain Laurie's lack of combat experience worked to his and his men's disadvantage. He began issuing a series of confusing and sometimes contradictory orders that quickly had his men moving in several directions at once. While two of the companies attempted to form in columns for street firing – a mistake in and of itself in that it would fail to bring to bear all of the muskets of his men at one time – the third company began spreading itself out for volley fire under the orders of a different officer. The ultimate result was an almost complete disarray of men clearly panicked by the approach of a sizable enemy force.

Suddenly, much to the dismay of all parties involved – both British and Rebel – several shots began to ring out sporadically from the disorganized British soldiers. Captain Laurie, sensing that he was quickly losing control of the situation, ordered his hundred or so men to prepare to fire a complete volley at the approaching enemy.

"Companies, to the front – take aim – fire!" Laurie shouted into the suddenly tense April morning air. All at once, nearly a hundred British muskets fired in unison in the direction of what would turn out to be the first truly organized force of Americans to face their British adversary.

Laurie noted with disappointment that the effect was less than dramatic, as a scant few members of the approaching force dropped to the ground. He was further alarmed to see that the Americans had quickly formed their own line of fire, and a return volley from across the bridge shattered the air.

Private Green, a young soldier of no more than eighteen, cried out in agony as two musket balls struck his midsection. He doubled over in sudden intense pain, clutching his stomach as blood gushed out from between his desperately groping fingers. A corporal, attempting to organize the few men in his charge, had his orders cut instantly short as a musket ball struck the side of his head with a sickening thud. He had no time to make so much as a single sound as he dropped to the ground, dead as he made awkward contact with the earth.

Several other British soldiers became the unfortunate victims of the whistling musket balls that suddenly seemed to fill the air in all directions. An older sergeant gasped as a bullet struck his upper thigh, watching in horror as the blood began to spurt from his leg in tremendous torrents. Others were struck or grazed by the flying projectiles, and their pitiful cries arose from the battlefield.

All of this became too much for the small British force to bear, as the enemy continued to bear down relentlessly on their now obviously untenable position. Despite the orders of Captain Laurie and other officers, the soldiers began to gradually move back toward the town in a disorganized manner. This movement soon became a panicked rout, as more musket balls were fired at them and several other comrades became victims of their deadly flights.

Captain Laurie made one final, feeble attempt to rally his men, but they were now long past the ability to respond to orders, however direct those orders may have been. With just the slightest hesitation, Walter Laurie joined the mad dash that had ensued back toward the town of Concord, stopping just long enough to spit the first bitter taste of combat from his mouth.

Major John Pitcairn

Commanding Officer, His Majesty's Marine Forces

Concord

12:00 P.M. April 19, 1775

Things had begun to settle down after the fight between the Rebels and Captain Laurie's men at the North Bridge. Lieutenant Colonel Smith had received the frantic plea for reinforcements that had been sent by Laurie, and Smith had responded – surprisingly choosing to lead a relief column of men in the direction of the bridge himself. Although Captain Laurie's men had been extremely relieved to see their rescuers arrive, there had really been no need for the reinforcements. The Rebels had crossed the bridge, routed the British, and simply stopped. The inability to continue the attack had been much more a function of a lack of coordination on the part of the Rebels than any threat posed by the British.

Nevertheless, John Pitcairn had been shocked at what he had observed returning from the scene of the battle. Quite a few bloodied British soldiers were being dragged and carried, others limping painfully along on a variety of wounds, and virtually every man appearing for all the world to be a defeated soul.

Lieutenant Colonel Smith had called a war council with most of the senior officers, including Major Pitcairn. Pitcairn was furious at the manner in which things had begun to unravel. The fact that he had been right all along about just about everything; that they should have returned to Boston from Lexington instead of continuing on to Concord; that they should never have divided their forces; and that they had needed an experienced commander at the North Bridge; gave Pitcairn little consolation. For now, he sat on a chair amid a hastily assembled and poorly managed meeting of perhaps a dozen British officers inside Wright's Tavern.

"Well, gentlemen," Colonel Smith stated rather optimistically, "we appear to have completed our primary mission of capturing or destroying a good amount of the munitions of these Rebels. I believe they will think twice before they choose to tangle with the King's soldiers again, eh?"

Smith's attempt at bravado was as hollow as his head, and it was received by the officers with a coolness that betrayed their contempt for the man. Major Pitcairn, for one, was tired of the incompetence of his commanding officer, and he made no attempt to hide that fact with his next comment.

"Colonel Smith, I don't believe these so called 'Rebels' will hesitate for even a moment to face us again. And they will do so in the next few hours as we make our return march to Boston."

"Nonsense, Major," Colonel Smith responded with an almost dismissive tone. "The fact that a few of our men were overwhelmed at the bridge and forced to retire means nothing. You saw what they did after that scrape. They turned away and wandered off like lost little children, which is exactly what they are."

"Little children," Pitcairn responded pointedly, "don't fire muskets with the accuracy of these men, sir. We are on ground which is familiar to them, not us. And we must march over a route that offers us no alternatives, which makes our movements all too predictable. No, Colonel, these are not lost children – these are men that are going to make our lives a living hell for the next seventeen miles until we get back to Boston."

Pitcairn was clearly beyond the acceptable boundaries of military protocol, but he was past caring about such things when weighed against what he realized was the literal survival of this command. His bravery had been questioned, his counsel had been ignored, and his intelligence had been insulted. The last thing Major John Pitcairn was worried about was the anger of an obese, incompetent army colonel. All eyes turned to see what Colonel Smith's reaction would be, as Major Pitcairn had clearly challenged Smith's assessment of the situation and, therefore, his authority.

For Smith's part, he was now at a crossroads of sorts. He could continue to bluster on about accomplishing missions and scaring Rebels – or he could take the steps necessary to at least allow his men a chance to make it back to Boston in one piece. To the good fortune of all parties involved, he chose the latter.

"Very well, Major, perhaps my attempts at maintaining the morale of our expedition may be a bit – misplaced at this point in time. However, I will not allow a single man in this room to display anything that even smells of panic or fear, is that understood?"

"Sir," Pitcairn stated carefully, "there is not a man in this room; I would even say not a man on this expedition; who is prone to panic. Of that, you can be sure. But any man that does not at least harbor a hint of fear at our current situation is an idiot, the likes with whom I have no desire to serve!"

The slight chuckle that rippled around the room had the fortunate effect of lightening the mood just a bit, and Colonel Smith was at least smart enough to take advantage of the break in tension.

"Very well then, my pragmatic Marine," Smith smiled, "we shall make immediate preparations to depart Concord and return to Boston using the same route along which we arrived. And we shall most certainly do so with a level of discipline and caution commensurate with the seriousness of our condition. Major Pitcairn, if you please – I should desire that you issue the necessary orders to make ready for our departure."

An almost collective sigh of relief was issued forth from the group of assembled officers, as they realized that a true military professional was now in control of things.

"Of course, sir," Pitcairn responded to the order. "Gentlemen," Pitcairn now addressed the collected officers in the tavern, "I should like to speak with each of you individually. There can be absolutely no misunderstandings regarding your assignments."

The other officers nodded as a group, understanding the gravity of their situation. There was no doubt that the orders about to be issued by Major Pitcairn would be followed to the letter. These men were professionals to their very core, and they understood fully that their lives, and the lives of their men, depended on that professionalism.

***

Major Pitcairn strongly suspected that his men would have no opportunity to confront their enemy face to face. He suspected this because, if he had been in charge of the Rebel forces, he would have avoided such a confrontation at all costs. As always, the advantage the British held was in their discipline and training, both of which could be brought to bear in a traditional engagement. Meanwhile, the Rebels had the advantage of knowing the terrain and, arguably, marksmanship. Their best strategy would be to keep their distance from the marching column of British soldiers, and hide behind the hundreds of trees, rocks, fences, and buildings that lined the road between Concord and Boston.

In order to counter this strategy, Pitcairn ordered his grenadiers to form the core of the marching column on the road, with the light infantry deployed on both flanks in order to flush out any Rebel marksmen. The wounded would be placed at the very center of the column in order to afford them some semblance of protection from any incoming fire.

The men were exhausted. They had gone without sleep, marched dozens of miles, fought multiple engagements, and were now faced with a lengthy march back to their starting point. The fact that they also realized that they might serve as targets at some point during this return march certainly did nothing to improve their morale. Possibly the only saving grace that any of them recognized was the fact that

Marine Major John Pitcairn was now leading them.

Just after one o'clock, the British column began moving out of Concord in the direction of Lexington and, ultimately, the safety of Boston. Initially, Pitcairn could sense a bit of uneasiness in the men, as the fear of not knowing what to expect played upon their collective minds. But after they had marched for fifteen or twenty minutes without an incident, the men began to relax and fall into the rhythm of the journey. The light infantry on either side of the column had not seen a single Rebel, and even Major Pitcairn, marching at the head of the column, began to think that perhaps he had overstated the intentions and motivations of these Rebels. Perhaps they had been satisfied with boldly and successfully confronting their enemy, and were now returning to their homes until the next alarm rang out.

As these rather pleasant possibilities passed through his mind, Major Pitcairn looked ahead and saw a fork in the road just a few hundred yards away. The Lexington road; the road upon which they were traveling and which also led to Boston; made a slight bend to the right, at which point it crossed a narrow bridge. Casting his gaze to the fields on either side of the small bridge, Pitcairn involuntarily pulled up on the reins of his horse, causing the animal to stop sharply.

Behind every tree, rock, and hay bale was a Rebel with a musket pointed in the direction of the approaching British column. Even these inexperienced farmers had recognized the bridge for the natural chokepoint that it was. There was simply no way to continue down the Lexington road without crossing this narrow space that had suddenly been turned into a potentially brutal killing ground.

Private Robert Boyle

43rd Regiment, Light Infantry, British Army

Lexington Road to Boston

1:30 P.M. April 19, 1775

It had been a long, grueling, and terribly stressful day for the members of the British Expeditionary Force to Concord, and the effects of this stress were beginning to show on the men. Officers and sergeants displayed little or no patience with the junior enlisted men, and the soldiers were beginning to outwardly grumble at the constant prodding from their leaders.

Private Robert Boyle was not immune to the situation, and he had also started making quiet, snide remarks whenever one of the officers or sergeants barked out an order to be quiet, speed up, slow down, or any number of seemingly mindless directions. However, as a mere private, and one extremely new to the art of war, Robert made sure his comments were audible only to himself.

Most recently, Robert's unit had been ordered to spread out on the left flank of the marching British column, and had been told to keep an eye out for any Rebels that may be lurking about. Such an order would have given him no cause for concern twelve hours ago, as he was a member of a light infantry unit specifically trained for this sort of duty.

Douglas F. Shupinski

However, his most recent experiences with these Rebels had shown that they were not quite the idiots that Robert and his fellow soldiers had been led to believe. And while Robert had not been part of the confrontation at Lexington, nor had he been at the North Bridge at Concord, such direct participation had proven to be unnecessary. Not only had he talked to several of the soldiers that had been at one or both locations, but the significant number of dead and wounded British soldiers told the only story Robert needed to hear. These Rebels were serious about what they were doing, as well as that for which they stood.

***

As Private Boyle walked up the gradual slope of what seemed to be the hundredth rise since leaving Concord, he took note of the fact that several of his company mates just ahead of him had stopped at the crest of the hill they were climbing. Moving toward them at a trot, Robert was quickly faced with the cause of their halt. As the ground sloped gradually downward toward a small group of houses along the Lexington road, Robert noticed a small wooden bridge just beyond the houses. On either side of the bridge, hundreds and hundreds of Rebels had placed themselves in positions such that they could easily fire upon the bridge from a relatively short distance away.

"Sweet Jesus!" Robert exclaimed, as the full significance of what he was seeing quickly dawned on him.

"Jesus, indeed," replied Sergeant Wiley, one of the senior enlisted men in his company. "We'll be needing Jesus himself to get through this. Look at that narrow bridge. If we could walk on water like the Savior Himself, we could avoid going over that deathtrap!"

The use of the term "deathtrap" was probably not the best choice of words in their particular situation, and several of the newer men recoiled visibly at the Sergeant's comment.

As the light infantrymen watched, the leading units of British grenadiers had narrowed their ranks to four men abreast, and were preparing to cross the small bridge. Behind them were the wounded men from the North Bridge battle, and behind them the remainder of the British column.

The lead grenadiers, marching purposefully and without hesitation, began crossing the bridge. At first there was a surprising quiet, as not a single shot was fired. As the first of the grenadiers completed their crossing followed by the rest of the column, that quiet was suddenly replaced with the terrific blast of hundreds of muskets firing at the same time. The Rebels had held their fire until as many British soldiers as possible had been bunched up on the small bridge.

The results were as awful as they were predictable. Men threw up their arms involuntarily, as many of the musket balls found their intended marks. Men were thrown backwards into the arms of their comrades, some dying quickly and wordlessly on the spot, while others screamed out in agony.

Several British soldiers were thrown into the stream on either side of the bridge by the impact of the deadly projectiles. Similar to the victims on the bridge, some were killed instantly, hitting the water and floating lazily downstream. Others splashed and flailed desperately in the water, calling out to their comrades to save them. But their comrades had their own problems, and the men in the water were left to their own fates.

Private Boyle watched in amazement as a Marine officer in a brilliant red coat that had led the way across the bridge on his horse, turned and moved back into the worst of the killing zone in order to encourage the men forward. Robert waited for the inevitable moment at which this brave man would be struck down by an enemy bullet, but against all odds, that moment never came.

Suddenly, the officer's horse reared up on its hind legs in fear, as several musket balls slammed into the bridge, the ground, and the men all around him. The officer was thrown to the ground as his horse galloped away in panic. But the setback was only momentary for the brave Marine, as he was quickly back on his feet grabbing a musket from a dead soldier and continuing to exhort his men to keep moving and stay calm.

Sergeant Wiley chuckled appreciatively at the actions of the officer.

Douglas J. Shupinski

"Damn Marines," he smiled. "You generally can't stand those boys because of their arrogance, but you can't help but lovin' 'em at a time like this."

"Marines?" Robert asked. "But, those are soldiers on the bridge."

"Ay, that they are. But that officer out front there is Major Pitcairn of His Majesty's Marine Forces. A crazier bastard you'll never see," stated Wiley. "I know a few of the sergeants in his battalion – they say the Marines would get into a bayonet fight with Hell itself if ol' Johnny Pitcairn was leadin' 'em."

It occurred to Robert that Hell was exactly what they were contending with right now, as more and more British soldiers fell victim to the disturbingly accurate fire of the Rebels. A bit of panic was beginning to seep into the actions of the retreating soldiers, as wounded men were being left on the side of the road instead of being picked up and attended to by the others. There was simply too many wounded and too little time to show pity, as the surviving men had actually begun to run down the road away from the bridge.

"Bloody hell!" Sergeant Wiley cursed to no one in particular. "Those men have to stop running!"

"Stop running?" Robert said. "They need to get out of that killing area as quickly as possible, and running is the best way to do that."

Sergeant Wiley turned a steely eye on the inexperienced Boyle.

"And which 'killing zone' would you be referrin' to, boy? The one on the bridge there? Or maybe you're talkin' about the area a few hundred yards down that road where the next group of Rebels will be waitin'. Or maybe the spot a mile or so from here where the woods come up so close to the road on both sides that you can almost reach out and touch the trees."

Wiley paused briefly, a challenging sneer on his homely face.

"So I ask you again, Private – which 'killing zone' are you talkin' about?"

Boyle realized the sergeant was right. The British weren't facing a situation in which they needed to get through this tough spot in order to then march back to Boston. They were facing a reality in which the next fifteen miles would be lined with Rebels behind every rock, tree, and fence post. The enemy would occupy every house along the way, pouring a deadly rain of musket balls into the ever-dwindling ranks of the British column.

The only chance the British column had of survival was remaining together as a cohesive military unit. To break into small groups – which is what would occur if the men continued to panic and run recklessly down the road – would mean that they would be confronted piecemeal by the Rebels at every opportunity. Unfortunately, that was exactly what was happening.

The situation was hopeless. Robert realized with disturbing clarity that he was probably going to die on this miserable stretch of dusty American road. Ironically, the last artistic color Robert Boyle would contribute to the world would be the random patterns of his own blood pouring onto the ground around him when he fell.

Captain John Parker

Commanding Officer, Lexington Militia Company

Lexington Road to Boston

1:40 P.M. April 19, 1775

By every possible measure, it had been a long day for Captain John Parker and his small group of Minutemen. Most of the men had been up since the previous morning, and many of them had been part of the group that had faced the British on Lexington Green.

That awful memory seemed to be years ago in Parker's mind. He had seen too many of his family, friends, and neighbors shot down mercilessly by the advancing British, and he couldn't shake the feeling that he was at least partly responsible for what had happened. Had he placed his men in defensive positions behind walls and houses instead of standing out in the open; had he simply given the order earlier to disperse the men, giving them the opportunity to make their deserved escape; had he…

But such reflections were wasted energy, he knew. What was done was done, and nothing could change the events or bring those men back to life. What could be done, however, was to refuse to give in to the urge to feel sorry for oneself and simply quit. The men that had given their lives on the Lexington Green deserved to be avenged, and Captain John Parker had vowed to continue the fight not just today, but for however long it took to realize the ideals for which they had sacrificed themselves.

Parker had been pleased to see that almost all of the men present on the Common that morning had been willing to come with him to continue the fight. In addition, many of those unable or unwilling to make it to the fight that morning had come along as well. Now numbering over one hundred strong, the Minutemen of Lexington would make their presence known once again.

***

The men from Lexington had reorganized themselves by early afternoon, and had prepared themselves to head for Concord. However, they soon received word from hundreds of arriving Minutemen from the surrounding towns that the British had begun a retreat back along the Lexington road toward Boston. Assuming the British would take the same road back to Boston that they had taken out that morning – which was a logical assumption, being that it was the most direct route and the only road the British knew – this path would take them back through Lexington within the next hour or so.

That assumption being made and agreed upon by the men, the Lexington militia used their intimate knowledge of the surrounding countryside to place themselves in the most ideal locations from which to engage the enemy. They would clearly not make the same mistake again of facing the British in the open.

Captain Parker was moving amongst his men, offering them suggestions as to what positions offered the best combination of protection as well as ability to fire on the approaching enemy. He came upon Jedediah Munroe, who had already been wounded in the fighting at Lexington. In addition, Jedediah was grieving the loss of his cousin, old Ensign Robert Munroe, who had been one of the first men killed that morning. Jedediah has chosen to place himself in an open spot between a small stand of trees and some nearby buildings.

"Jedediah, I fear your position might not offer you the best protection from the enemy," Parker stated simply, as he approached the older man. "Perhaps if you were to take cover behind those trees there, you might be better served."

Munroe eyed him carefully, chewing on a cheekful of tobacco and absently massaging the leg that had been grazed by a British musket ball earlier that morning.

"I ain't afraid of no Redcoats, John," Jedediah said slowly. "They had their chance to kill this old man once – and now they're gonna regret the fact that they didn't take advantage of it."

"No one is suggesting you're afraid, Jedediah," replied Parker. "I'm simply suggesting that a few trees might help to – "

"Move along, Captain," Munroe interrupted. "No offense intended, but some of the younger lads might benefit from your experience more than me."

Turning away, Jedediah Munroe gazed hopefully down the road in the direction of Concord, defiantly willing the British to dare and make their way past him.

***

Heeding the "suggestion" from the old man, Parker continued to check the positions of his men, forming them into small groups in some cases, and spreading out larger groups as appropriate. After a short time, he was satisfied that he had done what he could to protect them, while also maintaining their ability to effectively engage the enemy.

Within minutes, word began to filter back from further down the road that the British column was approaching. In the distance, Parker could hear the sound of muskets being fired, sometimes in groups, but usually in sporadic individual shots. Several minutes later, the first British troops rounded a bend in the road and began making their way carefully toward Parker and his men.

Captain Parker was shocked at what he saw. What had earlier been a disciplined group of highly trained, professional soldiers moving with an almost arrogant stride, now looked like a pack of frightened dogs that had been beaten one too many times by their cruel master. The lead elements of the column consisted of men whose uniforms were dirty and dusty, literally soaked through with the sweat resulting from hours of constant marching and exposure to danger. Parker could almost smell the fear emanating from these wretched souls as they approached, their eyes wide with a terror that had been brought on from having seen more than enough violence to last a man a lifetime, let alone a single day.

As if that weren't enough, as more and more British soldiers continued to gradually come into Parker's view, he saw that many of them were limping painfully, or carrying the bloody bodies of their comrades. Bandages soaked through with blood had been quickly and almost haphazardly wrapped around heads, legs, and arms.

For a brief moment, Parker felt almost ashamed that he and his men were about to add to the considerable misery that this group had already obviously endured. But then his memory replayed the scene on the Lexington Green – men attempting to get away, being shot down by repeated volleys of the British. Even when it had become obvious that these Minutemen had no real intention of engaging them, the British had continued to fire, several men being struck down and killed from behind even after they had actually made it off of the Common.

No, Parker reflected, these men coming toward him, regardless of their current physical state, had started this fight. Now the Lexington Minutemen were going to have an opportunity to help finish it.

The officer at the front of the British column immediately caught Captain Parker's eye. Well, I'll be damned, he thought! That was the same officer that had been on the Lexington Common that morning. He was a major in the British Marines, and he was the one who had demanded they all lay down their arms and disperse. And then the firing had started.

Parker was about to order some of his men to give the Marine officer some special attention with their target practice, when he continued to relive the events of the morning in his mind. As Parker recalled, the Marine major had given no order to fire and, in fact, had been shouting orders to his men to cease firing on the Minutemen.

Very well, Parker thought grimly, I'll give no specific orders to my men to shoot you down. After all, by riding a horse at the head of the column, this apparently brave but foolhardy man had already signed his own death warrant.

***

There had been a brief lull in the sporadic firing as the Lexington road had opened up somewhat, allowing the British skirmishers sent out on either flank of the column an opportunity to flush out any possible resistance. As the effective range of the muskets being carried by the Minutemen was really only about seventy or eighty yards, this open ground allowed the light infantry troops on both sides of the main body to create a bit of a safe zone, pushing the Minutemen back such that their weapons were – at least temporarily – ineffective against the British column.

But now the road was entering an area that had woods, walls, and buildings that came within only twenty or thirty yards of the road, and in some cases, literally butted up against it. The job of the British light infantry was about to get considerably more difficult.

As the distance between the British column and his men continued to decrease, Parker had to admit that he was impressed with the discipline being shown by the Minutemen holding their fire until the enemy was well within range. It wasn't until the gap had closed to a mere forty yards that shots began to ring out all around from the various hiding places on either side of the road. While most of the shots, due to the relative inaccuracy of the muskets, flew harmlessly over or to the sides of the column, it didn't matter. There were enough musket balls flying around that even a very low success rate had an immediate and appalling effect on the British.

Soldiers throughout the column were being struck down by the projectiles, and Captain Parker realized that the British were literally being fired upon from all directions. Some of the British troops attempted to gamely form firing lines, but only briefly. Anytime a group got together, they received an increase of firing from the Minutemen in order to break them apart. It quickly became a matter of fending for oneself, as the enemy began spreading themselves out. This tactic was completely contrary to everything they had been trained to do, and things began to quickly fall apart.

Minutemen that had engaged the British earlier began to arrive on the scene, adding their firing to the volume that was already pouring down on the unfortunate men in red. Soldiers were sent flying onto their backs or crumpled to the ground as bullets inevitably found their marks. Men dropped their weapons and frantically grasped at their heads, their midsections, their appendages, as bullets viciously assaulted their bodies. Most disturbing were those British soldiers, already wounded and attempting to gain some protection by huddling together in the middle of the column, who were struck a second, third, or even fourth time by the rain of death on all sides. Screams of agony could be heard in all directions as the distressingly short lives of dozens of men came to an end.

The flankers on either side of the column made valiant but feeble attempts to drive the Minutemen away from the road, achieving only occasional success. One unit of British light infantry succeeded in making their way behind a group of seven Rebels positioned behind a low stone wall, surprising them completely. The Americans were brutally shot down by the light infantry, as bullet after bullet was fired from point blank range into their unsuspecting bodies. These seven men would be forever remembered by their families as heroes – however unwilling – of the Cause.

Surveying the scene all around him, Captain Parker took stock of how his men were faring. He was pleased to see that most of them remained safely behind their selected cover, with one exception. Jedediah Munroe continued to stand resolutely out in the open, exactly where Parker had left him several minutes before. As Parker watched, he was overcome with incredible sadness as Munroe was struck twice by British bullets, sending him sprawling onto his back. One look at the lifeless eyes that stared up into the blue New England sky told Parker all he needed to know. The British had taken full advantage of their second chance at killing the old man.

***

The scene was quickly becoming one of confusion and chaos, as the British soldiers began to break apart and make attempts to run haphazardly away from the ambush, most of them choosing to wisely go in the direction of Boston down the Lexington road. It appeared that the invaders into the New England countryside were about to be completely annihilated, literally within sight of their initial transgression at the Lexington Common that morning.

Suddenly, a loud, booming noise reverberated from the direction of Boston. A brief silence ensued for several seconds, as everyone stopped and looked toward the unfamiliar sound. It didn't take long for all to realize that what they were hearing was the sound of a British cannon posted on a small hill a few hundred yards away. The sound was followed by the crash of a cannon ball falling into one of the stands of trees just off the side of the road. While the tangible effect of the shot was negligible, landing nowhere near any of the Minutemen, the psychological effect was immediate and dramatic.

The Minutemen, not just in the small woods where the shot had fallen, but all around the road, instinctively moved further away from their positions. While the Americans were confident in their ability to engage their enemy with musket fire, this was a weapon for which the Minutemen had no response.

Meanwhile, the initial shot followed soon after by another, was like a jolt of energy to the British column. Such a sound could mean only one thing – reinforcements had arrived from Boston to save them! Immediately, the chaos began to subside, as the British officers finally gained some semblance of control over their men. Firing lines, however unsteady they may have been before, began to form, and the light infantry flankers pushed outward with bold determination to create some safety for their comrades.

Captain Parker, having seen his share of fighting throughout his life, realized with disappointment that the arrival of the British cannon and reinforcements completely changed the deadly game they were playing. Understanding the danger this new development posed to he and his men, he began shouting orders to fall back away from the road and regroup in the fields a safe distance away.

Douglas J. Shupinski

Major John Pitcairn

Commanding Officer, His Majesty's Marine Forces

Lexington Road to Boston

2:00 P.M. April 19, 1775

Things had become increasingly desperate over the last hour or so, such that the men were beginning to openly disobey the orders of their officers. While Major Pitcairn had occasionally seen an individual soldier fail to follow orders in the past, this was the first time in Pitcairn's career that he had seen such behavior on a wide scale. It was interesting, he reflected grimly, how the prospect of getting shot down like a dog in the road had that effect on a man.

The only bright spot of the entire march had been the nearly invisibility of Lieutenant Colonel Smith. Early on in the march, Smith had been wounded somewhat badly in the leg, and had abandoned what little pretense of leadership he had exhibited up to that point. For a short time Smith had ridden on a horse to keep the weight off of his wounded leg, but the sight of an officer's uniform high above the rest of the column had proved irresistible to the Rebel marksmen. After a few close calls of numerous musket balls narrowly missing Colonel Smith and striking the unfortunate other wounded men around him, he had made the decision that his leg didn't really hurt all that much.

Complete command of the expedition – for whatever that was worth – had therefore fallen squarely on the shoulders of Major Pitcairn. He realized that his column was literally fighting for its very survival, as these Rebels were displaying a level of courage and discipline that no one could have imagined. Even Pitcairn, who had warned against underestimating the resolve of these simple farmers and tradesmen, had failed to appreciate how determined they were to make their point and defend their homes.

Pitcairn understood that his only chance of successfully making it through this gauntlet of Rebels relied on two things. First, he needed to get his light infantry out on either side of the column in order to keep the enemy back from the road and out of musket range. And second, he needed to maintain cohesion within the rest of the column. Both of these imperatives had proven extremely difficult to achieve, as the sheer numbers of the Rebels and the nature of the surrounding terrain conspired to spell the potential death of his command.

**

"Captain Laurie, if you please," Pitcairn said by way of summoning the young company commander to his side. Captain Laurie, having been roughed up at the North Bridge back at Concord, had since demonstrated a level of resilience and control that had impressed Pitcairn. As a result, Pitcairn found himself relying more and more on the young officer to carry out some of his most critical orders.

"Sir," Captain Laurie stated breathlessly, riding up and taking position alongside his new commanding officer. "What is it, sir?" Laurie's mobility had also proven to be valuable, as he was one of the very few remaining officers willing and able to stay atop his horse without being shot down by the enemy.

"Captain, I wish for you to address our situation on the left. Our flankers continue to creep back to what they perceive to be the safety of the column. Inform them that not only are they no safer here than out there, but that the continued existence of this command requires them to do their duty."

Douglas J. Shupinski

"Yes, sir, right away," Laurie replied, but lingered for just a moment.

"You have something to say, Captain Laurie?" Pitcairn asked, eyeing the young man carefully.

Captain Laurie, visibly uncomfortable, remained silent next to his commander.

"Damn it, man!" Pitcairn swore, "If you have something to say you had best do it quickly! How long do you think these Rebels will allow two idiotic officers to stand next to each other on horseback before they shoot us both down?"

"Major Pitcairn," Laurie said, lowering the volume of his voice, "we cannot continue to stand up to this onslaught. It is only a matter of time, sir, before we – well, before we – "

"What are you suggesting, Captain? Are you suggesting that we surrender to this rabble?" Pitcairn asked incredulously.

Laurie was shocked by the assumption his commander had made regarding his remarks, and was quick to set the record straight.

"No sir, never!" Laurie exclaimed with emotion. "I am only thinking that if we were to perhaps find a defensible position and place our men in a better position to stave off this attack, we might be better off. Walking out in the open as we are, the Rebels will most certainly continue to hit their marks."

Major Pitcairn briefly pondered the young man's suggestion, as he himself had thought about utilizing such a tactic. But his instinct told him that the only chance they had of making it back to Boston and safety was to keep moving. The moment they became static, they would be surrounding by the vastly superior numbers of the enemy and annihilated.

"Captain Laurie," Pitcairn replied slowly, looking the man dead in the eye, "I know your military experience has taught you that you must obey the orders of your commander because he outranks you. But there are times in which you must also obey your commander because you *trust* him. This situation, Captain – " Pitcairn said pausing to insure he had the desired effect on the man – "is one such time."

Major Pitcairn was mildly amused to see, of all things, a smile cross the face of the young officer.

"Aye, sir," Laurie replied smartly, "I shall see to the disposition of our troops on the left flank immediately!"

With the smile still lingering strangely on his lips, Captain Walter Laurie rode off to do his duty, his trust resting fully with the Marine major.

***

When the cannon shot came, it took no one by surprise more than Major John Pitcairn. While he hadn't quite admitted that their situation was hopeless – Pitcairn was simply incapable of such a sentiment – he had grudgingly acknowledged that many of the members of his command would not be returning to Boston. As he had watched in just these last few minutes, dozens of his men had been struck down by the incoming Rebel bullets, and there were now too many casualties for the other men to carry. As a result, Pitcairn was able to turn around and look back down a road that was lined with dead and wounded British soldiers.

Pitcairn had resorted to the rather unprofessional tactic of placing many of his officers and senior enlisted men at the head of the column armed with muskets and bayonets. Any man who attempted to run down the road on his own toward the safety of Boston was to be bayoneted, by the order of Major John Pitcairn. Issued by such an individual, with the steel to back it up, no one doubted that it would be followed to the letter.

The effect of the cannon shot, and the ensuing understanding of its implications, was immediate. The soldiers knew that not only their lives, but their pride, were being rescued by a relief column sent from Boston by General Gage. The men began organizing themselves into the appropriate formations, the discipline returning quickly to their movements.

In the distance, a few hundred yards down the Lexington Road from the struggling column, a force of British soldiers had taken up position on either side of the road. To Pitcairn's relief, he saw that the reinforcements that had been sent were substantial in number, probably five hundred or more. Between those men and their cannon, and his bedraggled force, they should be able to make it back to Boston in one piece.

Pitcairn rode ahead of the column in order to make contact with the commander of the relief force. As he arrived within the relative safety of the relief column's lines, he was met by Lord Percy, the commanding officer of the British First Brigade. Percy's first comment was both direct and an acknowledgment of the obvious.

"Good God, man, you look like hell! And the rest of your column looks even worse from what I can see from here," Percy stated.

"My Lord, my men and I have been under fire from hundreds, if not thousands of Rebels for the last several miles. Since departing Concord, sir, we have suffered a level of casualties I would never have thought possible."

Lord Percy, a man with at least as much military and combat experience as Major Pitcairn, seemed unfazed by the statement.

"I have no doubt, Major," Percy replied. "We ourselves have suffered from a similar onslaught by these savages. We must combine our forces and return with all possible haste to Boston. I trust that my cannon will assist us in this endeavor. In case you haven't noticed, these Rebels may exhibit a modest level of bravery when facing a man with a musket, but artillery seems to unnerve them to a considerable degree."

Pitcairn was overwhelmed with relief as he realized that Percy had no intention of settling in and fighting it out with the enemy. Percy had come to the same conclusion: that movement meant survival.

As the two men discussed their plans further, Pitcairn's column began shuffling past them, many of the men saluting Lord Percy with genuine gratitude. Theirs was an experience that none of them would soon forget.

***

The march of the final eight miles back to Boston was, in many respects, no easier than what had been experienced by Pitcairn's column alone. The Rebels continued to exact their toll on the British soldiers marching down the open road, but with the added strength of several hundred men, along with the cannon so dreaded by the Americans, their return was accomplished successfully.

Upon reaching their barracks in Boston, the men grudgingly formed into their proper ranks on the parade ground, their officers insisting on this one final display of military protocol and discipline. Upon being dismissed, not a single man lingered for even a minute, as they all returned to their designated locations to address their physical or psychological wounds.

For his part, Major John Pitcairn took little consolation in the fact that it was primarily because of his actions that any of these men had succeeded in returning at all. Had he not suggested to Lieutenant Colonel Smith that he send back to Boston for reinforcements, Lord Percy would never have arrived as their Angel of Salvation. And had he not exerted his own personal will that his men continue marching down the deadly space of Lexington Road, they might not have ever reached their Rescuer.

What had started out as a simple mission to march out into the New England countryside and confiscate a supply of weapons and supplies had turned into an all-out battle for survival. The deadly drama of a war had begun. And Pitcairn couldn't shake the realization that he had been the one to raise the curtain.

Douglas J. Shupinski

Major General Artemus Ward

Commanding General, Massachusetts Militia

Outside of Boston

April 30, 1775

Men from the militia units throughout New England had been pouring into the areas surrounding Boston for the last several days, their anger raised by the events at Lexington and Concord. Men from all walks of life – farmers from Massachusetts; fishermen from Rhode Island; tradesmen from Connecticut; lumberjacks from New Hampshire – all had responded to the cry that had gone out throughout the Colonies to rise up and face the tyranny of the British attack upon their homes. Amazingly, within less than a week's time there were over 15,000 men assembled around the city of Boston.

The British, following their disastrous attempt to reach out and impose their will on the surrounding countryside, had determined that it was best to retreat to the relative safety of the city. Although they did make efforts to extend themselves to the edges of the city limits, there were no attempts to move out beyond the peninsula that made up the city of Boston. This decision allowed the Americans to form a semi-circle around the city, stretching from Dorchester Heights to the south of the city up to Prospect Hill to the northwest.

Forty-seven year old Major General Artemus Ward of the Massachusetts Militia was conflicted on how he felt about the situation. On one hand, the fact that the rebellion was actually beginning to gain momentum was a cause for celebration in his mind. On the other hand, the current state of affairs was a virtual stalemate. As the Americans around Boston outnumbered the British by a ratio of almost two to one, it wasn't realistic for the British to attempt an attack on the American positions. Likewise, the British not only had strong defensive positions, but literally hundreds of cannon supporting them from their ships anchored in Boston Harbor. These two facts made an attack by the Americans an almost suicidal venture. Hence, the aforementioned stalemate.

The so-called Rebel army forming the semi-circle around Boston consisted primarily of men from four New England colonies. New Hampshire, Connecticut, and Rhode Island had all sent significant numbers of men to Boston, and of course Massachusetts led the way in terms of volunteers. All of this resulted in the numerical advantage enjoyed by the Americans. But this advantage was somewhat tempered by a number of considerations.

Most notably, while Major General Ward was technically in command of the American forces surrounding Boston, his position held little significance to the gathered men. These citizen soldiers gave their loyalty to their respective home colonies as opposed to a cohesive force that might otherwise have been referred to as an army. The fact that they had crossed the imaginary boundaries from one colony into another in order to offer their services was surprising enough; to expect that they would then place themselves under the command and control of some officer they had never heard of from another colony was simply too much to ask right now. In many cases, if not most, men from one colony simply refused to obey the orders of any officer that was not from their own colony. In fact, some units responded to direction that only came from officers of their specific town's unit.

For his part, Artemus Ward was as true of an American as one could find. He had been born in Massachusetts in 1727, the sixth of seven children in his family. Unlike most children in the Colonies, who received virtually no formal education, Artemus had been formally tutored at a young age, eventually attending Harvard University and graduating in 1748. In addition to his academic proficiencies, Ward had also served with the British army during the French and Indian War, climbing to the rank of colonel in the militia. His combat experience consisted of a rather unremarkable participation in the attack upon Fort Ticonderoga in 1758, combined with garrison duty for much of the remainder of his time. Nevertheless, in comparison to most of the other men who had been commissioned as officers in the various militias, he was modestly qualified.

In addition to the issues with the command structure, there were other challenges faced by General Ward which were both immediate and significant. First, the logistics of maintaining such a large number of men quickly became apparent. As no one had foreseen the events at Lexington and Concord two days earlier, let alone the response from the surrounding colonies, no provision had been made to see to the rather basic matters of feeding these men and providing for their hygiene needs. From the start, the areas in which these men now resided had quickly become filthy and disorganized, as men did what they determined was necessary to both feed and relieve themselves.

Second, there was a remarkable lack of military experience, even within the ranks of the officers. While a few of the men had fought in the French and Indian War alongside their current adversaries, or had been involved in minor skirmishes with the Indian population, most had only used a musket for the purpose of hunting.

Third, all manner of disease had quickly begun to spread amongst the thousands of men now crammed into their small camps. The combination of poor camp hygiene, close quarters, and little former exposure to many of the diseases now present, resulted in a near epidemic. Hundreds of men quickly fell ill, and several even died, some of the first tragic casualties of the war.

But the most significant crisis was the inability of this fighting force to carry out the most basic of objectives: wage war upon the enemy. While most men had arrived armed with their own muskets, there were still several thousand men who lacked a weapon of any kind.

Artillery was limited to a few scattered cannon and mortars, and even fewer men with the knowledge of how to use these implements of battle. Worst of all, both muskets and cannon required gunpowder, a commodity that was in such short supply as to make any real military operations virtually impossible.

***

"My God, Israel, you'd think we were commanding a herd of wild animals! I haven't observed even the most basic display of military discipline since this band of ruffians came together."

Artemus Ward was addressing Israel Putnam, the commanding general of the militia that had recently arrived from Connecticut. Ward's statements, while blunt and unflattering, were essentially accurate. Thousands of men had spread themselves throughout the Massachusetts countryside, making every effort to get comfortable without the slightest thought to such things as defensive posture, organization, or cleanliness. The result was a gaggle of chaos that appalled the locals and horrified the generals.

"That's true, General, that's true," Putnam replied thoughtfully, "but these men have heart. I can teach a man to shoot or march or build a redoubt, but I can't teach him to have heart."

Ward gave a surprised glance in the direction of his old friend.

"I must admit, I wouldn't have expected such a reaction from you, Israel. A man with your experience surely appreciates the need for training and discipline in an army."

Truly, Israel Putnam was a man who had no lack of military experience. Now at the ripe old age of fifty seven, Putnam had seen action on numerous occasions throughout the French and Indian War. In 1758, he had been captured by a group of Indians and almost burned at the stake. In 1762 in a British expedition against Cuba, he had been shipwrecked for a time, surviving that ordeal as well. A variety of other minor and major engagements made up the past of this well respected officer. Upon hearing of the events at Lexington and Concord, Putnam had ridden one hundred miles in just over eight hours, arriving just in time to be commissioned a Major General in the Connecticut militia.

"No doubt, Artemus, there's no substitute for having the chance to whip a man into shape before you send him into a battle. But I'll tell you what concerns me most of all," replied Putnam. "We have almost no cannon. We have almost no mortars. We have nothing to make those British soldiers over there in Boston cringe in fear. Meanwhile, they have all those nice, fat ships sitting right there in the harbor, just ready to rip our heads off with more metal than this ragtag group of men can possibly imagine."

General Israel Putnam glanced over at his friend with a look that bordered on hunger – hunger for the tools of war.

"We need cannon, Artemus."

Colonel Ethan Allen

Commanding Officer, Green Mountain Boys

Fort Ticonderoga

4:00 AM May 10, 1775

It was a pitch black moonless night as the eighty-three men disembarked from the scowls they had commandeered for the crossing of Lake Champlain located in the very upper north of the New York colony. The first man to set foot on dry ground was, as always, Colonel Ethan Allen. The men that followed quickly after him were members of the infamous "Green Mountain Boys", a name chosen by the men themselves to advertise the fact that they were from the Green Mountains, part of the New Hampshire Grants.

Ethan Allen was a veritable legend in his own time. While the average man stood no more than five feet seven inches in height, Allen was a behemoth at six feet four inches. In addition, his strength was every bit the match for his height, and there were stories of him facing off in fights against as many as seven men at one time, leaving not a single man in a conscious state at the conclusion of the altercation. His irreverence toward formalized religion, his amazing penchant for swearing, and his ability to consume mass quantities of alcohol made him a most unwelcome personage among the ranks of the "civilized" –

but absolutely loved and revered by the men he now commanded.

The Green Mountain Boys were men that had banded together years earlier in order to oppose the territorial disputes that existed between New Hampshire and New York, both of whom laid claim to significant tracts of land that lay along their common borders. While the Boys had never engaged in anything remotely resembling actual combat in pursuit of their goals, they had nevertheless been victorious in numerous bar fights and street brawls. Such men demanded in a leader someone with supreme physical strength, as well as intelligence to determine when and how to employ that strength. In Ethan Allen, they found both.

***

The Continental Congress of the American colonies was looking for soldiers to perform a mission that was expected to be extremely dangerous. Further east, over 15,000 militiamen milled about outside of Boston, having no ability to impose their will on the British soldiers holed up in the city. This was due to the fact that this "army" of militia had no artillery of which to speak. At some point, someone had suggested that the British-held Fort Ticonderoga located in the upper reaches of New York just might be the answer to their prayers. Inside the fort, there was an unknown but significant quantity of cannon, mortars, and powder – exactly the solution to the problem faced by the Americans outside of Boston. If someone were bold enough to launch a surprise attack on this fortress, they might just be able to overpower the garrison guarding the fort, and take possession of the precious artillery located inside.

It was at that point that someone had thought of Ethan Allen and the Green Mountain Boys.

Allen had jumped at the opportunity to put his men to work on something that promised excitement and fame – not to mention a chance to strike a blow against the British, for whom none of these men had anything but disdain. The group had quickly organized themselves, and had set off to accomplish their assigned mission.

***

As the men clamored ashore, they quickly organized themselves into several ranks in preparation for their assault on the fort, now barely visible with the approach of dawn. In addition to these eighty-three men, there were perhaps a hundred more waiting back on the shoreline from which they had departed, and the small boats began making ready to return and fetch these men as additional reinforcements.

A deep, gruff voice hissed out of the darkness in the direction of the men in charge of the boats.

"Jim, stop right there, man," Ethan Allen commanded the boatman. "There's no time to get the others if we are to have any chance of surprising the garrison. It would be best for you to remain right here in the event we are compelled to – depart quickly."

"Ah, let 'em go, Colonel," a voice joked quietly from the darkness. "The way he 'bout near killed us all coming over, I think I'd just as soon swim back across the lake if it comes to that!"

A chorus of soft chuckles emanated from the group, providing a needed break from the tension.

"The hell with all of ya!" responded the boatman with quiet ferocity. "If you had all stopped whining and swaying back and forth like little schoolgirls, there wouldn'ta been any problems."

"Never mind that, Jim," Allen replied, unable to wipe a broad smile from his face, "just stay right here. Me and the Boys won't be needin' any reinforcements anyway."

"If I may, Mr. Allen, I would suggest that a bit less humor and a bit more focus might be in order, considering our situation," stated a man standing just a few feet away from Allen.

The comment had come from Captain Benedict Arnold, the ostensible second in command of the expedition.

At first glance, there could have been no greater contrast between two men than that which existed between Ethan Allen and Benedict

Arnold. While Allen was huge in terms of his sheer size, Benedict Arnold was somewhat diminutive in stature, although possessing a rather muscular build. Ethan Allen dressed in whatever "uniform" struck his fancy, often attiring himself in buckskin. Benedict Arnold was always immaculately dressed in a formal military uniform. Ethan Allen had come from a modest background, his father having died early in his life and leaving the family to fend for themselves. Benedict Arnold's family had been relatively well-off, allowing Arnold the opportunity to start himself off successfully in the business world. Ethan Allen had attempted several business ventures, none of which amounted to anything of substance. At the time of the current expedition, Benedict Arnold was a fairly rich businessman, having prospered in a variety of commercial ventures.

But there were also a number of similarities between the two men. Both Ethan Allen and Benedict Arnold were extremely intelligent men, with a knack for accurately sizing up a situation very quickly. Both had a certain charisma which compelled men to follow them despite the severity of the situation. Both had fought in the French and Indian War. Ethan Allen was thirty-seven years old; Benedict Arnold was thirty-four. But the most striking similarity, which also created the greatest amount of tension between Ethan Allen and Benedict Arnold, was their ambition.

Benedict Arnold had initially been assigned the job of attacking Fort Ticonderoga, having presented himself to the Massachusetts Committee of Safety and suggesting the attack. Arnold had quickly assembled a group of men to make the attack, and was informed that he would be reinforced by Ethan Allen and his Green Mountain Boys once he had gotten closer to the objective.

However, when the two forces had met up several miles from the fort a day earlier, Benedict Arnold was disappointed to find that the Green Mountain Boys – the larger group of the two – had absolutely no intention of placing themselves under the command of this rather foppish militia officer. In fact, the men had made it quite clear that were they to be forced to do any such thing, they would rather abandon the expedition. Their allegiance lay firmly with Colonel Ethan

Allen.

Benedict Arnold, while an ambitious man, was also smart enough to realize that this was a fight he simply could not win. He therefore reluctantly agreed to serve as Ethan Allen's second in command, provided he was able to stay right next to Allen during the upcoming attack. To the Green Mountain Boys, the location of this upstart from the city meant little, as long as their colonel remained firmly in command. They all quickly agreed to the arrangement.

***

Colonel Ethan Allen slowly turned his attention in the direction of Benedict Arnold, fixing him with a stare that burned through even the dissipating darkness.

"Captain Arnold, I would appreciate it if you would demonstrate a bit of respect towards your present company," Ethan Allen stated. "You are, after all, somewhat of an uninvited guest of ours."

The men unconsciously stopped moving, waiting to see the result of the first real challenge to Allen's command.

"There was no disrespect intended, Mr. Allen," Benedict Arnold cautiously replied, "merely a suggestion that may help us to avoid being discovered."

"First of all," Ethan Allen replied, "my men will be 'discovered' when we choose to be, and not before. And second, I would appreciate if you would refer to me as 'Colonel' Allen – not 'Mister'. Is that clear – Captain?"

With the formalities of establishing the pecking order now complete, the men continued organizing themselves for the assault on Fort Ticonderoga. Despite the fact that they were facing a completely unknown situation, not a single man displayed the slightest hesitation in carrying out the orders they were receiving.

The eighty-three men quickly covered the half mile distance between their landing spot and the south wall of the fort, Allen leading the way with Benedict Arnold close on his heels. Upon arriving at the wall, the men were surprised to see the ruinous condition of the fort.

Douglas J. Shupinski

While the reports they had received indicated that the structure was not in its best condition, they were still somewhat shocked at how much the fort had crumbled in contrast to its previous days of glory during the French and Indian War when it had held out in the face of attacks by literally thousands of soldiers.

The men quickly clambered over the collapsed wall, instinctively spreading out as they reached the other side. Ethan Allen had covered only a few yards when he spotted a British sentry standing watch a short distance away. The sentry, having not seen another soul for months outside of those who resided in the fort, nearly had a heart attack at the sight of the mob that now presented itself. He stumbled to his feet, hastily pointing his musket in the general direction of the approaching men as he ran away, and pulled the trigger.

Fortunately for the Green Mountain Boys – and probably as well for the sentry – the musket merely flashed the gunpowder in its pan, failing to ignite the gunpowder in the muzzle of the weapon necessary to propel the bullet from the barrel. The sentry quickly fled into the center of the fort, shouting at the top of his lungs that they were under attack.

Allen's men were close on the heels of the terrified sentry, shouting like madmen now that there was no longer a need for silence and stealth. Another sentry appeared, stunned by what he saw. This man at least had the presence of mind to face his attackers, and actually managed to thrust his bayonet at a passing Green Mountain Boy, wounding him slightly.

An incensed Colonel Allen roared in anger at this second sentry, and raised his huge sword as he hurtled himself in the direction of the man who had possessed the temerity to assault one of his men. But at the last minute, Allen had mercy on this wretched soul who had at least demonstrated a shred of bravery. Instead of slashing the sentry across the head or chest, Allen merely thumped the man on the top of the head with the flat of his sword, nearly knocking the man unconscious.

"Damn you to Hell, man!" Ethan Allen shouted at the sentry. "You will take me to your officers' quarters, or I will kill you where you stand! Green Mountain Boys, draw yourselves into ranks and prepare for the surrender of the fort. Captain Arnold, if you would be so kind as to accompany me."

Without so much as a word, the British sentry led the way up a set of stairs which made its way into the interior of the fort, followed closely by Ethan Allen and Benedict Arnold. Again, they were surprised to note the extremely poor condition of the fort, especially in light of the fact that it was supposedly home to such a rich harvest of artillery.

As the three men made their way up the battered stairwell, they suddenly came face to face with a British lieutenant standing in the doorway of what was most likely his quarters. The officer had clearly not expected any visitors, as he was only half dressed and carrying his pants in his hands.

"Come out of there, you damned old rascal!" shouted Allen.

The lieutenant, although initially shocked at the order, composed himself enough to address his attackers.

"By what authority do you give such an order to an officer of the King's army!" demanded the lieutenant.

"In the name of the Great Jehovah and the Continental Congress!" replied Colonel Allen. "My men and I hereby demand the surrender of this fort and all of the effects contained therein. A failure to comply with these demands immediately shall see the massacre of every man, woman, and child inside of these walls!"

At that moment, a British captain arrived breathlessly, at least in this case having the good manners to present himself fully clothed. He had even had the presence of mind to arm himself with his sword.

"What in God's name is going on here?" questioned the captain.

"Sir," the British lieutenant replied, "this man demands the surrender of the fort and its contents, or he claims he will massacre everyone within our walls!"

To the British captain, it was a situation beyond his ability to comprehend or control. He had been awakened from a dead sleep and accosted by this giant of a man armed with the largest sword he had ever seen. The entire garrison of this fort consisted of less than fifty soldiers, most of them unfit for service. It was hardly a formidable force to bring to bear. And finally, there were also numerous women and children – the wives and children of some of the soldiers – that made their home inside Fort Ticonderoga. The threat of a massacre was simply too much to bear.

As the shocked lieutenant looked on, the British captain bowed his head and presented his sword to Colonel Ethan Allen in surrender.

***

One shot had been fired. One American had been slightly grazed by a bayonet. The result was the capture of an entire fort that held nearly a hundred pieces of artillery including cannon, mortars, and howitzers. In addition, the other supplies confiscated included thousands of cannon balls, tons of musket balls, and various other items that would come in quite handy to the Americans around Boston.

Although the significant issue of how to get these cannon and supplies to Boston over three hundred miles away still existed, the first significant step had been taken.

General Artemus Ward had his cannon.

Major General William Howe

British Army

Boston

June 1, 1775

It had been exactly a week since Major General William Howe had arrived in America aboard the HMS Cerberus. Generals John Burgoyne and Henry Clinton had also traveled to the Colonies with Howe, and together the three generals had been tasked with lending their expertise and experience to what was becoming a challenging situation for the British government.

This was, by no means, William Howe's first time in America. Born in August of 1729, Howe had joined the army in 1746. Howe had built a distinguished reputation based on his bravery and coolness in combat, and his time fighting in North America during the French and Indian War was only one of a number of experiences that had added significantly to his legend. It was during such engagements as Louisburg and The Plains of Abraham against the French that Howe had become famous – and respected – for his propensity to lead from the front. It was a habit that he had found difficult to break, even after having attained the lofty rank of Major General, and it was a constant source of concern to his subordinates.

Douglas J. Shupinski

Physically, Howe was tall, carried himself erect at all times, and looked every inch the general that had won the admiration of his soldiers. To some degree, his appearance was beginning to show the effects of years of eating and drinking well, sometimes to excess, but at the age of forty-five he still looked imposing. In addition, he also exhibited the stereotypical behaviors of many of his colleagues with respect to a love of gambling and the fairer sex.

In addition to his military endeavors, William Howe had also gained a great deal of experience in working and dealing with the Colonists, fighting alongside them on more than one occasion. There were even stories of Howe having donned the colonists' "uniform" of buckskin and camouflage when going into battle. This experience had caused him to develop a connection with these colonists, and he had found himself sympathetic to their current situation. In fact, as a powerful politician in his own right, Howe had repeatedly spoken out against almost all of the policies being forced upon the American Colonies by the British government, instead preaching the need to pursue reconciliation. Howe had gone so far as to state publicly that he would never willingly engage in military action against the American Colonies, and if called upon to do so, he would resign his commission.

However, when General Howe was ordered to proceed to America in order to aid in putting down the rebellion there, he reluctantly acquiesced. While a man of strong personal values, his allegiance to the British army was simply greater than any compulsion he may have had to remain neutral toward the Colonies.

***

Howe's companions, General John Burgoyne and General Henry Clinton, had proven to be a study in contrasts. John Burgoyne, whose nickname with his troops was "Gentleman Johnny", was the quintessential socialite. In addition to being a military leader, the handsome yet portly general was also fairly well known for his writing abilities, having written several plays that had enjoyed modest success in England.

Unlike a vast majority of his fellow British officers who were rarely shy about exercising heavy-handed discipline on their men, Burgoyne was a proponent of treating the enlisted man with a level of respect that was almost unheard of in the British military. As a means of enlightening his officers to understand this relatively humanitarian approach to military life, he insisted that they not only be well educated, but that they also continue their learning through reading and discussion amongst one another. He was, in a phrase, a Renaissance Man.

On the other hand, Henry Clinton's personality could only be described as direct, to a degree that made him appear almost coarse at times. Despite the fact that he was only thirty-seven years old at the time he arrived in Boston – the youngest of the three generals - he possessed a level of cynicism and negativity that would normally be expected from a much older man who had seen the dark side of the world one too many times.

While the earlier military careers of Howe and Burgoyne had been marked by heroism and audacity, Clinton had displayed less of such behaviors. His rather meteoric rise to his current rank had been more a matter of his reputation for taking careful consideration of all options before taking action, and he was better known for his abilities to plan operations more so than their actual execution. He was a "caretaker" officer, who may not have improved many situations with his actions, but at least had not made them any worse.

Regardless of their individual strengths and flaws, as a group these three men personified the best that the British military had to offer in terms of sheer experience and leadership. This was one of the reasons that they had been dispatched to America. The other reason – not so directly acknowledged by the King – was to become sufficiently familiar with what was going on in the Colonies such that they could replace General Thomas Gage should the situation require it.

The relationship between these men was rife with competition, as no formal command structure within the group had been established other than the fact that General Gage was in charge. In effect, the King had purposely created an environment in which he would allow the other three subordinate generals to joust for position while the King looked on and evaluated their actions. If and when the time came to replace Gage, the King would wave his hand and promote the man he deemed most worthy.

***

The four generals – Gage, Howe, Burgoyne, and Clinton – had gathered in the main room of the Boston house that General Gage had appropriated as his headquarters. A heated discussion had taken place for the last hour on the topic of what should be done to address the situation the British army was facing. While all four men agreed that action needed to be taken, there was a difference of opinion on what that action should be.

"Gentlemen, surely you must appreciate the effect this – siege, if we must call it that – is having on the morale of our men," Clinton stated flatly. "Every day we sit idle, we risk becoming laughing stocks not only of our enemy, but of our own men!"

"What are you suggesting, General Clinton?" Gage asked, playing the role of facilitator of the conversation.

"I'm suggesting that we organize our troops, and launch an attack to break out of this embarrassing hole into which you – we, have crawled," Clinton responded, quickly avoiding any placement of blame.

"I must continue to disagree with your suggestion for immediate military action," Burgoyne said. "These people surrounding us have no comprehension of the seriousness of their actions. If we were to confront them with the obvious – that they have threatened the Crown and shown themselves to be treasonous to their government – the popular reaction would most assuredly be an abandonment of their positions. And," Burgoyne continued, warming to his own ideas, "we must also impose immediate and severe martial law on the city of Boston. Our actions must reflect our words."

Howe, having remained silent for the last several minutes while he listened and considered the words of his colleagues, spoke up. He realized that he needed to choose his words carefully in order to avoid sounding overly cautious.

"Gentlemen, I do not believe we have reached the point of no return with these colonists. While they have certainly committed a most egregious attack upon our troops and, therefore, our government, I believe we still have time and space to settle this dispute in a somewhat amicable manner. By lashing out at these farmers and tradesmen – whom I am still not prepared to refer to as 'the enemy' – we will be the ones to make the final decision to start a war. A war which, while we most certainly will win, will still be extremely costly to our country both in the short and long term."

Because of the high regard with which the other generals held Howe, they paused for several seconds to consider his comments. The first to respond was General Burgoyne.

"General Howe, I am about to pay you the compliment of being direct. Perhaps you are not the most objective source of an opinion on this particular matter, in that you have already made your emotions well known as it relates to these Colonists. And while we have all had the opportunity to interact with these people in the past, I believe it would be safe to say that you have demonstrated a more sympathetic view to their Cause than the rest of us."

There was a somewhat stunned silence in the room, punctuated only by the ticking of a large grandfather clock sitting in the far corner of the room. Burgoyne's comments had stepped over the line of being candid, and had insinuated that Howe was incapable of making a rational decision. William Howe could feel his face burning, but his years as a politician allowed him to keep his temper in check, at least for the time being.

General Gage, always the peacemaker in these types of situations, attempted to smooth over what were obviously inflammatory comments from General Burgoyne.

"Gentlemen, clearly we all have personal and professional experiences that influence the opinions we have on any number of issues, this current one notwithstanding," Gage stated in a conciliatory tone. "I would ask that we..."

"No, General Gage, I believe that General Burgoyne has a valid point," Howe responded, choosing to take the high road. "I do have a strong connection to these Colonists for a variety of reasons. I have fought beside them, as have all of you, and found them to be of solid character. I admire their industrious nature, having literally built something from nothing. When my brother was tragically killed in combat, these Colonists honored him with a statue that stands to this day."

Howe paused for effect, looking each of the other three generals in the eye in order to drive his point home.

"However, that fact does not change my belief that a war will be both costly and unnecessary. Therefore, I feel extremely confident in standing by both my sentiments as well as my suggestions."

William Howe realized that he was beginning to dislike John Burgoyne, starting as far back as the commencement of their voyage from England. He was simply too much the showman for Howe, relying more on bluster and less on substance. However, it wasn't until this moment that he realized that he would never get along with John Burgoyne. Howe worried that his distaste for Burgoyne might even be a temptation to take overt actions to make this man look bad.

"Gentlemen, obviously it is not necessary for us to make a decision just yet," Gage said. "There is no immediate threat to the safety of either our troops nor to the city, therefore we are afforded the opportunity to continue our discussions and come to the best course of action."

"Action, sir, that is the key word here," stated General Clinton, wanting there to be no doubt regarding his counsel. "I only wish I had the opportunity to attack these rogues straight on; they would crack like a walnut."

"I suggest that you be careful what you wish for, General Clinton," warned Howe. "We have all fought alongside many of these men that now surround us. While they may not possess the ideal level of military professionalism, the one thing I have rarely seen them do is 'crack'."

Colonel William Prescott

Massachusetts Militia Forces

Outside of Boston

6:00 P.M. June 16, 1775

After weeks of waiting and indecision, action was finally being taken by the Americans surrounding Boston. The American Militia had been ordered to seize the heights located on the Charlestown peninsula to the immediate north of Boston, and to then prepare those same heights to be defended against a possible British attack.

A significant number of the members of the Massachusetts Committee of Safety had been hesitant to order such an action. Despite the fact that the skirmishes at Lexington and Concord had occurred a few weeks ago, many still held onto the hope that the differences between England and her American Colonies could be resolved in a peaceful manner. These same individuals believed that a move to fortify the Charlestown peninsula would force the British army in Boston to attack, the British no doubt perceiving the move as a direct threat.

However, several days earlier on June 13, the Massachusetts Committee of Safety had learned that the British had threatening plans of their own. Not only were they planning to occupy the heights of the Charlestown peninsula north of the city, but their plan also called for an occupation of the Dorchester Heights immediately south of the city. These maneuvers were designed to drastically decrease the control the Americans held over the city of Boston and, by definition, their control over the British Army located there.

The receipt of this information, in effect, forced the hand of the Americans. They were faced with having to either launch a preemptive occupation of one or both of these positions, or abandon any pretense of continuing the siege.

On June 15, the Massachusetts Committee had finally issued their orders. They directed Artemus Ward, commander of all American forces surrounding Boston, to select an American officer to move troops onto the Charlestown peninsula north of the city and make whatever preparations were deemed appropriate for defense. The man General Ward selected for the job was Colonel William Prescott of the Massachusetts Militia.

***

Colonel William Prescott could be described as somewhat of a gentle giant to those who knew him in civilian life. Although he had always maintained a leadership involvement in the local Pepperell, Massachusetts militia, Prescott had satisfied himself with being a hard-working and modestly successful farmer.

However, the other side of William Prescott was one of military experience and battle-tested bravery. He had fought in the French and Indian War with the British, and had so distinguished himself in combat that he had been offered a commission in the British army at the age of only nineteen. He had respectfully turned down the offer in favor of a quieter, calmer existence back on his farm.

However, when the call had gone out on the night of April 18, 1775 that the British were advancing out of Boston toward Concord, Prescott - now well into his forties - had rallied his men from their beds and set off to join the fray. Despite the fact that he and his unit arrived too late to participate in the day's events, the ire of the man had been raised — he had pledged himself to fight for the Colonies, come what may.

William Prescott was a natural leader, in that men trusted his judgment and respected his experience, separate from any formal rank or position that he may or may not have held. He had neither the need nor the desire to engage in behaviors of self-promotion, which made him an ideal candidate to lead this army of farmers and tradesmen who had no time for such things.

***

The late June sun was beginning to disappear from the sky as three regiments of American militia stood formed on the Cambridge Common. The regiments, one of which was fittingly his own, gave Colonel Prescott a force of about eight hundred men with which to work. Prescott realized that this was nowhere near the number that would be needed to defend against a determined attack by the British, but he wasn't overly concerned. First, he had been promised a significant number of reinforcements in the very near future, such that his current strength would be nearly tripled. And second, much like many of the other men assembled on the Common, in his heart he truly believed that a full-scale war simply wasn't in the cards.

"Colonel Prescott, I beg to report the formation of the regiments, and their readiness to move out upon your orders." Colonel Ebenezer Bridge breathed rather heavily as he gave his report, no doubt due to the considerable amount of activity and effort that had been required to achieve the current state of preparedness.

While the patriotism of these men assembled here could not be questioned, their level of logistical acumen was still woefully inadequate. Many of the men had reported without weapons, without ammunition, without food or water – in a word, without much thought being put into this evolution. After all, in their minds they weren't really going to be required to do anything of significance. To date, they had struggled to occupy themselves with anything other than looking across the water at the city of Boston and its relatively inactive residents. Why should today be any different?

"Thank you, Colonel," Prescott replied, and then more quietly, "What do you think about the men's condition?"

Douglas F. Shupinski

"Their condition?" Bridge asked. "I think most of these men still consider what they're doing to be a break from the monotony of their normal lives. Just look at them," Bridge gestured with a hint of disgust.

Prescott's gaze revealed a mass of men that resembled anything but an army. There was such a variety of clothing and weapons that there appeared to be no two alike. Rather than standing at attention, they had assumed a variety of relaxed poses, some chatting with the men around them, others smoking pipes or chewing tobacco. Even their officers, elected mainly due to their popularity with the men, were conducting themselves in a most informal manner.

"Well Colonel, they may not be soldiers yet, but at least we know they're capable of work," Prescott noted. "And that will be the first order of business. By the time we reach our final position on the Charlestown peninsula, it will only be a few hours before daylight. By then, we must have completed a good portion of our defenses in the event the British navy decides to take exception to our actions."

Prescott was referring to the fact that the British had several well-armed warships floating on the Charles River to the east of the Charlestown peninsula, their numerous cannon having the potential to fire on the American positions depending on where they were located.

"Well then, we have that going for us, don't we?" Colonel Bridge said with a broad smile. "It's amazing how the sight of a few cannon balls flying in your direction can motivate a man to put his back into the shovel, eh?"

Both men laughed, an unlikely response to the first actual acknowledgment that they were about to place themselves and their men into a potentially deadly situation.

William Prescott was a fighter. He understood the seriousness of what he was about to do. But he also knew that the men looked to him for reassurance and strength as their leader. An apparent casual conversation with another regimental commander punctuated by some humor might go a long way to taking the edge off of any fear that might exist in the minds of these men. And were he to be honest with himself, Prescott could use some smoothing around the edges of his own fear.

***

The men had been marching for over two hours, the sun having set and thankfully taken with it much of the heat of the day. But it was still a muggy, windless night, and some of the men had begun to complain about the length of their evening stroll. Their displeasure was made even greater by the fact that not a single one of them had any real idea of what their final destination might be.

At one point, the men caught sight of some shadowy figures just ahead of them, and there were a few tense moments. But as they quickly closed the distance between themselves and these shadows, they revealed themselves to be several units of American militia waiting to join them on their march. These new men were a Connecticut regiment under the operational command of Captain Thomas Knowlton, a well-known and respected officer throughout much of the army surrounding Boston. His presence, along with the addition of his two hundred or so men, added a bit of much needed confidence, and the column continued forward breathing slightly easier. They now numbered over one thousand.

One other addition to the column created a lift to morale. Old Israel Putnam, the fifty-seven year old hero of the French and Indian War, was the regimental commander of the newly arrived Connecticut men. There was now little doubt among the men that between Prescott and Putnam there was no shortage of effective leadership.

Finally at about 11:30 PM, the column of men came to a fork in the road, well known to all of them. The fork to the left went off in the direction of any number of Massachusetts towns, and taking it would have provided little clue as to the ultimate destination. However, Colonel Prescott didn't go to the left, but rather headed down the right fork of the road.

To the thousand men who followed after him, the situation was now clear: they were moving onto the Charlestown peninsula, with their objective most likely being the rather prominent terrain feature known as Bunker Hill.

Colonel William Prescott

Massachusetts Militia Forces

Charlestown Peninsula

11:30 P.M. June 16, 1775

The column had been halted for the last few minutes, and the men took the opportunity to get a quick drink of water or bite of food – at least those who had possessed the presence of mind to bring such necessities with them.

Colonel William Prescott and General Israel Putnam had walked to the top of a slight rise that gave them a reasonably good view of the Charlestown peninsula that now presented itself in the starlight of the June night. Prescott adjusted his sword swinging from a scabbard on the left side of his body and looked thoughtfully out on the surrounding countryside

"Well, Israel, there you have it. Our objective is there for the taking. Our British friends may have had plans of occupying this place for themselves, but I suspect their job will be a bit more difficult now."

"Maybe so," Putnam replied slowly, chewing on a fresh plug of tobacco he had just inserted into his mouth. "But we have a lot of work in front of us if we have any hope of making Bunker Hill a defensive position the British will hesitate to attack. A redoubt, of course, will need to be erected, along with rifle pits, walls, supply paths – "

"Bunker Hill?" Prescott reacted, looking quickly at his counterpart. "My understanding was that we were to fortify Breed's Hill down there," he gestured further in the distance. "Breed's Hill is closer to the shoreline, and will present a much greater threat to the enemy. If the British awake in a few hours to the sight of a heavily fortified position so close to Boston, they will have no choice but to attack us."

"Yes, William, that may be true. But the fact that it is so close to Boston means that it will not be as easily defended as Bunker Hill. The guns of their ships, not to mention those located there on Copp's Hill, will have an easier time of focusing in on us."

Prescott was clearly vexed by the disagreement being voiced by Putnam, and it caused him to hesitate slightly before he responded.

"General," Prescott stated pointedly, wishing to acknowledge the fact that Putnam outranked him as a colonel, "I understand your opinion. But I believe my orders are to occupy Breed's Hill. One of the primary objectives of our mission is to goad the enemy into attacking us when we have the advantage of a strong position. In addition, I believe Breed's Hill also gives us the option of, well General…"

Prescott stopped talking and looked carefully at Putnam.

"The option of what, Colonel? Speak your mind man, this is no time to mince words!" demanded General Putnam.

"Well General, I was thinking that the occupation of Breed's Hill also allows us to place some of our men on Bunker Hill as a covering force in the event that we have to retreat."

Israel Putnam was clearly not convinced that Breed's Hill was the better choice, but he allowed his penchant for action over discussion to get the better of him.

"Very well, William," Putnam conceded. "Breed's Hill it shall be. Now let us conclude this incessant babbling between officers and get to the matter at hand. I shall give the order to my men to prepare to move onto Breed's Hill and get to work – I suggest you do the same with your men."

"Immediately, General," Prescott responded, relieved that the old general had no desire to pull rank on him. After all, eight hundred of

Douglas J. Shupinski

the thousand men now lounging comfortably behind them were under Prescott's direct command, and he believed that this expedition rightfully belonged to him. "Let us see to our responsibilities."

***

Many of the men were surprised as they took a small path directly over Bunker Hill without stopping, but rather continued on to the smaller Breed's Hill. Upon their arrival, the men were formed into small working parties and armed with picks, shovels, and any manner of digging tool that was available. However, their first order of business — as was almost always the case for soldiers — was to sit and wait.

Richard Gridley was the engineer that had been sent along with the expedition, and it was his responsibility to lay the plans for what would hopefully become a heavily fortified and formidable American defensive position. He began by staking out the ground that would serve as the "fort" of the position, and would therefore be the central location of all defensive efforts. In actuality, the structure would more appropriately be referred to as a redoubt, and would eventually be made of dirt walls reinforced with logs.

Gridley designed the redoubt to be about 140 feet long on each side, and he positioned it such that two of the flat edges of the boxlike structure would face the two most likely avenues of attack by the enemy. The wall facing south would defend against an attack coming from the town of Charlestown, a small grouping of about a hundred and fifty houses and buildings no more than a couple of hundred yards away from the hill. Meanwhile, the wall facing eastward covered a gentle slope rising up toward the hill, which also seemed to Prescott and Gridley to be a probable direction from which the enemy might launch an attack.

"Mr. Gridley," Prescott whispered as he approached the engineer in the darkness, "your assessment of the plans, please. Do we have the makings of a suitable defense?"

"If you're asking me about the *potential* of this position," replied Gridley, with noticeable concern straining his voice, "I would tell you that I'm quite pleased."

"I suspect there is more to your story, Gridley," prompted Prescott, now joined by Israel Putnam. "What is it that worries you?"

"Colonel Prescott, the suitable construction of a redoubt and its surrounding support network can often take several days, if not weeks!" hissed Gridley. "You are asking these men to complete such a task in just a few hours! If your objective is simply to erect some form of hollow threat to the enemy, then perhaps that can be done. But if you actually believe that this position will have to repel a determined attack by a sizable enemy force, well then Colonel, I don't believe – "

"You will keep what you believe to yourself, Mr. Gridley," Israel Putnam interrupted harshly. "These men have two weapons at their disposal – muskets and morale. One of these is already suspect, due to our relative lack of gunpowder and musket balls. I will not have you undermining the other. Is that clear?"

Gridley looked at Putnam, his eyes widening at the almost threatening remarks made by the general. He looked back to Prescott for some form of support, and was met with the same menacing glare.

"Qu–quite clear, General," Gridley stuttered. "I was merely making an observation based on my professional opinion regarding such matters."

"And they have been noted, Richard," Prescott responded, softening his tone slightly. "Now, if you please, I would appreciate you focusing your considerable talents on the construction of our position."

Gridley, somewhat placated by Prescott's compliment, saluted weakly and moved off to begin the direction of the work to be done.

***

These decisions and preparations having been made, the men set about the task of turning plans into reality under the extremely demanding eyes of William Prescott and Israel Putnam. As Colonel Prescott had predicted hours earlier, while these men might not have the greatest of military experience, their motivation to participate in good old fashioned hard labor was second to none. As the night wore on – much too fast for the liking of Colonel Prescott, he admitted to himself – the redoubt began to take shape with a rapidity that was almost magical.

By 3:30 AM, the men were completely exhausted, and most of them retired to the inside of the redoubt to catch their first relaxing moment in hours. Even at this early hour, the first streaks of daylight became visible in the distance of that great expanse known as the Atlantic Ocean just to the east of where they lay.

Soon thereafter, things began to happen quickly. At about 4:00 AM, one of the more observant lookouts aboard the British warship HMS Lively anchored in the Charles River only a few hundred yards away spotted the American position on Breed's Hill. His shouts of warning to his fellow crewmembers could be heard across the short distance of water separating that ship from the Charlestown peninsula, and everyone knew the element of surprise had finally run its course.

For William Prescott, this signaled the need to roust the men from their rest and get them back to work as quickly as possible. Now that the British were fully aware of what the Americans were up to, it meant that the clock was ticking until the British were able to organize and launch an assault on Breed's Hill.

"All right, men, on your feet!" Prescott shouted. "The British now know of our presence, and will most likely be paying us a visit in a short while. Company officers, I need half of the men to remain inside the redoubt and continue to strengthen that position. The other half will report to me on the double. Come on now men, backs to the shovels, let's get to work!"

As cannon balls from the British warships began to scream over their position, the men resting in relative safety within the redoubt looked at Colonel Prescott as if he must be some sort of mad man. Why, in God's name, would they be ordered to leave the redoubt and venture into what was quickly becoming a veritable killing ground of artillery fire?

While it may not have been apparent to the average soldier, the need to continue improving this defensive position was both obvious and shocking to William Prescott. As the morning had gradually dawned on this Massachusetts peninsula, he suddenly realized that while the darkness had been a Godsend in terms of providing them with concealment, this same darkness had hidden a fatal weakness in their position.

Israel Putnam strode purposefully up to Prescott, his eyes automatically drawn to the same area that was causing Prescott so much consternation.

"Our left flank is in the air, Israel," Prescott stated matter-of-factly, his penchant for getting directly to the heart of the matter showing itself as consistently as always.

What Prescott was referring to was the fact that between the redoubt and the shoreline to the left, there was a distance of over two hundred feet that was wide open. This meant that an enemy force could quite easily bypass the redoubt and attack the American position from behind. All of the planning and effort that had gone into protecting the southern and eastern facing sides of the redoubt would mean nothing if that were to occur.

"Yes, Colonel, you are correct," Putnam responded, his mind swirling with potential solutions to this alarming situation. "Our men need to create some form of defensive works from our position here down toward the shoreline," he stated, gesturing toward the wide gap to their left rear.

To his credit, the engineer Thomas Gridley had quickly noted the flaw as well, and had already begun putting the men to work digging breastworks in the exact locations in which they needed to exist.

"If the British were to attack right now, we would have no way of holding on to this position. It would quickly become a death trap for our men," noted Prescott, the slightest hint of panic creeping into his voice.

"There now, William," Putnam said in a reassuring tone, "but we know that the British will *not* attack right now, don't we? They have just discovered our presence, which means they will require time to form their men, cross the river, and organize themselves for an attack. And if our enemy is true to form, they will take their jolly old time in doing so, don't you think?"

Douglas J. Shupinski

For the countless time, Prescott was thankful for the presence of the wise old man, and he forced himself to breathe a sigh of relief. He even allowed himself just the hint of a smile, as a plan began to form in his mind.

"Of course, you're correct as always, Israel. Therefore, this is what I propose we do," suggested Prescott. "We will construct breastworks as far as that rail fence just there," he said, pointing at a low fence line that lay a hundred and fifty feet or so from the redoubt. "The men can reinforce those rails with mud and grass from the surrounding fields, providing some amount of cover. From there to the shoreline is only a short distance that then remains unfortified."

"Which the men can cover by using stones from the surrounding fields," Putnam said, completing the plan. "They won't be the sturdiest of structures, but remember that any attack will be coming over ground that is wide open. Any cover that we can create will give us an advantage over the enemy. While you manage what needs to be done here, I will return to Cambridge and see if I can't entice General Ward to provide us with some additional men."

"Very well, General," Prescott responded. "Good luck to you sir, and please be careful. God knows we cannot afford to lose you right now."

"You can't afford to lose me, or you can't afford to lose the reinforcements that I come back with?" Putnam jibed his colleague.

"Well now, Israel, we can't have one without the other, now can we?"

On that note, Israel Putnam turned and hurried to gather additional support for the coming fight, while William Prescott set off to drive his men to levels of effort even greater than what they had already demonstrated.

***

Unfortunately for the Americans on Breed's Hill, the situation was now much different from the one they had faced the last few hours. While it was one thing to ask men to work feverishly in the middle of the night while all around was dead silent, it was something quite different to ask them to do the same thing while hundreds of heavy cannon balls flew through the air aimed directly at their location.

For a while all went fine, as the men adapted surprisingly well to the enemy fire. Most of the cannon balls passed harmlessly overhead, and the men soon stopped their incessant cringing with each passing shot.

It was after an hour or so following the start of the enemy barrage that the first casualty occurred. Asa Pollard, a soldier in Ebenezer Bridge's regiment, was working outside of the redoubt constructing the necessary breastworks that had been ordered by Colonel Prescott. As Pollard stood up and stretched to his full height in order to relieve the heavy strain on his back, a cannon ball came whistling through the air and cleanly decapitated the man. His body remained grotesquely upright for what seemed like an eternity to the horrified men working around him, his torso jerking uncontrollably as a thick stream of deep red blood spurted violently from the now exposed neck of the man. Finally, the body fell with a dull thud onto the ground as every man within view watched in disbelief.

Prescott, witnessing the event from just a few yards away, moved quickly to the dead man's side, and was joined by a young officer from Pollard's unit.

"Dear God, sir!" exclaimed the young man, "Pollard is dead! What should we do?"

"You, lieutenant, should concern yourself with the efforts of your men. There is nothing more you can do for this man," Prescott stated coldly. "You men, there," Prescott ordered three soldiers standing nearby in shocked silence, "bury this man as quickly as possible, and return immediately to your work."

The men, numb from what they had just witnessed, dropped their shovels and moved to comply without so much as a word. Several others turned away from the gruesome sight and vomited into the rich, dark earth of the New England countryside.

Well then, Prescott thought to himself, the reality of this war has finally come home for these men. While he also felt slightly ill from

Douglas J. Shupinski

what he had just seen, it was not a reaction he could afford to display in front of these men. Instead, he walked back toward the redoubt, offering words of encouragement as he passed the various groups of men now looking at him with hollow, scared eyes.

It was a defining moment. These inexperienced soldiers had witnessed, for many of them, their first taste of what war truly meant, and there was hesitation in their movements. If allowed to fester, it could spell disaster if they decided to abandon their duties and stream headlong back from where they had come.

Colonel William Prescott arrived at the redoubt, and promptly mounted the wall that faced directly toward the British warships. At this increased elevation, cannon balls screamed by with dangerous proximity. But Prescott could not, and would not be concerned with such realities. As his men looked on with what started as surprise, and turned into awe, Colonel Prescott proceeded to walk calmly back and forth in full view of both the Americans and the British. He shouted orders to those in the redoubt and threatened those working on the breastworks, all the while remaining seemingly unaware of the metal threatening to snuff out his life with the same brutality as it had to Asa Pollard.

The men took heart. If this man was willing to face danger in this manner, couldn't they all? The men returned to their work, still shaken by the recent events, but somehow strengthened by the bravery of this one extraordinary man.

The four British generals; Gage, Clinton, Burgoyne, and Howe; had been rousted from their beds at about 5:30 AM with the news that the Americans had fortified the nearby Charlestown peninsula. Gage had ordered a conference of the four men thirty minutes later.

"Damn those Rebels!" he had vented. "They were just a step ahead of us in fortifying that location! I blame myself for not moving more quickly," Gage admitted in a rare showing of pure honesty.

I blame you as well, thought William Howe, but he judiciously kept the thought a private one. He had no intention of making himself out to be the rude dolt that John Burgoyne had shown himself to be just a few days earlier. General Clinton, however, was apparently unencumbered by any fears of appearing abrasive.

"Gentlemen," Clinton began in his normal matter of fact tone, "the necessary action is quite clear. We must assemble our army immediately and attack without hesitation. The reports say that the Rebel defenses are weak and incomplete, and to attack them now is to do so when they are unprepared to repel a determined assault."

Howe was forced to admit that he agreed with Clinton, and said so.

"I believe General Clinton is correct. A quick, massive strike directly against the redoubt they have constructed will most certainly force the Rebels to retreat back across the spit of land to the north, and we will have possession of the peninsula."

"No, no, General Howe," Clinton said, shaking his head vigorously. "Not a direct attack. We have the opportunity to encircle these troublemakers by moving in behind them. In this way we will cut off their route of retreat and bottle up their army like so many sheep."

"And how would you propose we accomplish such a maneuver," General Burgoyne asked, somewhat skeptical of the plan being laid out by his colleague.

"Why, I could take a force of several hundred soldiers by boat up the Mystic River and land to their rear. Or perhaps we could land a body of troops near the town on the peninsula and march them around the right flank of the Americans. Either of these maneuvers could be conducted at the same time that General Howe is leading his heroic assault on the redoubt. In either case, the result would be the same: we would have the enemy in a pincer between two of our forces and could then destroy them at our leisure."

The heated discussion continued for several minutes, Howe advocating that a direct assault would be more than enough to drive this ragtag group of "soldiers" from their position, Clinton arguing for a more comprehensive approach of attacking simultaneously from the front and rear. Both Gage and Burgoyne vacillated between the two plans, at times siding with one general or the other. Eventually, all four generals knew that Gage would need to make the decision, which he finally did.

"Gentlemen, I appreciate the fact that your considerable experience is being brought to bear in our discussion," Gage stated. "However, I must conclude that the primary objective here is a simple, decisive strike. To attempt to coordinate an attack on one side while conducting a landing, march, and attack on the other is simply too complicated for the objective with which we are faced. These are not soldiers – they are farmers and carpenters and shopkeepers. A massive showing of force by the greatest army in the world will have them tucking their tails between their legs and retreating in no time. I suspect this may be just what is needed to convince the rest of these Rebels that any continued attempts to face this army will be futile."

Howe was pleased by the decision made by Gage, but couldn't help but take note of the disgust displayed by General Clinton. Howe wondered briefly if he might be taking the situation too lightly. After all, Henry Clinton was regarded as one of the best strategists in the entire British army. But Howe quickly dismissed his doubts, and refocused on the matters at hand.

"General Gage," Howe stated stepping forward, "as it is my suggestion that we conduct a frontal assault on the enemy's redoubt, I request that I be allowed to lead the attack."

Gage looked Howe directly in the eye for several seconds, and then turned to the other two generals. Burgoyne gave an almost imperceptible nod of agreement. Clinton, still put off by the snubbing of his plan, refused to make eye contact. Returning his gaze to Howe, General Gage made his decision.

"Very well, General Howe. You have permission to organize and conduct the attack."

***

That conversation had occurred almost seven agonizing hours ago. During that time, while there had been a significant amount of activity within the British army, the actual progress had been painfully slow. In addition to assembling a large body of troops – a time consuming task regardless of their level of training and discipline – there was also the need to locate enough boats to transport the men over water for a distance of approximately a third of a mile.

Howe had decided to launch his assault from a point on the Boston side of the river called Long Wharf, landing his force at the base of a small rise on the Charlestown peninsula called Morton's Hill. While he had been studying the terrain from Boston, Howe saw that this location offered him the opportunity to land far enough away from both the redoubt located on Breed's Hill as well as the small town of Charlestown. This would insure that his men wouldn't be under fire during their landing, quite possibly the trickiest part of this evolution –

or so he thought.

Howe had selected his men carefully. Despite the fact that he had little respect for the ability of the Americans to fight, he nevertheless chose to use the cream of the British army. To that end, he had selected ten companies of light infantry and ten companies of grenadiers for the first wave, in addition to several other units of infantry and Marines which would follow in the second. All told, Howe would have over fifteen hundred men at his disposal for the assault.

Slowly, surely, with the greatest of care and coordination, the first wave of twenty-eight barges shoved off from Long Wharf, each of them loaded to capacity with British soldiers. There had not been enough barges to complete the passage all at once, but Howe was confident that his first wave would be in no danger while they waited for the remaining members of the attack force to arrive.

The sight of these twenty-eight barges, arranged in two columns of fourteen boats each, was awe inspiring, even to someone like Howe who had seen more than his share of military operations. Howe had chosen to place himself in one of the first barges near the front of the small flotilla, a fact that was of no surprise to anyone. Throughout his career, he had always prided himself that he was not an officer who directed from the rear, but rather led from the front. While this practice had made him a highly respected officer among the ranks of the enlisted men, it had also placed him in any number of dangerous situations – much to the chagrin of his seniors who relied on his leadership to be there throughout the entire engagement.

The barges were unable to come up onto the shoreline due to their draft, but they got the soldiers close enough that they would only have to wade through knee-deep water. As they ground to a halt, each barge quickly displaced its cargo of British soldiers and immediately turned around to retrieve the second wave.

Howe, wading ashore along with his men, was pleased to see that there was no sign of confusion or nervousness amongst the men. With almost cold precision, they quickly assembled themselves under the watchful eyes of their officers and sergeants, checking their equipment and preparing themselves for what was ahead.

With respect to equipment, the typical British soldier was well prepared. Their uniforms were immaculate, their weapons were well maintained, and the supplies they carried were carefully designed to insure that each man had sufficient food, ammunition, and assorted other items such that he would be able to sustain himself in the event of a protracted engagement.

Ironically, it was this level of preparedness that worried General Howe. He immediately realized that these men would have significant difficulty in moving quickly when the time came to do so. As he had pointed out to his fellow generals, this attack must be made swiftly and violently. The fact that each man carried well over one hundred pounds of gear would most certainly be an impediment to this need for rapid movement. For the moment, he put these concerns to the side, and focused on the organization of his men.

***

Upon making a reconnaissance of the peninsula, Howe saw that General Clinton had been correct at least in one respect – the strategy that offered the best chance of success was an assault on the front of the main Rebel defenses combined with a flank attack around the left of the American lines. Howe summoned his second-in-command, Brigadier General Robert Pigot.

General Pigot was, in the technical sense of the term, actually a lieutenant colonel. Arriving in America in 1774 as the second-in-command of the 38th Regiment, Pigot soon found himself the recipient of a brevet rank of brigadier general as a result of the absence of his commanding officer. In effect, this meant that while Pigot would be afforded this rank during his time in America, once he returned to other duties he would revert back to his status as a lieutenant colonel.

Nevertheless, Pigot was a modestly capable officer, his only previous criticisms having come in the form of a penchant for caution when faced with situations of significant adversity. In addition, Pigot harbored some resentment at the fact that he was almost ten years older than his current commanding officer, General Howe, but had clearly not enjoyed the same level of success and subsequent promotion.

Map #1: The Battle of Breed's Hill

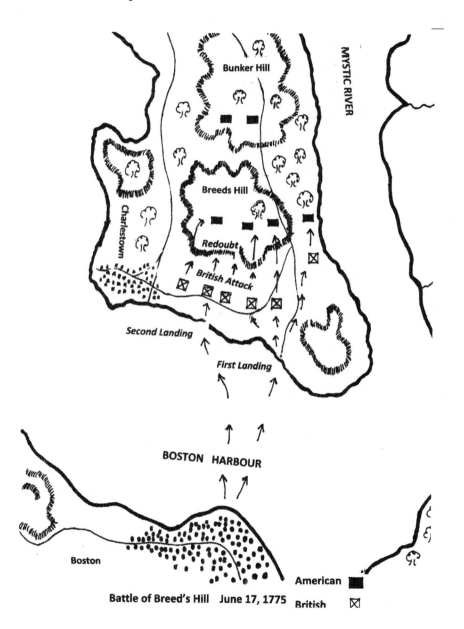

MYSTIC RIVER

Bunker Hill

Breeds Hill

Charlestown

Redoubt

British Attack

Second Landing

First Landing

BOSTON HARBOUR

Boston

Battle of Breed's Hill   June 17, 1775

American ■

British ⊠

"General Pigot, walk with me, if you please," Howe ordered his subordinate. The two men advanced a hundred yards or so inland, affording them a better view of the peninsula. "What is your initial impression?"

Pigot's experienced eye surveyed the topography of the area, as well as the fortifications of the Americans still clearly in progress.

"Sir, it would appear that the enemy is attempting to close a natural gap that exists between the redoubt on the top of that hill," Pigot gestured towards Breed's Hill, "and the shoreline just to their left."

"Precisely, General," Howe agreed. "I would propose that we separate our forces into two wings of equal size, with one demonstrating against the redoubt, while the other attacks simultaneously on the enemy's weaker left flank. Once we have broken through on their left, that wing can swing around behind the redoubt and attack it from the rear while the other wing turns their demonstration into a full assault."

Pigot smiled as he visualized the attack, his certainty of success complete.

"We will use the companies of light infantry and grenadiers for the assault on the enemy's vulnerable left, which I will lead," Howe stated. That will give me over a thousand men. In the meantime, I'm sending for additional reinforcements which, upon their arrival, will be assigned to the wing attacking the enemy redoubt, which will be under your command."

Pigot, confused as to why there was any need for reinforcements in the face of such an ill-prepared, disorganized enemy, nevertheless kept his face a mask devoid of emotion.

"Very well, sir," Pigot replied. "I will prepare the men I have now as the first line of attack, and form the reinforcements to their immediate rear when they arrive."

"Excellent, General. Once we have coordinated the wings, I shall attack first, which will be your signal to begin your demonstration to

Douglas F. Shupinski

hold the men in the redoubt in their location. Once I have gained a position to the rear of that hill," Howe gestured towards Breed's Hill," you will attack with everything you have. Is that clear?"

"Perfectly, sir. With your permission," Pigot stated formally, drawing himself up to a position of rigid attention and saluting Howe.

"God speed, General."

Colonel William Prescott

Massachusetts Militia Forces

Breed's Hill

2:30 P.M. June 17, 1775

The Americans had watched in stunned silence as the British soldiers crossed the river in their perfectly aligned boats, their buttons and bayonets glistening in the afternoon sunlight. Not a single man atop that small hill would ever forget that sight for the rest of their lives.

William Prescott had to force himself to appear as nonchalant as possible while the enemy soldiers disembarked on the Charlestown peninsula and began organizing themselves for an obvious attack. He knew that if he were to succumb to the gravity of the situation and appear unnerved in any way, it could start a panic that would never be halted. In a very real way, the future of this revolutionary movement rested heavily on his shoulders at this point in time.

Even a man of William Prescott's strength of character has doubts, and he was unable to drive those doubts out of his mind. Had he made the right choice in selecting Breed's Hill? Had he done everything possible to prepare this position and these men for the fight ahead? Had he placed his troops in the best positions from which to repel an attack?

Damn it, he chastised himself, stop with all of that. Focus on what

Douglas J. Shupinski

lies ahead. Still, he couldn't help but wish for someone with whom he could share the crushing burden of leadership just now.

"Colonel Prescott, you're looking particularly serious today, I must say."

The voice, coming from directly behind Prescott, caught him slightly by surprise, so deep in thought had he been. Prescott turned quickly and was overwhelmed with relief and gratitude by what he saw. Dr. Joseph Warren, arguably one of the most active and influential members of the revolutionary movement, was standing no more than ten feet away, an amused smile playing across his face.

Dear God, Prescott thought to himself, I have prayed for strength and support, and Providence has seen fit to answer my prayers!

***

Born in Roxbury, Massachusetts in 1741, Joseph Warren had graduated from Harvard in 1759 and studied medicine soon thereafter. Since that time, he had successfully built a large medical practice in Boston, gotten married, and sired four children. The greatest tragedy in his short life of thirty-four years had been the loss of his wife in 1772, leaving him to raise his four young children on his own.

None of this had prevented Warren from getting into the rebellion business on the ground floor. His beliefs led him to quickly conclude that the actions of the British government towards the American Colonies were unjust and immoral, and he found himself becoming close friends and allies of such individuals as John Hancock and Samuel Adams. Perhaps his greatest contribution to the Cause at this point had been the creation of the Suffolk Resolves, a document which had clearly and concisely laid out the issues that the colonists had with the actions of the British Crown. Written in September of 1774, it was both one of the earliest, as well as one of the boldest statements to the British, and it quickly put Warren at the top of the list of most notable Rebels.

Most recently, Warren had been primarily responsible for creating a network of riders that were to be prepared to travel throughout the surrounding countryside to spread the word in the event of a movement by the British to capture supplies and Rebel officials. This network had already demonstrated both its value, as well as its efficiency.

But perhaps the most significant fact about Dr. Joseph Warren – at least at this moment – was that he was exceedingly well known and respected by the average man who had chosen to join the forces now defending Breed's Hill. News of his arrival swept like wildfire throughout the ranks, and men could be seen peeking out from whatever cover they had chosen to verify that Dr. Joseph Warren had, in fact, arrived.

***

"Joseph, in God's name, what are you doing here?" Prescott asked, the relief clearly evident in his voice.

"Well, Colonel, that's an easy one," Warren replied. "I presented myself to General Putnam down there by those breastworks," he said, gesturing to his left. "The old man was foolish enough to offer me command of the troops there which, I suspect to everyone's relief, I refused."

Technically, Warren outranked both Israel Putnam as well as William Prescott, due to the fact that Warren had recently been appointed a major general by the Provincial Congress. As a result, it was appropriate for Putnam to have offered his command to a superior officer. Warren continued his story.

"So I asked General Putnam, 'tell me, where will the fighting be the hottest?' Old Israel paused for just a second, looked up here, and told me the redoubt was where the action would be. So, here I am, reporting for duty, Colonel."

"Doctor – I mean, General Warren," Prescott began, "you are the senior officer at our location, sir. I must insist that you assume command of – "

"And I must insist," interrupted Warren, "that you continue doing what you and I both know you are more qualified to do – lead men in battle. I may not be the most intelligent man in the Colonies, but I'm smart enough to realize that I'm much more capable of treating wounds than I am of knowing how to inflict them. And Colonel Prescott, it will truly be my honor to serve under you on this most glorious day."

Despite the fact that Prescott was still in command, he felt compelled to draw himself up and salute the young doctor.

"Now Colonel, if I have your permission, I should like to locate a musket. I don't believe throwing my scalpels at the enemy will do us much good," Warren joked.

"Perhaps not," Prescott replied, "but I do hope that your aim is as sharp as your surgical instruments."

On that surprisingly light note, Joseph Warren turned and marched off into the redoubt.

***

Colonel Prescott watched as the British soldiers continued to form themselves at the base of Morton's Hill, just a few hundred yards from where he stood. He could see that the enemy was forming into two separate units, which made complete sense to Prescott. Had he been in charge of the British attack, he would have organized two wings; one to attack the stronghold of the redoubt, and the other to move to his left and swing around behind the redoubt. Not exactly the most original plan of attack, but the most effective plans were rarely creative. Simplicity won battles. Creativity killed men.

Prescott had sent at least two messengers back to Cambridge, urging Artemus Ward to send reinforcements to Breed's Hill. At this point, only a few men had arrived, and Prescott was getting anxious about the fact that he was clearly outnumbered, even accounting for the fact that his men would be fighting from a prepared defensive position.

Unbeknownst to Prescott, a significant number of reinforcements had been ordered to Breed's Hill, but very few had actually made it that far. Some had been unwilling to cross the Charlestown Neck, the small strip of land that connected the mainland to the Charlestown peninsula, as this small area had been under almost constant bombardment from British ships sitting just offshore. Still others had made it across the Neck, but had only gone as far as Bunker Hill, realizing that Breed's Hill presented the most likely target for a large force of British soldiers quickly gathering nearby.

But the most common cause of the lack of reinforcements was simply the inability of the Americans to communicate and coordinate their actions. Those officers that possessed the willingness to go to Breed's Hill were given conflicting orders or often no orders at all. Still others received the appropriate orders, but still held on to the unwillingness to obey any directives given by men from a colony other than their own.

The result was that Colonel Prescott basically had those men that had arrived with him over twelve hours earlier – now exhausted, thirsty, and hungry from heavy labor – and a precious few others that had streamed into his position over the last couple of hours.

Prescott decided to make one final inspection of his position prior to the attack everyone now knew to be imminent. He walked down the left portion of his line, leaving the shelter of the redoubt and coming immediately to a line of breastworks that had been hastily constructed. These consisted of mud, grass, and rocks that had been placed between two rows of fencing a few feet apart from one another, creating what looked to be a thick wall. However, upon closer inspection, this breastwork was lacking in any real substance, and provided precious little cover for those men who had taken up position behind it. Continuing to his left toward the river, Prescott saw that a small fence made of the rocks gathered from the nearby shoreline and fields had been constructed. This wall, barely three feet tall, stretched all the way to the water. Again, the fact that it was hastily built insured that it provided only minimal protection to its defenders.

Arriving back at the redoubt, Prescott gazed out on the right side of his position, which was where the small cluster of houses known as Charlestown was situated. There had simply not been enough time to do much of anything on that side, and Prescott had to content himself that the few snipers he had placed in amongst the houses would be enough to dissuade the enemy from attempting a flank attack in that direction.

To make matters even worse, Prescott saw another row of boats coming from the Boston side of the river, heavily laden with what looked to be more British soldiers as well as a large contingent of Marines. The British were clearly taking no chances before they launched their assault. If only they knew what I know, thought Prescott, they might not see the need to be so cautious.

Weak fortifications, incomplete coverage of his flanks, a bone-tired group of defenders, enemy reinforcements; what else could be wrong with this situation, a despondent Prescott asked himself. Oh yes, the biggest problem of all: his small army was poorly equipped and had limited ammunition. Well, Prescott smiled grimly, other than these few issues, everything seemed to be just fine.

**

The Americans were settling into their positions, all pretenses of continuing to work having been abandoned mainly due to their level of exhaustion. The only thing to do now was wait.

As Prescott watched from his position atop the redoubt, it appeared that their waiting was to be brief. With sudden ferocity, dozens of British cannon from warships and land-based positions opened up on the American positions. At the same time, the enemy soldiers had separated themselves into two groups, and had begun their movement in the direction of the Americans.

The Battle of Breed's Hill was about to begin.

Major General William Howe

British Army

Breed's Hill

3:00 P.M. June 17, 1775

William Howe's plan of attack had, by this point, crystallized in his mind's eye. While General Pigot kept the redoubt and breastworks busy with his demonstration, Howe would lead his men against the poorly constructed rail fence and the even weaker rock wall. His men would sweep around behind the American lines, and he would have them in a trap. It was a simple case of elite troops against a ragged force of rabble – almost too easy.

But something continued to nag at the back of Howe's mind. What was it, he demanded of himself? His strategy was simple, his men were well trained, and the enemy was weak…

That's it, he thought. This plan relies on my enemy being weak. It relies on my enemy being unwilling to stand up to the onslaught of a direct attack carried out by the greatest army in the world.

William Howe was, if nothing else, an educated and intelligent man. And most of that education was in the art of war; some learned in the safety of academic study and discussion, but a great deal more in the bloody and deadly classroom of combat. How many other commanders throughout history had fallen prey to their own arrogance, overly confident in the abilities of their army and the inabilities of their adversary? Was he about to become the next chapter in history that future officers would study in order to learn the folly of such beliefs?

Damn it, man, stop thinking about such things, Howe cursed to himself! At this point, whatever mistakes or erroneous assumptions that I have made are water under the bridge. Now is the time for action, and swift, decisive action always outweighs the value of a carefully constructed plan. And there is no general in the world better than William Howe at taking action! Yes, that's the attitude I *must* have right now.

With that thought firmly in his mind, Howe prepared himself and his men to attack.

***

Howe had formed his men into three lines. The front line consisted of his elite light infantry, men accustomed to moving quickly and striking the enemy with extreme force. Behind this line he had formed his grenadiers. These large, hulking men would follow up on the success of the light infantry which would pierce the enemy line at numerous locations. Finally, the third line formed by the 5th and 52nd infantry regiments would pass through the light infantry and grenadiers, and form the main line of attack against the enemy's rear. All in all, it was a force of almost a thousand soldiers.

His orders were to move fast, not stopping to fire at the enemy positions. The objective was to close the distance between his men and the defenders as quickly as possible, and overwhelm the enemy with the use of their bayonets when they made contact. Cold steel and hot tempers, he had instructed his men.

Howe had also given his men other encouragement as they had formed up for their attack several minutes earlier.

"Men, I have every belief that you will behave like Englishmen, and as becometh good soldiers. And know that I will not ask you to go a step further than where I go myself at your head."

The men had cheered heartily at this speech, knowing that General

William Howe was as good as his word. For this reason, not a single British soldier was surprised by the fact that Howe had placed himself and his staff officers in the front rank with the light infantry.

"Colonel Fallon," Howe called out to one of the regimental commanders, "you may begin the attack." Howe was forced to shout his orders to the colonel, as the constant sound of booming cannon and shrieking cannon balls made it difficult to be heard.

"Aye, sir," Fallon replied, and turned to face his lead company, the 23rd Welsh Fusiliers. The Fusiliers were one of the best trained and most feared units in the entire British army, most of them no stranger to the violence of battle.

"All right, you bloody animals," Fallon ordered his men, "let's show these scoundrels what Welshmen are made of!"

With a deep-throated shout, the 23rd moved out at a measured pace, the rest of the light infantry on either side of them following their lead. Behind them, the massive grenadiers and the remaining grim faced infantry paused briefly to allow for a space to form between their ranks, and then stepped off themselves.

The British drummers beat an agonizingly slow staccato, as the men began what appeared to be an almost leisurely approach toward their enemy. To the remainder of the British army watching from the other side of the river in Boston, the movement looked as if it was at a snail's pace.

General Howe had placed himself such that he was approaching the rail fence portion of the enemy line. He was attempting to keep his eye on everything, from the manner in which the lead regiments dressed their ranks, to the spacing between his three lines, to what General Pigot's men were doing off to his left. But the one thing that he was unable to assess was the intentions of the enemy. As the gap between his men and the American lines continued to decrease, there was absolutely no sign of movement from behind the rail fence. Perhaps these Americans had finally given in to the inevitable and abandoned their position, recognizing that they had no chance in standing up to the British. That would certainly make their work today a lot easier. Perhaps...

The distance to the enemy had now decreased to less than a hundred yards. The day had taken on an almost eerie quality, as the only sounds were the steady beat of the drums and the swishing sound made by the British soldiers making their way through the waist high grass. The cannon on the ships and on Copps Hill had ceased their fire to avoid hitting their own men as they got close to the Americans.

The British were now within about 30 yards of the enemy position, and Howe observed the first movement behind the rail fence. As he watched in dismay, hundreds of musket barrels appeared above the rail fence, and were leveled directly at the oncoming ranks. The Americans had apparently not abandoned their positions.

Off to his right, the other units of light infantry were closing in on the rock wall when the wall suddenly erupted in a sheet of flame and smoke. Dozens of men in their proud scarlet coats crumpled to the ground, but they were quickly replaced by other men. A second volley from behind the wall had the same effect as the first, and the line shuddered to a halt.

General Howe was considering whether or not he should move to the wall and take command of the situation when the rail fence directly in front of him erupted with its own violence. All around him, Howe witnessed the horrific effects of the volley. Some men grabbed their chest, or a leg, or their head, as a musket ball struck home with awful results. Other men, sometimes struck by two or three bullets simultaneously, were hurled back, landing on the ground in a variety of awkward positions.

Lieutenant Cowley, a young officer who served as a member of Howe's staff, cried out in pain as a musket ball struck his shoulder, spinning him around and knocking him to the ground. Captain Sparles was not so lucky, as two bullets struck in quick succession into his stomach. His eyes wide in disbelief, Sparles watched as portions of his intestines suddenly protruded from the gaping wounds.

Despite the orders that Howe had given not to stand and fire but to continue to their objective with all possible speed, most of the men gave in to the natural inclination to defend themselves. Leveling their weapons at the rail fence, they fired a somewhat sporadic, unaimed volley, most of which sailed well over the heads of the Americans.

Meanwhile, the Americans were taking advantage of what had become a large grouping of stationary targets, and were pouring a steady fire into the closely packed ranks of the British. Even though the grenadiers were quickly filling the gaps left by the fallen light infantry, they too fell victim to the surprising ferocity of the enemy's fire. Men were falling in groups of two, three, and even four at a time, as the ground was quickly becoming carpeted with dead and dying British soldiers. The shrieking of cannon balls had been replaced with the screams of men who had suffered wounds they had only envisioned before in their worst nightmares.

Howe was shouting at the top of his lungs, urging his men forward, cursing at them to stop firing and attack the enemy with their bayonets. But his orders were lost in the confusion that inevitably occurs when men are locked in desperate combat. Looking quickly toward the attack on the rock wall off to the right, Howe was shocked to see that these men had broken off their assault and were streaming with unbridled haste back toward their starting point at the base of Morton's Hill.

Very well, then, Howe conceded, you Americans have won this first round. We will regroup and come at you again. But this time you will be facing a bloodied, angry animal bent on avenging your ridiculous arrogance.

Even as men continued to fall in staggering numbers to his right and left, William Howe calmly gave the necessary orders for a retreat. His men, relieved to be given the opportunity to escape this hellish moment, began retreating quickly toward safety. Even as they moved back, two other members of Howe's staff were hit, one screaming as a bullet shattered his thigh, while another dropped to the ground without making a sound, a musket ball nearly exploding the right side of his head.

The high grass was literally covered with the blood and splattered body parts of British soldiers, and even General Howe, with his vast experience in warfare, had to suppress the urge to add his own vomit to this grisly mess.

Private Robert Boyle

43rd Regiment, Light Infantry, British Army

Breed's Hill

3:15 P.M. June 17, 1775

For at least the thousandth time, Private Robert Boyle cursed himself for being so stupid and naïve as to leave England for these God forsaken colonies. Not only had he never had even the semblance of an opportunity to continue practicing his love of drawing, but he had been subjected to the most deplorable conditions and situations anyone could have ever imagined.

This most recent adventure for Robert was proving to be, by far, the worst of all. His unit, the Forty-Third Regiment, had been ordered to form up on the left of a massive display of British troops. In the near distance, everyone could make out what appeared to be almost comical defenses, behind which stood several hundred Rebels. A small fort had been hastily constructed atop a hill, and the Rebels were crowded within its cramped confines.

At first, Robert had assumed that this display of might on the part of the British would be sufficient to send these Rebels high-tailing to the rear. Orders had been given, ranks had been formed, and everyone had stepped off smartly and began moving toward the American lines.

But as the Forty-Third Regiment, which was formed as the second of two lines approaching the small fort, got closer and closer, the Americans gave no indication of turning and running away.

Excellent, thought Robert. This will be our chance to get some revenge for that embarrassment at Lexington and Concord several months earlier. Private Boyle's unit had suffered significant casualties during that little excursion, and all the men had thought about since that day was the time when they would be given the opportunity to pay back the Rebels for what they had done. Perhaps today would be that day.

At first, things today had gone fairly well. Despite the fact that Robert could see that the British soldiers to his right were being greeted with a fairly heated reception, there had been virtually no firing coming from the small fort. The only issue they were having here on the left was the enemy snipers that had been placed in the houses of the small town located on the western edge of the peninsula. The constant potshots these snipers were taking had at first been just an annoyance, but as the British lines had continued advancing, these potshots became painfully accurate. Several of the men in both the first and second ranks had fallen victim to the cowardly actions of these sharpshooters.

As the British lines had gotten closer to the Americans, Boyle had noticed that the officers were ordering the lines to slow down to little more than a crawl. What in God's name, thought Robert? Why are we slowing down?

"Sergeant Wiley," Boyle had yelled over the din of the firing, addressing the grizzled man to his immediate left, "what's going on? Why aren't we moving at the quick step? The firing isn't that bad! We could overrun that fort if the officers would just take our leashes off."

"We ain't supposed to take that fort, at least not right now. Are you daft, man?" Wiley had replied in disgust.

"What do you mean, Sergeant? Are we just supposed to stand here like a bunch of stupid, fat hens and get picked off by those rats over there in the town?"

"Aye, Private, that there is your job right now," Wiley had replied, a disturbing smile curling his lips. "While we stand here, General Howe and the boys over there," he gestured to the right, "will break through those lines and swing around behind this here tiny fort. That's when we

Douglas F. Shupinski

attack for real."

The strategy suddenly became clear in Robert's mind, and he nodded in understanding. "So we're a diversion, to hold this side of the enemy line in place."

Wiley turned to look at Boyle, an expression of amusement on his face.

"You best watch yourself, there Boyle," Sergeant Wiley had quipped. "You keep figuring out what's going on, and you'll never have a chance of becoming an officer."

Wiley had roared in laughter at his own remark, and Boyle had been forced to acknowledge the comment with a chuckle of his own.

But the situation had quickly taken a turn for the worse. It became increasingly obvious that General Howe on the right was having a dreadful time of it, as dozens and dozens of men could be seen falling to the ground in grisly heaps of writhing humanity. In just a few minutes, Howe's men had turned back and actually began running to the rear!

General Pigot, in command of the British troops making the diversionary attack on the left, had no choice but to order a similar withdraw. Boyle and the other members of his regiment had been given the order to make an about face and perform an orderly retreat to their starting point.

But this withdraw was to be extremely short lived. Almost immediately upon returning to their original location, the order was given to reform and prepare for another attack. And this time, the word had been passed, there was to be no diversion. This time, the units on the left had been ordered to assault and capture the American redoubt atop the small hill. Simultaneously on the right, the British troops would perform a similar attack and sweep over that portion of the enemy's lines.

This was no longer an attempt to outmaneuver the enemy and catch them in a trap. This had become an all-out frontal assault designed to overpower and destroy the enemy through superior training, discipline, and firepower.

***

"First rank, dress your ranks and prepare to advance," a British major shouted across the lines of soldiers which formed the left wing of the British force. "Forward, march!"

On that command, hundreds and hundreds of scarlet-clad men stepped off and began moving toward the American lines to the beat of their drummers. Off to the right, similar commands were being given by officers of that portion of the British attack commanded by General William Howe.

Private Boyle had chosen to remain close to Sergeant Wiley, reasoning that the experience of the sergeant was a most valuable asset at a time like this. Wiley glanced over at Boyle, whose face must have looked as if he'd seen a ghost.

"Easy, lad," Wiley said calmly. "Things are about to get exciting, so you best have your wits about you. Fix your eyes on that redoubt ahead of us, and don't be looking around to either side of you – you may not be happy with what you see."

"Sergeant Wiley," Boyle protested, "I've seen....combat before. This doesn't.....bother me....at all. I'm perfectly fine." Robert had to stop talking at several points during his reply to catch his breath, which seemed to be escaping him at the moment.

"Of course you are, laddie, of course you are," Wiley replied with a smug grin on his face.

By now, the first British column had come within about a hundred feet of the redoubt, and the men let out a boisterous shout as they prepared to close with the enemy. However, it was at that moment that the entire front of the redoubt became a sheet of flame, followed by a thunderous blast. The air was filled with the high-pitched whine of flying metal, as the Americans unleashed their first volley at the attacking British.

Robert had been unable to get a clear look at the American lines, due to the fact that the first rank of British soldiers had obstructed his view. Suddenly, huge gaps appeared in the first rank, caused by dozens of men collapsing clumsily to the ground as the enemy bullets found their mark. Robert was able to see the American redoubt clearly now, muskets bristling from every part of the structure. What had seemed to be a pathetic, poorly defended structure from a distance, suddenly took on a much more menacing character when seen up close.

"Move forward, men, and fill the gaps!" shouted the major who had given the initial order to move out. His command was just barely audible to Robert, despite the fact that the major was no more than fifteen or twenty yards away with his back to the enemy lines. "Push up and form a solid line – " the major continued shouting, but he was suddenly cut short as a musket ball struck him squarely in the middle of the back. He dropped to his knees, his eyes a picture of surprise as blood began pouring from his mouth.

Almost without hesitation, a British captain took over and continued urging the men to move forward, fill the ranks, keeping focused on the enemy position. Soldiers began falling at an increasing rate, as the Americans continued to deliver another, and yet another volley into the closely massed attackers.

"Let's go, men, dress your ranks. You're British soldiers, not some group of hooligans from the streets of Boston!" the captain shouted, and his remarks were rewarded with a loud response that was a mixture of laughter and misery all at once.

With a precision that can only be achieved through countless hours of brutal drill, the British closed up and dressed their ranks, the entire time under fire by the Americans just a few yards away. In some cases, a man would move forward to fill an opening, only to be violently cut down, with yet another man filling the gap yet again. As those who survived the ordeal would later claim, it was a display of bravery unmatched in the history of war.

Robert was now on the front line of the attack, still clinging desperately to the side of Sergeant Wiley. The men were literally leaning forward as they continued their assault, as if they were walking into a stiff wind. The soldier to Robert's right suddenly pitched backwards, having been struck by bullets on both the right and left side of his chest in rapid succession. Private Boyle, failing to heed the previous advice of Wiley to keep his eyes on the objective, looked down at the bloody mess on the ground that had been, until only a few seconds ago, a vibrant young man.

Shaken by the sight, Boyle hesitated, and immediately fell behind the attacking column. Sergeant Wiley, ever vigilant to the actions of his underlings, broke from the ranks and came back to the side of Private Boyle.

"What the hell are you doing, lad?" Wiley snarled. "This here attack needs every man to do his duty, which don't include standing here and gawking at a dead man. Now either move your arse, or you'll know what it feels like to be run through by a British bayonet!"

Private Boyle looked away from the dead man on the ground into the eyes of Sergeant Wiley, and knew in an instant that the threat was not an idle one.

"Aye, Sergeant," Boyle stammered, and began to stumble forward to take his place back in the front rank, Sergeant Wiley close by his side.

The two men had walked no more than a few paces when Sergeant Wiley suddenly collapsed to the ground, crying out in pain as he grasped his right thigh.

"Ah, damn it," Wiley shouted to no one in particular, "them bastards actually hit *me*, of all people. Sergeant Thomas Wiley ain't meant to get shot!"

Boyle stopped and knelt at the side of the wounded man, a look of distress on his face as he saw the bloody hole in Sergeant Wiley's leg.

"For God's sake, Boyle, don't just look at me!" the Sergeant growled. "Help me to my feet – there's work to be done here."

Obediently, Boyle put the sergeant's arm around his shoulder, and raised him painfully off the ground until he was back on his feet. Wiley bent over with a grimace, and picked his musket up off of the ground.

"Now lad, it's I who need you by my side if I'm to have any satisfaction of killing me some Rebels. So find me something I can use as – "

Wiley's words were drowned out by the eruption of yet more firing from the American redoubt. This time the bullet that struck Wiley was less accommodating, leaving a clean hole in the middle of his forehead. The man fell to the ground dead, an angry scowl on his face as if he knew in his dying moment that he would never have the chance to reap his revenge on the enemy.

Robert stared in disbelief at the dead sergeant, the man whom he had relied on to get him through this awful ordeal. Now what do I do, he thought to himself, a brief wave of panic coursing over him.

But he knew what to do. "Move your arse and attack the enemy," the sergeant would have ordered, and so that's what Boyle did.

But on this day, even valor was not an adequate shield, as Private Boyle felt a shuddering jolt to his right arm. Looking down, he was met with the sight of bright red blood coursing from his body, just above the elbow. Without even a hint of panic, Robert dropped his rifle and took one of the bandages out of his pocket that the men had been ordered to prepare before the attack. If anything, he was annoyed at this most recent obstacle to his ability to carry on with his duty, and he began to calmly wrap the bandage around the wound.

But the combination of blood loss and unrealized shock was more than even his young, healthy body could handle, and his world quickly began to swim around him. The last thing Private Boyle saw before he passed out and collapsed to the ground was the sight of hundreds of British soldiers retreating all around him, streaming past him without a pause, leaving him to his own personal fate on that horrible stretch of ground.

Colonel William Prescott

Massachusetts Militia Forces

Breed's Hill

4:30 P.M. June 17, 1775

All around Colonel Prescott, men were cheering at the tops of their lungs as the British retreated back down the hill for a second time. The tiny redoubt at the top of Breed's Hill was holding on!

"By God, Colonel, I believe we have whipped the British this day!" exclaimed a jubilant Colonel Ebenezer Bridge. "The greatest army in the world, eh? Obviously they are not great enough to stand up to the marksmanship of Rebels, it would appear."

Bridge's comments rousted Prescott from an almost unconscious state brought on by extreme exhaustion. It seemed like years since the two colonels had talked about what might lie ahead of them on the Charlestown peninsula, but that conversation had occurred just last night.

"The men have done well, Colonel," Prescott acknowledged carefully, "but I do not believe our work for today has been completed. The British are proud and stubborn, if nothing else – I doubt they are handling the results of this battle very well, and I have no doubt they will return.

Douglas J. Shupinski

"At the risk of appearing overconfident, Colonel Prescott, I'm not so sure about that," disputed Bridge. "Just look at the ground to our front. Surely, an army cannot bear such losses yet again!"

The ground that Colonel Bridge was referring to was, indeed, a grisly sight. Starting just a short distance from the redoubt and stretching back at least sixty or seventy yards, there were red-clad bodies strewn about so thick that in almost every case they were physically touching the body next to them. Some of the bodies were writhing in place, groaning and begging for some kind of mercy. Sometimes the desired form of mercy was water or medical help; in many cases, it was to be allowed to die. Other wounded soldiers were attempting to crawl back down the hill, or creep into a depression in the ground for a bit of cover. However, most of the bodies were still and silent, well beyond the need for water, comfort, or protection.

Prescott and Bridge were joined by Dr. Joseph Warren, who strangely appeared no worse for wear despite the fact that he had been in the thick of the fighting during both of the first two attacks. His clothes were almost immaculate, and he was carrying himself with a casual nonchalance that would have been more consistent with a man enjoying a walk in the park as opposed to fighting a desperate battle.

"Gentlemen, my regards," Warren greeted them brightly. "A fabulous day for our Cause, is it not? I should think King George will now realize that we are serious about what we have been saying!"

The two colonels, surprised by the almost giddiness of the man, turned to look at one another briefly, and then looked back at Warren in amusement. Despite the grim nature of their situation, they were forced to smile just slightly at the infectious energy of this amazing man.

"A fabulous day so far," agreed Colonel Prescott, "but I would be much closer to your apparent state of mind, Dr. Warren, if we had more ammunition. At the risk of ruining your jocular mood, look at the condition of the men around you."

A quick survey of the men remaining in the redoubt revealed a precarious situation. There were only about one hundred and fifty men left in the small fort, many of the others having retreated to the relative safety of nearby Bunker Hill when either their powder or their nerve had run out. Those that remained were either completely out of powder and musket balls, or were very nearly so. The men were scrounging for anything that could be fired from their weapons, to include nails, scraps of metal, even tiny pebbles that would fit down the barrel of their musket. In addition, they had been awake in many cases for over thirty-six hours, and had had little to eat or drink during that time. In short, they were exhausted.

Warren's jubilant mood became somewhat more sober, fully comprehending the situation. However, he refused to completely abandon his optimism.

"I see, Colonel Prescott, that our men are ill-prepared to repel another determined attack by the enemy. But, perhaps the enemy has had enough for one day."

"Exactly what I was saying just a moment ago, Dr. Warren," Colonel Bridge chimed in. "We have dealt them two rather nasty blows to the chin. Maybe they will choose the more prudent course of action and retreat to fight another day."

"At the risk of being a wet blanket," Colonel Prescott said, "I'm afraid your predictions and optimism are unfounded. Apparently, someone has neglected to inform the British of their expected behavior."

Colonel Prescott nodded in the direction of the bloody slope rising up to where the three men were standing, causing Warren and Bridge to turn around. At the base of the hill, hundreds and hundreds of British soldiers were quickly reforming their ranks, having been joined by a large contingent of newly arrived reinforcements.

***

The relative calm of the redoubt was suddenly filled with men moving about briskly, their exhaustion evaporating with the flood of adrenaline that comes with the knowledge of facing imminent danger. Officers were shouting orders at the men, directing them to abandon their search for ammunition and take their places along the edge of the

Douglas F. Shupinski

redoubt facing the oncoming attack.

Colonel Bridge, who had left Prescott and began circulating among the men, returned to make his report.

"Colonel Prescott, I would estimate that each man is able to fire between two and four shots at the enemy. After that, it will be every man for himself."

"Then we must make every one of those shots count, Colonel Bridge," Prescott stated firmly. "We must force the British to retreat again, so that we may retire to our positions on Bunker Hill. We are simply no match for the British if it comes to hand to hand combat."

"Very well, Colonel, I shall pass the word along to wait until the British are within a few yards, and to then aim low." On that note, Bridge moved off to see to his business.

Turning back to look down the slope of the hill, Prescott was unable to stop a shiver from running through his body. Despite the horrific losses that the British had already suffered, their oncoming lines were straight and disciplined, their drummers beating a steady staccato, their fifers putting out a tune that could only be described as jaunty. Despite what any man in that redoubt felt about the policies and actions of the British government, there could be nothing but respect for the men that were coming toward them now.

Off to his left, Prescott could see a similar assault being made against the breastworks and the rail fence. Interestingly, there didn't appear to be any enemy troops moving against the rock wall on the extreme left of the American line. Apparently the British had determined that the wall was simply too strong of a position to attack. No matter – they only needed to break through at one location in order to jeopardize the integrity of the entire American defenses.

The gap between the advancing red lines and the redoubt had closed to less than one hundred yards, and still the Americans held their fire. Prescott could now see that the second line of the British formation was made up of Marines. So, apparently they were pulling out all of the stops. Anytime the Marines were involved, it meant the British were deadly serious.

The enemy lines quickly closed to less than forty yards, and Prescott could hear the American officers throughout the redoubt giving the preparatory commands to fire. Good, he thought, the men were exhibiting excellent fire discipline. Had anyone told him days ago that these men would be standing toe to toe with the elite of the British army and holding their fire in this manner, he would have thought them out of their minds. But here he was, Colonel William Prescott, a witness to the indomitable spirit of a group of men defending their homes.

Despite the fact that he heard the command to fire being given, Prescott couldn't stop himself from jumping at the sound of over a hundred muskets being fired almost simultaneously. His view of the approaching enemy columns was temporarily obscured, as the smoke roiled over the edges of the rampart and drifted down the slope of the hill. As it slowly began to clear, Prescott was again appalled at what he saw, despite the fact that he was seeing the same scene repeated for the third time today.

Most of the front rank had disappeared, having dropped to the ground with wounds to every conceivable part of their bodies. Just as before, the men behind them had replaced their fallen comrades, calmly stepping over the bodies. It suddenly seemed to Prescott that the advancing enemy soldiers were moving more quickly than they had during the first two attacks, and he realized this time there would be no stopping them from gaining the redoubt.

"Prepare to retreat from the redoubt!" Prescott began shouting to the men around him. "Pass the word along, make your way to the back of the redoubt and retreat to Bunker Hill!"

As the word was quickly passed, many of the men began doing as they were ordered, while others continued to remain stubbornly in place at the front edge of the small fort firing at the oncoming enemy. Having moved to the center of the small enclosure in order to make his orders heard by as many men as possible, Prescott had lost sight of the attacking column. Therefore, he was shocked when he turned and faced the front of the redoubt and saw a number of red coated soldiers appearing at the top of one of the walls, intent on making their way inside.

Douglas J. Shupinski

"Retreat, damn it!" Prescott shouted toward the few men still maintaining their positions, "make your way out of the opening to the rear!"

But as Prescott turned to check on the progress of the men attempting to do as they were told, he saw that the smoke and confusion had made his seemingly simple directions exceedingly difficult to complete. Despite the fact that he was only a few yards from the rear opening, Prescott was unable to see exactly where it was located, and many of his men were experiencing the same difficulty. Prescott cursed himself for allowing the redoubt to be constructed with just a single means of escape, but such second guessing was wasted energy at this point.

Prescott turned back to face the enemy soldiers that had now gained entry into the redoubt, their numbers beginning to increase with disturbing speed. The Americans were now engaged in the hand to hand combat that Prescott had so greatly feared, and his fears were confirmed by what he saw. Americans, no match for the experience, discipline, and bayonets of the British, were being systematically cut to pieces by the enemy.

Prescott's adjutant, Lieutenant Rossing, parried the thrust of one bayonet, only to be cut down by two others that were driven ruthlessly into his torso. Several other men, cornered in one small area by a dozen British soldiers, attempted to surrender, but were shown no quarter by men whose blood had risen to the boiling point by the violence of the moment. The Americans were bayoneted, one by one, their pitiful screams being added to the deafening noise of the battle.

As Prescott himself began to counter the thrusts of oncoming bayonets, he witnessed one of the saddest events of the day. Dr. Joseph Warren, father to four small, motherless children, was shouting amidst the most desperate fighting, swinging his sword in every direction, urging the men around him to continue their struggle. His face was set in a mask of determination as he warded off one enemy soldier after another.

To Prescott, it suddenly seemed as if the whole scene was frozen as a British soldier several feet away from Warren leveled his musket and fired. Warren's body jerked upward in an involuntary spasm, as the bullet struck the side of his head. Warren dropped to his knees and remained there for several seconds, with a look on his face that Prescott could only describe as being one of − satisfaction. He then collapsed forward, marking the end of a brief, but extraordinary life.

At this point the redoubt had become a deathtrap for the Americans, who faced one of three unenviable prospects; face a numerically superior and better trained enemy in hand to hand combat; attempt to surrender and risk being butchered by the crazed British soldiers; or make a desperate attempt to flee through the small opening of the redoubt, at which point they would be subjected to the fire of the pursuing enemy.

***

Eventually, all of the Americans that had manned the redoubt had been either killed, captured, or had escaped. Despite this fact, the casualties continued to mount for the Americans as the British engaged in a dogged pursuit of their retreating enemy. In fact, a significant number of losses experienced by the Rebels would eventually result during this final retreat to Bunker Hill.

Colonel Prescott arrived at Bunker Hill, and immediately searched for Artemus Ward, the officer in charge of the men that had remained there. Prescott was furious at the fact that not a single man under Ward's command had made even the slightest attempt to reinforce the position on Breed's Hill, despite the fact that they had enjoyed a front row seat to the entire battle.

Prescott found Ward on the back side of the hill, attempting to organize his men for an orderly retreat from their position, which would almost certainly come under attack in the next few minutes by the jubilant British.

"General Ward!" Prescott called out. "If you please, sir, a word."

"What is it, Colonel. I am extremely busy at the moment preparing for our withdrawal."

"Withdrawal, indeed," Prescott said, making no attempt to hide the

Douglas F. Shupinski

disdain on his face and in his voice. "General, had reinforcements been dispatched to us on Breed's Hill, we would have almost certainly been able to hold that position!"

"Colonel, I made every attempt to drive these men from their position here in order to do just that," Ward countered defensively, "But not a single man would budge."

Prescott's shoulders slumped at the excuse offered by the Commanding General. His men had fought and died like true soldiers, and they had not been given the full support that their efforts had deserved. Prescott looked directly into the eyes of Ward, his voice lowered to just above a whisper.

"If you could not *drive* these men, General, then why did you not *lead* them?"

With the direct accusation hanging heavily in the air, Colonel William Prescott turned and walked off.

Major John Pitcairn

Commanding Officer, His Majesty's Marine Forces

Breed's Hill

4:55 P.M. June 17, 1775

The air was literally alive with flying metal as the British soldiers and marines made yet another attempt to overrun the tiny redoubt manned by the stubborn Rebels. Being the consummate warrior himself, Major John Pitcairn couldn't help but feel a grudging respect for the small group of Americans that refused to give in to the overwhelming odds that had been stacked against them.

"Dress your lines, men, fill the gaps," he shouted to the marines all around him, many of whom would no doubt soon become the latest casualties in a day of terrible losses. "Don't stop to fire at the enemy — keep moving toward the fort!"

Despite his orders, some of the soldiers and marines had, in fact, stopped and formed themselves into ragged firing lines. The human instinct for survival in this type of situation screamed out against continuing to move in the direction of danger, and despite their training to follow orders without question, this most basic instinct had taken over in these men.

"For God's sake, men, you're nothing but targets if you remain

Douglas J. Shupinski

here," Pitcairn shouted. "Victory — and survival — is there!" he urged, pointing directly at the walls of the redoubt.

With a resounding shout, the men resumed their attack, in spite of the fact that many of them were cut down almost immediately by yet another blast of musket fire from the Americans.

The scene had taken on an almost slow motion quality as Pitcairn continued forward, urging his men when he could, threatening them when necessary. He felt as if his whole life had been leading up to this moment, and he realized that he had never felt more alive than he did just now.

With a start, Pitcairn remembered that his son, James, had been positioned just off to his right at the start of the attack, and he looked around anxiously for the young man. He was relieved to see that James, a Marine lieutenant, was bravely mirroring the efforts of his father just a few yards away, pushing the men forward toward their objective. James caught the eye of Major Pitcairn, and moved in his direction.

"Major!" James Pitcairn shouted above the roar of the battle, "I believe the enemy is attempting to retreat from their position! If we give them one final push, we shall reach our objective!"

Turning his attention back to the redoubt, Pitcairn could see that his son was correct. Many of the muskets protruding from the wall of the small fort had begun to disappear, clearly indicating that the enemy was attempting to retreat.

"Marines!" Pitcairn shouted, "See there! The Americans have retreated! Push forward, and the day is ours!"

At that moment, a voice called out from within the redoubt, challenging Major Pitcairn's assessment of the situation.

"We ain't retreated yet!" shouted an American from within the redoubt, and with that statement several dozen musket barrels appeared above the wall and let loose with a ragged, but well aimed volley in the direction of the attacking marines.

Major Pitcairn, his sword raised high in the air as a signal for his men to attack, suddenly felt as if a sledgehammer had punched him in the chest. Looking down, he was mildly surprised to see the front of his crimson uniform taking on a much darker shade of red.

"Well, I'll be bloody damned," Pitcairn cursed, immediately feeling the strength beginning to ebb from his body. He struggled to remain standing, but he felt dizzy and began to fall backwards. His fall was broken by the firm grasp of someone catching him from behind, and he turned and looked into the eyes of his son.

"Thank you, Lieutenant," Major Pitcairn gasped weakly, ever the stickler for military protocol, even at a moment like this. But Lieutenant Pitcairn was not so inclined to observe such formalities.

"Father," he said gently, "you've been injured. You must be taken to the rear immediately and get the proper medical attention." The look on James Pitcairn's face clearly indicated that his father's wound was of a most serious nature.

"I will not be removed from this battlefield until I know the outcome," Major Pitcairn stated firmly, a level of strength returning to his voice. "That, Lieutenant, is an order!"

"Major Pitcairn," James replied, nodding in the direction of the redoubt, "the outcome of the day has been determined."

Looking up, Major Pitcairn was pleased to see his men swarming over the walls of the redoubt, while others circled around behind the small fort in an attempt to catch the Americans in a trap. His son was right – the outcome of the day was assured.

"Very well then, Lieutenant, I shall submit to your wishes. After all, we both know whose side your Mother would be on – yours, as always."

Major John Pitcairn suddenly felt his eyes welling up with tears, as he pictured the beautiful woman he had been married to for so many years. He understood instinctively that he would never see her again. He knew a mortal wound when he saw one, and his was of such a nature.

"James, please insure that my wounded men are taken from the field first. Once that has taken place, you may remove me at your discretion."

"Of course, Father," James replied. As Lieutenant Pitcairn looked around, he realized that several dozen Marines had gathered around their commanding officer, genuine concern on the face of every man looking on.

"Damn it, you men!" Lieutenant Pitcairn barked at the staring marines, "resume your attack! If you have any intention of honoring this man, you will do so by defeating the enemy!"

Shocked out of their worried moment, the men quickly gathered themselves and did exactly as they were ordered. With a menacing shout that clearly indicated the intention for revenge, they moved forward to take their retribution on those that had dared to take their beloved leader from their ranks.

"By God, Lieutenant," Major Pitcairn said quietly, a look of admiration on his face, "you have become quite the ogre. Now, if you please, I am ordering you to rejoin your men and insure that this day ends in victory."

"This day has already ended in victory, Father," James replied. "And with all due respect, sir, that is an order that I will refuse to obey. My place right now is with you."

***

Lieutenant James Pitcairn would remain with his father for the next few hours, watching as the man he loved and respected like no other fought courageously for his life. But it was a battle whose outcome had been determined from the very moment an American musket ball had struck home.

Early the next morning, his son by his side, Major John Pitcairn passed peacefully from this world, joining hundreds of other British soldiers and marines that had made the ultimate sacrifice the previous day in the name of duty and service to their country.

Private Robert Boyle

43rd Regiment, Light Infantry, British Army

British Army Hospital, Boston

June 18, 1775

The first thing that struck a person when they entered the makeshift hospital set up in the middle of Boston was the sound. Dozens of men were crammed into the space afforded by the relatively small house, and their pitiful moans and screams of pain assaulted the ears. Some cried out for food or water; others, in their delirium, asked to see wives, mothers, children. Many simply begged to die, asking anyone for assistance in doing so.

Next was the appearance of the place. It seemed that one was unable to look in any direction without seeing blood – pools of it, splatters along the walls and the floor, caked and oozing from the men lying about. The men themselves were often hideous to behold. Most of them had blood-soaked bandages attempting to stem the bleeding from every imaginable part of the body. Others, beyond help, and therefore not worthy of wasting valuable bandages, laid on the floor with the insides of their heads and bodies clearly visible to anyone with the stomach to observe such a thing.

Finally, the unlucky visitor was hit like a hammer by the stench. Despite the fact that the battle had occurred just the day before, the heat insured that the dead had begun to decay, and the wounds of those still alive had begun to putrefy. Added to this was the fact that the men were almost always unable to move themselves, and therefore were forced to urinate and defecate where they lay. The overworked doctors, nurses, and attendants simply didn't have the time to see to the personal hygiene needs of each man.

A number of people were moving throughout the rooms of the house, engaged in various medically-related functions. Nurses, many of whom were simply women that had volunteered their time and had absolutely no medical training whatsoever, made any attempt to ease the suffering of the wounded. Their actions ranged from giving the men water, to reading a letter from a loved one to holding the hand of a frightened soldier as he passed away.

Medical orderlies, who were officially part of the British army, were primarily responsible for the logistical and administrative aspects of running a hospital, however temporary it may be. Soldiers needed to be brought in and taken out, supplies needed to be organized, and records had to be maintained with respect to names, units, types of wounds and, with disturbing regularity – deaths.

But the worst duty by far was that of being a surgeon under these circumstances. At the rear of the house, a rather large kitchen had been established as an operating area. This arrangement had worked out rather nicely, as a mammoth fireplace had served to boil the hundreds of gallons of water used during the operations. In addition, when a soldier died during the course of an operation – which happened quite frequently – the body could be removed through the back door without having to cart it back through the hospital. Watching a steady parade of obvious operating room failures tended to have a negative effect on the morale of those men waiting their turn.

Within the operating area, a large table had been cleared off and pressed into service as an operating table. As the surgeon finished with one man, a second was quickly brought in and laid out. The surgeon conducted a quick visual inspection of the patient, combined with some information provided by the orderly regarding the nature and severity of the man's wounds. With that process completed in a minute or two, it was time to operate.

Due to the fact that there was virtually nothing to be used as an anesthetic, the next step was to place a sturdy stick or a bullet between the teeth of the patient. This was to prevent the man from both breaking his teeth by gnashing them together due to the intense pain, as well as stifling the volume of his screams. Next, two or three orderlies positioned themselves at various locations around the unfortunate man, and pinned down his arms and legs. The purpose for this was obvious – especially to the soldier lying on the table.

Almost all of the procedures were performed on the limbs, as wounds to the head and torso were considered mortal and therefore didn't warrant the attention of a doctor. As the typical musket ball was a rather large piece of metal, the effects to the human body when the two came together were catastrophic. Bones weren't so much broken as they were shattered, with dozens of splinters often spraying themselves within the victim's body. Such wounds often quickly became infected, and the only course of action to save the man's life was to amputate the limb.

This procedure began with the surgeon selecting a scalpel which he used to slice through the flesh of the limb until he had exposed the bone. If the surgeon was working on an arm or the lower leg, he would then select a somewhat smaller saw which would be used to cut through the bone. An amputation of the upper part of the leg would require a much larger saw which looked a great deal like a simple hacksaw. Once the bone had been completely cut through, the previously used scalpel would finish the amputation by cutting through any final shreds of flesh that continued to stubbornly attach the limb to the rest of the body.

Once the procedure was completed, the instruments that had been used by the surgeon were placed back on a nearby table. When the next patient was laid out on the operating table, the same instruments would be selected by the surgeon, wiped off haphazardly with a dirty, bloody rag, and used for the next amputation.

As one might imagine, the shock to the body of a soldier undergoing these procedures was overwhelming, and often resulted in

Douglas J. Shupinski

death within a few minutes to a few hours. Those that survived the initial shock often contracted an infection, which was usually worse than dying outright. Such men often lingered for several days, experiencing unimaginable pain, eventually lapsing into a delirious state before dying. In fact, the survival rate of a man subjected to the barbaric experience of amputation was about one in three.

***

Private Robert Boyle had arrived at the hospital approximately twelve hours earlier, and had been lying uncomfortably for that amount of time on the wooden floor of one of the upstairs bedrooms. He had been informed by one of the orderlies that his wound was, "not so serious, Mate," and as a result had been placed at the bottom of the list for receiving medical attention. Based on the screams emanating from the operating room directly below him, he had considered that lack of attention to be a true blessing indeed.

But his good fortune had apparently come to an end, as two orderlies walked into Boyle's room and somewhat clumsily placed him on a stretcher.

"All right there, lad," one of the orderlies said, "it's time to go down and see the good doctor, eh? He'll 'ave you fixed up and back to your unit in no time."

Boyle wasn't so sure that he wanted to see the doctor, or go back to his unit, but his options appeared to be somewhat limited at this point in time.

"What's going to happen to me now?" Boyle asked, unable to keep his voice from shaking in fear.

"Oh now, not to worry, me Boy. Barney's seen his share of wounded men in his day," the orderly stated, referring to himself in the third person. "That pesky Rebel musket ball missed the bone, praise be to God. You won't be needin' an amputation, no sir, not you. The doctor will most likely just clean things up a bit and stop that bleedin' you been doin' for the last few hours."

While Robert had no idea of the orderly's qualifications in making such an assessment, he desperately latched onto the hope that the man was correct. Robert was painfully aware – both literally and figuratively – that an amputation to his wounded right arm meant the end of his career as an artist.

As Robert was brought into the operating area, he caught sight of the surgeon seated in the corner, his back resting against the wall. With a start, Robert realized that the doctor had passed out!

"What in God's name!" Boyle exclaimed. "What kind of a doctor is this? He's fainted, by God, at a time like this?"

"At a time like this, indeed," replied the orderly, his voice dripping with disdain for Boyle. "That there man has been on his feet, operating and amputating for the better part of twenty-four hours. He hasn't fainted, you sap – he's asleep. He tries to catch four or five minutes between operations. I hope that's alright with you – Private."

Robert felt suddenly embarrassed by his grossly inaccurate assessment of the situation. The doctor was exhausted, plain and simple.

"Begging your pardon, sir," Robert stammered to the surgeon. "I had no idea – I didn't mean to show any disrespect – "

"Save your breath, Private," the orderly said. "That man can't hear a word you're sayin'. Sometimes it takes us three or four good shakes just to get him up and about, so don't think your little apology is making even a dent in his slumber."

To prove his point, the orderly walked over to the surgeon and began jostling the man with the barest of military reverence.

"Alright, sir, another man needs your skills. Rise up, sir, time to go back to work."

The surgeon gradually stirred himself back to life, hoisted himself onto his somewhat wobbly legs, and made his way toward Boyle. He slowly examined Robert's wounded arm through his bleary eyes, and then turned toward the orderly.

"All right then, hand me the scalpel there on the left, as well as the small saw. You two men," the doctor said as he gestured to two orderlies standing at the doorway, "come here and hold this man down."

Robert's eyes widened in panic, as he realized what the surgeon intended to do. The orderly had lied to him! They were going to cut off his arm after all, and with it, any hope Robert might have had for being an artist!

"Excuse me, sir," the orderly said quietly to the doctor, just as Robert was about to begin screaming at the top of his lungs, "but perhaps this one could do with a bit more of an examination."

The surgeon's bleary eyes suddenly became ablaze with anger at the orderly's comment.

"Who do you bloody think you are, Corporal, telling a surgeon how to do his job?" the doctor lashed out viciously. "You're an orderly, for God's sake! Mind your place!"

"An orderly indeed, sir, and a good one," he replied in an even tone, not wanting to rankle the doctor any more than he already had. "And one of my jobs is to take care of my doctors; try and make things a bit easier for you gentlemen when I can. I'm just thinking, sir, that you may not have to go to the trouble of doing yet another amputation on this here lad."

Robert, sensing an opportunity to avoid disaster, addressed the doctor as well, his voice calm, but deeply intense with emotion.

"Sir, I'm an artist. I draw and sketch and paint. I'm not a professional soldier, sir. I only joined the army because I was told that I would have a chance to see and draw things from around the world if I became a soldier. Please, sir, don't take my arm – *please!*"

The surgeon, placated by the comments of the two men, immediately lost his anger, and he nodded slowly in acknowledgement. And then, to the surprise of everyone in the room, the doctor's face broke into a wide grin, and he began to actually laugh.

"See the world and draw it, eh?" the surgeon chuckled. "Now that's one I hadn't heard before, I'll say. I can see our recruiters haven't lost their touch. See the world – draw it. Dear God, that's funny!"

The men in the room all broke into smiles of their own, and even Robert managed a painful grin as he realized how ridiculous it sounded.

"Very well, my young Michelangelo," the doctor said, "Let's see if we can save the career of a budding artist."

Pulling aside some of the bloody cloth that covered Boyle's wounded arm, the surgeon looked more carefully at his patient. As the orderly had observed earlier, the bullet had, in fact, missed the bone. After washing off some of the surrounding blood, the surgeon could see that Robert's wound was much more superficial than he had earlier surmised.

"Well, well," the surgeon stated slowly, "it appears that some cleaning and bandaging may be all you need, Private. You've obviously lost quite a bit of blood, but that's nothing that a few days of rest won't cure. Orderly, hand me that basin of water, and rip off a healthy strip of that bed sheet."

Robert was relieved beyond words, and he looked directly at the orderly, an unspoken message of gratitude more clearly reflected in his eyes than any words could have possibly conveyed. In the middle of this place of overwhelming pain and death, a single act of kindness had saved more than a man's future profession – it had saved his soul.

General George Washington

Commanding General, American Forces

Cambridge, Massachusetts

July 3, 1775

The man who walked confidently into the headquarters of the American army located in Cambridge was clearly a man of both power and wealth. The manner in which he carried himself indicated that he was accustomed to being in control, and the quality of his impeccable uniform clearly demonstrated he was a man of means. Finally, the fact that he was at least four or five inches taller than anyone else in the room insured that his entrance was one worthy of notice.

Several officers looked up casually, having become used to the comings and goings of dozens of officers and messengers during the course of a typical day. However, they quickly found themselves unconsciously coming to attention in the unannounced presence of this visitor.

"Excuse me, gentlemen," the tall stranger said in an almost quiet voice, "but I would greatly appreciate the opportunity to introduce myself to your Commanding General."

A colonel from one of the Massachusetts units was the first to overcome his surprise, and moved quickly to greet their visitor. Not knowing whether he should salute this man or shake his hand, he simply stood at attention in front of him.

"Sir, if I may," the colonel began, just a hint of hesitation in his voice, "may I tell the Commanding General who he will have the pleasure of meeting?"

A slight smile of amusement crossed the tall man's face as he answered the man.

"Colonel, General Ward and I have known one another for many years. I truly hope your prediction of this meeting being a pleasure is accurate. Please inform your commander that General Washington has arrived from Philadelphia."

***

Despite the fact that it had been just over two weeks since Washington had been appointed as the Commanding General of the "Continental Army" located outside of Boston, his rather eventful journey from Philadelphia to his current location seemed much longer. This journey had been lengthy, both literally and figuratively.

The Continental Congress had quickly realized the need to appoint someone to assume overall command of the American forces, but the debate over who that individual should be had raged long and loud for many days. During that time, Washington had attended virtually every meeting held by the Congress, but he had chosen to remain silent most of the time. At no point had he publicly verbalized a desire to receive the appointment of Commanding General. However, the fact that he had attended each and every meeting adorned in his full military uniform spoke volumes about his true ambitions, and this fact was lost on no one. While understatement may have been a quality of George Washington, subtlety most certainly was not.

Ultimately, the decision became relatively easy. Washington was a Virginia aristocrat, which insured his ability to develop relationships with not just the other wealthy men who came predominantly from the New England colonies, but also the wealthy men from the southern colonies. The Continental Congress realized that this potential to exert both social and regional influence would be a key to establishing some semblance of unity in support of the war that had now been thrust rather unexpectedly upon them.

Washington had had limited participation in earlier debates within the Continental Congress, which ultimately worked in favor of his appointment. First, his peers viewed him as being somewhat moderate in his opinion of the British government. The last thing the Congress needed was a fire-breathing warmonger, intent on gaining revenge against England. Second, Washington's silence had insured that he had made very few enemies during the debates; debates which had strained the bonds of friendship between many of its participants.

However, far and away the greatest attribute brought to the table by George Washington was his military experience. And at the end of the day, what the Continental Congress was looking for wasn't a man who could speak with passion and eloquence on the tyranny of the British government – they were in desperate need of a man who knew how to fight.

Washington had acquired this experience as a result of having served for many years alongside the British, primarily just before and during the French and Indian War. Most notably, Washington had achieved an almost legendary level of fame from his participation in the disastrous campaign against Fort Duquesne in 1755.

In that year, the British had ordered Major General Edward Braddock to sail from England to America with two regiments of troops, and direction to take command of all British forces in North America. Braddock's objective was to deal a blow to the French and their Indian allies, such that both of these groups would lose the appetite for continuing the conflict. This would insure that England would have control of North America once and for all.

Unfortunately, on the march to Fort Duquesne, located in western Pennsylvania, Braddock's command had been attacked by a sizable force of French and Indians which had employed "Indian style" tactics. The British, stubbornly clinging to their European brand of fighting, had been overwhelmed by the enemy, and the result had been a bloodbath that had claimed the lives of nearly all of the British soldiers who had been present, to include General Braddock.

Washington, demonstrating an amazing coolness under fire, successfully rallied the few survivors and fought his way out of the ambush. During the course of the engagement, Washington had not suffered even so much as a scratch, despite the fact that two horses had been shot out from under him, and there were no less than four bullet holes in his uniform.

***

On June 15, 1775, the Continental Congress officially announced their decision. John Hancock, the president of the Congress rose from his chair and made the proclamation.

"The President has the order of Congress," Hancock stated formally, "to inform George Washington, Esquire, of the unanimous vote in choosing him to be General and Commander-in-Chief of the forces raised and to be raised in defense of American liberty. The Congress hopes the gentleman will accept."

Washington, despite the fact that he had silently lobbied for the position for weeks, was suddenly overcome by the enormity of what he was being asked to do. With characteristic humility, he slowly raised himself from his chair and drew himself up to his full, imposing height.

"Mr. President, I declare with the utmost sincerity, I do not think myself equal to the command I am honored with. As to pay, Sir, I beg leave to assure the Congress that as no pecuniary consideration could have tempted me to have accepted this arduous employment at the expense of my domestic ease and happiness, I do not wish to make any profit from it."

George Washington had achieved his objective. He had been given complete command of all American forces now at war with Great Britain. His elation was severely tempered by one nagging question in the back of his mind: What had he gotten himself into?

In and Around Boston

Winter 1775-76

As the momentous year of 1775 came to a close and 1776 began, a sort of stalemate settled over the Boston area. The two sides eyed one another warily across small stretches of land and water, but neither dared to take any kind of major offensive action against the other.

For the Americans, such offensive plans were thwarted primarily by the fact that they simply didn't have enough ammunition. Most of all, their supply of gunpowder was so small that there was a constant concern that the British would launch an all-out attack if they were to become aware of how dire this situation was for the Continental Army.

In addition, the British had received reinforcements in the last few months, and had also taken the time to strengthen their defenses surrounding Boston. Should the Americans be so foolish as to attack their enemy, they would find significant numbers of British soldiers well entrenched behind these defenses. In short, despite the fact that the Continental Army was inexperienced in the art of war, they were smart enough to know a losing proposition when they saw one. On September 11, General Washington presented his generals with the option of launching a full scale assault: to a man, they voted against it.

However, there were much greater problems being faced by the Continental Army than just an inability to attack. As the year came to a close, they faced the very real possibility of their entire army simply ceasing to exist. For the most part, the men had signed up to serve until the end of the year, and no longer. When the officers discussed the possibility of reenlistment with their men, they were met with an almost unanimous refusal.

The members of the Continental Army were not, after all, really soldiers. They were farmers, tradesmen, business owners and – most importantly – the heads of families. They had been gone for months now, and the pinch of homesickness was as rampant as the various diseases that had ripped through the camps.

The fact that conditions in these camps were horrendous only reinforced the desire of the men to be over and done with this grand adventure. The food was becoming scarce, and had always been of questionable quality. The weather had turned cold, and there were few building materials with which to construct living quarters. The romantic vision of fighting for liberty was quickly becoming a nightmarish reality.

Many of the men chose not to wait until the end of the year, and took matters into their own hands. Soldiers deserted by the dozens each week, despite the fact that the punishment if caught was often death. Many days began with the formation of the men around a freshly dug grave, next to which sat a coffin. The soldier guilty of desertion would be marched to the edge of the grave, where he would face a firing squad of twelve men. Commands would be given, muskets would shatter the silence of the morning, and the guilty man's bullet-riddled body would be hurtled back into the grave where it would eventually be placed in the coffin and given some semblance of a proper burial.

Other men, guilty of a variety of minor to major infractions, were subjected to the rather brutal practice of flogging. Almost any offense, ranging from theft to disobeying an order carried with it an associated number of lashes with the cat-o'-nine tails, and this number could be as high as two hundred.

The true seriousness of the situation became apparent when, on November 12, General Washington called upon the army for official reenlistments. Of the nearly seven thousand men under his command, exactly 966 agreed to continue their service.

The generals of the Continental Army issued a rather patriotic proclamation, in which they promised the men that their efforts and sacrifice would not be in vain. Their very freedom depended on their willingness to continue the struggle against the tyranny of the British. The proclamation was somewhat effective; by the end of the week, the number of reenlistments was up to about 3500.

As 1775 ended, thousands of men picked up their weapons and belongings and returned to their homes. There was no fanfare, either positively or negatively. Men simply bid their comrades farewell, most of them secure in the belief that they had done more than their fair share. With a hasty step, they headed anxiously back to their families and homes, eager to return to their previous lives.

Washington, now desperate to save his army, called upon the surrounding colonies to supply him with militia in order to buy some time. Massachusetts and New Hampshire responded with enthusiasm, and thousands of men from those two colonies arrived in time to fill out the ranks, if only temporarily.

Distraught by the seemingly endless challenges of his command, General Washington wrote to a friend in Philadelphia:

"How happier I should have been, if instead of accepting a command under such circumstances, I had taken my musket on my shoulder and entered the ranks, or, if I could have justified the measure to posterity and my own conscience, had retired to the back country, and lived in a wigwam."

Slowly but steadily, additional recruits began to arrive into the various camps situated around Boston. By early 1776, the Continental Army had returned to roughly the same number of men that had been present at the end of 1775. But this was a new army that consisted of an unstable combination of experienced men remaining from the previous year, new recruits that had just arrived in the last several weeks, and militia whose mercurial nature made them continuously suspect.

The future was unclear, with one exception; General George Washington and his corps of generals and officers knew they had a great deal of work to do.

***

As for the British, their situation was not much better. They had already learned a painful lesson about attacking these Americans when they were behind walls and fences, and the British had no desire to repeat that mistake. Therefore, their military actions consisted primarily of reinforcing their defensive positions, and conducting limited patrols just outside the city limits.

This lack of military operations had a severe negative impact on the common soldier. Without any real purpose or responsibilities, the men began to display their lack of motivation and morale in a variety of predictable – and unpredictable ways. Their appearance began to decline, as the strict rules regarding the maintenance of their uniforms were often not enforced with the typical level of rigor. Men began drinking and gambling, with even more than the normal enthusiastic participation they traditionally displayed. Finally, to the horror of their officers, many of the soldiers acquired the most unsavory habit of chewing tobacco, a trait thought to be practiced only by the vulgar members of the American Continental Army.

Major General Gage had been recalled to London, ostensibly to provide a detailed report to the British Parliament on the conditions that existed in the American colonies. However, everyone knew what it looked like when a general was sacked, and this was it. In his place, Major General Howe assumed command.

Bottled up in a city that had long since run out of most of its supplies, the British had come to the uncomfortable realization that virtually everything they needed to survive would have to come from England. This resulted in the men having to subsist almost exclusively on salted meat, with the occasional addition of fish to their diet. In order to keep warm as the weather turned cold, the men resorted to tearing down any structure that might provide them with the necessary wood for their fires.

To make matters worse, what few ships that were sent from England with supplies for the impoverished army were often intercepted by the upstart American Navy, or more often by the privateers that had been commissioned by the Continental Congress to prey upon exactly these kinds of seafaring targets.

By the middle of the winter of 1775-76, these conditions had

Douglas J. Shupinski

resulted in the British hospitals being filled to capacity with men suffering from everything from smallpox to scurvy to dysentery.

The previously referenced patrols sent out by the British resulted, on a number of occasions, in encounters with the Americans. Several of these encounters turned into rather sharp and bloody engagements which more often than not ended with the Americans – better suited for this type of hit-and-run fighting – coming out on top. The lopsided British casualties that occurred during these engagements served to further deteriorate the already shaky morale of the men.

***

Clearly, this situation of common misery experienced by both armies could not continue indefinitely. But neither side indicated a willingness to abandon their positions, however unsavory they may have been.

Something had to break. But it would take the introduction of something significant to change the status quo.

Colonel Henry Knox

Artillery Commander, American Forces

Cambridge, Massachusetts

January 24, 1776

The face of Colonel Henry Knox reflected a strange combination of utter exhaustion and total triumph as his band of ragged men trudged into the American headquarters in Cambridge. This look of exhaustion was the result of having endured fifty-six days of some of the most grueling conditions any man had ever known. The look of triumph was the result of the thunderous cheers of hundreds of American soldiers that had turned out to verify that the rumors regarding Knox and his men were, in fact, accurate. Most notably, the soldier that had just now come into the view of Colonel Knox was none other than General George Washington himself, the smile on his face so wide that it gave him the rather uncharacteristic appearance of being almost giddy.

Behind Knox stretched a parade of sleds, each being pulled by two oxen. Even with these massive beasts strapped to the sleds, they moved at a plodding pace as a result of the considerable weight each sled was forced to bear. It was the source of this weight that had caused Washington to grin so broadly. Unmistakable in their appearance –

despite the fact that they were each covered with a coating of fresh snow – were fifty-nine pieces of artillery that had arrived from Fort Ticonderoga – nearly three hundred miles away.

Colonel Knox approached General Washington with a sudden flourish of energy and formality, drawing his massive six foot, 250 pound frame up to full attention in front of the Commanding General.

"General Washington," Knox reported proudly, "I present to His Excellency a most noble train of artillery. It consists of a variety of weapons and sizes, with a total of fifty-nine..."

Knox suddenly wavered back and forth, and Washington thought the man was about to lose his balance. But he regained his composure, and continued his presentation.

"My apologies, General," Knox said slowly. "But the journey has been a bit challenging, and sleep has been at a premium for my men and me over these last few weeks."

Despite the gravity of the moment, a ripple of laughter went through the men watching the scene unfold in front of them. After all, it wasn't every day that one saw a man almost faint directly in front of the commanding general; especially one with the significant proportions of Henry Knox.

"Colonel Knox, I assure you that no apologies are necessary," Washington said quietly to the man who was quickly gaining his confidence. "I am both amazed and gratified by the efforts of you and your men. I must admit," Washington said, lowering his voice so that only Knox could hear him, "I was never really sure until this very moment that your idea was possible. Perhaps I should place more faith in your obviously considerable abilities."

***

Henry Knox had been born in Boston on July 25, 1750, the seventh of ten sons born to William Knox. Henry's father had passed away at an early age, as had several of his brothers, while other siblings had moved away or gone to sea. When all was said and done, it had been nine year old Henry who was left with the responsibility of providing financially for himself, his mother, and his younger brother.

Henry had managed the situation by quitting school and getting a job in a local bookstore, a vocation that would occupy Henry for the next fifteen years. It was during this time that Henry became a voracious reader, specifically in the area of military disciplines, and even more specifically in the employment of artillery and the construction of fortifications.

As Knox had grown into a young man, he found himself drawn to the ideals being espoused by the Sons of Liberty, the rather radical organization that advocated for rebellion against the British Crown up to and possibly even including an independent country.

In addition, Knox had become totally smitten by the charms of one Lucy Fluckers, the daughter of the wealthy Thomas Fluckers, who just happened to be the Royal Secretary of Massachusetts Bay. To make matters even more uncomfortable, Lucy's brother was a lieutenant in the British army. Despite the apparent conflict of values, Henry and Lucy were married in June, 1775, just days after the battle at Breed's Hill had occurred.

After failing in his attempts to forbid his daughter to have anything to do with Knox, Thomas Fluckers used his considerable influence to have Knox offered a commission in the British army. Several days later, Lucy and Henry took a carriage in the middle of the night, slipped past the British guards posted at the outskirts of Boston, and made their way to Cambridge where Henry offered his services to the fledgling Continental Army.

Knox's response to Thomas Fluckers' offer of a British commission had clearly been a resounding "no".

***

General Washington had complained long and loud to Colonel Knox about the lack of any big guns at his disposal. Knox, recently appointed by Washington to be the Chief of Artillery of the Continental Army, had responded with a suggestion that had seemed, at the time, ludicrous.

Douglas J. Shupinski

"General Washington," Knox had implored, "there are numerous pieces of artillery sitting idle at Fort Ticonderoga. If we were able to bring those guns here to Boston, we could place them in such a manner as to force the British to evacuate the city!"

"Colonel Knox, your passion is compelling," Washington had acknowledged, "but the reality of accomplishing such a feat is simply too much of a stretch for the imagination."

Knox, one of the few men in the Continental Army tall enough to almost look Washington directly in the eye, did just that.

"General Washington, I beg you to give me the opportunity to make this happen. If I were to fail, then we have lost nothing in the attempt. However, sir, if I were to succeed..."

Knox left the possibilities hang in the air, and he saw immediately that he had hooked his prey.

"Very well, Colonel, you have my permission to attempt to retrieve the artillery," Washington had replied, a slight smile of admiration on his face. Washington knew only too well when he was being manipulated, and this had been one of those occasions.

"I ask that you supply frequent reports on your progress," Washington had ordered sternly. "After all, we don't want to miss the opportunity to offer you a fitting welcome upon your ultimate arrival!"

***

Knox had set out immediately for Fort Ticonderoga, arriving on December 5th. With the assistance of the small contingent of soldiers manning the fort, Knox began a thorough inventory of the available cannon and ammunition. The bad news was that many of the artillery pieces were in such poor condition as to be unusable. The good news was that there were still nearly sixty cannon of various sizes that would almost certainly function satisfactorily.

Knox and his men began disassembling the guns from their mounts in order to make them slightly easier to transport, and by December 9th they were positioned at the northern end of Lake George. There, the cannon were loaded onto flat bottomed boats and floated to Fort

George at the southern end of the lake where they would continue the remainder of their journey which would be primarily over land.

Knox had sent several men ahead of the main party with instructions to commission the construction of forty sleds capable of carrying loads weighing up to 5400 pounds. In addition, as many as eighty oxen were to be purchased for pulling these massive sleds. Amazingly, both of these critical items were ready and waiting upon Knox's arrival at Fort George.

Unfortunately, the weather was not cooperating. In order for the sleds to be of any use, there needed to be snow on the ground, but as of December 11th when Knox and his party were ready to go there was none. Knox stomped and cursed every day, furious at the inactivity of his expedition. On December 17th he attempted to calm any concerns that General Washington may have had, informing his commander that, "I have 42 strong sleds." Undoubtedly, Washington noticed the absence of any report regarding the actual *progress* of these sleds.

Finally, on Christmas morning, 1775, Henry Knox awoke to the glorious scene of nearly two feet of snow having been deposited overnight. It was the best Christmas present the former bookseller had ever received.

It was at this point that the true test began. The movement of the sleds was painfully slow, as even the slightest obstacle proved to be challenging when transporting objects of such gigantic proportions. Small hills became mountains, as the men and oxen labored mightily to move their cargo up and over these rises. Actual mountains – of which there were many – seemed nearly insurmountable. But the emphasis for Knox was on the term "*nearly* insurmountable", as he drove the men and animals to accomplish feats they would never have believed possible just a few weeks earlier.

By January 5th, Knox's party had reached Albany, and they now faced the task of having to cross the Hudson River. Fortunately, the river had frozen over to a degree that allowed the group to cross, even with their heavy burden. Although one cannon broke through the ice, it was close enough to the shoreline that the men were able to retrieve it and get it safely across.

Douglas J. Shupinski

At one point during the arduous retrieval process, one of the soldiers unwisely suggested that they simply leave the cannon at the bottom of the river. After all, reasoned the man, there were still nearly sixty other cannon to be delivered.

Colonel Knox reacted to the man's comment almost violently, suggesting that, given the option, he would rather leave the soldier at the bottom of the river instead of the precious cannon. The foolish soldier was wise enough to keep any further comments to himself, and the man threw himself mightily into the task of pulling the cannon out of the water.

***

On January 24th, 1776, Colonel Henry Knox's "noble train of artillery" as he called it, arrived triumphantly at the American headquarters in Cambridge, Massachusetts, having traveled a total distance of three hundred miles in fifty-six days.

Knox had accomplished what appeared to be impossible. The tables were about to be turned on the British huddled miserably in Boston. And George Washington would never again view Henry Knox in the same way.

General William Howe

Commanding General, British Army

Boston

March 17, 1776

Major General William Howe had witnessed many unbelievable events throughout his rather lengthy military career. But he was forced to admit that none had been as unlikely as the scene playing out before him right now.

Thousands of British soldiers and sailors, as well as hundreds of civilians who had remained loyal to the Crown, were hastily boarding over one hundred and fifty British ships, intent on leaving the city of Boston. And although there was not really a sense of panic about their movements, they were certainly moving with a speed that indicated, at the very least, a significant sense of urgency.

"General Howe, we shall be prepared to depart in just a few minutes, sir," reported Captain Brillings, one of the members of Howe's staff. "I wonder if I could request, with all due respect, sir, that the General make his way up the gangplank and onto the flagship."

Howe couldn't quite decide whether or not he liked the young Captain, a quandary he realized existed with most of the other members of his reconstituted staff. The men that had gone into battle with him at Breed's Hill had been men he had served with for quite some time, and he had literally trusted them with his life. But too many of those brave men had been killed on that fateful day, with many others receiving wounds that required their return to England. This new group of staff officers seemed efficient enough – but they were untested in combat. And that, Howe knew, was the truly definitive measure of any soldier.

However, additional opportunities to test anyone in combat would have to be put on hold for the time being. The reason for that was simple: the British army and navy were evacuating the city of Boston and its surrounding waters. And they were doing so because the Continental Army had made it impossible for them to remain there safely.

***

The beginning of the end of the British occupation of Boston had occurred on the morning of March 5th. Howe had been awakened from a peaceful slumber just as the sun was beginning to rise on what promised to be another mild day in the city.

"General Howe, General Howe," one of his staff officers had stated insistently, his voice a confused mixture of whispering and controlled panic. "Sir, if I might request your presence at your observation point."

The "observation point" being referred to by the staff officer was nothing more than a position on the roof of the house that Howe had utilized as his headquarters for several months. The rooftop gave Howe the opportunity to not only see the main positions of his army throughout most of the city, but it also allowed him to see many of the American positions. These positions formed a wide arc in the shape of the letter 'C' that extended from directly north of the city at a place called Lechmere's point, traveled southwest to the middle of the arc at Cambridge, and ended directly south of Boston at Roxbury.

Several minutes later as Howe stepped onto the platform that had been erected on the rooftop, he was handed a telescope by yet another member of his staff.

"If you would, sir, please take a look in that direction toward Dorchester Heights," the officer requested, pointing almost directly south.

Howe knew from many previous hours of observation that where he was being directed to look was a small peninsula jutting eastward out into the Boston harbor, upon which rested two small hills. Howe was perturbed at the fact that he was wasting his time looking at this stretch of land. As of last night this peninsula, including its two small hills, had been deserted.

"Major, I'm aware of the location of Dorchester Heights," Howe stated bitterly, as he raised the telescope to his right eye. "Surely, you didn't need me to confirm that it hadn't escaped at some point..."

With a start, Howe realized that he was staring into the dark, menacing barrels of dozens of artillery pieces placed on the tops of the two small hills located on Dorchester Heights. These cannon were sitting within the perimeters of two redoubts which, at least at this distance, appeared to be surprisingly well constructed.

But how could this be? Howe made it a point to survey both the positions of his men as well as the American positions every night before the sun went down. Last night had certainly been no exception, and his survey had not taken note of these new emplacements. Surely, he could not have missed something so – dangerous.

"Good Lord," Howe said absently, almost to himself. "The rebels have done more in one night, than my whole army could do in months."

***

Technically, General Howe was correct. However, the plans for occupying Dorchester Heights had begun the moment Henry Knox had arrived from Fort Ticonderoga with his precious cargo.

General Washington realized that if he were able to place heavy cannon on those two small hills south of Boston, they would be capable of bombarding the city due to their relative height advantage. Meanwhile, the British would be unable to return their fire with any

Douglas J. Shupinski

degree of effectiveness, as they would almost certainly have difficulty elevating their cannon to the necessary angle.

Washington had decided to fortify the hills. He also decided that, similar to what had been done on Breed's Hill months earlier, he would do so in one night.

However, constructing the fortifications necessary to protect the cannon would be much more difficult than things had been on Breed's Hill. The ground was frozen to a depth of eighteen inches, which would make construction efforts difficult and time consuming.

The problem had been solved when Colonel Rufus Putnam, a relative and close friend of Israel Putnam, had suggested a rather innovative solution. As opposed to building the fortifications out of the ground of the two small hills, he suggested constructing most of the fortifications out of other materials at a separate location. Then, on the appointed evening, these previously constructed breastworks could be moved under cover of darkness to Dorchester Heights.

These portable breastworks had been constructed out of heavy timber frames which would eventually be filled in with hay bales and barrels filled with dirt and rocks. Ingeniously, these barrels were placed at the front of the fortifications so that they could also be rolled down at any advancing columns of enemy soldiers.

Over the period of several weeks, the necessary materials had been gathered and transformed into something of a prefabricated fortification. However, the real trick would be in the ability of the Continental Army to transport these materials to the two hills on Dorchester Heights and get them assembled in one night – all without the British being alerted to what was transpiring.

Beginning on the night of March 2nd, the Americans initiated an artillery barrage, utilizing the few guns they had placed to the north on Lechmere Point. This served to cover the sounds of any movements or digging. Finally, on the night of March 4th, over two thousand American soldiers began the laborious task of moving hundreds of pieces of fortification to the two small hills on Dorchester Heights. At three o'clock in the morning, an additional force of soldiers came and relieved the first work party.

By the time the sun peeked over the horizon of the Atlantic Ocean to the east, over eight hundred soldiers and nearly fifty artillery pieces had been moved into place along Dorchester Heights. This unwelcome sight was what had greeted General Howe.

***

It was this series of events that had brought General William Howe and the British army to this place on the morning of March 17th. The greatest army in the world, supported by the most powerful navy in the world, had been unable to hold one city in the face of a rebel siege.

The fleet of British ships was headed for the city of Halifax, Nova Scotia. Many of the Loyalists that were being forced to leave Boston would never return to their native city, some remaining in Canada while others returned to England.

But General William Howe vowed that he would return. Perhaps to the city of Boston, or perhaps to some other location that offered the British army the greatest opportunity to end this revolt once and for all.

This war was far from being over. In the mind of William Howe, it had just begun.

Douglas J. Shupinski

Part Two

New York

Captain Nathaniel Horne

Pennsylvania State Riflemen, Continental Army

New York City

April 23, 1776

The army had been marching almost continuously since their departure from Boston over two weeks earlier. It wasn't uncommon for the men to travel twenty miles in a day, and it hadn't taken long for the effects of this constant exertion to show themselves.

The first noticeable result wasn't what had appeared in the men's behavior, but rather what had disappeared. The recent euphoria of having forced the most powerful army in the world to retreat from Boston quickly faded into the past, as the realities of regular army life began to settle in.

While the food the men had eaten during their siege of Boston had certainly been nothing to write home about, the rations they had received during their march had been even worse. The newly formed Continental Army simply hadn't figured out the complexities associated with keeping an army properly supplied while on the move. Accordingly, the men who had been asked to complete this arduous journey were chronically tired and hungry. The result was predictable: the best cases involved unauthorized foraging from the farms, orchards and fields that had lined the route of the army's march. The worst cases ended with men simply abandoning their grand adventure, and returning home to their families.

Fortunately, many of the local citizens had turned out to cheer the men as they marched through the countless towns and villages along their path, and many of these kind people offered food and drink to the exhausted soldiers. Even so, these bright spots occurred all too infrequently to eliminate some of the former dysfunctional behaviors.

***

Captain Nathaniel Horne was an officer in the Pennsylvania State Riflemen, a unit that had been raised in and around Philadelphia the previous summer. Its Commanding Officer, Colonel Samuel Atlee, was an experienced officer, having served alongside the British during the French and Indian War.

Like so many of the American units which were now converging on New York City, the Pennsylvania State Riflemen had been initially organized to serve their role as militia. This meant that their purpose, as was the purpose of all militia units throughout the Colonies, was to defend their home colony as needed. However, when the plea had gone out from the forces surrounding Boston that additional troops were needed, the state of Pennsylvania had graciously – albeit, with a great deal of hesitation – allowed some of their militia units to travel to New England in support of that cause. Many other colonies had seen fit to do the same.

Finally, the men had reached their destination of New York City, a place so foreign to Nathaniel and the rest of the men in his unit that it might as well have been the moon. The differences between the small towns that many of them had come from and this city were overwhelming, and even those men that had come from the city of Philadelphia were struck by the culture of this city at the confluence of the Hudson and East rivers. It somehow seemed less conservative and much more full of itself, a fact demonstrated by the relative extravagance of its citizens. The houses were more grandiose and the buildings better appointed and constructed, all courtesy of the financial power wielded by this thriving community nestled at the tip of what was known as York Island.

More disturbing to many of the men – or interesting to them, depending on their moral character – was the existence of literally hundreds of prostitutes throughout the city. These women inhabited a seemingly endless number of questionable establishments centered in some of the seedier sections of town. Both the number of prostitutes and the number of bars had logically increased with the arrival of thousands of men who were lonely, bored, and far from the accountabilities associated with their previous home lives.

***

Captain Horne had recently made the acquaintance of another Captain, a William Smith from Connecticut. Captain Smith was the chief engineering officer in New York City and, as a result, had been tasked with designing and implementing the plans for fortifying the city against a possible British attack. That was all well and good, Nathaniel had reasoned – he just appreciated the fact that Smith was roughly the same age and had some worldly experience, unlike most of the other junior officers around him.

"As I was explaining, William," Nathaniel said, following up on an earlier conversation the two had been having, "it all depends on the amount of rain during the growing season. Too much rain means great big grapes without much flavor. Too little, and you get no juice. But that perfect amount – "

"For God's sake, Nate, you always act as if wine is the center of the universe!" replied Smith, having been subjected to some form of this discussion many times before. "It's just a drink, man."

Nathaniel could have appeared no more shocked had he seen a ghost.

"Just a drink? Just a drink? Why, that's like saying that tobacco is just another weed! Were it not for that little gem of the plant world, we would never have the ability to enjoy the pleasure of a finely rolled

Douglas J. Shupinski

cigar."

Smith merely rolled his eyes, his lack of appreciation for the proclivities of Nathaniel Horne complete.

"Now, Captain Smith," continued Nathaniel, "I suggest you begin demonstrating the proper respect for these finer things in life, or I shall be forced to find someone else with which to share my considerably enjoyable company."

"God forbid," responded Smith, feigning a horrified look. "Whatever was I thinking? Of course, Captain Horne, there can be no greater aspiration in life than the frequent and continuous enjoyment of wine and cigars."

"Finally," Nathaniel said with a heavy sigh of relief, "you've seen the light. But you have much to learn, my friend. Your work must begin now."

"Actually, Nate, it's your work that must soon begin," Smith stated, his previously light tone quickly becoming serious. "We're not making the progress I would like to see over on Long Island, so we're going to need more men. As most of the soldiers in your unit are experienced farmers and tradesmen, they're exactly what I need – hardworking men, accustomed to days of heavy labor."

The work that Captain Smith was referring to was the construction of fortifications on the high ground just across the river to the east of New York City. The area was known as Brooklyn Heights, and anyone with even the semblance of a brain in their head realized that control of Brooklyn Heights meant control over the city.

"What do you mean, 'hard working men'?" Nathaniel responded sharply. "These men are soldiers, who came here to fight the British, not toil away at the whim of an engineer from Connecticut!"

"Easy, Nate," William replied calmly, "I meant no insult by my comment. I rather meant it as a compliment to the quality of their backgrounds."

What Smith was referring to was the unfortunate fact that not every member of the American forces was an upstanding citizen, so to speak. Quite a few of the men that had opted to join the American army had done so in order to escape something. Perhaps they were wanted for a crime, or were overwhelmingly in debt. Some were nothing more than common bums, who had lived on the streets and saw the opportunity to have a meal and a place to sleep. Certainly, these types of men weren't the majority of the army by any stretch; but they were numerous enough that some units had already gained an unsavory reputation for shirking responsibilities at every opportunity.

Nathaniel smiled uncomfortably, realizing he had been just a bit sensitive.

"I'm sorry, William. It's just that I want my men to be known as fighters, not farmers. I suppose they can be both, eh? Now, explain to me what you're trying to do over there across the river, and perhaps I can give you some suggestions on how to best put my men to good use."

Captain Smith smiled broadly at his new friend. This was a good man, he knew almost instinctively. And if the Americans were to be successful in their fight against the British, they would need many more men just like Nathaniel Horne.

"Very well then, my wine-drinking, cigar-smoking Captain. Look here at what I'm proposing as a most unpleasant surprise to our British friends," Smith offered.

As Nathaniel looked on, Captain Smith proceeded to unroll a map of Brooklyn Heights that revealed information known to very few men indeed.

General William Howe

Commanding General, British Army

Halifax, Nova Scotia

June 1, 1776

Enough was enough – it was about damned time.

William Howe had been chomping at the bit to get back at the Americans ever since he had been forced to make a rather inglorious departure from Boston three months earlier. Finally, he had assembled everything necessary to repay the debt of revenge that had been gnawing at him for longer than he cared to acknowledge.

The British army had departed Boston with its proverbial tail between its legs, having been forced to evacuate their position as a result of a menacing number of cannon that had appeared almost miraculously on the heights overlooking the city. But even as the last of the British fleet turned north toward Nova Scotia, Howe had already begun planning his return.

There were times when a man hated to be right, and this was one such time for William Howe. He had made it clear to the British Parliament and his colleagues in the British army that these Americans were more than just a band of rabble that would go away at the first sign of conflict. Howe had been correct, to a greater degree than he had ever imagined.

Let's see, thought Howe, what have these farmers and tradesmen done so far? Nearly annihilated a British force sent to Concord, Massachusetts to disarm them; stood toe to toe with the cream of the British army at Breed's Hill, a feat that Howe had witnessed more closely than he cared to recall; and strategically outmaneuvered the British bottled up in Boston.

Yes, enough was enough, indeed.

Upon reaching the port of Halifax in Nova Scotia, General Howe had begun coordinating the actions necessary to put an end to this insurrection.

First, he had attended to the needs of his own men. Not only had they suffered a blow to their pride, but they had also been compelled to leave a significant amount of their weapons and supplies in Boston. Howe's first order of business had been to get his men properly outfitted, and back to the business of being soldiers. This had taken the form of endless hours of drill and discipline, followed by more hours of the same.

Second, the necessary weapons, ammunition, uniforms, and myriad other items necessary to send an army into combat were procured for the men. A well-equipped soldier was a confident soldier. And a confident, well-equipped soldier was deadly.

Third, Howe had received word that the British force that had been tasked with attacking Charleston, South Carolina had completed its task and was now making its way north. He immediately dispatched a ship with orders to intercept that fleet and direct it to New York City.

Finally, Howe had also received the rather unexpected, but extremely gratifying news that a fleet containing thousands of British and Hessian troops had departed England bound for the American colonies. Again, ships were sent to find that fleet and order it to make its way to New York City.

If the British were successful at coordinating the three forces coming from Halifax, Charleston, and England to arrive in New York

Douglas J. Shupinski

City at roughly the same time, they would have an overwhelming force of both ships and troops. Howe wasn't completely sure of the size of the American army located there, but he was certain that it would be no match for the awesome force that was now bearing down upon it.

***

"General Howe, you wished to see me, sir."

General Howe looked up from the maps he had been studying to be greeted by the sight of Major General Charles Cornwallis.

"I did, General. Please join me over here. I have some plans I would like to discuss with you."

Cornwallis, always ready and willing to share his opinions, made his way briskly to the table where Howe was standing.

Howe and Cornwallis had enjoyed a relatively stable, albeit cool, relationship since Howe had been appointed the Commanding General of the British forces in America. While Cornwallis believed he himself was the best choice to serve as the overall commander, at least Howe seemed to have a better grasp of the situation here in the colonies as compared to the previous commander, General Gage. As a result, Cornwallis was determined to show his value to Howe as a means of gaining his trust and confidence.

From Howe's perspective, he was pleased that Cornwallis had proven to be a competent and reliable ally, especially at times like this. The perspectives and experience of someone like Cornwallis could prove invaluable in determining the best course of action when there were so many options from which to choose.

All that being said, both men shared the unspoken but clear understanding that, given the opportunity, Cornwallis would jump at the chance to replace Howe as Commanding General. It was the type of politically charged environment that typified the realities of being a general in the British army.

"General Cornwallis, you are aware of my plans to set sail for New York City in the next few days, I assume," Howe stated matter of factly.

"I am, sir. The General was kind enough to share his plans with me in the recent past," Cornwallis responded formally.

"And what are your thoughts regarding this decision?" Howe asked, looking directly at Cornwallis.

"I'm sure the General has sound reasons for making such a decision. As always, sir, I stand ready to do my duty in support of whatever orders you see fit to publish."

"Damn it, man!" Howe exploded, "for just a moment stop telling me what you think I want to hear and tell me what you think! Our fortunes are locked together on this, General. If *my* plans are successful, then so shall you be. And if they are not..."

Howe left the completion of his statement hanging in the air.

Cornwallis was slightly taken aback by the uncharacteristic candor of Howe, and he took a moment to gather himself and his thoughts.

"At the risk of sounding condescending, sir, I would agree that New York City is the correct objective. It is there that the American army is located; therefore that is where I believe we must go. The traditional strategy of simply taking control of major cities – such as Boston or Philadelphia – and hoping for eventual capitulation by our enemy will not work in this situation."

Cornwallis paused briefly, and then concluded his thoughts.

"In my humble opinion, sir, I do not believe that these rebels either understand or respect the accepted rules of warfare."

General Howe chuckled slightly, amused at both the fact that Cornwallis had opened up so willingly, as well as at the idea that Cornwallis was capable of anything even approaching humility.

"Very well, then," Howe replied slowly, "New York City it shall be. I was considering a landing on the large island just to the east of New York City – Long Island, I believe it's called," Howe said, pointing to that land mass on the map in front of him.

"Certainly, sir, that is one possible landing point for our army," Cornwallis replied cautiously.

Howe looked at his subordinate in mild surprise. Cornwallis clearly had other ideas, and wished to share them. Well, thought Howe, I wanted honesty.

"But I suspect, General, that you see other options as well?" Howe asked.

This deference being shown to him by Howe was a bit unsettling to Cornwallis, and he shifted his stance uncomfortably. He wasn't quite sure exactly how much latitude he was being given in speaking his mind. Finally, however, his belief in his own experience and abilities got the best of him.

"Sir, I would strongly consider landing our army here," Cornwallis said pointing at Staten Island located to the south of New York City. "From that position, we will confuse the enemy by hiding our intentions of whether we intend to take control of Long Island, or move directly against the city itself. In addition, Staten Island is far enough away from the American army such that the arrival of our reinforcements from Charleston and England can be accomplished in safety."

Returning his gaze to the map, Howe quickly realized that Cornwallis' plan had genuine merit. Still, Howe was the Commanding General, and his superiority needed to remain intact.

"I appreciate your honesty, General Cornwallis. I will certainly take your suggestions into consideration as I make my final decision."

General Howe returned his gaze to the maps on the table, a clear indication to his subordinate that the meeting was over.

Cornwallis came to attention smartly and saluted General Howe, turned on his heel, and departed the room in much the same manner in which he had entered.

General George Washington

Commanding General, Continental Army

New York City

June 27, 1776

It had been two and a half months since George Washington had arrived in New York City, but the time had seemingly passed in an instant. There was simply so much to do to make ready for what Washington suspected was the inevitable arrival of the British, and that arrival might come at any time.

Washington had made his headquarters at the southernmost tip of York Island in a spacious house located on Broadway, the main thoroughfare running down the middle of the city. From this location he was overseeing the almost overwhelming number of details that needed to be addressed if his army was to have any hope of successfully repelling a British attack.

***

Washington had been poring over a multitude of maps that showed the various islands, rivers, and bays that constituted the area surrounding New York City. He stood painfully erect, his massive six foot four inch frame having been hunched over for what felt like days.

Douglas J. Shupinski

His bones screamed in protest, and Washington realized again that he was no longer the young man that had so enthusiastically entered into the military life so many years ago.

His challenges in defending this city were many and significant. In many respects, the tables had been turned in terms of the situations the British and Americans had dealt with in Boston.

For one thing, the Americans were now the ones in a central, static position, awaiting the arrival of a military force that had the opportunity to place itself wherever it saw fit. This dramatically limited the options of his army, and Washington knew from hard experience that options were often the key to victory.

Also troubling to Washington was the fact that most of the population in and around New York City was Loyalist. In the best of circumstances, these people sympathetic to the British would sit idly by, feeding information and insights to the invading British. The worst case would be these same individuals actually taking up arms against the Americans, potentially swelling the ranks of the enemy. Either of these possibilities was most unsettling.

Finally, the geography around New York City was tailor made for a joint force of infantry and warships. New York City was on an island, just barely separated from the mainland by a narrow strip of water to the north of the city. If the enemy was to successfully place its naval forces in the rivers on either side of the city, and then land its troops at any number of locations on York Island – well, that was a scenario that Washington chose to block from his mind just now.

Washington allowed his mind to drift back to a conversation he had had with General Nathaniel Greene, possibly his most trusted and capable subordinate. This conversation had taken place soon after Washington had arrived in New York City back on April 13th.

***

"General Washington, I have taken the liberty of surveying the area around the city at your request, sir," Greene had stated. "I believe that we find ourselves in a most precarious position with respect to our ability to establish an effective defensive position."

"Please continue," Washington had replied, eager to hear the thoughts of someone so insightful and capable. Greene had pressed on, comfortable in the confidence being displayed in him by his commander.

"Sir, I believe that the key to our success does not lie here within the confines of the city, but rather across the river at the western-most tip of Long Island."

Despite the fact that there were only a few years difference in their age, Washington felt an almost paternal affection for this man and he smiled warmly at the self-assurance Greene was displaying.

"Please continue, General Greene."

"Sir, as the General can clearly see," Greene stated, pointing to a large map of the area comprising New York City and its surroundings, "if the enemy were to occupy these heights just across the river to the east of the city, they would have complete control over our current position."

Greene paused and looked purposely at Washington.

"In effect, sir, they would have the same advantage over us as we had over them in Boston. That is to say, their artillery would have complete dominance over our army."

Looking at the map, Washington saw that not only was this true, but glaringly so. This meant that a man as experienced as the British Commander, General Howe, would almost certainly attempt to take advantage of the terrain.

"What do you suggest, General Greene?"

"Well, sir," Greene responded as if on cue, "I believe that a well-entrenched force on this prominent terrain feature known as Brooklyn Heights would be able to effectively repel a major attack. But the first key would be the preparation and organization of that defensive position."

Washington looked thoughtfully at the map for a few seconds, and then reached out and swept his finger over a small section.

"I see that Brooklyn Heights sits on this piece of land that bulges out from the main part of Long Island," Washington noted. "Where the

Douglas J. Shupinski

bulge meets the rest of the island appears to be a slightly narrower area to defend – perhaps that is our opportunity."

General Greene smiled broadly at Washington for just a moment, and then pulled a piece of paper from his breast pocket. With just the hint of a flourish, Greene unfolded the paper and laid it on top of the map. On the paper was a hand drawn version of what was clearly the same area as on the map. And across the relatively narrow piece of land that Washington had referred to was a series of small boxes, each of which was labeled, "fort". Connecting each of these forts were straight lines labeled, "entrenchments". General Greene had already come to the exact same conclusion as Washington, and had taken the initiative of designing a defensive system.

Washington looked up with mild surprise, a slight smile of admiration on his face.

"Well, General Greene, it would appear my presence here is quite unnecessary. You seem to have things well in hand."

"Wh–why, not at all, sir," Greene stuttered, hoping his borderline dramatic actions had not insulted the man he held in such high regard. "I'm merely honored that the General agrees with my rather basic attempt at – "

"Enough, General Greene," Washington chuckled. "You have every right to be pleased at having devised such a sound strategy."

Greene relaxed visibly, and even mustered a nervous smile.

"Just a moment ago, General Greene, I heard you say that the defense of Brooklyn Heights would be the first key to our success. What might the second one be?"

Greene directed General Washington's eyes back to his hand drawn map, to an area at the northern end of York Island.

"Sir, in addition to defending ourselves from an attack over land, we must also defend ourselves from an attack coming from the water," Greene explained. "To that end, I believe we will need to construct forts lining the rivers on either side of York Island to prevent the British navy from coming down behind us on Brooklyn Heights."

"Yes," conceded Washington, "I can see that being a most disturbing situation. British troops in front of us, British warships behind us – not only would we receive fire from both sides, but we would also have no avenue of escape."

"Exactly, sir," agreed Greene. "Finally, we would need to place cannon on the tip of York Island here, on this small island called Governor's Island here, and on this small spit of land jutting out into the bay from the New Jersey coast called Red Hook, located here," Greene explained, pointing out each of the locations on his map as he spoke.

Washington turned away and walked several steps, deep in thought. After several seconds, he turned and faced Greene.

"Very well, General Greene, I believe your strategy to be a sound one. However, this isn't something that we can accomplish overnight as we did in Boston. These plans will take literally months to turn into a reality."

"Yes, sir, that is true," acknowledged Greene. "That is exactly why we must have the entire army here as quickly as possible."

"Indeed," replied Washington. "We have no idea how long the British will favor us with their absence."

***

That conversation had occurred over two months ago. Since that time, the Americans had accomplished an amazing amount of work in the creation of their defenses. The forts on Brooklyn Heights; some of which were given such names as Fort Putnam, Fort Stirling, and Fort Greene; had been painstakingly constructed and connected by entrenchments, exactly as planned.

Further upriver, Forts Washington, Lee, and Thompson had been constructed on either side of York Island. These forts were slightly larger and even better constructed than those located on Brooklyn Heights, as they contained quite a number of cannon to repel British warships coming down the river.

The British had given the Americans the precious gift of time. But the generosity of General William Howe was about to come to an end.

Corporal Robert Boyle

93rd Regiment, Light Infantry, British Army

Staten Island

June 29, 1776

As always, the soldiers were ecstatic at the prospect of getting off the ships they had been forced to inhabit these last three weeks. Cramped conditions, constant seasickness, and food that was even worse than normal – a feat not easy to accomplish – left the men exhausted and demoralized. Returning to dry land was the first literal and figurative step to reviving their lagging spirits.

Newly promoted Corporal Robert Boyle resisted the urge to drop to his knees and kiss the ground as he departed the HMS Randolph, a forty-eight gun British warship that had been his prison for the last twenty days along with almost two hundred other British soldiers. Such a display of childishness would simply not befit the rank of corporal, a rather lofty station in life after having been at the bottom of the rank structure for so long.

Robert's arm had healed quite nicely, with nothing but a rather nasty scar as proof that he had participated in one of the most deadly engagements of the war so far. Unlike many of the soldiers who developed dangerous infections after being treated for their wounds,

Boyle had required only a couple of weeks to fully recover from his injuries. This rapid return to health had been in no small part due to the excellent work that the surgeon had performed on the young artist to whom, for some reason, he had taken a shine.

Upon returning to his unit, he had been ordered to make an appearance in front of Captain Moore, his company commander. Robert was terrified, wondering what he had done wrong to be subjected to such an awful fate. But his fears had turned out to be unfounded, and he recalled the rather surprising meeting in his mind.

***

"Private Boyle, sir, reporting as ordered," Robert had said, barely keeping the fear from his voice as he presented himself to the Captain.

"Ah, Private Boyle," Captain Moore had acknowledged, looking up briefly from some papers he had been reading. "Stand at ease, Private."

Boyle had been standing at rigid attention, as was dictated by protocol when addressing an officer. He quickly shifted his position to one of just slightly less formality, but remained at a form of attention and avoided direct eye contact with the Captain.

"Boyle, are you aware of why I wanted to see you?" Captain Moore asked.

"No sir, that information was not shared with me, sir."

"Well Boyle, I have been told by a number of individuals – to include the late Sergeant Wiley – that you are an excellent soldier. I have been told that you possess fine qualities such as self-discipline, bravery, and honesty. These are the qualities of a leader in this army, Private Boyle."

Robert remained silent, as he had no idea of how to respond to such revelations.

"I have therefore made the decision, Private Boyle," Captain Moore continued, "to promote you to the rank of corporal. God knows, after that awful experience at Breed's Hill, there are opportunities for advancement, and you have proven yourself worthy of such opportunities."

Douglas F. Shupinski

Captain Moore stood up and extended his hand to Robert. Stunned at such a gesture coming from an officer, Robert remained motionless for a second before reaching out and shaking the hand of the captain.

"Th-thank you, sir" Robert stammered, scarcely able to believe what was happening. But as the seconds passed, the significance of the responsibility he was being given began to gradually sink in. He realized that he would no longer simply be responsible for taking care of himself, but would have the task of looking out for the well-being of other British soldiers. It was an honor not to be taken lightly, and he drew himself up to full attention as he released the Captain's hand and rendered a crisp salute.

"Sir, I thank you for this opportunity," Robert stated forcefully. "I will do everything within my power to earn this position."

"Oh, you've already earned the position, Corporal," Captain Moore replied. "The trick these days seems to be staying alive long enough to enjoy it."

***

Robert had since taken to his role as a Corporal with relative ease. The fact that many of the enlisted men had already respected him prior to his promotion had made it an easier transition. The privates in his company willingly followed his orders, not just because they had to, but because they believed that Corporal Boyle was genuinely looking out for them.

Captain Moore had been right; not only did Robert Boyle have many of the qualities of a natural leader, but the men around him knew it.

Surrounding the personal life of Corporal Robert Boyle was the larger story of what would be in store for the future of this army. Rumors flew around the camp like paper in a windstorm – the army was landing on the southern tip of York Island within a week; the army would await the arrival of reinforcements, and then attack Long Island; the army would re-embark on the ships and sail north of New York

City, landing and attacking from that direction.

There were many rumors, but they were really just different versions of the same story: the British army was going to attack the Americans, and they would do so in the very near future.

***

Robert had just completed an inspection of the area around the encampment of his company, satisfied that they were complying with all of the regulations of hygiene and organization. While most of the soldiers willingly followed the rules, understanding that these rules were in place for their own safety and well-being, there was still the occasional lapse of discipline. However, it always seemed that the closer the army got to going into combat, the more compliant the men became.

Robert was passing by one of the many campfires that had been built around the tents of his company. Several Privates were sitting and talking amongst themselves when one of them spotted Robert and called out to him.

"Corporal Boyle! Do you 'ave a moment?"

Robert, lost in his own thoughts, took a second to respond.

"Of course, Private Barnes, what is it?"

"Corporal Boyle, we was just talkin' here about what's goin' on these last few days," Private Barnes stated somewhat hesitantly. "And we was thinkin' – well, Corporal, we was thinkin' that you might have heard somethin' about what General Howe might 'ave in mind for us."

Robert's initial reaction of surprise at the question was quickly replaced by amusement. Apparently these men assumed that his promotion to Corporal carried with it some insight as to what plans were being made by the Commanding General. It drove home in an instant two critical lessons for Robert; first, how desperate these men were for some level of comprehension about their future; and second, how much they overestimated the power of a position that was but a single rank above them. He made a mental note to always keep these lessons in mind.

"Private Barnes," Robert replied, "believe me when I tell you I would love to have that knowledge as much as you all. But alas, I have neither a direct connection to General Howe, nor do I have the wisdom of the late Sergeant Wiley."

The men became instantly sober at the mention of the Sergeant's name. Wiley's experience had been a continuous source of insight to the men, and his actions on the battlefield had saved the lives of more than one of the men now seated around the campfire.

"Aye, lads," one of the other Privates remarked, "Sergeant Wiley was a good man, he was. This company will miss the likes of him during this next fight, that's for sure."

"This *army* will miss the likes of him in the next fight, Private," Boyle responded quickly. "But the loss of a man like Wiley leaves a hole that has to be filled. Sometimes you try and fill it by promoting someone else to do the same job. Captain Moore has seen fit to ask me to try and do that, to some small degree. And I pray to God Almighty that He gives me the strength to be half as good a man as Sergeant Wallace Wiley was."

The men looked at Boyle in surprise, not used to having a non-commissioned officer speak so openly and honestly.

"But here's a secret, lads, that perhaps even Sergeant Wiley didn't know," Boyle continued, a deep seriousness creeping into his voice.

The men around the fire were completely still now, their eyes fixed on Corporal Boyle, awaiting this revelation.

"Not a single man in this army – not Corporal Robert Boyle, for sure – can replace that kind of a soldier. That's something that must be done by every one of us. By remembering what he stood for. By honoring what he did. And by carrying on the pride he had in himself and in this army."

Several of the men shifted uncomfortably, knowing that Robert was right, and that the responsibility they all had was of great significance.

"Gentlemen," Robert continued, "I promise you that I will give you everything I have within me to do those things. All I ask – all that this army *demands* – is that you do the same."

Robert suddenly felt exhausted, and he allowed his chin to drop to his chest for just a moment. Regaining his composure and coming to attention, he saluted the group of men.

"Good night, gentlemen."

The men immediately assumed a position of attention, and returned the salute of their Corporal as he made his way into the gathering darkness. And as they resumed their seats around the fire, each of them had the same thought echoing in their minds: they had found their new Sergeant Wiley.

Douglas J. Shupinski

American Continental Army

New York City

July 8, 1776

As the late afternoon gradually made its way into the early evening, hundreds of troops had gathered in a large open area just off of Broadway, told they were to be informed of a resolution that had recently been passed by the Continental Congress in Philadelphia. A number of other similar gatherings were taking place throughout the city, some attended by soldiers, some by civilians, and some by both. Word had it that this resolution would have a direct impact on the manner in which the war would be conducted in the future.

Some of the more outlandish rumors hinted that it had something to do with declaring independence from England.

But such rumors of independence were clearly just that – rumors. Every soldier knew that the Continental Congress, made up of delegates clearly unwilling to put on a uniform and face the enemy, would never have the guts to make such a bold statement.

A colonel from one of the Connecticut units strode purposefully to the center of the crowd, and climbed up on a bench that had been placed there for that very purpose. In his left hand he carried a large piece of paper rolled into a tight tube. It was the contents of this paper, ostensibly, that contained the reason for the many gatherings.

As the colonel unrolled the paper, the low murmuring throughout the group of men gradually died down until it was completely silent.

"By order of George Washington, Commanding General, Continental Army, the following document is to be read to all members of his command on this day, the 8th of July, 1776."

The day was still warm, but it was late enough that the worst of the heat was beginning to dissipate. The only sounds were those being made by the various conveyances moving down Broadway just a short distance away, as well as the birds roosting in the nearby trees. The men were relaxed, but curious.

"The following declaration has been communicated to King George the Third of England, to be effective immediately," continued the colonel. With that preamble, he began to read directly from the document in his hands, which he had unrolled and was holding directly in front of himself.

"When, in the course of human events, it becomes necessary for one people to dissolve the political bands which have connected them with another, and to assume among the powers of the earth, the separate and equal station to which the laws of nature and of nature's God entitle them, a decent respect to the opinions of mankind requires that they should declare the causes which impel them to the separation."

The effect was as if a bolt of lightning had been sent through the crowd. Men gazing idly about suddenly had their eyes riveted on the colonel. Men who had been seated on the ground or leaning against trees and walls were on their feet, leaning forward to hear the remainder of the announcement.

Well, I'll be damned, the men thought to themselves. They actually did it. Those men in Philadelphia that we all thought were cowards actually did it. They had declared that the American Colonies were an independent nation.

***

However, the journey to this day had not been an easy one for the members of the Continental Congress by any means.

As recently as a few months ago, most of the delegates to Congress

Douglas J. Shupinski

were heavily in favor of reconciliation with England. The belief was that there was simply too much for both parties to lose if the colonies separated from the Crown. England needed the natural resources of the colonies, and the colonies required the lucrative marketplace that England provided for the goods that they produced.

However, there were a number of extremely influential men who were working hard behind the scenes to drive the colonies to a break from the Motherland. And there was no one more influential or more hard-working than John and Samuel Adams, second cousins from Massachusetts. These two had made every possible effort to convince their colleagues that independence was the only path that made any sense.

These two men, along with others fighting for independence, rested their logic on the fact that England had engaged in numerous underhanded and tyrannical acts, including taxing the colonies without allowing them any political representation, forcing private citizens to quarter unwanted British soldiers in their homes, and turning the colonial civilian legal authorities into virtual puppets beholden to the whims of the King.

Ironically, these radicals for independence had utilized their own share of underhanded methods in order to advance their cause, rationalizing that the end result would justify the means utilized. An example was a recent poll conducted in Pennsylvania, during which the populace (that is to say, the male populace) was asked to vote on whether or not they were in favor of breaking ties with England. During the debates that preceded the vote, the Adams' and their colleagues shouted down anyone who attempted to speak out against independence. In some cases, individuals were even threatened with bodily injury.

Despite these questionable efforts, the poll eventually yielded a victory for those in favor of reconciliation. Pennsylvania remained unconvinced of the wisdom of independence, and several other colonies including New York, Delaware, and South Carolina maintained a similar stance on the matter.

***

It was, ironically, the actions of the King himself that brought things to a head. For weeks, those in favor of reconciliation had heard rumors that a Peace Commission was on its way to the Colonies to discuss the best way to bring the colonies back into the Royal fold. Instead, on May 6, reliable sources reported that the King had not sent a Peace Commission, but instead he had sent a sizable army to New York City. And, to add insult to injury, this army contained thousands of mercenaries – hired soldiers from several German provinces who were known throughout Europe as some of the most vicious and bloodthirsty fighters in the world.

Soon thereafter, the radicals for independence decided the time was right to force the issue. On June 7, 1776, John Adams and Richard Henry Lee introduced a motion to the Continental Congress which read, in part, as follows:

"That these united colonies are, and of right ought to be, free and independent states, that they are absolved from all allegiance to the British Crown, and that all political connection between them and the state of Great Britain is, and ought to be, totally dissolved."

The effect of the motion was predictably polarizing to the members of the Continental Congress. Those in favor of independence flush with the momentum they had gained from the arrival of the British army and its mercenaries, wanted to strike while the iron was hot, and demanded an immediate vote. Meanwhile, those in favor of reconciliation felt that a lengthy delay would eventually allow cooler heads to prevail.

After much debate, a compromise was reached: the Continental Congress would reconvene and vote on the motion on July 1st.

***

As the July 1st vote got closer, the positions of each of the colonies became more evident. As a group, all of the New England colonies

Douglas J. Shupinski

would vote for independence. Pennsylvania, Delaware, and New Jersey delegates were told by their respective legislative bodies back home to vote as their consciences dictated. Maryland and New York delegates were specifically forbidden to vote in favor of independence.

It was time for the Adams cousins to get to work. Operating behind the scenes, often with individual members of the Congress, they gradually eroded the will of various delegates to resist the tide in favor of independence. The carrot they often used was pointing out to the delegates that, if the colonies were to become independent, they would all become extremely influential members of a governing body presiding over a potentially powerful country. The stick they wielded was warning men that if their particular colony refused to jump on the independence bandwagon, they would be left behind as the rest of the country moved forward.

Whether or not the efforts of the Adams' would be sufficient to sway the vote in favor of independence remained to be seen. In the meantime, a much less dramatic issue became evident.

***

The members of the Continental Congress realized that, should the colonies declare their independence, there needed to be some proclamation to make England and the citizens of the colonies aware of the news. To that end, a committee of five men; Benjamin Franklin from Pennsylvania, Roger Sherman from Connecticut, John Adams from Massachusetts, Robert Livingston from New York, and Thomas Jefferson from Virginia; were instructed to draft a document that would accomplish this objective.

Almost immediately, the four older and more influential members of this committee; Franklin, Sherman, Adams, and Livingston; indicated that they had little time to participate in what they perceived to be the most pedestrian of tasks. Instead, they delegated the responsibility to young Thomas Jefferson, only thirty-two years old, to accomplish this administrative triviality. Meanwhile, the other four moved off to busy themselves with much more important tasks related to the war and the eventual independence they hoped would arrive.

Jefferson was furious, believing he had been relegated to the role of a simple secretary while other critical items were attended to by the others. Nevertheless, he sequestered himself into the tiny, hot room he had rented in Philadelphia, and began composing the document.

***

Finally, July 1st arrived, at the absolute height of the hot summer season in Philadelphia. The members of the Continental Congress packed themselves into the tiny Pennsylvania State Building and began the debates which would last for hours.

The vote taken at the end of the day was inconclusive. While there was a significant majority in favor of independence; nine of the thirteen colonies had voted in favor of the resolution; the result had not been the unanimous decision that everyone knew to be critical. Under enormous pressure, those in favor of reconciliation were convinced to participate in another vote the very next day, after they had had an opportunity to think things over yet again.

That night, more work was done behind the scenes. A delegate from Delaware in favor of independence was called from his home to Philadelphia to break the stalemate in that colony. New York's legislative body had a sudden and unexpected change of heart, and ordered their delegates to vote for independence. South Carolina, having long been on the fence, gave in to the argument that unity was the paramount priority. And two delegates from Pennsylvania, John Dickinson and Robert Morris, decided to remain at home the next day so that a majority vote for independence could be achieved in that critical colony.

On July 2, 1776, the thirteen colonies of America voted unanimously to declare themselves independent of England. The declaration was read in public for the first time on July 4th, and the first appearance of the declaration in newspapers occurred on July 6th.

Ironically, when the document which became known as the Declaration of Independence was passed on July 2nd, not a single member of the Continental Congress signed it. Everyone agreed that there was a need for certain edits to be made to the document before it

Douglas J. Shupinski

could be signed and made official.

Specifically, some of the language describing the charges against England needed to be softened just a bit. After all, while these men yearned for independence, they also recognized that there would always be a need for strong economic ties with their old Masters. In addition, Thomas Jefferson had overstepped his bounds when he included language that was critical of the institution of slavery. Many of the members of the Continental Congress not only supported that particular practice, but they actively engaged in it.

It wasn't until August 2nd that a final version of the document was ready for signature. Over the next six months or so, as members of the Continental Congress passed through Philadelphia, they stopped and signed the declaration.

The colonel standing on the bench at the center of the group of soldiers had nearly completed the reading of the document in his hands. His voice rose in volume as he attempted to add weight and significance to the final lines:

"We, therefore, the Representatives of the united States of America, in General Congress, Assembled, appealing to the Supreme Judge of the world for the rectitude of our intentions, do, in the Name, and by Authority of the good People of these Colonies, solemnly publish and declare, That these United Colonies are, and of Right ought to be Free and Independent States; that they are Absolved from all Allegiance to the British Crown, and that all political connection between them and the State of Great Britain, is and ought to be totally dissolved; and that as Free and Independent States, they have full Power to levy War, conclude Peace, contract Alliances, establish Commerce, and to do all other Acts and Things which Independent States may of right do. And for the support of this Declaration, with a firm reliance on the protection of divine Providence, we mutually pledge to each other our Lives, our Fortunes and our sacred Honor."

***

On July 12th, the long awaited Peace Commission from England finally landed on Staten Island. The Howe brothers – General William Howe and Admiral Richard Howe – had desperately hoped that a peace could be brokered between the colonies and the King. But both men realized that their hopes were now almost certainly in vain.

The thirteen colonies were now galvanized in a way they had never been before. Whereas they had referred to themselves as the thirteen colonies, they now referred to themselves as the united States of America. And they were no longer simply fighting for the rights and protection of their respective colonies – they were fighting for the independence of a new nation.

The Declaration of Independence had changed the game.

Douglas F. Shupinski

Sergeant Alexander Bickell

Hesse-Cassell Division, British Army

Staten Island

August 15, 1776

It appeared as if the last of the British forces had finally arrived on Staten Island. For the past six weeks there had been a steady stream of British ships arriving to the island, each one carrying either the firepower of cannon, a load of soldiers, or often both. The assembled army that now awaited its further orders was truly awesome.

The British fleets had arrived from three locations. First, Admiral Richard Howe, along with his brother Major General William Howe, had come down from Halifax, Nova Scotia, having been chased out of Boston several months ago. On August 1st, a fleet arrived from Charleston, South Carolina, bringing three thousand additional troops and the important personages of Generals Cornwallis and Clinton. Finally, a few days earlier a fleet from England had appeared on the horizon, eventually landing its horrendously seasick and miserable cargo of an additional 11,000 troops.

All told, the waters around Staten Island were now literally crammed with nearly four hundred ships, and the island was close to bursting with its 32,000 soldiers. It was the largest invasion force ever assembled and deployed by any country in the history of modern warfare. If these rebels thought for a moment that they had faced the best and greatest that Britain was able to offer, they were sorely mistaken.

This was a calculated display of strength on the part of the King. The logic was that these numbers of ships and soldiers would be simply too much for the Americans to fathom, and abject terror would compel these farmers and tradesmen charading as soldiers to pack their bags and return to their homes. With any luck at all, none of these British soldiers would need to engage in combat.

***

For Sergeant Alexander Bickell, such strategic machinations were beyond his knowledge, as well as beyond his caring. He was a Hessian soldier who had been trained to close with and destroy his enemy with superior firepower, discipline, and ruthlessness. And while a cessation of hostilities here in America was certainly not distasteful to him, it would seem like a bit of a shame if he and his men had come all this way without being given an opportunity to do what they did best.

Alexander Bickell was one of eight thousand mercenaries that had been recruited from several principalities within Germany, most from the Hesse–Cassell region. As a result, all of the German mercenaries had been conveniently but inaccurately dubbed "Hessians" by their British counterparts. To a man, these Hessians were extremely disciplined, highly trained, and imbued with a certain esprit de corps. In addition, the Hessians had a reputation – well deserved – of conducting themselves in ways that were considered outside of the bounds of proper military behavior.

The British commanders knew they were taking a risk by employing the likes of such men. The Hessians were known to show little or no regard for the personal property of their enemies, and civilians were often subjected to acts of heartless brutality. In addition, they paid little attention to the time-honored concept of allowing an enemy soldier to surrender himself, choosing to use the points of their bayonets as a response to a man raising his arms in capitulation. But the decision had been made at the highest levels of the British government to take these chances in favor of the cruel effectiveness provided to their army by these Hessians.

Sergeant Bickell would have smiled in amusement had he been told that he had been "recruited" for this assignment. In fact, his father had chosen to offer his oldest son up for military service in exchange for a bounty – a bounty that his father had immediately stuffed into his own pocket as he walked away from his son without so much as a backward glance of farewell. That was just fine with Bickell; he never could stand the bastard anyway, having been subjected to his father's merciless beatings for as long as he could remember.

For now, Sergeant Alexander Bickell had but one priority; to prepare his men for the fighting that might lie ahead.

***

"You there!" Sergeant Bickell barked as he approached a Hessian soldier relaxing on the ground. "What in God's name do you think you're doing?"

The unsuspecting man jumped to his feet, realizing that he had already violated the rule of never getting on the bad side of this demon coming towards him.

"Why aren't you on duty with the rest of your squad," Bickell demanded, his black eyes boring a hole through the man.

"S–Sergeant Bickell," the man stammered, "I have been placed on light duty by the battalion surgeon. I was told to remain in camp until further notice."

"Light duty?" Bickell hissed, a menacing look on his face. "Hessian soldiers in my unit are not permitted to be placed on 'light duty' unless they have been wounded in combat – *seriously* wounded. And it seems to me that since we have yet to be in combat, you have no excuse for your situation!"

"Yes, Sergeant – I mean, no Sergeant," the man responded fearfully, clearly unaware of the appropriate response.

"Where is your weapon, soldier?" Bickell demanded.

"Sergeant, I believe it's stacked over there," the soldier said, pointing toward a stand of arms nearby.

"You *believe?*" Bickell shouted, clearly incredulous at the response. "You *believe* it's over there? Private, if I don't see you in full uniform and standing guard with your squad in two minutes – and that means carrying your elusive musket – I will have you strapped to a cannon and lashed until your back is a shred of flesh! Is that understood?"

"Yes, Sergeant, completely!"

The hapless soldier sprinted into a nearby tent, then re-emerged a second later and sprinted to the stand of arms where he hastily retrieved a musket, and then sprinted back to the tent to complete his preparations.

Sergeant Bickell moved on, knowing there was no need to remain and insure that the man followed his orders to the letter. He knew that his men understood that the only thing more dangerous than facing the enemy in combat was facing Sergeant Bickell when he was angry.

***

Several hours had passed since Bickell had reprimanded the malingering soldier, and the men that had been standing guard from Bickell's company were returning from their duty. These men were hot, tired, and hungry, and generally in a bad mood. In short, in Bickell's opinion this was the perfect time for an inspection of their weapons and uniforms.

"You men coming off of guard duty, fall in for inspection," shouted Corporal Brenhoffen, one of the senior enlisted members of the battalion. "You have thirty seconds to prepare yourselves – you had best make good use of that time."

Not a single complaint was heard from the men; they were too aware of the consequences for giving even the slightest impression of complaining. But the strained looks on their faces was a clear indication that the men weren't happy with the situation.

Sergeant Bickell had been sitting in his tent listening to the orders being given by Corporal Brenhoffen, as well as listening for any undisciplined comments from the men. Waiting exactly thirty seconds, Bickell emerged from his tent and strode purposefully toward the assembled men.

"Detail, attention!" Corporal Brenhoffen shouted, and the men immediately complied with the order.

Bickell came to a stop exactly three yards in front of the detail, just as protocol dictated. Looking to his left at Corporal Brenhoffen, he nodded almost imperceptibly.

"Exchange weapons with the man next to you!" ordered Brenhoffen. After doing so, the men immediately returned to their positions of attention.

Sergeant Bickell occasionally utilized this practice of exchanging weapons prior to an inspection as a means of instilling interdependence and accountability within his unit. The concept was simple, but effective. You were personally responsible for the condition of whatever weapon was in your hands at the time of the inspection, whether that weapon belonged to you or the man next to you. If that weapon was deemed to be in poor condition, you would receive extra duty or, in extreme cases, thirty lashes.

The result was that every man not only concerned himself with the maintenance of his own weapon, but also kept a sharp eye on how his fellow soldiers were maintaining theirs. Sergeant Bickell wasn't able to watch these men every second of the day – there was only one of him. But this strategy had created countless pairs of watchful eyes, and the consequence had been a more cohesive unit, and better maintained weapons and equipment.

The weapon being inspected was officially known by the British supply system as the Long Land Service Musket, but the troops referred to it as the "Brown Bess". While no one exactly knew the origin of the nickname, it was assumed that the "Brown" came from the color of the stock as well as the metal (which was brown as a result of having been treated with a substance to prevent rust.) The "Bess" portion of the name was less apparent, but probably came from the practice of soldiers giving their weapons some moniker of affection; and 'Brown' and 'Bess' seemed to naturally go together.

The Brown Bess was an extremely durable and sturdy weapon, which was important in light of the rough treatment they often received. Traveling long distances over difficult terrain, constantly being banged around, the musket could take a beating and still remain operational. Also, in combat situations it made for a formidable weapon in the hands of a skilled soldier, either as a platform for the fearful bayonet that could be as long as twelve inches, or as a simple club.

That was the good news.

The bad news was that the Brown Bess weighed over eleven pounds with a barrel that was forty-six inches long, thus making it both tiring to carry on the march, and sometimes tough to wield in the tight conditions often experienced during hand–to–hand combat.

Sergeant Bickell began moving methodically down the row of men, his eyes constantly roaming over their uniforms, their weapons, and their personal hygiene. Nothing escaped the experienced eye of Bickell, and while the men remained motionless and seemingly emotionally detached, every one of them was in abject fear that their sergeant would notice some slight imperfection.

To the universal relief of the detachment, Bickell was unable to find anything to dissatisfy him. With just a hint of disappointment, he concluded his inspection and addressed Corporal Brenhoffen.

"You may dismiss the detachment, Corporal. Insure their sleeping areas are in proper order before they are permitted to turn in for the evening."

"Yes, Sergeant!" Brenhoffen responded, as he came to attention and rendered a crisp salute.

As Sergeant Bickell walked off into the evening, he had to grudgingly admit that his men were exactly where he needed them to be in terms of their training and preparation. They were learning and developing their military skills to such a degree that life would be very dangerous for their enemy when the fighting began.

General William Howe

Commanding General, British Army

Long Island

2:00 P.M. August 26, 1776

General William Howe surveyed his surroundings with a feeling of great satisfaction. His men, always the picture of discipline and military decorum, seemed to be at a heightened degree of preparedness for a number of reasons.

First, at the most basic level, the men were simply happy to be off of those damned Royal Navy ships, where some had suffered for weeks, while others had suffered for months. The absence of seasickness, the improved diet, and the room to move about all contributed to the high morale. Second, if the population on Staten Island had been friendly to the arriving British army, the Long Islanders had been literally overjoyed at the presence of these red-clad warriors. Cheers from the men, kisses from the women, and gifts of food had been theirs for the taking. Nothing makes a man feel better about himself than knowing what he was doing was popular with the local citizenry. But most significantly, when casting his gaze around a British soldier was able to see thousands and thousands of his counterparts, endless rows of artillery, and a sea filled to capacity with warships ready to throw their weight into the fight when necessary. Such a display of power would fill even the most timid soul with confidence.

The landing on Long Island had taken place like a well-rehearsed play. The warships had provided oversight as the hundreds of troop transports had pushed off from their places on Staten Island, the headquarters of the army. Crossing the three miles of open water had been child's play, the bay a virtual sheet of glass, the weather cooperating completely. The landings on the opposite shore had been completely unopposed, as the few Rebels ordered to occupy the shoreline had immediately run for the hills at the sight of the incredible power rowing in their direction.

However, unknown to General Howe there was even better news. His adversary, General George Washington, was completely misinformed as to the size of the British invasion force. Normally, the inexperience of the Americans caused them to grossly overestimate the number of enemy troops they were facing. But in this case, the few Rebel scouts that had remained long enough to get a rough count of the arriving British had sent word that the enemy coming ashore probably numbered around seven or eight thousand men. Such misinformation had the potential to create dire consequences for the Americans.

***

General Howe had established his headquarters just a few hundred yards inland from where the successful landing had taken place four days earlier. In addition to the massive numbers of men and equipment that surrounded him, Howe was also fortunate to have his two key commanders by his side. Lieutenant General Charles Cornwallis and Lieutenant General Henry Clinton had also made the crossing and were now standing with him as he made final preparations for his attack.

"Gentlemen," Howe began, "I know you may feel as if we have discussed our intentions already a thousand times, but I feel it is appropriate to insure we are all in agreement at this final hour – especially in light some new information we have received."

Douglas J. Shupinski

The two generals nodded in unison, having learned from previous painful experiences that even a slight misunderstanding could lead to disaster when it came to sending men into combat.

"We will be dividing our army into three sections in an attempt to confuse and overwhelm the enemy," Howe continued. "General Clinton, I know that this decision has been a point of concern for you in the past, but I trust that you are now comfortable with this course of action."

All three men knew that anyone's discomfort with the plan was, at this point, completely irrelevant. However, Clinton appreciated the unusual display of deference being shown by his commander.

"Sir, having had the opportunity to ruminate on this plan, I am fully in support of it," General Clinton replied respectfully. "I have no doubts with respect to its wisdom, nor to its ultimate success."

"Excellent," Howe replied automatically, relieved that the charade of collegiality could finally be put to rest. "Now, as we all know, gentlemen, our ultimate objective is to attack the system of fortified works that the enemy has built on Brooklyn Heights. Control of these heights will force the Americans to evacuate New York City – much like those bastards did to us in Boston."

Cornwallis and Clinton looked at their commander in surprise. While Howe's use of profanity was somewhat commonplace, the fact that he had acknowledged the British retreat from Boston was the truly shocking part. Howe had basically ordered his staff to avoid any references to that rather inglorious episode from the past.

"However, before we get to the fortifications, we must first address the small matter of several thousand enemy troops being spread out in front of Brooklyn Heights," Howe continued on, almost as a monologue.

"Apparently, there is at least one fairly intelligent person in the Continental Army who has devised a strategy that requires us to defeat not one, but two layers of defense," remarked General Cornwallis.

"Perhaps, General," Howe replied cryptically, "perhaps."

"Have we received any new intelligence regarding the size and placement of these forward troops, sir?" Clinton asked.

"We have, General Clinton. If you please," Howe ordered, indicating to his two generals that they were to follow him to a large map of Long Island that was hanging on a wall nearby.

"Local citizens have reported that there might be as many as two thousand troops on the American right flank guarding the Gowanus Road," Howe stated, pointing to a position on the map labeled as such. "Meanwhile, there are reportedly two smaller forces of approximately one thousand troops each located here and here at the Flatbush Pass and the Bedford Pass, which form the center of the American position" he said, indicating these locations on the map as well.

"Excellent, sir," Cornwallis commented with a smile. "These are almost insignificant numbers of troops for our army to face on the right and center of the enemy position. What do we know about their concentration on the left flank?"

General Howe turned and faced his two comrades, unable to keep an evil grin from spreading across his face.

"Apparently, that fairly intelligent individual responsible for the design of the Rebel defenses has opted to place no troops on his own left flank."

A stunned silence hung in the air, as Clinton and Cornwallis took several seconds to process this information.

"But, General Howe," Cornwallis blurted out, "that is foolhardy to the point of being almost criminal!"

"Take caution in drawing your conclusions, General," Howe warned. "The Americans have no doubt placed a number of patrols in that area with orders to screen that flank for any movement. As you can see on the map, that flank is fairly close to the main enemy fortifications on Brooklyn Heights, therefore allowing them to move troops forward in response to an attack on their left."

Clinton and Cornwallis nodded thoughtfully, fully aware that overconfidence was the deadliest of vices in the art of war.

"Your plans, sir?" Clinton asked.

"As we had previously decided, we will have General Grant move against the right flank of the Americans with his force of approximately five thousand men," Howe began. "However, as opposed to an all-out attack, he will be ordered to make a demonstration against the enemy in order to hold them in place. Grant will be given strict orders that his force is not to be brought into a full engagement until given the command to do so."

"Sir, if I may," General Cornwallis stated, "are we confident that General Grant will be able to simply 'demonstrate', as you say, without being pulled prematurely into a full confrontation? While these Rebels clearly lack any military discipline, we have already seen their penchant for – well, sir – for enthusiasm."

"James Grant is a general in His Majesty's army," Howe replied with just a hint of disdain at the question. "If he is ordered to avoid a full engagement until the appropriate time, then he will do so."

"Yes, My Lord," Cornwallis replied, receiving his commander's message loud and clear. Everyone was expected to do his duty – there was no room for error.

"At the same time," Howe continued, "General von Heister and his five thousand Hessians will stage a similar demonstration at the center of the American position. And despite the somewhat heathen nature of he and his men," Howe stated, casting a meaningful look in the direction of Cornwallis, "he too will restrain his attack until given the signal to do otherwise."

There was just a moment of uncomfortable silence, as the three men contemplated the insinuation that had been made by General Howe. They all knew that when the Hessians got their blood up in a combat situation, restraint was not always the easiest of orders to have them carry out.

"Finally," Howe said, "our remaining ten thousand soldiers will loop around on the Old Jamaica Road, travel through the unguarded Jamaica Pass, and come down upon the left flank of the Americans. If our comrades are doing their job well against the right and at the center, we should take the Americans from behind, and crush them in a vice."

"Sir, if I may ask," Clinton ventured, "where would you like General Cornwallis and me to be during the engagement?"

"You shall both accompany me with the portion of our army

swinging around behind the Americans on their left. As I believe that wing of the attack to be the most critical, your experience will best serve us from that position. The demonstrations on the part of Generals Grant and von Heister are scheduled to begin soon after midnight tonight. Therefore, in order to be in position at the necessary time, we will be departing with our ten thousand men in the next few hours."

A brief silence ensued as all three generals looked thoughtfully at the map on the wall, their minds going over the countless details that would need to be addressed in the very near future.

"Are there any other questions?" General Howe asked, turning his gaze back to his commanders.

"Yes sir," Cornwallis replied. "Once we have crushed the enemy with your three-pronged attack, what will our next move be?"

"One thing at a time, General Cornwallis," Howe responded firmly, "one thing at a time."

Douglas F. Shupinski

Map #2: The Battle of Long Island

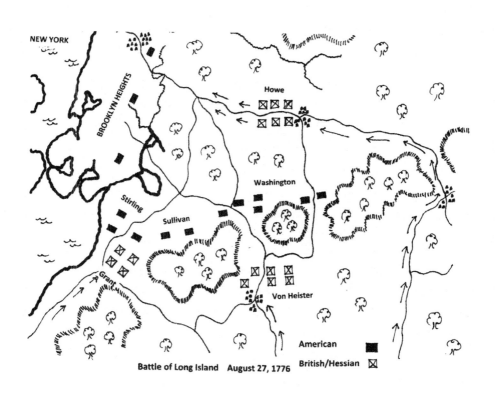

Battle of Long Island   August 27, 1776

American

British/Hessian

Captain Nathaniel Horne

Pennsylvania State Riflemen, Continental Army

Gowanus Road, American Right Flank

4:30 AM August 27, 1776

The Pennsylvania troops were marching at a blistering pace in the dim moonlight with orders to move with all possible speed to the Gowanus Road. Just a short time ago, word had arrived at the fortifications on Brooklyn Heights that the British had launched a sizable attack against the American right flank, and the small detachment of militia posted there had wisely turned and fled almost immediately in the face of overwhelming odds.

***

Thirty minutes earlier, Captain Nathaniel Horne had quickly organized his company into their three platoons, holding a brief meeting with the three young lieutenants in charge of these units.

"Gentlemen," he had stated at the conclusion of this meeting, "I have been told by our commander, Lord Stirling, that reports from the patrols to our front indicate that we are marching to face General Grant of the British army. I need not remind you of the comments made in the past by this scoundrel of a man."

"No Captain, his remarks were most unappreciated by the men, as I recall. Stating that he could defeat the entire Continental Army with but five thousand troops was an insult to this army — and to this country, as well."

Horne was struck by the man's reference to "this country", a concept that was still forming in the minds of many. For some reason, it caused him to experience a brief tingling down his spine, perhaps in the realization that he was part of something much larger than he had ever anticipated.

"Indeed, Lieutenant Springs," replied Horne. "Perhaps tonight we shall see if the good General Grant is up to the task of making good on his boasts. Personally, if I were in his position, I would be soiling my trousers at the thought of this many men from Pennsylvania coming to greet him."

The men chuckled in appreciation at their commander's comment, taking a much needed measure of comfort from his obvious confidence.

"What other units are going with us, Captain?" one of the other lieutenants asked hopefully.

"I've been told that Colonel Smallwood's Marylanders will be with us, as well as Colonel Huntington and his Connecticut regiment. All told, we should have over fifteen hundred men."

"And the British, sir — how many men do they have?" asked the same lieutenant.

Nathaniel paused before he answered. He firmly believed that his men deserved to know what they were about to face, but he also knew that too much information could cripple a man with fear.

"I would guess that we shall be outnumbered to some degree," replied Horne carefully, "however, to what degree I am unaware. But this I know — it has been said that a man defending his home is worth ten men attacking it. If that is truly the case, we outnumber our enemy to a greater degree than they could ever imagine."

Despite the darkness of the night, the eyes of each of the three lieutenants suddenly lit up with a brightness borne only of a deep sense of pride.

"Now," Captain Horne ordered, "return to your men and prepare to march. We must make great haste if we are to prevent the British from making too much headway."

***

That conversation seemed to have taken place days ago in the mind of Nathaniel Horne as he marched at the head of the column of men under his command. Nathaniel could sense, rather than actually see or hear, the other Pennsylvania troops directly to his front, which were being led by their commanding officer, Colonel Samuel Atlee.

A figure appeared out of the darkness, and Horne was momentarily startled by its sudden arrival. It was a corporal from one of the other Pennsylvania companies, a man that Nathaniel recognized but whose name he couldn't recall. The man quickly recognized Horne, and presented himself to the young officer.

"Captain Horne," the corporal hissed, careful to keep his voice barely above a whisper, "I have instructions from Colonel Atlee that your men are to form up in a line of battle on the edge of the tree line just ahead," he stated. "We have reports from our forward patrols that the British are no more than a few hundred yards beyond that, and appear to be moving in this direction."

"Corporal, with all due respect to the Colonel, if the British are only a short distance away and moving towards us, I am at risk of not reaching my assigned position before they do," Horne replied insistently.

"Yes, sir, the Colonel anticipated that concern," replied the corporal quietly, "and he asked me to inform you that the British are moving at 'a most leisurely pace' in his words. He instructed me to tell you that if you were to make all possible speed, keeping the need for silence in mind, that your men would have enough time to safely position themselves as ordered."

Nathaniel wasn't completely convinced of the safety of what he was being ordered to do, but they were orders nonetheless.

"Corporal, please inform Colonel Atlee that my men and I will be in position within five minutes."

"Very good, sir. The Colonel also asked that I tell you that Colonel Haslett's Delaware men will be on your left, and the remainder of Colonel Atlee's regiment will be on your right. You are to insure that you have linked up with each of those units upon posting your men. Good luck, Captain Horne," the corporal stated, having already turned and started moving back to his forward position with his unit just ahead.

***

True to his word, Horne and his Pennsylvanians had found their way to a small wood which ended at the edge of an open field as predicted. Nathaniel had spread his men out into a thin battle line, insuring that his left flank was connected to the Delaware troops and his right to the other Pennsylvanians under Atlee. Having personally checked that his company was situated in the best possible position, he returned to the center of the line where he would have the best ability to direct their actions once the shooting began.

The saying goes that the waiting is the most difficult part of any stressful situation. By that definition, it was a mercifully short period of time before Nathaniel could hear an obvious movement of a large number of troops immediately to his front.

"Pass the word along the line," Horne ordered in steady voice, "prepare to fire only on my command."

Horne could hear his orders being passed down the line on either side of him, and he marveled for the hundredth time that these men were so capable of conducting themselves in a military manner. They had, for the most part, no experience as soldiers, and little training to speak of. Yet, here they were, in the middle of the night, about to engage an enemy force that was superior in numbers, experience, and training. What drove a man to do such a thing? What drove Nathaniel Horne to do such a thing? Perhaps at some later time he would contemplate these philosophical questions more deeply. For now, he needed to focus on keeping himself and his men alive.

Out of the darkness directly ahead, a blast of cannon and musket fire erupted. The air was suddenly filled with whistling projectiles, most flying harmlessly overhead, but some making a whacking sound as they struck the trees all around Nathaniel's men. At least two men cried out in pain as the enemy fire hit its intended targets, but the darkness prevented Nathaniel from seeing who was hit, or to what degree of severity.

The need for silence clearly a thing of the past, Nathaniel shouted out to his men.

"Stay low, men, find cover behind trees or rocks if you can! Another volley is on its way!"

Captain Horne was quickly proven correct, as the crash of a second round of cannon and musket fire erupted out of the night. This time the projectiles were lower and slightly better aimed, but the men had heeded their Captain's advice and found cover. The result was no less terrifying psychologically to the Pennsylvanians, but thankfully, no one was hit.

"Remember men, no one fires until I give the order!" Horne shouted into the darkness. "We will wait until they have closed upon us and are in the open field!"

The faintest streaks of dawn were beginning to spread themselves over the landscape, as the blackness of the night gradually gave way to the gray tones of the approaching day. Just barely, Nathaniel could begin to see the outlines of the enemy formation to his front, but the individual figures of the soldiers still escaped him. No matter; the compact nature of the European style of fighting practiced by the British required that the Americans merely fire at the mass now approaching them.

In Horne's judgment, the enemy was probably one hundred and fifty yards or so away from his men. Colonel Atlee had given specific orders to wait until the enemy had closed to within seventy-five yards before any firing occurred. Assuming the British were advancing at a standard pace, that meant that it would be less than a minute before they would be in the prescribed range.

Douglas J. Shupinski

Silently counting down, Nathaniel waited impatiently for that time to pass. He knew that there would be no more volleys from the British, as their artillery would be afraid of hitting their own men, and the infantry wouldn't stop and take the time to reload after their second volley. The tactics of the enemy dictated that this engagement would be carried by the bayonet, as the British closed in on the Americans and employed their superior military discipline in a bloody, brutal display of hand-to-hand fighting. Horne understood, as did every American crouching resolutely in the gathering dawn, that the only chance of victory lay in their ability to keep the enemy at a distance through massed, accurate fire that would stop the enemy advance in its tracks.

"Company!" Horne shouted at the top of his lungs, "prepare to fire!"

The sound of dozens of muskets being leveled bristled through the air, as men stood up off of the ground or moved from behind the cover of the trees in order to give themselves the best firing position.

"Fire!" Nathaniel shouted, as a similar command was echoed down the line from other company commanders. The startling blast of hundreds of muskets being discharged almost simultaneously crashed throughout the dawn. The increasing light allowed Horne to clearly see the bodies of dozens of British soldiers crumple to the ground, an audible groan of pain and anguish emanating from the British lines as men died.

"Re-load, men, quickly!" Nathaniel shouted, urging his men to prepare for the next volley. "Prepare to fire on my command!"

Nathaniel paused just a few more seconds to insure as many men as possible would be prepared to add their bullets to the sheet of death they were about to send across the field. Satisfied that he had waited as long as he dared, he bellowed the order to fire.

Again, the result was similar, as more British soldiers fell to the ground, some in pain, some dead. The remainder of the enemy soldiers stopped in their tracks, then began an orderly retreat back in the direction from which they had come. This resulted in a ragged cheer being let out by the Americans.

"Don't celebrate too much," Horne warned his men. "They'll be back, and this time they know what to expect."

***

The British did come back, several times over the next few hours; but it was not with the vengeance that Captain Horne would have guessed. Their ensuing attacks seemed almost tentative, with a limited number of soldiers advancing partway across the field, firing their weapons, and then returning to their original location.

"Look at those rotten Lobsterbacks!" one of the Pennsylvanians shouted after a most recent advance by the enemy. "They're afraid to come any closer, knowing what's waitin' for 'em!"

Many of the other men in Horne's company shouted and laughed in agreement. It was clearly a good time to be a member of the Continental Army.

However, something was nagging at Nathaniel. The enemy attacks were almost *too* structured and calculated. There was a consistency to them that made them appear to be part of a bigger plan.

Ah, what do I know, Nathaniel thought to himself. I should stop thinking so much and just fight the enemy.

William Glanville Evelyn had been born in Ireland in 1842, the son of an influential father who had both strong political connections as well as significant financial resources. When William had decided to make the military his calling, his father had been more than capable of securing him a commission in the British army. Since that time, William had proven to be a reliable, intelligent officer who had a knack for quickly gaining the trust of the men around him. But that trust had always been earned on the parade field or on the training ground. This mission had been the first time that this trust had been put to the true test of combat.

As the rest of the British army filed into their assigned positions in preparation for an attack on the unsuspecting Americans, it was with grim satisfaction that he knew the ensuing victory would be, to some degree, the result of his efforts. Captain Evelyn had been responsible for leading the column of British soldiers against the unguarded left flank of the American position. This was to be the proverbial hammer that General Howe planned to bring down on the rest of the Rebel army. Allowing himself just a moment of reflection, Evelyn reviewed in his mind the events he had been part of over the last few hours.

***

By 2:00 AM the British contingent on horseback had been moving quietly through the unfamiliar countryside for many hours. So far, things had gone exactly as planned. There had been no enemy patrols to deal with, and the few civilians that had been encountered had quickly been gathered up and sent to the rear of the column that stretched back nearly two miles.

For his part, Captain William Glanville Evelyn would have to admit that he felt that this situation was just a bit over his head. While he was confident of his abilities as an officer in the British army, he had virtually no combat experience. As a result, he was basically learning the ropes of this business as the seemingly endless night went along.

Captain Evelyn had been placed in charge of a small group of officers, charged with leading the way for the ten thousand or so British soldiers to their immediate rear. This small group in the lead had no way of knowing whether or not they would come in contact with any Rebels, despite the fact that they had been assured that the Jamaica Pass was completely unguarded. The backwoods farmers who had been the source of this information had an unfortunate way of seeing what they wanted to see, and conveying that which was most consistent with their political affiliations.

Captain Evelyn and his group, responsible for the safety of thousands of men behind them, could ill afford the luxury of such tenuous optimism.

Captain Evelyn's mounted group included another captain by the name of Oliver DeLancey, who had shown himself to be most valuable for the last several, stressful hours. DeLancey had agreed to serve as the messenger, so to speak, between the scouting party led by Captain Evelyn, and the rest of the column to their rear. DeLancey had already made two trips back to speak with General Clinton who had positioned himself at the front of the main column, providing Clinton with updates on the progress and circumstances being encountered out in

Douglas F. Shupinski

front of the army.

"Captain DeLancey," William whispered into the darkness, "if you please, sir."

Almost magically, DeLancey appeared out of the pitch blackness of the night, his horse sidling up next to Captain Evelyn's mount. "Yes, Captain," DeLancey responded, ready as always to perform his duty as perhaps the most important soldier in the British army on this night.

"Captain DeLancey, please inform General Clinton that we have arrived at a place known to the locals as Howard's Tavern. Our three guides tell me that we are but a few hundred yards away from the entrance to the Jamaica Pass."

The guides that Captain Evelyn was referring to were three local farmers who claimed allegiance to the Crown. While William was fairly certain of their reliability – a man would have to be crazy to ride alongside a group of men as he led them into an ambush – he still conducted himself with the utmost caution. After all, one didn't place his life into the hands of three complete strangers without some degree of hesitation, regardless of the circumstances.

This spot marked the final checkpoint before Captain Evelyn and his party would enter the Jamaica Pass, a virtual gateway to the rear of the American forces which had been deployed to the front of Brooklyn Heights. If the British force chomping at the bit behind William could safely and successfully navigate this final stretch of road, the Americans would find themselves trapped between the ten thousand men led by Generals Clinton, Howe, and Cornwallis behind them, and the two other groups of British soldiers led by Generals von Heister and Grant in front of them. The Americans would have no choice but to either surrender or be annihilated.

**

Captain DeLancey had quickly departed, and had just as quickly returned. That was good news, in and of itself. It meant that the rest of the army was immediately behind Evelyn and his party, and would be able to take immediate advantage of any opportunity that presented itself.

"Captain Evelyn," DeLancey whispered into the darkness, "General Clinton wishes to inform you that you are to proceed through the Jamaica Pass with all possible speed, however, keeping the safety of your party and those behind it as your highest priority."

William was glad that the darkness hid the expression on his face as he received the report from DeLancey. If ever a man had been the benefactor of an order that indicated the ultimate grasp of the obvious, this would have to be such a time. Evelyn may have been inexperienced in combat, but he wasn't an idiot.

"Very well, Captain DeLancey," William replied smoothly, "thank you for the guidance from the General."

William could almost sense the smirk on the face of DeLancey, indicating his fellow officer appreciated as well the obvious nature of the order he had just delivered. Nevertheless, it was always a good idea to be reminded of one's duty.

The small group of officers moved out quietly, fanning out in such a manner as to have the greatest coverage of what may lay in front of them. They had been traveling for only a few minutes when the silence of the evening was broken by the sudden sound of horses approaching from their direct front. The British officers immediately drew their weapons, mainly in the form of swords, to greet whatever was coming their way.

Out of the darkness, five figures appeared on horseback, but William was unable to definitively determine the identity of the men. In a quiet voice, assuming the most convincing American accent he could muster, he called out into the night.

"Who goes there?" he commanded.

"Easy, lads," a calm American voice responded. "We're the patrol responsible for watching this pass in case the British get any idea of heading this way."

This was almost too good to be true. Not only did the response of the American indicate that he thought he was addressing other members of his own army, but it also revealed that there was no significant force waiting to ambush the British. Never had so much information been provided in so few words.

The British officers, quick to appreciate the gravity of the situation, had quietly surrounded the group of enemy soldiers such that they now had no way of escaping without a fight. Captain Evelyn closed the distance between himself and the lead rider in the enemy party until their horses were almost touching one another. It wasn't until that point that the man who had spoken realized the folly of his actions.

"Very well, then," Captain Evelyn said quietly to the man, "you have fulfilled your duty of watching this pass. Unfortunately for you, by the time your General Washington is aware of what you know, it will be too late."

Immediately, the members of the American patrol reached for their weapons, the sound of steel being unsheathed clearly evident in the night. Captain Evelyn responded quickly to their actions.

"Don't be fools!" he hissed urgently. "Anything you do now will be worthless! Surrender yourselves, or you will all be butchered on the spot for no good reason!"

The frustration of the Americans was almost palpable, as they realized that this British officer was correct. There were no reinforcements anywhere nearby that would hear their struggles, thus providing a warning to the rest of their army. They would simply be killed in the middle of the night, sacrificial lambs to a poorly planned defense on the part of their leaders.

Slowly, the Americans returned their sabers to their scabbards, submitting themselves to their inevitable fate. Their bodies sagged in their saddles, disgusted at themselves for having failed to perform their appointed duty on this most critical night.

"Now," Captain Evelyn continued calmly, "if you would be so kind as to surrender your weapons and accompany my officers, there is someone who I believe would be most interested in making your acquaintance."

***

Bringing himself back to the present, William realized that he had a broad smile on his face. And why not? The resulting interrogation of the five Americans by General Clinton had confirmed that the Americans had neglected to guard the Jamaica Pass. They had mistakenly placed their confidence in the belief that the attack by the British would come either up the Gowanus Road, through the Flatbush Pass, or both. It never occurred to them that the enemy might break itself into three pieces, sending one of these pieces on such a looping trek through the Long Island countryside. Surely, no one was capable of pulling off that kind of maneuver.

However, thanks to the efforts of many individuals, not the least of which was Captain William Glanville Evelyn, that's exactly what the British had been able to accomplish. Now all that remained was for the order to be given to all three prongs of the plan to launch all out attacks on the unsuspecting enemy.

The ten thousand men under the command of General Howe had positioned themselves at Bedford. This location allowed them to move southwest against the rear of the American forces deployed in front of the Brooklyn Heights. At the same time, it allowed these same ten thousand British soldiers to move northwest directly against the American forces on Brooklyn Heights, if the opportunity presented itself.

For the time being, General Howe had determined that he would first focus on the enemy forces trapped to the southwest. After defeating these troops, he could then turn the full attention of the British army against the Brooklyn Heights. It was a logical, calculated plan – and it was poised to begin.

Captain Evelyn was mildly startled by the discharge of two cannon located just a short distance away. William knew that this was a signal to General von Heister and his Hessians at the center of the American lines, as well as General Grant located at the right of the American lines. Upon hearing the discharge of these cannon, von Heister and Grant would know two things: first, that Howe and his ten thousand men had successfully reached their designated location at Bedford; and second that the demonstrations that these two generals had been conducting over the last six hours were to be turned into full-blown attacks.

At the same time these demonstrations would become full attacks, General Howe and his force of ten thousand would come sweeping down from the north

As far as Captain William Glanville Evelyn could see, it was the beginning of the end for the Americans on Long Island.

Major General John Sullivan

Division Commander, Continental Army

Flatbush Pass, American Center

9:15 A.M. August 27, 1776

John Sullivan was acutely aware of the fact that he was the second choice with respect to his current position.

General Washington had selected Major General Nathaniel Greene to be the Commanding General of the forces on Long Island, at least during those times when Washington himself wasn't present. However, General Greene had taken ill several days earlier, and had been forced to remove himself to the relative safety and available medical care located in New York City.

That meant that someone would have to replace the extremely capable and well respected General Greene. And that replacement had been Major General John Sullivan.

John Sullivan was somewhat unique as a general in the Continental Army. Generally speaking, when a man of affluence had chosen to support the cause of independence, he had done so in one of two ways. Either he served in the fledgling military of the Colonies, or he entered into the political arena. John Sullivan had seen fit to do both.

As a politician, Sullivan had participated in many of the earliest debates regarding the most plausible courses of action for the Colonies.

Douglas F. Shupinski

He had been well known and well respected in this role and, as a result, many of his colleagues were shocked when he made the rather fateful decision to leave politics and enter the military.

Sullivan had subsequently participated in the action around Boston at the very start of the conflict, and had eventually been sent north to fight the British in Canada. While this didn't necessarily constitute a significant amount of combat experience, it was more than many of the other generals, and quite a bit more than most of the troops.

***

While John Sullivan may have had a limited amount of combat experience, his enthusiasm and bravery were virtually limitless. He had a genuine desire – for better or for worse, depending on how one viewed such things – to lead men to victory in battle. And he believed that the way such things were accomplished was to lead by example.

To that end, when Sullivan had been informed that the British were attacking at a number of locations throughout Long Island, he determined that the best place for him to be was at the center of the American lines. His reasoning, sound as it was, was that the center of one's army generally held the key to victory. Little did he know that the key to victory on this day was not only on his left, but it had already been irreversibly exploited by the enemy.

Regardless, Sullivan arrived at the Flatbush Pass in a flurry of activity and a cloud of dust, accompanied by his small group of staff officers. The morning was already alive with the sounds of cannon and musket fire, and lines of opposing American and British soldiers were clearly visible a short distance away.

"Who is in charge here?" Sullivan demanded, as he approached a group of men conferring just behind the closest American lines.

"I am, sir," replied a tall officer sitting astride a horse. "Brigadier General Malcolm Tidings, 4th Maryland Brigade."

"General Tidings, what is your situation?" Sullivan inquired.

"As you can see, sir, we are being opposed by several brigades of what I believe to be Hessians, based on their uniforms," replied Tidings. "They have not yet launched a full attack, but rather seem to be sending small units to probe our positions for weaknesses."

"Very well," acknowledged Sullivan. "What of the American units off to your right? It appears that there is activity on that front as well."

"Indeed, sir. We have received several requests for reinforcements from General Stirling and the Delaware and Maryland boys over there who seem to believe they are the focus of the main enemy attack."

Sullivan thought through the information he was receiving, and decided that General Stirling was correct.

"Major Grimes," Sullivan said, turning to one of the members of his staff. "Take Colonel Stanley's regiment as well as Colonel Marcum's regiment, and lead them off to the right toward the sound of the guns. If we are going to hold the center here, we must insure that our flank does not give way. Is that clear?"

"Completely, sir!" Major Grimes replied, and immediately galloped off to carry out his orders.

"Now, General Tidings, I should like to ride forward and get a closer look at what we are facing today," Sullivan stated firmly.

General Tidings looked about quickly at their current position, which was no more than a hundred and fifty yards from the front line. Exactly how close, Tidings thought to himself, does this madman want to get?

"Of course, sir," Tidings replied tightly. "If you will follow me, it shouldn't take more than a few seconds to get as close as you like."

***

Generals Sullivan and Tidings, along with their respective staffs, gazed out across an open field that stretched out approximately a hundred or so yards, ending at a wood line. Clearly visible, despite their green uniforms, were hundreds of Hessian troops who seemed to be waiting patiently in their positions.

"They've been in those positions for the better part of an hour now, sir," Tidings explained. "They have taken the opportunity to fire a number of volleys at our lines, but the damage inflicted has been minor. Likewise, we've sent several volleys in their direction, but I suspect the effect has been the same."

"They're either waiting for the order to coordinate their attack with the enemy troops to our right," reasoned Sullivan, "or else they're simply serving as a diversion to keep us in place. Either way, I suspect the last thing they would expect would be for us to attack."

General Tidings looked at Sullivan in alarm.

"Attack? General Sullivan, with all due respect, most of these men have never seen a shot fired in anger in their lives! It's one thing to ask them to assume a defensive position and wait for the enemy to cross that open field. It's something quite different to expect them to cross that field into the teeth of veteran Hessian regiments!"

Sullivan turned and looked coldly at Tidings, his contempt clearly apparent.

"General Tidings, these men are soldiers. They will do what they are ordered to do and I, for one, have every confidence that they are capable of making such an attack."

At that moment, two cannon shots sounded clearly off to the left and slightly behind where the two men were talking. So fixed had their attention been to their front and right that neither man had taken the time to look in the direction of this new threat. Now, however, every man in the American lines turned reflexively and looked to their left rear. What they saw made them shudder in fear.

The morning sun reflected brightly off of thousands of British bayonets, and Sullivan realized immediately that he was faced with an enemy force to his front as well as an enemy of unknown size coming down on him almost directly from the rear. At almost the exact same time, drums could be heard across the field to their front, and the Hessian units began moving slowly towards them.

"General Tidings, we must move quickly!" shouted Sullivan. "Leave a covering force to the front to stall the Hessians, and turn the bulk of your men to face the enemy coming at us from the left rear!"

"Yes, sir, I'll see to it immediately," Tidings responded, and galloped off quickly to carry out his orders.

But both men knew in their hearts that there was little chance of successfully defending against both threats. Not only were they hopelessly outnumbered, but to ask grossly inexperienced troops to execute this type of command quickly with any degree of discipline was almost impossible.

For Major General John Sullivan and the men that he commanded, this was not going to be a matter of victory or defeat – this was going to be a matter of survival.

Douglas J. Shupinski

Sergeant Alexander Bickell

Hesse-Cassell Division, British Army

Flatbush Pass, American Center

9:45 AM August 27, 1776

The moment of truth had finally arrived for the Hessian soldiers, and Sergeant Alexander Bickell felt the familiar surge of adrenaline running through his body. The smell of the gunpowder, the sounds of weapons firing and men shouting, the sight of the enemy poised to receive the assault; all of these things flooded Bickell's senses, and he became focused in a way that could only be achieved through the anticipation of impending battle.

Bickell assumed his position immediately behind the advancing lines of Hessian infantry. His responsibilities there were two-fold: first, to echo the orders of the officers directing the battle so that his men would clearly understand what they were supposed to do; and second, to run through with his bayonet any Hessian that attempted to turn and run for the rear. While Bickell wasn't thrilled with this second responsibility, it was one that he had carried out in the past, and would have no hesitation in repeating on this day.

Bickell noted with grim satisfaction that his men were maintaining their lines with proper military discipline, despite the fact that the

Americans in the tree line to their front had begun a rather sporadic fire. Excellent, Bickell thought to himself. Uncoordinated firing would never stop an attack by these men. Only massed, well-aimed volleys had any chance of inflicting the kind of casualties that would cause this attack to grind to a halt, and surely these inexperienced Americans weren't capable of effectively executing such tactics.

Even as that thought was passing through his mind, the unmistakable crash of a coordinated volley shattered the morning air. Much to his dismay, Bickell watched in surprise as a number of his men tumbled to the ground clutching various parts of their body in pain and anger.

Some of the Hessians hesitated, and began preparing to fire their own weapons in return. It was a common response in battle, the instinct to lash back immediately at one's attacker with the only thing that was available. But the weapon that was most important right now was the bayonet, and that weapon could not be brought to bear unless the distance between the Hessians and the Americans could be closed with the greatest possible speed.

"Keep moving, you bastards!" Bickell shouted at his men. "No stopping to fire your musket. Keep moving at the double time and close with the enemy! Come on, boys, you are Hessians – show your mettle!"

Bickell's exhortations galvanized the men, and they continued to move forward with a new purpose. However, within just a few seconds, a second volley was let loose by the enemy, and more men collapsed to the ground, dead or dying.

This time, even the fear of their own Sergeant Bickell wasn't enough to prevent the Hessian lines from coming to a halt, and a few men even turned and began running back to their departure point. Bickell focused his attention on one man in particular who was shouting incoherently and running to the rear with a look of madness in his eyes.

"Soldier, stop right there and return to your position!" Bickell shouted, as the man got closer and closer to where Bickell was standing. But there was no way to reason with the man, who had clearly become

Douglas J. Shupinski

overcome with panic. The Hessian continued on his headlong flight to what he believed to be safety, and Bickell shouted his order to halt yet again, but it was to no avail.

Coldly, Bickell stepped into the path of the panicked soldier, leveled his bayonet, and drove it cleanly through the man's abdomen. The soldier came to an abrupt halt at the end of Bickell's musket, his panic suddenly gone and replaced with a look of pain and confusion.

As blood began to pour out of the dying man's gaping mouth, Bickell was briefly overcome with self-disgust at his barbaric act. But he quickly recovered his composure, knowing from hard experience that the death of this one man might very well save the lives of countless others.

Bickell withdrew his bayonet from the man's body, and he toppled to the ground, now only several painful minutes away from death. Looking up, Bickell could see the fear in the eyes of the others coming towards him that had chosen a similar course of action. These men came to an immediate halt, executed an about face, and returned to their positions in the battle line.

Satisfied that he had stemmed the tide of retreat at least for the moment, Sergeant Bickell now concentrated on renewing the attack.

"All right now, you Hessian scoundrels, it's either my bayonet in you, or your bayonet in them!" he shouted, gesturing toward the line of Americans no more than fifty yards away. Despite the fact that another volley from the enemy had inflicted additional casualties on the Hessians, they now turned their full rage on the Americans to their front.

With a deep-throated roar, the Hessians picked up their pace, quickly closing on the enemy lines before they were able to get off another stinging volley. While some of the Americans had predictably chosen to retreat in the face of the violent onslaught, Bickell was more than a bit surprised to see that most of the enemy troops were resolutely holding their positions. Just as well, he thought; we'll make these Rebels pay for their foolhardy bravery. Even so, Bickell couldn't help but feel just a twinge of respect for these inexperienced men in his vengeful path.

***

Inexplicably to many of the Hessians, the firing from the enemy lines had slackened considerably in just the last few minutes. Whereas they had previously been on the receiving end of numerous concentrated, well-aimed volleys, they were now experiencing only sporadic musket fire from the rapidly approaching tree line. The effect on the morale of the Hessians was immediate, as their advance became more rapid and purposeful. Their confidence soared, as they believed that they had rattled the Americans into retreating in the face of their vicious assault.

For his part, Sergeant Bickell quickly realized that this was only a small part of the real story. Soon after the sounding of the two cannon shots, Bickell had taken notice of the clear signs of another force of British soldiers advancing to the left and rear of the American lines. It didn't take a genius to realize that the enemy had suddenly found themselves in the unenviable position of being caught between two attacks from both in front and behind. Bickell experienced an involuntary shudder at what that must feel like to find oneself in such a position.

Shaking himself away from such destructive thoughts, he focused on the task at hand. There was still much work to be done, as the opportunity to literally annihilate the enemy had presented itself. Urging his men forward with threats and curses consistent with the finest traditions of the Hessian philosophy, Bickell quickly passed through the front line of his men and assumed his favorite position – at the very point of the attack.

"Come on men!" Bickell shouted into the muggy, morning air, "Follow me to victory!"

His men, with yet another shout of pure brutality, did exactly as they were ordered, and the Hessian line was suddenly into the tree line and face to face with dozens of American soldiers who had foolishly chosen to remain in their positions.

Overwhelmed and outnumbered, most of the Americans

immediately assumed a position of surrender, either placing their weapons on the ground, or raising them above their heads. Some of these men were quickly surrounded by the advancing Hessians, their weapons snatched away and corralled into small, defenseless groups for eventual removal to the rear of the British lines.

However, many other Americans were not nearly so fortunate. In the heat of battle, self-control was simply beyond the capacity of many of the Hessians and they continued to engage their enemy with ruthless efficiency.

One group of seven or eight Americans had huddled into a small group, weapons discarded and arms reaching for the sky. Such a defenseless posture was meaningless to a group of advancing Hessian soldiers, as they encircled their enemy and began to slaughter them with repeated thrusts of their bayonets. The Americans begged pitifully for mercy, but none was shown, as one by one the high-pitched screams turned into sickly gurglings of death followed by eventual silence.

Stepping back, covered in the blood of their helpless prey, the Hessians nodded grimly in satisfaction at one another and proceeded to move on to their next victims. Such were the misfortunes, they reasoned, of being stupid enough to wage war against Hessians.

To the far right of the advancing Hessian lines, yet another atrocity was playing itself out. Three Americans were lying helplessly on the ground, having been wounded earlier in the exchange of fire that had preceded this final assault. One had been shot in the stomach, and the chalky-white pall of death had already begun to form on the unlucky man's face. The other two had been wounded less severely, but in such a way as they were unable to retreat from their position.

A squad of Hessian soldiers approached these men, and began laughing at the obvious helpless nature of their situation.

"Look at these useless bastards!" one of the Hessians remarked. "So much for standing up to the finest fighting unit in the world! Maybe a bullet in the ass would get them off their feet and moving."

The other Hessians standing around erupted in laughter at the comments of their colleague.

"Don't waste a bullet on them," stated another. "The weight of the lead would only serve to make them even slower!"

Still more laughter burst out, as the pitiful wounded men looked up in terror at their captors. The Americans were unable to understand a single word being directed at them, as the conversation was being conducted in German.

A small, wiry corporal with mean eyes ceased his laughter, but a cruel smile remained on his lips.

"If we take these worthless rats as prisoners, they'll probably die anyway," the corporal rationalized. "Either that or they'll get paroled in a few weeks and probably be taking shots at us from some other spot in this God forsaken land. Best to end it now, and be done with it."

Several of the Hessians looked uncomfortably at the corporal as they realized what he was suggesting, but no one said a word in protest. To do so would appear weak in the face of one's fellow soldiers, and such weakness was not to be tolerated. Not with Hessians.

With a sudden viciousness, the corporal stepped forward and drove his bayonet into the midsection of the most grievously wounded American. The man's eyes briefly went wide in astonishment, but soon became pale and lifeless in death.

The two other wounded men stared at their now dead comrade in disbelief, their eyes quickly turning toward their captors.

"You two," the corporal ordered in a flat, emotionless voice to a pair of privates standing next to him, "finish this business."

The two privates hesitated, looking first at the corporal and then at their comrades standing nearby for some indication of support against the barbaric order they had just been given.

"Now, Privates!" the corporal nearly shouted, "or you'll both be lying next to that worthless lump I just took care of!"

The two privates moved in on the remaining wounded Americans, who immediately clawed frantically at the ground in an attempt to move backward in escape. They shouted out for their lives to be spared, but the die had been cast. With much less enthusiasm than had been displayed by the corporal, the privates drove their bayonets into the helpless men, their screams echoing throughout the suddenly quiet field that had ceased to be a scene of battle. It was now a field of murder.

***

Sergeant Bickell could see that the situation was quickly getting out of control. While he had every desire to crush the enemy at least as much as anyone else, he also understood the need to maintain proper military discipline at all times – especially now. To allow these men to commit such acts of cold violence that he was witnessing meant a breakdown in the system of checks and balances that defined a professional army.

Off to Bickell's left he watched as several Hessians surrounded yet another group of Americans attempting to surrender themselves. Moving quickly in their direction, he shouted out to the group.

"You men, there! Remove the weapons of the enemy, and prepare to move them to the rear!"

Several of the Hessians, suddenly aware of the appearance of a senior enlisted man, lowered their raised muskets and backed away from their quarry. However, three of the soldiers remained focused on their prisoners, their bayonets aimed ominously at the Americans.

Bickell, now just a few feet away, stopped and stared at these men.

"I said, remove their weapons and move them to the rear," Bickell repeated, a cold sternness creeping into his voice.

One of the threatening Hessians, a private, looked up at Bickell, a look of disgust clearly visible on his face.

"Move them to the rear, Sergeant? These bastards are no better than sniveling dogs, and deserve to die where they stand," said the sneering Hessian soldier. Looking back at the Americans, he moved towards them, his intent clear to all.

Bickell felt his face flush red, incensed at the fact that a mere private was daring to question his commands. He briefly considered shooting the man on the spot, but the memory of having already killed one of his own on this day caused him to hesitate.

Bickell took several quick strides in the direction of the Hessian, closing the distance until he was no more than three feet away from the man. Raising his own musket, Bickell placed the tip of his bayonet in the small of the man's back.

"Stand down, soldier," Bickell said, his voice a low, menacing growl. "If you do not, the last man to die on this field will be you."

At this point, all of the other Hessians had moved back from their original positions, leaving Bickell and the private at center stage. All eyes were on the two men, as the drama played out in front of them.

The American prisoners, despite the fact that they were unable to understand a single word being spoken, nevertheless understood what was at stake here. They looked quickly back and forth between their executioner and their savior, at least as far as it seemed to them.

The private was clearly flustered, unwilling to back down and lose face in front of his comrades, but also unsure as to what this sergeant was capable of doing. Bickell took the opportunity to push his bayonet ever more insistently into the man's back.

"Stand down, Private," Bickell repeated, this time with just a hint of calmness and finality in his tone. "There will be many other chances to take your revenge on these Americans – of that you can be sure."

The man took the opportunity afforded by Bickell to walk away from the situation with his dignity intact.

"Of course, Sergeant. Why kill just these few today, when tomorrow will give us the chance to kill a thousand others," he said, lowering his weapon, and stepping back away from the Americans.

With a brutal slash, Bickell sent the butt of his musket whistling through the air, impacting the private's jaw with a sickening crack. The man collapsed to the ground, blood pouring from a huge gash that had been opened along the side of his face. He gazed up at Bickell, his eyes wide in fear of this man who seemed to be completely incapable of mercy.

"Let that be a lesson to you all," Bickell stated firmly, his eyes sweeping along the group of Hessians. "When a sergeant gives you an order – when *I* give you an order – you will obey it immediately. Without question. Without hesitation."

The Hessians looked at Bickell with wide eyes, then down at the injured private, then back again at Bickell.

"Now," Bickell ordered, "remove these prisoners to the rear. And remove that Hessian piece of filth off of the ground," he said, nodding toward the private on the ground, "before I change my mind and slit his throat where he lay."

This time, there was no hesitation on the part of the Hessian soldiers, as they quickly complied with the orders of their Sergeant.

Major General John Sullivan

Division Commander, Continental Army

Flatbush Pass, American Center

10:15 AM August 27, 1776

The previously promising situation had gone to hell in a hand basket in a matter of ten minutes, as General Sullivan and his few remaining troops suddenly found themselves in the middle of a hailstorm of flying lead and enemy bayonets. Americans, attempting to surrender, were being murdered by the advancing Hessians, who had become nothing more than a band of marauding killers with no semblance of dignity or discipline.

The remnants of the Continental Army here at the Flatbush Pass had retreated several hundred yards such that they were just beyond the advancing enemy and out of immediate danger. But the sounds of approaching troops made it clear to everyone that this moment of reprieve was fleeting, to say the least.

Sullivan knew that the only chance of saving even a portion of his command was to use a portion of his men to establish a stable line of defense that would allow the other American soldiers to scamper back to Brooklyn Heights and the relative safety of that position. Calling out to several of his junior officers, he ordered them to come to his side.

"Gentlemen!" Sullivan shouted above the confusion of the

battlefield, "Assemble on me!"

With surprising composure, a half dozen or so captains and majors made their way toward Sullivan, forming a small circle around their commander. Their sweat-streaked faces, some of which were also covered with the blood of their soldiers, looked hopefully on, imploring this man to give them the orders that would allow them to retreat and perhaps live to fight another day. But no such orders were forthcoming.

"Men, we have a responsibility to save whatever portion of this army that is capable of making its way back to Brooklyn Heights," Sullivan began. "But in order to do that, we must form a line and stop the enemy advance, at least for a few minutes."

"Stop the enemy advance?" a major asked, his disbelief blatantly apparent. "Sir, with all due respect, the enemy outnumbers us by at least four to one, and our men have been routed from their positions! If any of us are to survive, we must retreat now!"

Sullivan eyed the man coldly, feeling his anger rising up within him at the cowardice being displayed. But he quickly remembered that these were novice soldiers, many of whom had never before experienced such a violent and confusing situation. To expect them to conduct themselves with perfect military decorum was, he realized, simply beyond the bounds of reality.

"It is no longer a matter of *any* of us surviving today, Major," Sullivan replied calmly. "It has now become a matter of *some* of us surviving. The orders I am giving you mean that perhaps today – "

At this point Sullivan paused, the emotion suddenly caught in his throat preventing him from completing his statement. Regaining his composure, he finished his statement.

"The orders I am giving you means that today, perhaps we shall not be the ones to survive. But our actions may save not only the lives of the men around us, but may save the very existence of this army."

Almost as if the hand of God had passed over them, a calm resolve settled among the small group of officers standing in the circle. They knew what their commander was saying was true, and in that moment, they committed themselves to their assigned duty.

"What are your orders, General?" a young captain no more than twenty-five years old asked. His expression was one of a man resigned to the likelihood that he would never see the sun rise on another day.

"All right, then," Sullivan stated firmly. "Each of you are to gather as many men as you can in the next two minutes. Encourage them, threaten them, do whatever you must do to get them back here. We will be forming a line along this small rise directly behind us," he said, looking back at the area immediately to their rear that rose up perhaps no more than a few feet. "Our position may not look like much, but it will provide us a position from which to repel the enemy."

A look of disbelief briefly crossed the faces now looking at him, but Sullivan had no doubts that his orders would be carried out.

"Now, move! Sullivan commanded, putting as much confidence behind his words that he could muster.

***

Within a matter of minutes, the officers had returned, some bringing several dozen soldiers, others followed by no more than a handful of frightened, confused men. As each officer arrived with his offering, Sullivan placed them into positions that provided the greatest protection for the moment, but also allowed them to move quickly with a semblance of coordination.

The sounds of the approaching enemy were getting closer by the second, and Sullivan knew that there was precious little time to prepare for the attack they all knew to be imminent. Sullivan was pleased, at some level, to see that many other soldiers had continued to move to the rear, and knew that his ability to delay the pursuit of these men would result in their successful retreat.

Just as the last of the Americans had formed themselves into a ragged line, a solid line of green-coated Hessians appeared to their direct front. A collective shiver of fear ran through this small group of men who were brave enough – or foolish enough – to stand in their path, and Sullivan was not exempt from this same reaction.

"All right, men, here they come!" Sullivan shouted, as the Hessians continued to advance on their position. "Prepare for volley fire. On my command, ready – fire!"

A rather weak volley of musket fire rang out, but it nevertheless stung the enemy, and there was a brief halt to their lines. Quickly regrouping, the Hessians renewed their assault, and the distance between the two groups narrowed with dangerous speed. Sullivan ordered a second volley to be fired, and then a third, but the advancing enemy troops had gained critical momentum and never wavered for an instant.

Sullivan could see that the Hessians had no intention of making a straightforward frontal assault. With calm precision, two wings of enemy soldiers broke off from the main line, each making its way in a wide arc around both sides of the American position. Sullivan had suspected that the Hessians might make such a move, as he had absolutely no support on either of his flanks to protect against such a maneuver. Despite this knowledge, there was nothing that Sullivan could do in opposition, and he made a snap decision.

Looking to his rear, Sullivan could barely make out the shapes of the retreating American soldiers in the distance, indicating that they were well on their way to Brooklyn Heights and ultimate safety. The work of this small group of Americans was done, and it was time to see to their possible survival.

While any type of coordinated volley fire had ceased from the Americans, individual soldiers continued to fire. But the fear in these men was obvious, as they watched the two groups of Hessians continue to circle around them on both sides.

"Men, cease fire and retreat to Brooklyn Heights!" Sullivan shouted. "Now, men! Abandon your positions and retreat to the rear!"

Initially, one or two men began to move back, then small groups of three or four, and finally a general retreat occurred. To Sullivan's surprise, he observed that there was almost no panic, and many of them even continued to pause briefly to fire a final defiant shot at the pursuing enemy. The orderly fighting withdrawal of the Americans forced the Hessians to remain in a line of battle, which kept the speed of their advance to a relative crawl. Most of these men would make it, Sullivan realized. Despite the odds being drastically against them, they had allowed a good portion of the Continental Army to escape, and even now were making their own way to safety.

However, that was not to be the fate of Major General John

Sullivan. Having remained in position to insure that as many men as possible had moved to the rear, he suddenly found himself surrounded by at least a dozen Hessian soldiers, their bayonets leveled as they continued to close the noose around him.

"Come on, you filthy German bastards," Sullivan hissed, brandishing his sword. "Which one of you wants their head split open?"

The Hessian soldiers, while not able to understand what this madman was saying, could clearly see that he was not giving up without a fight. They continued to close in on Sullivan, and were now ready to end the matter with the finality of multiple bayonet thrusts.

Several yards away, Sullivan could hear a man shouting orders in German. Almost immediately, the Hessians lowered their muskets and opened the circle for a man to pass through.

Sullivan was presented with an enlisted man, but obviously one who commanded significant respect, almost fear, from these soldiers. With absolutely no hesitation, the man approached Sullivan until he was no more than three feet away. Sullivan raised his sword in anticipation of a fight, but the Hessian simply stopped and stared at him.

With complete calm, the Hessian turned and surveyed the numerous soldiers surrounding them, then slowly returned his gaze to Sullivan. The message was clear – there is no hope for you, American General. For today, at least – it is over.

Raising his right hand, the Hessian reached out to Sullivan, bidding the American to relinquish his sword and surrender. While surrender was against every inclination he had, Sullivan couldn't help but notice the look in the eyes of this Hessian standing in front of him. There was an odd balance of compassion and indifference which seemed to say, "Don't be foolish. Live another day. But should you choose otherwise, it would cause me no discomfort to kill you myself."

Bowing his head in resignation, John Sullivan handed his sword to the Hessian.

Captain Nathaniel Horne

Pennsylvania State Riflemen, Continental Army

Gowanus Road, American Right Flank

12:15 P.M. August 27, 1776

Nathaniel now understood why the British attacks had seemed tentative up to this point. Horne and his Pennsylvanians here on the right flank of the Continental Army had been facing nothing more than a demonstration of force, designed to hold their attention so that the British could focus on other areas of the battlefield. Those areas had turned out to be the left and center of the American lines, which had apparently been overwhelmed by the attacking enemy.

That meant that General Stirling here on the right was the last remaining part of the Continental Army still actively engaging the enemy. It also meant that the British were now able to concentrate their entire army on this small group of men along the Gowanus Road.

Nathaniel's men had begun to glance with greater and greater frequency to their rear, as the sounds of musket and artillery fire continued getting closer from that direction. Meanwhile, General Grant's British soldiers to their front had clearly changed from limited probing attacks to an all-out offensive. Thousands of enemy troops were now moving directly at the Pennsylvanians, their lines sharp and disciplined, their fearful bayonets brightly reflecting the noontime sun.

The sounds to the rear and the sights to the front indicated one thing: there was no way that the Americans would be able to hold their current position. The only way for Nathaniel to save his men was to stage an orderly retreat. But before he could do that, Nathaniel needed to be given those orders. And even if he received such orders, in which direction should he retreat? He and his men appeared to be surrounded.

Almost as if God Almighty had been reading his mind, a lieutenant suddenly appeared at his elbow, the sound of the man's approach covered by the din of battle in every direction.

"Captain Horne!" the lieutenant shouted above the noise, "Colonel Atlee wishes to inform you that you are to execute a retreat to the army's lines at Brooklyn Heights. The Colonel is issuing similar orders to the other units in his command, as General Stirling has given the order for retreat to this entire section of battlefield."

"That's all well and good, Lieutenant," Nathaniel replied with an edge to his voice, "but exactly how are we supposed to make our way to Brooklyn Heights? It appears to me that there are a rather large number of enemy soldiers in our path!"

The young lieutenant sheepishly acknowledged the reality of the situation by looking at the ground, unable to meet this captain's intense gaze. Nathaniel realized that the man was only carrying out his orders, and he regretted his hostile tone and demeanor toward the man.

"Lieutenant," Horne said calmly, "has either General Stirling or Colonel Atlee provided any orders regarding the suggested line of retreat?"

"Yes, sir," replied the lieutenant, happy to be spared from the searing gaze of just a moment ago. "General Stirling has indicated that his men are to navigate through the swamp to our left, then make your way to the Brooklyn Heights. In the meantime, he and a small group of Colonel Smallwood's Maryland battalion have formed a line to stop the British advance."

Well, I'll be damned, Nathaniel marveled. The man has guts, that's for sure.

"Very well, Lieutenant, consider the General's orders received and

Douglas F. Shupinski

obeyed. I'll begin moving my men through the swamp immediately."

The young lieutenant said something in reply, but it was lost in the sound of the battle which had suddenly become dramatically louder. Looking to his front, Nathaniel was shocked to see that the enemy had advanced to no more than forty or fifty yards from his lines, and some of his men had begun to prematurely execute the order to retreat.

Looking to his rear, the appearance of hundreds of enemy soldiers told Nathaniel that his situation was truly desperate. If he and his men had any chance at all to escape, it would have to happen in the next two minutes.

"Men, prepare to retreat through the swamp to our left," Horne shouted. "We must move as one, and we must move now!"

But even as his men rose to move out of their positions, the British were upon them. Several of Nathaniel's men had remained in their spots just long enough to deliver a final musket shot, in hopes that this might slow down the enemy advance. These few men were rewarded with an entire volley from the advancing British, and Nathaniel watched as several of his men were riddled with multiple musket balls, their bodies dropping silently to the ground without so much as a groan of agony. So grievous and overwhelming had been the sudden and violent damage to their bodies that they were killed instantly.

Still others were not so fortunate as to receive such a quick demise. Two of Nathaniel's men had been wounded by the enemy volley, one in the leg and one in the back. Both men were attempting to painfully make their way toward the swamp when the advancing British soldiers caught up with them. Never seeing their enemy, the Americans made no attempt to surrender, and the British made no attempt to convince them to do so. Instead, the two men were ruthlessly bayoneted by several men each, the ends of their lives not nearly as quick and silent as the others. Nathaniel could hear their high pitched screams above the sound of the battle, and he knew that if he lived, he would hear those screams for the rest of his life.

Somehow, almost all of the rest of Horne's men had made their way to the swamp, and they had begun to retreat deeper and deeper into the muck, placing valuable distance and safety between themselves and their tormentors. At least two men were the unlucky recipients of a group of scattered, unaimed shots from the British. One of the men stumbled for a few steps, desperately trying to maintain his balance, finally collapsing and disappearing below the surface of the quagmire.

The other man, Private Cronin, had been walking no more than a few feet away from Nathaniel when he pitched face forward into the swamp. Nathaniel quickly rushed over to the man, lifting him back to his feet. The man, clearly disoriented, began frantically clutching at the back of his head, pushing his long braided pony tail off to the side in order to conduct his panicked self-examination.

"I've been shot in the head, Cap'n!" he cried. "For God's sake, I've been shot in the head! Help me!"

Nathaniel pushed Cronin's hands away, and began feeling for a wound on the man's head, dreading what he might find. After several seconds of fruitless searching, Nathaniel suddenly looked at the center of the man's ponytail. Nestled comfortably amongst the tight braids was a British musket ball!

"Why, you lucky bastard!" Nathaniel almost laughed. "That bullet never made it to your head. It must've been fired from too far away and didn't have enough power to make it through that thick skull of yours!"

Nathaniel popped the musket ball out of the Private's ponytail and handed it to him as he walked away, the private almost fainting with relief. Calling over his shoulder, Nathaniel gave the man a final word of encouragement.

"I wouldn't worry too much about the British, Private Cronin. Why, they obviously wouldn't harm a hair on your head!"

***

Against all odds, most of Captain Nathaniel Horne's company made it back to the safety of the fortifications along Brooklyn Heights, as did most of the other men that had faced the British that day. Despite the fact that the enemy had completed a perfectly executed flanking movement to the American left, coming down almost behind the Continental Army, the Americans had escaped the potentially devastating trap that had been sprung by General Howe.

That being said, everyone knew that their current position at Brooklyn Heights was a tenuous one at best. Behind the Continental Army lay the East river, with any number of British warships patrolling there with complete impunity. Any attempt at crossing the river to New York City in the available long boats was nothing short of suicide. To their front was a consolidated, rapidly advancing British army, consisting of no less than 20,000 men as compared to their own force of perhaps 6,000.

In the minds of many, the easiest part of this battle had already occurred. The real trick would be in surviving the impending onslaught of a well-trained, well supplied, and numerically superior enemy.

General George Washington

Commanding General, Continental Army

Brooklyn Heights, American Headquarters

9:00 P.M. August 29, 1776

General George Washington had arrived at Brooklyn Heights two days earlier, just as the British army had launched its coordinated assault on the hapless Continental Army. Washington had been frustrated at the superior strategy being employed by his enemy, realizing that he had been out-generaled by his counterpart, William Howe. However, at the same time, he couldn't help but marvel at the discipline and bravery that he had witnessed first-hand by these amateur soldiers that had been placed under his command. Time and again, Washington had watched from Brooklyn Heights as the Americans had stood their ground in the face of overwhelming odds, grudgingly holding their positions until their situation had become completely hopeless. The fact that so many had successfully made their way back to the fortifications where he now stood continued to astonish him.

So much for what had already occurred, thought Washington to himself. The real question was what would he do next? To answer that question, he had sought the counsel of his most trusted generals, virtually all of whom had urged the retreat of the Continental Army across the East River to New York City. That was all well and good, and certainly made the most sense. The real question was – how?

For some inexplicable reason, General William Howe had presented the Americans with the incredibly valuable gift of time. Rather than force the issue and attack the fortifications on Brooklyn Heights immediately on the heels of their victory two days earlier, the British had halted and consolidated their army. They had begun digging trenches that were inching their way toward the American positions, apparently intent on decreasing the distance of open ground they would have to cross in their eventual attack. While such a strategy wasn't completely foolhardy, it certainly demonstrated a lack of appreciation for the dismal condition of the Continental Army.

Specifically, the Americans had very little ammunition remaining for either their muskets or, even more importantly, for their artillery. A drenching rain had blanketed the island during much of the last two days, rendering what limited ammunition that had been available completely useless. Furthermore, the troops had little or no food to the point that a significant number of men had not eaten a substantial meal in over three days. Add to these facts the situation of little or no opportunity to sleep, and it resulted in an army that was close to being defenseless.

Washington had ordered all of his senior commanders to a meeting at his headquarters, the purpose of which was to make a final decision on the next steps for the Continental Army. While he himself could see little alternative to an attempt at escaping across the East River, Washington knew he needed the agreement and support of these generals who were so critical to the ultimate success or failure of the army.

***

The men fell silent as General Washington made his way to the front of the room. He turned and faced the assembled generals with a look on his face that he hoped conveyed both the seriousness of the situation, as well as his confidence in their ability to do the right thing.

"Gentlemen," he began, his voice echoing off the walls of the small room, "we are faced with a momentous decision. As you are all aware, we are facing an enemy that outnumbers us by a reported margin of better than three to one. However, we are well entrenched, and the British must cross an open area of some six or seven hundred yards before they reach our lines."

Major General Israel Putnam respectfully cleared his throat as an indication that he wished to speak.

"General Putnam, you have something to say?" Washington asked.

"I do, sir," Putnam responded with deference. "While I agree that the enemy would face quite a warm welcome from our men, I must tell you that it is my opinion that our lack of significant artillery − not to mention the limited ammunition we have at our disposal − will make any type of sustained defense almost impossible."

"Add to that, General," another commander chimed in, "the fact that it is most likely only a matter of time before the bulk of the British navy is able to navigate past our meager defenses on the East River. This would result in the enemy's ability to bombard us from the rear with a most impressive number of cannon."

Washington was forced to concede that both of these comments were accurate, and only reinforced what he believed to be the only plausible course of action. However, he needed these men to come to that conclusion on their own. Only such a realization would result in the full support of his subordinates and, ultimately, their men. After all, the Continental Army wasn't really a professional fighting force that would automatically follow the orders of their overall commander - at least not yet. Such were the challenges faced by Washington.

"Very well, then," responded Washington. "Assuming your comments to be accurate − and I personally believe that they are − what would be your recommended course of action."

A silence fell upon the room, no man being willing to state the obvious. The Continental Army needed to retreat in order to survive, but that very movement to safety might result in its destruction. It was a difficult choice.

Washington sensed a slight commotion near the back of the room,

Douglas J. Shupinski

as several of the officers moved aside to let a man step forward. It was Colonel John Glover, one of the more junior officers in the room.

"Sir, if it pleases the General, I have a suggestion that he might wish to consider," Glover stated firmly, but respectfully.

"By all means, Colonel," Washington invited. "We are assembled to find a solution to our dilemma. Any and all ideas are more than welcome."

John Glover was from Marblehead, Massachusetts, and had been an active member in the American forces opposing the British from the very beginning. He had spent most of his life as a fisherman in his home colony, but the lack of any significant navy had compelled him to offer his services to the army. The fact that he always spoke his mind with little filtering of his opinions meant that he was not the most popular officer in the Continental Army. But his professionalism and military abilities were well respected, and no one doubted his passion for the cause of independence.

"General Washington," Glover stated, "I believe my Marblehead men could successfully evacuate the army across the East River to New York City. We have quite a few boats at our disposal, the night ahead of us promises to be foggy, and my men are excellent seamen."

Colonel Glover was referring to his unit, the 14th Continental Regiment, which was almost entirely made up of fishermen from Marblehead, Massachusetts. However, while the nautical skills of these men were supposedly superb, they had never been put to a test quite like this. The East River had notoriously rapid and unexpected currents, the crossing would be occurring in the dead of night without any light whatsoever, and the nearby British warships might be alerted to the crossing at any moment.

A murmur of obvious concern swept through the room, as the officers considered the danger of such a strategy. General Washington, however, remained stone faced, staring openly at the man who had the courage to make such a suggestion.

"How confident are you in the ability of your men to carry out this crossing," Washington asked directly, his gaze never leaving the man standing in front of him.

There was an extended silence in the room, as every man stopped talking to hear the response. Glover's stare never flinched away from Washington, he and his commanding general seemingly intent on seeing into the very soul of one another.

"Only a fool would make a guarantee of success on something as dangerous and unpredictable as what I'm proposing," replied Glover, ever the pragmatist. "However, if your question, General, is whether we have a better chance of saving this army by evacuating our position or remaining in place to face the attack of the British tomorrow – well, sir, then I stand behind my proposal."

Washington continued to stare at Glover, internally amazed at the audacity and bravery of this man. He broke his gaze away and swept it over the room of assembled officers.

"By a show of hands, then – who is in favor of evacuating our army tonight," Washington asked bluntly.

Several hands shot up immediately, several others following slowly. After several seconds, every hand in the room had been raised in agreement.

Washington looked back at Glover, just a hint of satisfaction and relief in his eyes.

"Very well then, Colonel Glover. It appears that we are to place the fate of our army into your capable hands. Gentlemen, if you please, remain here for a short time while I draw up the necessary orders. Colonel Harrison, front and center!" Washington barked, summoning his Chief of Staff. "We have work to do."

***

Orders had been given for various units to begin moving at 7:00 PM toward the boats that had been assembled at a nearby ferrying point. The plan called for those units remaining within the fortifications to spread out as the other units departed. Therefore, the lines were to become thinner and thinner as the evening progressed and more men were evacuated. The honor – such as it was – of being the final unit to evacuate the fortifications was given to General Thomas

Mifflin's Philadelphia troops.

Things progressed well as the night wore on, the only obstacle occurring when a northeast wind whipped up around 9:00 PM, making it extremely difficult for Glover's men to navigate their human cargo across the river. But Glover's promise regarding the excellent seamanship of his men proved to be well-founded, and the crossing continued, albeit at a considerably slower pace.

Finally around midnight the wind and rain abated, and the East River became as calm as a sheet of glass. Boatload after boatload of American soldiers glided silently across the water to be deposited safely on the opposite shore. At that point, Glover's Marblehead men would turn about and return for the countless time across the river. It was a marvel of seamanship, endurance, and pure bravery.

General Washington was seemingly everywhere throughout the night. At one point he could be seen urging the men to move quickly and silently from the fortifications. At another time he would be at the ferry helping to organize the mass of humanity trying to embark on one boat or another. To his men, he never appeared flustered or anxious. He never appeared tired or afraid. The men reasoned, if their commander wasn't afraid, then perhaps there was no reason for them to be either.

***

At long last, it was time for General Mifflin's troops to depart the fortifications on Brooklyn Heights, leaving the positions utterly deserted. However, by now it was 7:00 AM and the sun was up, depriving these final troops of the benefit of the darkness.

But Providence chose to turn its smiling face upon these men from Philadelphia, as a thick, heavy fog had settled over the area just after dawn. So blanketing was this fog that it made it impossible to see from the American lines to the British lines just a few hundred yards away. This allowed Mifflin's men to quietly move to the ferry and quickly board the last remaining boats. This same fog made their final passage invisible to the nearby British warships anchored just south of the crossing.

A final longboat remained anchored at the ferry along Brooklyn Heights. A dozen or so men had climbed aboard, ready to depart now that they were satisfied that all of the American troops had been successfully evacuated. An officer called out to the soldier who would be piloting the longboat on this final crossing of the East River.

"Sergeant, if you please," ordered the officer, "let us make our way to New York City, and away from this devilish piece of ground. I'll be damned if I ever accept another invitation to visit here!"

The small group of men on the longboat chuckled at the remark, both because of its humor as well as out of respect for the speaker. The sergeant chuckled as well as he replied, pushing the boat out into the mild current of the river.

"As you wish, General Washington, sir, as you wish."

American Continental Army

In and Around New York City

September - November, 1776

Events had clearly not favored the Americans during the month of August at Brooklyn Heights. Having been forced to retreat his badly beaten army across the river to New York City, General George Washington hoped to rally his men and prepare them for their first successful confrontation with the British.

Unfortunately for the Americans, things would only get worse.

***

By mid-September, the British had assembled a force of ships and troops the likes of which had literally never been seen in the long and storied military past of that country. Literally hundreds of ships carrying thousands of cannon had assembled for what was obviously to be an invasion of New York City. Immediately behind these ships, waiting rather impatiently, were tens of thousands of British and Hessian troops, anxious to finally put an end to this bothersome conflict.

Washington had prepared defensive positions directly across the river from the British at a place called Kip's Bay. However, when he saw the full power of the enemy facing him just a few hundred yards away, the decision was made to evacuate the city rather than risk annihilation.

To that end, Washington left approximately 4,000 troops, many of them militia, to man the positions along the shore at Kip's Bay, while the remainder of his army beat an organized but hasty retreat north to King's Bridge and Harlem Heights. It was a Herculean task, as the Americans first had to evacuate the numerous wounded men, followed by the bulky cannon, then hundreds of wagons of precious supplies and ammunition, and finally the remaining soldiers.

The retreat had been accomplished not a day too early. On the morning of September 15th, eighty flatboats carrying 4,000 British troops set out from across the river, heading straight for Kip's Bay. However, instead of going directly to the shore and off-loading their human cargo, the boats formed an ominous line just parallel to the American defensive positions. At that point, the summer morning was shattered by the sound of eighty cannon that began pounding away at the pathetic American positions. The barrage continued for over an hour, during which time the inexperienced Americans on the receiving end fled in terror.

At least most of them fled. Dozens of men were caught in the hellish teeth of the cannonade, their bodies literally blown apart as hundreds of solid shot and shells landed in their midst. Some men were caught in the open as they attempted to escape, their bodies tumbling crazily in the air as a shell landed nearby, ripping off their arms, their legs, their heads. Others, too terrified to move, became victims of a well-placed shot that landed in the shallow holes and trenches that had been dug. Most of these unlucky men died an anonymous death, as there was nothing left of them to identify.

By the time the British flatboats completed their journey to the shore and the soldiers disembarked, there was little remaining to be done. A few of the bravest Americans had remained long enough to meet their attackers, but the British quickly captured or killed these hearty souls. In several instances, the British brutally decapitated the Americans, placing their heads on long pikes at various locations along the shoreline. The intent of the British was to terrorize their enemy and send a clear message: if you oppose the King, the price you pay will be high indeed.

***

On the night of September 20th, a fire broke out in New York City. The Americans claimed it had been set by the British as punishment to the city's inhabitants for having the temerity to house the Continental Army. The British claimed it had been set by the Americans as a means of depriving their enemy of the supplies and housing contained there.

Either way, it was a devastating affair, as over five hundred buildings – nearly a quarter of the entire city – was consumed by the flames. Only a fortuitous shift in the wind at about 2:00 AM prevented the entire city from being burned to the ground. By late morning on September 21st, the blaze had burned itself out. For weeks after, bodies were still being recovered from the charred ruins of what had once been a thriving part of one of the most prosperous cities in America.

Whether by accident or design, the conflict had ratcheted up to a new horrifying level. The fight for independence between the American Colonies and the most powerful country in the world had officially become a total war.

***

The British continued their dogged pursuit of the Continental Army for the remainder of September, as well as throughout October, pushing them further and further north of the city. On October 28th, General Washington and his ever dwindling army finally turned to face their pursuers at a place called White Plains.

General William Howe formed his 13,000 men into two columns, apparently planning to attack the Americans in a frontal assault.

However, the British had learned their lesson in that terrible encounter at Breed's Hill the previous year, and had no intentions of repeating it. Instead, one of Howe's columns executed a perfect movement to their left in an attempt to occupy the heights of Chatterton's Hill on the right flank of the American position.

Despite the fact that Washington was able to move some of his troops to counter the maneuver, it was a classic case of too little, too late. The enemy attack on Chatterton's Hill was conducted by 7,000 Hessians under the command of a hard, experienced Hessian officer named Colonel Johann Rall. Demonstrating their trademark combination of discipline and brutality, the Hessians quickly overran the heights, thereby making it virtually impossible for Washington to hold his position.

Over the next several days while Howe awaited additional reinforcements to press his advantage, Washington executed yet another skillful retreat, moving his men across the Bronx River to relative safety. The Americans began constructing defensive positions, fully convinced that the British would cross the river when they were fully prepared, and launch yet another attack against the exhausted Continental Army.

But on this occasion it was Washington's turn to awake on the morning of November 5th to a surprising scenario. The British had vanished from their position, Howe moving his army southward to an as yet unknown destination.

***

Fort Washington, as it had come to be called, sat on the New York side of the Hudson River, several miles north of New York City. In June of 1776, a number of American officers including General Washington himself had surveyed the ground in this area, and determined that a fort placed at this location could be the key to defending the Hudson River and, ultimately, everything south of New York City. Fort Washington was ultimately constructed at the highest point along the shoreline, and was also located at the narrowest part of the Hudson River. The Americans could simply not conceive of a more ideal spot for a fort.

For months after, thousands of men labored to construct the fort, which ultimately enclosed an area of about four acres. The shape of the fort was roughly a pentagon, with dozens of guns poking out of its earthen walls at every conceivable angle. Trees were felled and placed around the outside of the fort, their ends sharpened and angled in such a way as to be a severe impediment to any attacking force. It was, by any measure, a formidable defensive position.

It did, however, have its drawbacks. Most significantly, there was no source of water internal to the fort. This made the Hudson River, nearly one thousand yards away, the closest water. This meant that in the event of a siege on the fort, the men would potentially run out of an obvious necessity rather quickly, with no safe way to replenish themselves. In addition, no magazines had been built to house the gunpowder needed for the numerous cannon. The fact that the gunpowder would need to be situated, for the most part out in the open, meant that it would take just one lucky shot from an enemy artillery piece to blow up the whole place.

Following the confrontation with General George Washington at White Plains, General Howe had chosen to move his troops to oppose Fort Washington. The British knew, just as the Americans did, that this fort could not remain in the hands of the Americans if the British had any intentions of freely navigating their way up and down the Hudson River.

**

However, as the fortunes of war would have it, it was neither the strength of its construction, nor its logistical weaknesses that would ultimately determine the fate of Fort Washington.

On the evening of November 2, a man from Pennsylvania named William Demont slipped out of Fort Washington under the cover of darkness and made his way to the British lines that had just recently been established a short distance from the fort. Normally, such an event would have been almost routine, as many Americans had deserted to the enemy for any number of reasons. In this case, however, the desertion of Demont was to prove to be disastrous for the Americans.

Fort Washington was under the command of a Scotch-Irish officer from Pennsylvania named Colonel Robert Magaw. He was well respected by his men, as well as by General Washington, who had been completely confident in leaving Magaw in charge of such a crucial location. Magaw had been in charge of the fort for a number of months, and had become intimately familiar with its construction, the placement of its cannon, and the disposition of the men charged with the fort's defense. The only other man that had a similar level of knowledge of the fort was Colonel Magaw's adjutant: William Demont.

While the Americans had a considerable number of men manning the fort itself, a key part of their defense was over a thousand soldiers that had been deployed outside of the fort. The idea was that these men, supported by the cannon located within the fort, would prevent the British from getting close enough to Fort Washington to launch a concerted attack.

Based on the information brought to him by Demont, General William Howe not only knew how many men and cannon were in and around Fort Washington, but he also knew specifically where they were placed. General Howe developed a plan to launch a three-pronged assault on the fort. The strategy was designed to systematically drive the Americans in the outer defenses back into the fort, which was simply not large enough to accommodate such a large number of troops. At that point, it would be a simple matter of gradually closing the ring, to the point that the British cannon could lob shell after shell at the unprotected men crammed into the fort.

The strategy, despite the fact that the Americans resisted fiercely, worked like a charm. Once again, the Hessians under Colonel Johann Rall showed why they were considered the most disciplined troops in the world, driving the Americans out of their strongest positions and back into the fort.

After several hours of some of the bloodiest and deadliest fighting the war had yet seen, General Howe demanded the surrender of the Americans. On November 16th, Colonel Magaw realized that any continued resistance would result in the senseless slaughter of hundreds, if not thousands of American soldiers. Reluctantly, he agreed to the terms of unconditional surrender.

While the Americans had only suffered approximately one hundred and fifty men killed and wounded in the battle, the real tragedy was the number of men who became prisoners of war. In all, nearly 3,000 officers and men marched out of Fort Washington and into British captivity. It was a blow to the Continental Army that could scarcely be absorbed.

***

From Fort Lee, located just across the river on the New Jersey side of the Hudson River, General George Washington watched with tears in his eyes. He was the one that had ultimately made the decision to defend the fort, despite the fact that many of his officers had urged that he abandon the location and save its defenders for another day. However, he had been convinced that the strength of its defenses, its men, and its commander would make it almost impregnable to enemy assault.

He had, quite obviously, been grievously mistaken.

Unwilling to make the same mistake twice, General Washington ordered the abandonment of Fort Lee. When the British crossed the river the next day intending to attack and conquer Fort Lee in much the same way they had conquered its partner across the river, they found the position deserted with the exception of a few Continental soldiers who had gotten drunk the night before and passed out inside the walls of the fort.

***

Washington had ordered his men to organize whatever supplies, ammunition, and artillery that could be moved, and head southwest toward Philadelphia.

The long retreat across New Jersey had begun.

Part Three

New Jersey

Douglas F. Shupinski

General George Washington

Commanding General, Continental Army

Trenton, New Jersey

9:00 P.M. December 7, 1776

The last few weeks had been the worst of George Washington's life. Embarrassed and outraged at the numerous defeats that his army had suffered over the last several months, insult had been added to injury.

As usual, the Continental Army was suffering horribly due to the now routine lack of supplies, clothing and – most importantly – ammunition. Many of the men had no winter clothing, others had no shoes. All of this as the temperatures continued to drop closer and closer to the freezing point.

The result was an exodus of desertions from the ranks. With little hope of ever winning a battle, and even less hope of receiving the items necessary to survive the rapidly approaching heart of the upcoming winter, men simply gave up and began the long trek back to their homes.

As a human being, Washington understood their plight. These men had given everything they had in pursuit of a vague dream of independence. But those that were charged with supporting them in the form of money and supplies had quite simply failed to do so. The Continental Congress, always wary of allowing the largest standing

American army to become too strong, had failed to provide the promised meager pay to the soldiers. The Quartermaster of the army had been incapable of appropriating the necessary clothing and food to keep the men warm and fed. And – to Washington, this was personally the most disturbing – these brave men had not been given the leadership necessary to achieve victory.

Despite these facts, General Washington was compelled to put aside his humanity and view the situation with the cold detachment of a commanding general. Were he to allow these desertions to go unchecked and unpunished, the result could quite possibly be the complete disintegration of his army. Therefore, Washington had ordered the distasteful punishments of dozens of men caught while attempting to desert. Most of these punishments took the form of men being given as many as one hundred lashes across their bare backs, administered while their comrades stood by and observed in grim silence. While these punishments had resulted in a slight decrease in the number of men deserting, the resulting drop in morale was almost as debilitating to the army.

However, all of these immediate concerns paled in comparison to what was about to occur in just over three weeks. As of January 1, 1777, the enlistments of almost every member of the Continental Army were due to expire. Based on the number of men attempting to get an early jump on these expiring enlistments, along with the reports from his generals, Washington knew that his precious army would soon cease to exist.

Thank God the British are not aware of the precarious position we are in, Washington thought to himself. Nevertheless, the Continental Congress needed to be made aware of the seriousness of the situation. To do this, Washington dispatched a messenger to the Board of War, carrying a communication which described in absolute detail what was likely to occur in the very near future.

***

"Colonel Harrison!" Washington called out to his Chief of Staff. Washington was seated at a large desk in the middle of the library of the house he had selected as his headquarters. The owner of the house, a

Douglas J. Shupinski

reported Loyalist, had made the rather prudent decision to move himself and his family to New York City in order to enjoy the protection of the British army.

Colonel Robert Harrison appeared, as always, within a matter of seconds, looking for all the world as if he had just taken hours to compose himself especially for this summons by the Commanding General. The colonel's military bearing and uniform were always impeccable, and Washington found himself oddly irritated on occasion at his inability to catch Harrison in anything resembling a state of unpreparedness.

"Yes, sir?" Colonel Harrison asked, coming to formal attention in front of Washington. "How may be of assistance to the General?"

"Colonel, what information have we received with respect to the positions of our army?" Washington asked. "I must be kept constantly aware of the most recent locations of each of its sections."

Several weeks earlier, Washington had chosen to divide his army into four units, the largest of which he had placed under the command of Major General Charles Lee at White Castle, New York. Washington's orders to Lee and his approximately 7,000 troops were to guard against any British attempts to move north into New England, predictably for the purpose of re-capturing Boston. In addition, if General Howe and the British decided to invade New Jersey, General Lee was instructed to re-join General Washington and his 2,000 troops who would already be in position in New Jersey.

In fact, invading New Jersey is exactly what Howe had done on November 20th, and as early as November 21st Washington had written to Lee requesting that he join Washington. When General Lee exhibited no intention to do as instructed, this first "request" was followed up a week later with a more direct order – move your army *now* to southern New Jersey and link up with Washington's men. Finally on December 2nd, General Lee had begun moving toward Washington in a manner that could only be described as lethargic.

"Sir," Colonel Harrison ventured cautiously, "may I presume that your most immediate concern is in regard to the current location of General Lee?"

Washington looked carefully at Harrison. Despite the fact that the man was clearly a relatively junior officer, the relationship that often existed between a Commanding General and his Chief of Staff was one that required a high degree of trust, as sensitive matters were often the topic of interactions. This was one such case.

"Yes, General Lee," Washington said slowly, careful to try and keep any type of emotion from his voice. His efforts were fruitless, as Washington's tone and body language revealed the frustration he had with Lee.

***

Major General Charles Lee was, without a doubt, one of the most interesting and intriguing members of the Continental Army. Born and raised in England to a rather affluent family, Lee had been commissioned as an ensign in the British army at the age of fourteen. Through a rare combination of political connections and actual military competence, Lee had quickly moved up through the ranks, adding to his credentials by actively participating in several engagements during the French and Indian War in America.

It was during this time that Lee met and married the daughter of an Indian chief named White Thunder. He was anointed with his own Indian title which roughly translated into "boiling water", a reference to his constantly restless spirit, penchant for bold action, and sometimes violent temper.

Soon thereafter, Lee began a somewhat gradual fall from the graces of the British military, as his often blatant criticisms against several senior officers began to take their toll. Following a modest level of success serving under General Charles Burgoyne while fighting in Portugal, Lee became a colonel in the Portugese army. He followed this adventure with his acquisition of the rank of General in the Polish army in 1763, serving as the aide-de-camp to the King of that country.

Officially resigning his commission in the British army in 1773, Lee returned to America where he quickly became a key figure in the revolutionary movement. By the outbreak of hostilities at Lexington and Concord, many members of the Continental Congress considered him to be the best candidate for command of the fledgling Continental Army. However, the fact that he was not a native-born American worked against him, and Washington's ability to potentially influence the southern colonies into supporting the independence movement ultimately led to Lee being named a subordinate to Washington. This, quite predictably, had never sat well with the overly ambitious Lee.

***

"Yes, my clever colonel," Washington remarked to Harrison, "I suppose the location of General Lee and his men would be of significant interest to me. What news do you have?"

"Sir, I am told that he is moving in this direction with − in his words − 'the greatest possible speed.' However, General Lee was clear that he no longer has a force of 7,000 men due to sickness and desertion. His reports indicate that he may have less than half of his original number by the time he arrives."

Harrison was startled at a brief display of uncharacteristic temper by Washington, as he pounded his fist loudly on the desk in front of him. Quickly composing himself, Washington replied to Harrison.

"Very well, then. Please continue to keep me apprised of that situation. In the meantime, I should like to see Colonel Glover immediately."

***

Colonel John Glover presented himself to General Washington, the ever-present look of disgust on Glover's face.

"General Washington, I wish to report that the shuttling of the men across the river back to the Pennsylvania side has begun as ordered. God willing, and with the favor of the weather, they should all be across by tomorrow morning."

"Very well, Colonel," Washington responded. "Please keep me informed with respect to your progress, or if any difficulties arise. Also, I am interested in hearing about your ability to prevent the enemy from continuing their pursuit of this army once we have successfully re-located to the Pennsylvania shore."

Once again, Glover's group of fishermen from Marblehead, Massachusetts were being called upon to demonstrate their seamanship skills. Washington had determined that he needed to place a natural boundary – in this case, the Delaware River – between his army and the pursuing British. The trick this time, however, was two-fold. First, the retreat needed to be accomplished before the enemy arrived and trapped the Americans with their backs to the river. And second, any attempt by the British to pursue the Americans across the river needed to be eliminated. To that end, Washington had ordered that any and all boats within seventy miles of the Continental Army be confiscated and removed to the opposite shore.

"Aye, sir," Glover responded. "Begging your pardon, General, but I believe we have successfully taken possession of pretty much anything that can float." Glover gave a rare, devious smile. "If the British want to come after us, General, they'll have to swim."

Washington allowed himself a tight smile in return, refusing to allow this man to see the overwhelming relief he felt. Knowing that his army was on the verge of enjoying its first moment of safety in many weeks was the best news he had heard in quite some time.

"Very well, Colonel Glover. As always, your men have demonstrated the professionalism of soldiers who are clearly being commanded by a true leader. Perhaps someday this country will have the opportunity to properly express its gratitude to you and them."

Glover looked quickly at the ground, slightly embarrassed by the praise being given by a man he held in great esteem. Looking up and staring Washington directly in the eye, Glover gave his response.

"The only gratitude my men and I request, sir, is the chance to pay back these British bastards for what they've done to us."

General William Howe

Commanding General, British Army

New Jersey Bank of the Delaware River

6:00 AM December 14, 1776

As usual when he was in the field, William Howe had awakened early, the darkness just now beginning to relinquish itself to an almost-winter dawn. He had developed this habit, as many military leaders did, as a means of reviewing the upcoming day's plans. While he wasn't necessarily a man who second guessed himself, Howe was a firm believer in checking the numerous details that went with the job of commanding a large army.

However, this particular early morning found Howe with no details to check, as any initiative he might take with his army had been snatched away from him by the Americans. Having arrived at the New Jersey bank of the Delaware River the previous day, the British had found themselves once again confounded by the seemingly endless ability of the Continental Army to make good its escape across yet another waterway.

The British Army had chased the Americans across the entire colony of New Jersey with an almost relentless pursuit. Howe had placed Major General Charles Cornwallis in charge of the operation, and as always, Cornwallis had driven his men past the point of exhaustion, cursing, threatening, and cajoling them the entire way.

But the British had been the victim of two unlikely circumstances. First, for the entire war, the British had always been better fed, better clothed, and better equipped. They had more supplies, artillery, and ammunition than the Americans could have hoped for in their wildest dreams. And it was exactly this excess of resources that had bogged down the British as they force-marched across the countryside. Meanwhile the Americans, poorly equipped and always hungry, had been unburdened by the normally necessary accoutrements of war. Their privations had become their advantage, making them able to move more quickly than their enemy. Second, much to the surprise of the British, the Americans apparently had a few leaders who possessed at least a rudimentary level of military skill. These men had exercised an almost innate ability to wage a fighting retreat that constantly frustrated the pursuing British. Bridges had been destroyed, small but effective ambushes had been executed, and the British were continuously on the alert for a major attack that was forever being threatened, but never really materialized.

The ultimate frustration had been the arrival of the British army on the banks of the Delaware, fully prepared to make a quick crossing to the Pennsylvania side of the river, under fire if necessary. But calling upon the bravery of the troops had been unnecessary. A search for miles and miles up and down the river had revealed the fact that the Americans had taken possession of every boat, big and small, that might allow such a crossing.

The final result was General Howe standing alone on this bitterly cold December morning, looking across the Delaware River into Pennsylvania – the current sanctuary of his elusive enemy.

***

General Howe had grudgingly allowed his army to have breakfast before ordering a meeting of his senior officers. Why not, Howe had reasoned – the need for haste no longer existed, and his men had certainly suffered these last few weeks. It was approaching eight o'clock as the last of the dozen or so officers crowded themselves into the field tent Howe had ordered erected as his acting headquarters.

Howe waited a minute or two, allowing the men to jostle themselves into some semblance of order, the most senior officers nearest to the front, junior to the rear. This arrangement was, in this case, a combination of both military etiquette and practicality. Those officers closest to the front were in a better position to hear their commanding general, as well as being placed farthest away from the tent flap and the biting cold attempting to force its way inside.

"Gentlemen," Howe began, "it appears that we have come to the unfortunate end of our race, at least for the moment. As you are aware, the Americans have withdrawn to the Pennsylvania side of the river, taking all of the boats in the area with them."

While this was certainly not news to the officers, many of them looked at the ground in frustration and embarrassment, having been reminded of their failure to confront and destroy the Americans yet again.

"However," Howe continued, "I believe we all realize that this cowardly retreat by our enemy is only a brief reprieve for this so called army. As the saying goes, you may run, but ultimately, you cannot hide."

The men mumbled in agreement, their embarrassment of a moment ago quickly forgotten, the spark returning to their eyes and spirits as quickly as it had departed.

General Cornwallis, standing directly in front of Howe, spoke up.

"Sir, is it your intention that we expand our search for boats further up and down the river? Clearly, the Americans cannot have covered the entire length of the Delaware."

Many of the officers grunted in agreement, and several sidebar conversations between the men began discussing plans on how to accomplish this feat. Raising his hand to command silence, Howe responded.

"No, General Cornwallis, I don't believe that is the most prudent course of action at this moment, nor in the longer term. I believe the time has come for us to end our campaigning for the winter. We will return the main body of the army to New York City where we will make our winter quarters. In addition, I intend to establish a series of supporting positions between here and our main base in the event that the Americans make the poor decision of attempting to return to New Jersey. However, I believe that possibility to be highly unlikely."

Several of the officers were clearly surprised by this pronouncement from their commander. The assumption among both the officers and the enlisted men had been that the pursuit of the Americans would continue, given the significant advantages the British held in numbers and readiness for battle.

General James Grant stepped forward, placing himself directly next to Cornwallis. It was obvious the man had something to say.

"General Grant," Howe said, acknowledging his subordinate, "you have something to offer?"

"Sir, with all due respect," Grant began cautiously, "the enemy is clearly exhausted and disorganized. A final push across the river may catch the Americans by surprise and completely incapable of mounting a serious defense. Such a situation – "

"While it is obviously unnecessary for me to explain my orders," Howe interrupted, mildly perturbed by Grant's comments, "allow me to share some information with you that I believe will demonstrate the wisdom of our strategy."

General Grant bowed his head and retreated a step, having been clearly put into his appropriate place by the commanding general.

"I must stress the sensitivity of this information, as it was obtained through somewhat – shall we say – unconventional means," Howe continued.

"Several days ago, Mr. Washington sent a dispatch to that group of criminals sometimes referred to as the American Continental Congress. In this dispatch, he conveyed his serious concerns regarding the expiration of the enlistments of most of his army – specifically, almost all of the men under his command who have any degree of combat experience. This dispatch was intercepted by someone who has wisely chosen to remain loyal to England."

A buzz of excitement filled the tent, and Howe was obliged to once again raise his hand for silence.

"It seems Mr. Washington believes that there is very little possibility that any of these men will choose to continue fighting against the Crown. To paraphrase his words, Mr. Washington believes that as of the end of the year, the Continental Army will virtually cease to exist!"

The group was suddenly alive with energy with the realization that the war might be nearing its conclusion. Men smiled at one another, an occasional chuckle and backslap punctuating the cold morning air.

"So, as you can see, gentlemen," Howe concluded, "I find it most distasteful to send our men across the river in this ungodly weather to fight a battle – regardless of how assured our victory would be – when patience and the coming of spring may deliver us a scenario in which there are simply no more battles remaining to fight."

His logic impeccable, his information sound, General Howe had clearly convinced his senior officers that now was the time for withdrawal and restraint. Howe turned his back away from the group, returning to the small writing table that had been placed in the corner. It was an unspoken order that the decision had been made, and the meeting was officially concluded.

A minute later, all of the officers had left the tent, with the exception of General Cornwallis. He remained in the same position he had occupied throughout the meeting, waiting patiently to be recognized. After a minute had passed, it became clear to Howe that General Cornwallis would not be ignored.

"General Cornwallis, I truly hope you are not remaining in my presence as a simple means of avoiding the cold outside."

"Sir," Cornwallis spoke, "I request permission to speak freely."

While General Howe was not accustomed to entertaining the thoughts and suggestions of his subordinates, he also realized that Cornwallis was not only his second in command, but an officer who had a great deal of experience and ability. Sighing deeply, Howe dipped his head slightly communicating his willingness to allow the man to speak.

Sir," Cornwallis began, "you know I would never disagree with you in front of the other officers. But I must admit a slight discomfort in not taking advantage of the opportunity with which we are faced. While I understand the potential for the American army to collapse on its own,

I would much prefer to accomplish that feat ourselves, here and now. In addition to the possibility that Washington may not have an army in the spring, there is also the possibility that he will strike while his army is still intact, before the enlistments expire."

"Strike? Strike with what, General? He has barely enough men to guard his own encampment, and those men are tired, beaten, and without sufficient means to fight!"

"Yes, sir," Cornwallis acknowledged, "all of that is true. That is exactly why we should continue our pursuit and end this thing here and now!"

Howe had to admit a grudging admiration for the man's fighting spirit. God knew, Charles Cornwallis had never shied away from a battle, and this situation was no different. Howe took several steps across the tent, and placed his hand on the shoulder of Cornwallis in an uncharacteristic display of familiarity.

"General," Howe said slowly, "as always I appreciate your insights and, even more so, your willingness to share them with me. However, in this case, I am firm in my orders."

Cornwallis allowed his gaze to remain fixed on his commander, an unspoken sign that he still wasn't convinced. It was time for Howe to play his trump card.

"General Cornwallis, I have been contemplating a suggestion for you that I believe I will now make. I know it has been an extremely long time since you have had the opportunity to see that beautiful wife of yours back in England. Perhaps this period of inactivity over the next several months will afford you the opportunity to take some well-deserved leave and return to see her."

Cornwallis' demeanor changed instantly, as the thought of seeing his wife washed over him. The legendary beauty of Cornwallis' wife was exceeded only by the well-known deep love he had for the woman. With an almost sheepish smile on his face, he responded to Howe.

"Sir, I believe your wisdom extends beyond those matters pertaining to war. I will begin making preparations immediately for our return to New York."

General George Washington

Commanding General, Continental Army

Pennsylvania Side of the Delaware River

7:15 P.M December 20, 1776

General George Washington shook his head in wonder as he paced back and forth. It never ceased to amaze him how quickly things could change during wartime. It was almost as if the normal pace of events was drastically accelerated to a breakneck speed, cramming dozens of major and minor occurrences into the span of a few short days.

Such was the case at this point in time.

Just a week earlier, Washington had been frustrated by the fact that his dwindling army was receiving none of the reinforcements he had ordered to join him. General Charles Lee, clearly intentionally dragging his feet, had been somewhere in New Jersey with his force of nearly 4,000 men. Instead of marching with all speed to join Washington, Lee had sent repeated requests that he be allowed to attack the flanks of the scattered British army. Washington had refused, continuing to issue his original orders with greater and greater severity to the point that he had become almost threatening to his tardy subordinate. It was a leadership style with which Washington was extremely uncomfortable; but General Lee had left the Commanding General with no choice.

Then, on December 13th, a most unexpected event had occurred. Lee had chosen to take overnight lodging in a tavern near Basking Ridge, New Jersey, probably because it afforded him a great deal more comfort than the tents being occupied by the rest of his men. The tavern was located about three miles to the rear of his army and, under normal circumstances, should have been a relatively safe location.

However, on December 12th, British General Cornwallis had decided he needed to know the whereabouts of General Lee's force, suspecting that it might be located on his flank or even to his rear. Such a situation was unacceptable to Cornwallis, so he dispatched a small detachment of about twenty-five British cavalrymen to scout the area and determine Lee's position.

In command of this small cavalry contingent was a twenty-two year old British officer named Banastre Tarleton. Despite the fact that Tarleton was relatively new to warfare, having had his commission purchased by his mother just over a year earlier, he had already gained the reputation of being brave, reckless, and heartless. During several previous engagements, both large and small, Tarleton had demonstrated not only the talent for chasing down and hacking to death enemy soldiers attempting to escape, but also the apparent *love* of it.

While scouting the countryside, Tarleton and his men had come upon several American soldiers who had been ordered to provide a screen around the rest of Lee's army, as well as protection for Lee himself. Threatening to decapitate them if they refused to speak, Tarleton quickly learned that General Lee was just a few miles away, sitting unsuspectingly in his comfortable tavern.

On the morning of December 13th, General Lee had arisen and enjoyed a rather leisurely breakfast while the remainder of his army had broken camp at about eight o'clock and begun their painfully slow march in the direction of Washington's force. Tarleton and his men had quickly surrounded the tavern, fired a volley through the windows, and loudly ordered the immediate surrender of anyone inside. Clearly, this Friday the 13th was an unlucky day for Charles Lee.

General Charles Lee had been taken into custody, and returned with all possible speed to the headquarters of General Cornwallis. To the surprise of everyone present, Charles Lee had not only been treated well by Cornwallis, but had been received as the old friend that he actually was, the two men having served together in the past as fellow British officers.

Washington had received the news the next day, with understandably mixed emotions. On one hand, Charles Lee provided experience and confidence to an army that drastically lacked both of these things. On the other hand, Lee had displayed a continuing unwillingness to follow the orders of Washington, and had even made it known that he believed that he should be the commanding general of the Continental Army. To Washington, who valued a man's penchant for loyalty above all else, such a situation was simply unacceptable. In effect, the capture of General Charles Lee by the British removed the need for Washington to make a decision regarding the man's fitness to remain in command of a portion of the Continental Army.

In addition to this dramatic turn of events, General John Sullivan, now in charge of the soldiers previously commanded by Charles Lee, had arrived at Washington's camp this very day, in the midst of a terrible snowstorm that had caused his men to suffer considerably during their march. However, much to Washington's dismay, instead of arriving with the expected and much needed 4,000 troops, Sullivan's command had consisted of only half that number. The rest had either been too sick to travel, or had deserted somewhere along the march.

General Horatio Gates had also been successful at making his way to join Washington, despite the horrific weather. But again, Washington had been disappointed at the number of troops he had brought compared to the number that had been expected. Gates was able to add perhaps 600 healthy men to the ranks of the Continental Army now camped along the Pennsylvania side of the Delaware River.

All told, Washington theoretically commanded between 7,000 and 8,000 men. However, when those on the sick rolls and otherwise unavailable for combat were factored into the equation, Washington would be lucky to muster 6,000 troops for any potential action.

***

Surprisingly, all of this apparently mattered little to George Washington. For at least a week now, he had been contemplating a bold strike against the British in New Jersey, and the loss of Charles Lee and a good number of his troops had failed to dampen his schemes. As Washington walked along the edge of the river gazing thoughtfully at the distant shoreline, his plans began to coalesce in his mind.

As always, Washington's chief of staff, Colonel Harrison, was a short distance away. Stamping his feet against the bitter cold and attempting to wrap himself even tighter in his overcoat, Harrison stood resolutely by, awaiting any orders from his commander. The fact that Washington appeared impervious to the elements was a continuing source of amazement to him.

"Colonel, if you please," Washington ordered abruptly, shaking himself out of his previous contemplations.

"Yes, sir," Harrison responded, moving quickly to Washington's side. "What is it, sir? Can I order the cook to prepare you something to eat? Perhaps a warm fire may be in order, sir."

Washington looked at Harrison strangely, an odd glow on his face.

"What are you rambling on about, Colonel? Food? Fires? I want an immediate report on the number of men we have fit for duty – and I want it to be absolutely accurate, is that understood? I also need to know the status of our ammunition for both the artillery as well as the men's muskets."

"Completely, sir," Harrison replied, beginning to get swept up in the sudden energy being exhibited by his commander. "I shall see to it immediately."

Colonel Harrison turned and began walking briskly away, knowing that Washington had little patience when he was hot on the trail of something – which he clearly was now.

"Colonel!" Washington called out after the bustling chief of staff.

"Yes, sir, what is it?" Harrison asked as he quickly returned to Washington's side.

Washington turned to face Harrison, a nearby campfire casting an eerie light across the Commanding General's face. To Harrison's surprise, there was an almost evil grin on the man's face, a countenance in complete contrast to the usual calm expression he displayed at virtually all times.

"There is one other item that I need located and distributed to the men, Colonel Harrison," Washington stated slowly, placing emphasis on every word.

"What would that item be?" Harrison asked.

"I need every man to have – a bayonet."

Colonel Johann Rall

Hessian Regimental Commander, British Army

Trenton, New Jersey

9:30 P.M December 24, 1776

The last two weeks had been most infuriating to Colonel Johann Rall, the commanding officer of the 1,500 Hessians that had been stationed in Trenton since December 13th. Although he was extremely pleased that he had been given his current assignment, things simply weren't going the way he had envisioned.

Johann Rall was a fifty-six year old professional soldier, having seen more combat in more parts of the world than almost any other man in the British army. He had relished the opportunity to come to the Colonies in order to fight the Americans and, to date had proven himself to be a courageous and reliable officer under fire. His actions, and the actions of his regiment had figured quite prominently in the British victories at White Plains and Fort Washington. It was for these reasons that Rall had actively lobbied to be given command of this most forward of British outposts, and it was for these same reasons that his request had been granted by General Howe.

***

Douglas F. Shupinski

Howe had made several decisions in the last two weeks. First, he had established several outposts stretching from the original British headquarters at Staten Island to Rall's post in Trenton. These posts, Howe believed, would make any possible movement into New Jersey by the Americans almost impossible. Second, he had replaced General Cornwallis with General James Grant, allowing Cornwallis to make his plans to return to England for a well-deserved leave. This made Grant the overall commander of the Hessian and British forces stationed throughout New Jersey. And finally, Howe had chosen to not only separate the Hessians and British soldiers to their own respective outposts – there was frequent bad blood between the two groups – but he had also placed the Hessians closest to the Rebel army located just across the river in Pennsylvania.

In charge of all of the Hessian positions was Colonel Carl Emil Kurt von Donop, yet another in a long line of disciplined, battle-hardened Hessian officers. Unlike Colonel Rall, Donop was a calculating, thoughtful officer who considered his every move very carefully before making it. In addition, he had a certain level of respect for the Americans, having seen them perform rather well against his men on a number of occasions.

On the other hand, Rall tended to be impulsive, making quick decisions based on instinct rather than a genuine analysis of the situation. And Rall believed the Americans were nothing more than amateurs, military misfits who didn't belong on any battlefield, let alone facing the greatest soldiers in the world.

These differences of characteristics and opinions made for a stormy relationship between Donop and Rall, and both would just as soon rather not deal with one another unless absolutely necessary. As a result, Donop's orders to Rall over the last two weeks had been infrequent, and fairly vague.

***

Colonel Rall was just now returning from yet another trip into the countryside surrounding the small village of Trenton, a town of no more than about one hundred houses and other buildings. Over the last two weeks, Rall had been sending out patrols in the direction of the nearby Delaware River in an attempt to ascertain the presence of any enemy soldiers there. Not only had his men seen the enemy, but they had been repeatedly ambushed by them. Barely a day had failed to pass without several casualties being reported to Rall at his headquarters at the center of town. Whenever he would receive one of these reports, he would curse loudly in German – Rall spoke virtually no English – and vow to the men around him that these Americans would pay for their actions.

Several hours earlier, it was one of these enemy ambushes that had compelled him to see for himself what was happening in his area of operations. Taking a group of over a hundred men down to the river, he had seen nothing – as he knew would be the case. Despite his low opinion of the enemy, he was forced to admit that these Americans were fairly adept at disappearing when the situation demanded it.

Dismounting just outside of his headquarters, Rall was approached out of the darkness by Captain Johann Ewald, a young but experienced officer whom Rall tended to trust deeply.

"Sir, what was the result of your patrol, if I may ask?" Ewald said.

"Nothing, Captain Ewald, absolutely nothing!" Colonel Rall spit out bitterly. "Just like every other damned patrol I've made in the last two weeks! These Americans appear out of nowhere, ambush my men, and then melt into the countryside like the cowards that they are."

"Sir," Ewald said quietly, moving away from the other members of Rall's headquarters command, "I know we have discussed this in the past, but perhaps you will allow me to begin to – "

"No, damn it!" Rall exploded. "I will not reconsider my decision regarding fortifications around this wretched little town! Despite what Colonel Donop may have suggested, a defensive posture will do nothing but sap the morale and fighting spirit right out of these men!"

Despite the fact that Captain Ewald was no stranger to his commander's violent outbursts, he nevertheless shrank visibly away from the man.

"We must continue to send patrols out to find this conniving

Douglas J. Shupinski

enemy, and draw him into a proper battle!" Rall continued, his anger growing."

Even as the words were leaving his mouth, Rall reflected that his refusal to act defensively was somewhat ironic. He had already ordered six outposts to be set up around Trenton, some of them manned by as many as one hundred men. His cannon had been deployed in the center of the town, constantly manned by their crews. And of the three regiments that Colonel Rall commanded in Trenton, he had mandated that one of them be available for combat at all times at a moment's notice. This meant that the regiment on duty slept in their full uniforms, and had their loaded muskets within arm's reach. Despite his verbal bravado, Colonel Johann Rall was taking few chances when it came to the defensive preparations of his command for an attack.

"Now, Captain Ewald, if you are quite finished questioning my abilities as a commander, I shall retire for the evening," Colonel Rall stated bitterly. "I shall eventually return to my quarters, but for a short time I will be at Mr. Hunt's residence."

Of course you will, thought Ewald. Colonel Rall had been spending almost every evening at the home of Abraham Hunt, a local Tory who had been more than happy to entertain the Colonel over the last two weeks. While most of the remainder of the town's population had chosen to depart rather quickly upon the arrival of the Hessians, Mr. Hunt had instead adapted to the new occupants, providing a warm spot to pass the time during the day for the soldiers, and a comfortable sanctuary accented with spirits and card games for Colonel Rall and a few other officers in the evening.

Throwing his cape contemptuously over his right shoulder, Colonel Rall stomped off into the evening. These Americans may be able to make his life a living hell, but they were not about to ruin a perfectly good evening of drinking and gambling.

***

Christmas morning dawned bright and brutally cold. While many of the Germans had enjoyed a modest level of celebration the previous night, the required level of alertness ordered by Colonel Rall had not been compromised. Hessian soldiers were the consummate professionals – something as trivial as Christmas Eve wasn't nearly enough to make them let down their guard.

This was not necessarily the case for Johann Rall. As usual, he had stayed up until the early morning hours, playing cards and drinking. It was for this reason that the incessant banging on the door of his quarters at the ungodly hour of ten o'clock was received by Rall with a somewhat groggy anger.

"Enter, you Swine!" Rall shouted. "This had better be good, or I'll have you beaten within an inch of your life!"

The door opened gently, and Captain Ewald poked his head into the room with the greatest of trepidation.

"Sir, I assumed the Colonel would require a report regarding the disposition of our men, and the events of the previous evening," Ewald stated haltingly.

Captain Ewald had arisen very early, which was to say that he had never really turned in for the night. By sunrise, he had taken it upon himself to inspect the various outposts around Trenton, and was satisfied that the evening had been mercifully uneventful. Perhaps the Rebels, who never seemed to take a respite from the constant harassment of the Hessians, had finally seen fit to enjoy the Holiday season, if only for the time being.

Rall sat up in his bed, rubbing his face and his bald head with both hands, clearly attempting to erase the cobwebs from his brain.

"Make your report, Captain" Rall ordered, gradually composing himself after his initial outburst.

"Sir, I beg to report that last evening was quiet. Several of the outposts reported hearing movement to their fronts along the river, but there were no attacks by the enemy."

Rall breathed a heavy sigh of relief that he hoped went unnoticed by the junior officer. While he chose to display an appearance of casual indifference to his men, Rall was genuinely concerned that the Americans might just be foolish enough to try something desperate and rash. He had even gone so far as to send several messages to his

Douglas J. Shupinski

Commanding Officer, General Donop, sharing these exact sentiments in no uncertain terms. The fact that Christmas Eve had passed without incident gave him significant consolation, and he visibly relaxed. Perhaps his low opinion of the enemy was well founded after all.

"Very well, Captain," Rall responded. "Have my mount prepared immediately. I shall take my breakfast here in my quarters, and then I intend to inspect my entire command, both inside and outside of the town. While I doubt the necessity of my actions, I suppose it is important that the men see their commander up and about on Christmas Day."

Captain Ewald came to sharp attention and, with a look that was just barely tinged with contempt, saluted and departed the room.

Rising from his bed, Rall went to the nearby window and gazed outside. The ground was covered with a fresh snowfall, but the bright sunlight suggested that it might not be quite as cold as previous days. Inspect my command, Rall mused. Yes, I suppose that would be the proper thing to do. Let me complete these trivial displays of command – an afternoon nap can wait for a few hours. Those wretched Americans are no doubt buried in their threadbare blankets, hoping to God that *we* don't attack *them*.

General George Washington

Commanding General, Continental Army

Buckingham, Pennsylvania

3:00 P.M. December 25, 1776

The Continental Army was finally on the move. Tramping out of the woods and down toward the shore of the Delaware River, the men looked nothing like the professional army they were intending to attack. Few of the men had anything that resembled a proper uniform, but rather were wrapped in any of a number of combinations of coats, cloaks, and blankets. At least one in every four or five soldiers had no shoes, instead wrapping their feet in rags in a feeble attempt to protect them from the biting cold of the Pennsylvania winter. In fact, the path from the army's tents to the Durham boats waiting at the shore could be clearly identified by the snow that had been marked with the blood of the men's feet.

***

General George Washington had met with his most senior and trusted officers the evening before, and had informed them of his plan. While several of them had initially appeared incredulous at the boldness of Washington's intentions, they had eventually been convinced of its potential for success. In any case, as their commander had noted, it was either victory or death for the Continental Army. So true was this fact that Washington had declared that the password for the army was, "Victory or Death".

The objective of the attack was the Hessian stronghold located at Trenton. Washington had selected this as his target for three very logical reasons. First, it was the enemy position closest to the river, thereby making it easiest to reach after crossing the waterway. Second, the roughly fifteen hundred Hessians manning that position would be a reasonable force for the Americans to engage, given the Americans' nearly three to one numerical superiority. And finally, Washington had received several reliable reports that the troops in Trenton had made virtually no attempts at fortifying the town.

Specifically, the plan called for the army to be separated into three columns, each of which would cross the Delaware River at different locations. One column, consisting of approximately 1,500 men under the command of Lieutenant Colonel John Cadwalader, would cross the river some distance south of Trenton and make diversionary attacks on several Hessian outposts located in that area. This would help prevent the garrison at Trenton from receiving any reinforcements. The second column, seven hundred men under the command of Brigadier General James Ewing, would cross the Delaware immediately south of Trenton and position itself at the Assunpink Creek bridge. This position would cut off the most obvious retreat route of the Hessians at Trenton, and would also serve as a blocking force for any enemy reinforcements.

General Washington himself would command the main column which would consist of about 2,400 men. This column would cross the river north of Trenton, at which point it would separate into two groups. One group would be led by Major General John Sullivan, who would take the River Road and enter Trenton from the south. The other group under Major General Nathaniel Greene would take the Pennington Road and enter Trenton from the north. The obvious plan was to catch the enemy between two attacking forces, thereby creating confusion and eliminating their ability to coordinate a focused counterattack.

All of this looked good, of course, on paper. However, Washington and his commanders were painfully aware of the fact that there were inherent challenges to successfully carrying out this rather elaborate plan. The weather was awful, the troops would be moving at night in pitch darkness, and all of the columns needed to arrive at their appointed locations at basically the same time. Even then, there was no way of knowing how prepared and alert the enemy might be.

As Washington watched his men move silently toward the waiting boats, he reflected on how desperate this attack truly was. Despite the fact that he had displayed a confident face to his commanders, certain they would do the same with their men, Washington had serious doubts about the ultimate outcome of his plan. However, he was facing a situation that makes any army and its commander extremely dangerous – he had nothing to lose. It was either win this battle, or the army would disintegrate in a week.

***

General Washington had opted to place himself in one of the first boats to cross the river. In his mind, it was more important to make himself immediately visible to the arriving troops, who would be justifiably nervous about their exposed position upon landing on the New Jersey shore. If the landing was detected at this point, the Hessians might just have enough time to assemble the entire garrison at Trenton, move the few miles to where the Americans had landed, and attack and annihilate what would almost certainly be a fragmented and disorganized army. Washington would have to trust that some of his other generals, who would remain on the Pennsylvania side of the river until the crossing was complete, would be up to the task of driving the men to keep moving.

Moving down to the water's edge for perhaps the third or fourth time to check on the progress, Washington caught sight of Colonel John Glover, the Massachusetts man who was ultimately responsible for the boats that were carrying the men across. Glover was disembarking from one of the boats for what had already been several trips for the former fisherman. Washington approached the colonel, motioning for Glover to join him several yards away where they could have a private conversation.

"How are things progressing, Colonel Glover?" Washington asked, the tenseness apparent in his voice. Checking his watch, Washington saw that it was already nearly eleven o'clock. The plan called for the army to begin moving toward Trenton no later than midnight, so that everything would be in place for an attack at dawn.

Glover took a second to gather himself. The work of moving the men had been tedious and physical, as the boatmen had been obliged to use long poles to both propel and steer the boats, as well as guide the large chunks of ice that had formed on the river away from the bows of the vessels. The fact that it was a bitterly cold night did nothing to help the situation, further sapping the strength of his men.

"It's going as well as can be expected, considering the conditions, General," remarked the ever-pragmatic Glover. "My men are keeping a steady pace across the river, thanks to these Durhams."

Glover was referring to the Durham boats, which were the main craft being used for the crossing. These boats had been built years earlier when iron ore had been discovered in the local area. In order to transport their amazingly heavy loads down the river and across the river's rapids just north of Philadelphia, the miners had needed boats that were both capable of carrying a large amount of ore while also maintaining a minimal draft on the shallow Delaware River. The Durham boats had just a five inch draft when empty, and only about thirty inches when loaded with up to fifteen tons. This meant that each boat could transport either fifty to sixty men in a single trip, or could safely carry the heavy artillery that would follow, once all of the men had crossed. It was the transportation of these cannon that had worried Washington from the start. He suspected they would pose the greatest challenge to Glover's men, but to attack Trenton without them would be almost suicide.

"Very well, Colonel. Continue with your work. And Colonel Glover — " Washington stated, temporarily halting the man's departure and causing him to turn and face Washington. "Do you remember what you said to me several weeks ago when we discussed our previous retreat across the river? You said the only thing your men wanted was an opportunity to pay back the enemy."

Glover gave a slight smile, his memory recalling the brief conversation he had had with the Commanding General.

"Ay, that I did, General. That I did."

As Glover turned and walked back toward the river and his men, Washington could barely make out the man's parting comment.

"I suppose I should have learned a long time ago to be careful what you wish for."

***

Several hours had passed since his update from Glover, and much to Washington's dismay things had begun to unravel. Just as he had suspected, getting the cannon across the partially frozen river had turned out to be arduous and time consuming, and precious hours were wasted as that process continued at an agonizingly slow pace. Now at almost 4:00 AM the army was not only disastrously behind schedule, but the men had been forced to huddle in small groups trying desperately to fend off the biting cold. To their credit, Washington overheard not a single complaint during his constant movement in and around the landing point. Whether this was due to their fortitude, or the fact that their chattering teeth made speech difficult, was not known.

However, even this critical lapse in the schedule paled in comparison to the other news that Washington had just received. Apparently, neither of the other two detachments of his army had been successful in crossing the river. General Ewing, tasked with setting up a defense at the Assunpink Creek to block the Hessians retreat, had determined that the crossing was impossible. And Lieutenant Colonel Cadwalader and his fifteen hundred men had fared only slightly better attempting to cross the river from their location. Amazingly, Cadwalader had crossed most of his men over, and then had decided that he would be unable to get his artillery across. He had, therefore, crossed his men *back over* the river to their starting point on the Pennsylvania side.

As a result of all of this, not only would Washington be forced to attack the Hessians in broad daylight, but he would be doing so with not three columns of his army, but only one. This had become not only a desperate plan, but it was a plan that had a dwindling chance of success with each passing minute.

Despite these setbacks, Washington was resolved in his decision to attack. There was no turning back now. The very fate of the new independent nation was hanging in the balance, and General George Washington simply refused to give up without a fight.

Appearing out of the darkness was Colonel Henry Knox, the Chief of Artillery for the Continental Army. He approached Washington with just the slightest hesitation, having been made aware just a moment earlier of the failure of the supporting sections of the army to successfully cross the river.

"General, I thought it would be prudent for us to call a meeting of the senior officers, sir, and discuss our options at this point. As you are aware, we are badly behind schedule, and General Ewell and Lieutenant Colonel Cadwalader – "

"Yes, Colonel, I am aware of the situation," Washington snapped impatiently, and immediately regretted his momentary lapse of control. The last thing this army needed right now was for its Commanding General to demonstrate a lack of restraint and discipline, especially when addressing someone like Henry Knox. Few men had done so much to earn respect as had the portly artillery commander. Taking a deep breath, he addressed the colonel with renewed patience in his voice.

"I am aware of our challenges, Colonel Knox. But there will be no need to hold a meeting. Our course of action at this time is dictated by the evening's password – 'Victory or Death'. Now, if you please, issue the necessary orders to begin our movement toward Trenton."

With Knox looking on with a combination of disbelief and deep respect, Washington stomped off into the darkness in search of his mount. Come hell or high water, General George Washington would be at the head of this column of soldiers as they marched their way to Trenton. Tonight, this army didn't need a general – they needed a Leader.

Captain Nathaniel Horne

Pennsylvania State Riflemen, Continental Army

Pennington Road, New Jersey

4:30 AM December 26, 1776

The men had been marching for what felt like weeks, numbly placing one foot in front of the other in a seemingly endless journey that had lost any significance save for its merciful conclusion. A myriad of difficulties contributed to the misery the men were experiencing. Obviously, the bitter cold of the Pennsylvania night sapped a man's strength as quickly as any blistering heat might have done. Many of the men hadn't slept in almost twenty-four hours, having been roused from their slumber before dawn on the previous day to begin preparing for this night's mission. In addition to marching, the men were constantly required to assist with a massive cannon stuck here, a wagon that had fallen into a ditch there. As if the movement of their own pathetic frames wasn't effort enough, they were also responsible for these pieces of equipment so critical to the success of their army.

But ultimately, it was the cold – always the cold.

Despite stringent orders to keep moving under all circumstances, some of the men had given in to their exhaustion and had sat down on the side of the road. As the officers on horseback came upon these men,

Douglas J. Shupinski

they quietly cursed them back onto the road, threatening them with some future punishment worse than what they were going through now. Some of these men simply returned to their previous resting places once the officers had passed, their minds simply not able to envision anything worse than this.

On two occasions, officers were forced to dismount and accost a malingering soldier who simply refused to respond to any orders and threats. Upon further investigation, it had become quickly apparent why the soldiers were being so obstinate – they had frozen to death.

***

Captain Nathaniel Horne was not so fortunate to be one of the officers with a horse. As always, he was marching ahead of the men in his company, enduring the same conditions as they were. His Pennsylvanians had been given the assignment of leading the entire column along these roads, that decision having been made under the misperception that his men might be familiar with these roads and the surrounding terrain. With a very few exceptions, this was simply not the case.

Nathaniel wondered how the rest of the Pennsylvania Riflemen were making out with respect to their part of this undertaking. For reasons that no one chose to share with Nathaniel, he and his company had been temporarily detached from their unit and assigned to General Stirling's Brigade, while the rest of his unit had remained further downriver. This most recent assignment had not sat well with many of Horne's men, who felt uncomfortable being surrounded by soldiers from other colonies. Of course, they knew they could trust a Pennsylvanian next to them in a fight, but a man from Delaware or Maryland or – God forbid, New England – now that was another story.

At least they were no longer in those wretched boats crossing the river. The men had been wedged in so tightly they were barely able to move an inch. The wind had come whipping down the river at a truly horrific speed, immediately sweeping away any body heat that was generated by the closely packed groups. Nathaniel had marveled at the men from Massachusetts who had been tasked with pushing and guiding the boats across the river. Bad enough that he and his men had been forced to endure their single crossing – he simply couldn't imagine the cruel agony of repeating that same journey over and over again. Perhaps these men from New England deserved the benefit of a second opinion.

***

Despite the continuing stormy weather, the first light of dawn came clawing across the New Jersey sky at about seven-thirty, causing mixed emotions in Nathaniel's mind. The approaching day promised at least some relief from the biting cold. But he also knew that the army's plan had been to attack the Hessians in Trenton at daybreak in order to take full advantage of their sleepy confusion. While Nathaniel didn't know exactly where they were, he knew that they weren't coming into position to launch an attack. Apparently, the surprise of a dawn attack was not to be.

However, just a short time later Horne sensed a thinning of the woods that had surrounded them for the last few hours. Sure enough, Nathaniel suddenly found himself at the edge of an open field which stretched off into the distance. Despite the poor visibility caused by the weather, he could just make out a building about 600 hundred yards away that was obviously occupied, evidenced by the thick smoke pouring from its single chimney. And just beyond this structure, perhaps another half mile in the distance, lay a cluster of buildings. Dispersed throughout this cluster of buildings were the massive hulks of artillery pieces arranged in neat rows. Nathaniel felt a sudden rush of adrenaline through his body, the fatigue and cold being washed away and replaced with an immediate anticipation. Trenton!

From behind him, Horne could hear the frantic approach of an officer on horseback. The man arrived beside Horne with a combination of harsh commands and anxious snorts of the animal.

"Captain!" the officer shouted, addressing Nathaniel, "You will immediately deploy your men into line of battle and prepare to advance on that building to our direct front," he said, pointing at the building with the smoking chimney. "That would be a Hessian outpost, and we must attack and silence it before they are able to spread the alarm to the town!"

"Yes, sir!" Horne responded, and began issuing the necessary commands to carry out the order. "Pennsylvanians, form a line of battle on my position! You will form two lines and prepare to advance!"

With remarkable efficiency, considering the agony of the last hours, the men responded automatically to the commands given by their company commander. Sergeants began bellowing their profanity-laden orders, all need for stealth and silence now abandoned.

But even as the men formed as they were directed, Horne saw a man exit the door of the building to their front, lazily buttoning his coat against the early morning cold. With sudden alarm, the man looked directly at the Americans just a short distance away, and immediately returned into the building, all thoughts of tending to his biological needs forgotten.

"Pennsylvanians, advance!" Captain Horne shouted, and his men began moving forward at a steady pace. Within a minute, twenty or so men began pouring out of the building, hastily dressing themselves as they appeared, frantically attempting to organize themselves. One man, clearly the officer in charge of the detachment, began shouting orders, attempting to establish a ragged line of defense.

Captain Horne and his men had continued to advance, and by now had closed the distance to no more than two hundred yards. Horne gave the order to halt and prepare to fire.

"Company, prepare to volley fire!" Horne shouted. "Take aim! Fire!"

The quiet winter morning was shattered with the sound of over a hundred muskets pouring forth their deadly cargo.

"Reload!" Horne shouted. "Prepare for another volley!"

In a matter of seconds, the line of men had reloaded and was anxiously awaiting additional instructions.

"Take aim! Fire!"

A second volley erupted in the direction of the Hessians. But

Nathaniel could clearly see that the distance was too great, the musket balls falling harmlessly to the ground before they could reap their deadly harvest.

This was all the Hessian officer needed to see to know that he was not facing a small raiding party. The arrival of hundreds of additional American soldiers at the edge of the woods indicated that this was, indeed, the impossible enemy attack that he had been told by his commander would never materialize.

With the discipline of true professionals, the Hessians began moving quickly back toward Trenton. Their commanding officer understood clearly that his job was not to engage the enemy, but to provide a warning to the rest of the army located throughout the town.

General George Washington had bet everything on the coming battle. The wisdom of that decision was about to be determined.

Colonel Johann Rall

Hessian Regimental Commander, British Army

Trenton, New Jersey

8:15 AM December 26, 1776

Colonel Rall was awakened, most unceremoniously, by an insistent banging on the front door of the house that served as his quarters. Shaking the sleep from his head, Rall became immediately aware of the sound of nearby firing. His first reaction was one of almost indifference, assuming that one of the American patrols had simply ventured a bit too close to the Hessian stronghold. But a moment later, he was shocked to hear the deep-throated blast of cannon fire. What in God's name?

Colonel Rall jumped from his bed and quickly crossed the room to a nearby window. Throwing it open to the immediately bitter cold, he leaned out to survey the situation. Directly below him was the figure of his adjutant, Lieutenant Jacob Piel. The man looked up at his commander with the expression of someone who had just seen a ghost.

"Lieutenant Piel, what is the meaning of allowing our artillery to waste their ammunition firing at the shadows of – "

"Sir!" Piel interrupted urgently, "that is not *our* artillery that is firing!"

The adjutant's words struck Rall like a thunderbolt, as the implications of that statement quickly organized themselves in his mind.

"Lieutenant Piel," Rall asked, staring down intently at the trembling young officer below him on the street, "do you mean to tell me that what I hear is the firing of *enemy* cannon?"

"Yes, sir," Piel replied, his voice oddly apologetic as if it were in any way the young man's fault. "That is exactly what I beg to report, sir."

"Lieutenant, have my horse brought to my door immediately!" Rall ordered. "Give the order for all units to immediately deploy for combat!"

The stunned adjutant, unable to process the enormity of the situation, stood completely still and continued to stare up at Rall.

"Now, Lieutenant!"

Regaining his senses, Lieutenant Piel gave a hasty salute and scrambled away to issue the directives of the Commanding Officer.

Colonel Rall pulled himself back into the room and angrily slammed the window shut. He grabbed the various pieces of his uniform, quickly getting dressed, choosing not to take his normal fastidious efforts in preparing himself for presentation to his men. Apparently today, action would have to take priority over protocols.

***

Exiting the front door of his quarters, Rall was confronted with a scene that bordered on controlled chaos. Hessian soldiers were running in every direction, some clearly going to their duties, others clearly running away from them. There were the sounds of hundreds of muskets being fired, and dozens of cannon blasts rocked the stormy morning. Johann Rall was well known for his violent temper, but the rage that he could now feel boiling up inside of him was unlike anything he had ever experienced.

An orderly arrived leading Rall's horse, and the commander quickly jumped aboard the animal. Turning in circles to give himself an all-around awareness of the situation, Rall was perturbed at his inability to quickly assess what was happening. A soldier with extensive combat experience, Rall had always prided himself in his battlefield intelligence, possessing an uncanny ability to size up a situation and quickly determine the most appropriate course of action. But something about this current scene forced Rall to pause, desperately attempting to gather additional information with his eyes and ears.

And then it occurred to him. The town wasn't just being attacked from one direction: they were being attacked from at least two different directions, perhaps three. The situation was clearly more serious than he initially believed.

Two main streets called King and Queen Street ran parallel to one another through the town, dividing Trenton from roughly north to south. Facing himself so that he could look southward down King Street, it sounded as if an attack was coming from that direction. However, there also seemed to be some significant activity off to Rall's right, to the west of Trenton. All of this was confused by the fact that the sounds of the battle were echoing off of the tightly packed houses, and a howling wind was whipping down the streets.

Major von Dechow, Rall's second in command, rode up at a full gallop, pulling his mount up sharply as he arrived in front of Rall. Saluting crisply, he addressed the Commanding Officer.

"Colonel Rall, I wish to report, sir, that we are being attacked from several directions by several thousand enemy soldiers who also have a number of cannon at their disposal."

Barely keeping his rage in check, Rall was unable to keep the agitation out of his voice.

"Several directions, several thousand, a number of cannon – damn you, Major, I need more accurate information! We cannot effectively form a defensive line and counterattack with your wispy shots in the dark!"

Major von Dechow, clearly not appreciating Rall's insinuations of incompetence, narrowed his eyes and replied evenly.

"They are not 'shots in the dark', Colonel. This action began no more than a few minutes ago, and it is all of the information that is currently available. Also," von Dechow said carefully, "we are having some difficulty in forming the defensive line of which you speak, as we have no breastworks or fortifications constructed."

Rall gave an evil, hard look at von Dechow, fully appreciating the accusation that was being hurled at him. Rall had received numerous orders from his Hessian commanding officer, Colonel von Donop, to erect defensive positions for his troops and artillery in and around Trenton. In addition, Major von Dechow had practically begged Rall to be allowed to create some protection for the troops throughout the town in the event of an attack. Rall had refused these requests, and had practically laughed at von Dechow's caution. Now, that decision was coming back to haunt Rall, and this subordinate standing in front of him was making sure that it did so.

As the two Hessian officers traded barbs, a battery of American cannon made a sudden appearance at the northern end of King Street, no more than a hundred yards from where Rall and von Dechow were standing. The Americans began to unlimber the guns, and were quickly ready to fire.

At almost the exact same moment, a regiment of Hessian infantry appeared at the southern end of King Street, and began marching in the direction of the enemy artillery. Rall was relieved to see that the Hessian soldiers approaching him were those of his own regiment. Having been the unit on duty the previous evening, these men had been fully armed and dressed, and were therefore able to respond most quickly to the enemy threat. Rall rode down the street to meet his men and take charge of the situation.

"Rall's Regiment!" Rall shouted into the teeth of the winter storm. "Rall's Regiment! Your honor is being attacked today by a pack of cowards! Who wishes to punish the enemy?"

The deep-throated shouts of hundreds of Hessian soldiers rumbled through the winter morning, and the men broke into a double-time step as they passed by Rall, moving quickly in the direction of the American artillery. But before they had gotten closer than about a hundred yards away from their objective, the enemy cannon suddenly erupted sending four rounds of canister fire into the ranks of the unlucky Hessians.

The Americans, apparently anticipating that the battle would take place in close quarters, had wisely chosen to load their artillery pieces with canister shot. This consisted of a metal container containing dozens and dozens of small metal balls. When the canister shell was fired from the cannon, it was like a giant shotgun, spraying those dozens of metal balls in a narrow arc out to a distance of 150 to 200 yards. Unfortunately for Rall's regiment, they were well within the effective range of the canister shots. Even worse, their ranks were closely packed together, the narrow street forcing them into an almost funnel-like attack formation. This first volley of cannon fire literally ripped through the first three or four ranks of the Hessians, tearing off limbs, decapitating men, saturating bodies with awful bits of hot metal.

Some soldiers were thrown backwards into the men immediately behind them, showering them with blood and brains and body parts. Other men, not killed outright by the blasts, but suffering some terrible wound, crawled off to the side of the street, desperately seeking shelter from the storm of metal.

Amazingly, the Hessians continued to advance, but only briefly. The Americans were able to quickly fire a second round, this time the Hessians being within about fifty yards. The effects were even more horrific than the first volley, as several of the closest soldiers virtually exploded as they absorbed the full impact of the canister shot. Blood and body parts were sprayed throughout the street, splattering on the walls of the nearby houses, covering the men in the rear, pouring onto the snow that covered King Street.

The effects of the cannon were simply too much for the Hessians to bear, and they broke and ran back down King Street in the direction of their waiting commander. To make matters worse, the retreating Hessians began receiving musket fire as enemy soldiers continued to pour into the town from several directions.

Rall could scarcely believe what he was seeing. His proud, disciplined men were running as fast as their legs would carry them back down King Street away from the enemy. An enemy that, in Rall's mind, was no army at all, but a band of ruffians. Could it really be these Americans that were attacking his command? The situation was suddenly overwhelming to Rall, and he began to rock back and forth on his horse, speaking to no one in particular.

Map #3: The Battle of Trenton

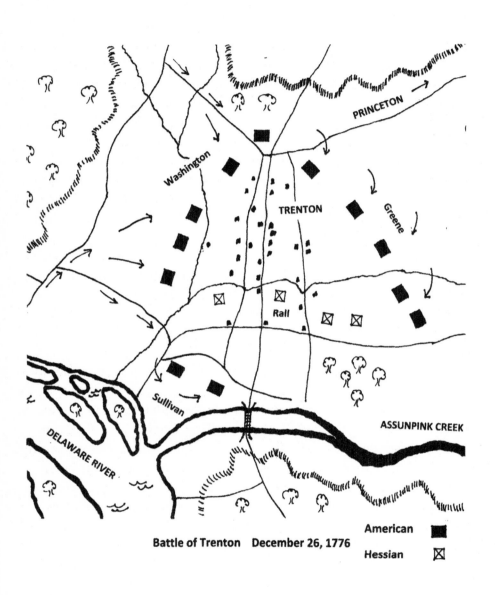

Battle of Trenton   December 26, 1776

American ■
Hessian ⊠

"Dear God, Dear God, what is happening? What is happening? This simply cannot be! These are *my* men! They don't run. They don't retreat. They are Hessians, for God's sake!"

Lieutenant Piel had remained at Rall's side the entire time, the perfect adjutant as always. He now spoke to his disoriented commander.

"Colonel Rall? Colonel Rall, sir. You must see to the disposition of your men, sir. You must issue orders to them. What do you want them to *do*, sir?"

The desperation in the voice of the young lieutenant shocked Colonel Rall out of his bewildered state, and he quickly composed himself. Surveying the situation, he realized that his options were extremely limited. He obviously could not head north up King Street, as that was the direction of the dreaded canister. To his left, he could see hundreds of enemy troops beginning to make their way toward the town, thus making retreat in that direction highly unlikely. Looking behind him, the Americans had already begun to make their way up King Street from that direction.

There was only one choice – he must quickly move his men east, out of the town and into the open where they would have the opportunity to reform and face the enemy in a coordinated defensive position.

"Lieutenant Piel, there is an apple orchard just a few hundred yards outside of town to the east of where we now stand," Rall stated firmly, his confidence beginning to return. "We shall make our way to that orchard, gathering any Hessian troops we encounter. Once we arrive there, we will form into battle lines and prepare to repel the enemy. Is that clear, Lieutenant?"

"Perfectly, sir."

"Good. Now let's move, Lieutenant Piel. If we have any intentions of winning this battle, we must do so in the next few minutes."

Captain Nathaniel Horne

Pennsylvania State Riflemen, Continental Army

Trenton, New Jersey

8:30 AM December 26, 1776

Until just a few minutes earlier, the only thing remarkable about this winter morning was the fact that a major storm was whipping through the area. At this point, that same storm had become the *least* remarkable event.

Captain Nathaniel Horne had been among the first of several hundred American soldiers to approach the town of Trenton from the north, coming down the Pennington Road with the fury of Hell on the unsuspecting Hessians. In addition, Captain Horne could hear the sounds of battle coming from the west, which Nathaniel knew to be the result of the other column of Continental soldiers that had taken the River Road toward Trenton.

Looking around him, Horne saw nothing but the adrenaline of battle evident on the faces of his men. Whereas, less than an hour ago these same men were on the verge of exhaustion, they now exhibited the actions of men who had seemingly enough energy to take on the entire British army.

But it wasn't necessary to take on the entire British army, simply the

Douglas F. Shupinski

Hessian detachment that had been all but marooned here at Trenton. And it had become immediately evident to the men that this attack had come as a complete surprise to the enemy. The obvious chaos, the lack of an organized defense, and the fear in the eyes of the fleeing enemy told them everything they needed to know. General George Washington and the Continental army had the chance to pull off one of the greatest victories in the history of warfare – and they were all a part of it.

However, Captain Horne continued to remind himself of one small detail: the actual battle had to be fought – and won. Despite the surprise achieved by the Americans, the Hessians were still a formidable group of soldiers, and more than capable of rallying themselves and conducting a vicious counterattack. The key to preventing such a maneuver was to press the attack with a violent resolve, not stopping to regroup, not even stopping to take prisoners.

Earlier, Captain Horne had reported up through the chain of command that the weather had caused the cartridges of most of his men's muskets to become wet and unusable. The response from General Washington had left no doubt: there was no turning back – they were to use the bayonet. Apparently, Washington had already considered this possibility.

Nathaniel had felt some concern with respect to that scenario. In previous engagements, the Americans had demonstrated an obvious lack of enthusiasm for using the rather barbaric pointed weapon at the ends of their muskets. The enemy, on the other hand, had been only too willing to subject the Americans to the effects of cold steel. In particular, the Hessians had displayed an almost giddy willingness to skewer their enemy with a callousness that, quite honestly, drove the fear of God into the Americans.

Well, now the tables were turned. The Continental Army was approaching these same Hessians, except now it was the Americans who had the opportunity to employ the bayonet. Captain Horne worried that his men might not have the stomach to take the battle to the enemy in a manner that would insure success.

Captain Nathaniel Horne need not have worried.

The Americans swept into Trenton with a force that made the existing winter storm seem like nothing more than a gentle breeze. Shouting at the tops of their lungs, their teeth bared in the anticipation of face to face combat, the Americans hurled themselves down King and Queen Streets. Anything in their path was destroyed with heartless impunity. A unit of Hessians had formed in a battle line in the middle of King Street, their faces set in an expression of determination. In a matter of seconds, the Americans had plowed into their ranks, slashing with the butts of their muskets, thrusting their bayonets into the bodies of the enemy. The Hessian defense lasted no more than a minute before the few survivors broke into a panicked dash away from their attackers.

Behind them, the retreating Hessians left a dozen or more of their comrades lying on the ground. Some were writhing painfully from the effects of the muskets and bayonets, blood pouring crazily onto the previously pure white snow, turning it into a macabre mixture of red gore. Others were splayed in a variety of grotesque positions, their bodies lying still, or twitching with the spasms of their final death throes.

"Come on, Pennsylvanians, follow me!" Horne shouted into the wind of the storm, and his men responded with a chorus of shouts and cheers. "Keep moving down the street – we must continue to drive them!"

Horne's men did as they were ordered, the fury of the battle providing all the energy that was necessary. Looking around him, Horne was pleased to see that his unit was still intact, and casualties appeared to be non-existent. No time to worry about such things right now, Nathaniel chastised himself. Counting the corpses and tending to the wounded could be done at the conclusion of the battle.

From one of the side streets that lined King Street, a group of Hessians appeared, apparently set on halting the advance of the Americans. Estimating their number to be no more than a hundred or so, Horne couldn't help but be impressed at the bravery of this small group of men willing to stand up to the onslaught of the attacking Americans that probably outnumbered them three to one. With a sound that was more of a growl than a shout, the Hessians leveled their bayonets and advanced toward Horne and his men.

Tragically for these Hessians, they were quickly attacked from three sides by the numerically superior Americans and the final result was only a matter of time. But it became immediately evident that these Hessians had no intention of going away quietly.

One Hessian, almost certainly a grenadier based on his massive size, bore down on Nathaniel, a look of sheer hatred in his dark eyes. Horne was just able to slash aside the thrust of the man's bayonet, its blade passing precariously close to the side of his head. Nathaniel swung the butt of his musket with all of his strength, feeling the dull crunch as it impacted with the man's jaw. The Hessian staggered backward, temporarily disoriented by the blow, but quickly gathered himself and renewed his attack.

This time, Nathaniel struck first, thrusting his bayonet at the center of the man's huge body. Despite the fact that the Hessian was able to slightly dodge the attack, it didn't prevent Horne from scoring a glancing slash to the man's side, laying open a ragged gash that began to spew blood into the air.

The Hessian looked down at his side in disbelief, unable to comprehend the fact that this rebel had actually bested him in the first round of their fight. Roaring with an almost animal-like sound, the Hessian hurled himself back at Horne, leveling his musket and driving Nathaniel to the ground. The man quickly brought his bayonet to bear, and launched himself at Horne for the final killing blow. All Nathaniel could do was to weakly raise his own musket in a defensive move that he knew would be futile.

For some unknown reason, the Hessian suddenly stopped in the middle of his attack, his eyes becoming confused and unfocused, his musket dropping to the ground. The man stumbled forward a step or two, and then fell to his knees, a thick stream of blood suddenly spewing forth from his open mouth. Then, as quickly as his rage had appeared, the Hessian's face took on an almost sleepy quality, and he toppled to the ground, face first.

Behind the massive Hessian stood an oddly grinning Private Cronin, the same soldier who had been shot harmlessly in the ponytail during the retreat from Brooklyn Heights. He had just pulled his bayonet, dripping with blood, from the back of the giant Hessian. Somehow out of context for the violently chaotic scene still playing out all around the two men, Cronin leaned down and offered his hand to Horne, helping him to his feet.

"You told me once that the enemy wouldn't harm a hair on my head, eh, sir?" Cronin asked. "Well Captain Horne, that didn't mean I felt the same way about them, now did it?"

Suddenly light-headed from the intensity of his recent encounter, Horne was only able to reply weakly to this man who had just saved his life.

"Apparently not, Private Cronin. Apparently not."

***

Small, vicious fights continued to swirl throughout the stormy streets of Trenton, some taking place on the main streets between larger groups of soldiers, others involving perhaps only seven or eight men on the numerous side streets of the town. In virtually every case, the Hessians found themselves uncharacteristically outnumbered, in some instances overwhelmingly so. The Americans began to see something they had rarely seen before in this war – the enemy surrendering. But this occurred only when the Hessians realized there was absolutely no other recourse other than death – and even then, many chose to die fighting rather than suffer the indignity of surrendering to the Americans.

However, for every Hessian that surrendered or was cut down, dozens of others were making their way eastward in an obvious attempt to organize themselves at some as yet unknown location. Captain Horne instinctively knew that the key to bringing this battle to a successful conclusion for the Americans was to prevent the enemy from doing just that.

"Come on, men, don't dally!" he shouted. "We've done some fine work, but we're far from being finished. Follow me!"

For the countless time this day, the brave men from Pennsylvania leaned into the biting winter wind, and followed their captain.

Douglas J. Shupinski

Sergeant Alexander Bickell

Hesse-Cassell Division, British Army

Trenton, New Jersey

8:45 AM December 26, 1776

It was as if the whole world had turned upside down, and all of the comforting rules of warfare had ceased to exist.

Sergeant Alexander Bickell had always known two things to be absolute truths during his time in America. First, a Rebel could never stand up to a Hessian in battle. And second, Hessian soldiers never surrendered. These facts, in Bickell's mind, were as unshakeable as the sun rising each morning.

Based on what had occurred in the last hour, Alexander Bickell was beginning to wonder if he would ever see the sun rise again. For the first time in his military career since becoming a sergeant, the men in Bickell's unit were more afraid of something else other than *him*.

Bickell was like a man deranged, shouting and cursing at the top of his lungs, grabbing retreating Hessians as they streamed by him in the street, ordering them into formation so they could halt the attack of the Americans. But he might have saved his energy. Although an occasional man stopped and took up a position on either side of him, most of the others continued to run past him in search of some safe haven in the terrible storm of flying lead and thrusting bayonets. Even those that stood by Bickell's side did so only briefly, some being almost immediately cut down by a musket ball, others losing their momentary bravery to the overwhelming violence of the situation.

Finally, however, Sergeant Bickell had succeeded in getting a group of men to stand together and offer something in the way of a line of defense. It was no more than fifty or sixty men, but it was enough to offer some amount of resistance to the surge of Americans that was making its way through the town.

Bickell knew from experience that this group had the potential to form the core around which an ultimate defense could be built. On numerous occasions in the past, Bickell had seen the tide of a battle changed by a surprisingly small group of men who chose to either make a stand or launch an attack against what appeared to be overwhelming odds. This small group could galvanize the rest of the army, giving them hope where none had existed just a few moments before.

Now was the time for that stand.

"Hessians, form to my right and left!" Bickell shouted, ordering the group to position themselves on either side of him. Now was not the time to lead from the rear. Bickell knew that if these men were to remain firm in the face of the enemy onslaught, it would have to be by his own example. Slowly, clearly against their instincts, the men took up positions on either side of this sergeant who apparently knew what he was doing.

Looking to his right and left, Bickell could see the fear on the faces of these men. He had seen it before. Eyes darting quickly in all directions; men continuously licking their lips; constant, unnecessary hand movements to touch the face, clearing it of some nonexistent pest; these were all the signs of men unsure of themselves at a time when self-confidence was perhaps the most important virtue of all.

Sergeant Bickell and his men were at the southernmost point of King Street, where it intersected with Second Street. From that position, Bickell was able to see enemy soldiers pouring down King Street directly at them. As if that weren't enough, off to the left there were more Americans coming at them, their wild shouts clearly audible in the bitterly cold morning. Bickell quickly made the decision to retreat the hundred yards or so to the intersection of Queen and Second Streets. This maneuver would result in the two enemy columns coming together, allowing his men to face only a frontal assault, as opposed to an attack from both their front and their flank.

"Hessians!" Bickell shouted, "retreat at the double time! We will re-form at the next intersection and prepare to repel the enemy!"

Sergeant Bickell was relieved to see that the men quickly and efficiently obeyed his orders, maintaining their formation as they moved back to the next intersection. Once there, Bickell had them execute an about face and confront the attacking Americans.

It was at that point that Sergeant Bickell realized how hopeless his situation really was. As the two enemy forces met one another at the intersection of King and Second Street and began moving toward him and his men, he saw that they were facing literally hundreds of Americans. The enemy force came to a brief halt just long enough to raise their muskets and fire a volley at this group of Hessians who had the audacity to stand up to their unstoppable force.

Despite the fact that the volley was fired quickly with little attempt at accuracy, the sheer volume of metal sent hurtling in their direction had an awful effect on Bickell's tiny group. Some men pitched backwards, in many cases hit by two, three, or even four musket balls on all parts of their bodies. These were the relatively lucky ones, as they were generally dead by the time they hit the frozen ground.

Other men suffered wounds to their arms and legs, which would almost certainly result in the amputation of the limb and, in many cases, an agonizingly slow death due to infection. The man to Bickell's immediate left suddenly dropped his musket and clawed at his stomach, eventually doubling over and collapsing to the ground. Glancing at the gushing gut wound, Bickell knew from experience that the man had no more than a few painful minutes of life remaining as his blood quickly exited his body in vicious crimson torrents onto the contrasting white snow.

The carnage all around them was simply more than the remaining Hessians could take, and they soon broke their formation and ran eastward down Second Street. They had no idea where they were going, but any place had to be better than this deathtrap they were now facing.

***

Quite unexpectedly, Sergeant Bickell found himself completely alone. Looking behind him, he could see the backs of dozens of Hessian soldiers making their way toward the small bridge that crossed the Assunpink Creek a short distance outside of the town. Looking back to his front, Bickell was shocked by the volume of shouting Americans who had renewed their advance and were heading quickly in his direction.

Sergeant Bickell came to the nauseating realization that there was no hope in continuing his stubborn defense. A one man stand on his part would be nothing more than a ridiculous gesture that would result in yet another notch on the belts of the enemy. Fighting back everything he had been taught as a proud Hessian soldier, he raised his musket and fired one final defiant shot in the direction of the Americans. Then, willing his legs to obey his brain's commands, he followed his fellow Hessians toward the creek and possible escape.

Colonel Johann Rall

Hessian Regimental Commander, British Army

Trenton, New Jersey

9:15 AM December 26, 1776

The orchard was a scene of chaos. Several hundred Hessian soldiers had obeyed the order they had received to escape from the town and re-form at their present location. However, despite the best efforts of a number of officers, the men were little more than a confused mob that wandered about and cursed at their situation, any semblance of unit cohesion lost in the jumble of soldiers that had arrived haphazardly to this small area just a few hundred yards east of Trenton.

Arriving on horseback at the orchard accompanied by what remained of his staff, Colonel Johann Rall was faced with a situation that was new and disturbing. Normally the epitome of good discipline and order, these men were conducting themselves in a manner that he had previously attributed to the inexperienced Americans that were now chasing them down. Rall had never accepted even the slightest deviation from proper military bearing from his troops, let alone this gross display of unprofessionalism he was seeing now. Despite the vicious cold that refused to release its grip on the morning, Rall could feel his face burning as if it were on fire.

Riding to the center of the roiling mass of humanity, Colonel Rall rose up in his saddle and shouted like a madman with all the force in his body.

"Damn you all to Hell!" he nearly screamed. "What is the meaning of this? You are Hessian soldiers, by God!"

The colonel's outburst caused many of the men to stop their own shouting and cursing, and gradually they began to focus on their Commanding Officer.

"You are the bravest, best trained fighting men in the world – in the world!" Rall shouted. "You have never given up on a fight before in your lives! You have never been afraid of anything!"

A low rumbling began to come from the men, as many of them lifted their heads and began straightening their uniforms into some form of military presentation. Others began picking up their recently discarded weapons, checking them for their serviceability.

Rall continued his tirade, his energy flowing like a powerful force through his own body and out into the bodies of the men around him.

"These Americans are not attacking Trenton! They are not attacking you as an individual! They are attacking the Honor of the Hessian military! Now, who will stand with me and show these rebels what it means to be a soldier?"

The roar of hundreds of German voices split the morning air, arms and muskets raised to the sky, a spark of bravery coming back into each man's eyes.

"I am Colonel Johann Rall! You are my men, and I am your commander! Organize around your officers and prepare to face the enemy with me now!"

With a precision borne of new found confidence, the Hessians quickly arranged themselves into makeshift units around officers who struggled mightily to prepare them to attack.

"Sir, I beg to report the situation," stuttered a flustered captain who had come riding at breakneck speed, skidding his horse to a halt directly in front of Rall.

Having regained his composure, Colonel Rall calmly addressed the young officer.

"Very well, Captain, make your report."

"Sir, the enemy has established very strong blocking forces to our north between us and the Princeton Road. In addition, they also have several hundred men positioned on either side of the bridge across the Assunpink Creek to our east."

The captain's eyes were nearly bulging from his head, indicating he clearly understood the significance of this information. Colonel Rall immediately grasped the meaning of the message as well; the Americans had effectively cut off any route of retreat out of Trenton.

"Damn it!" Rall cursed under his breath. Despite the sudden pang of fear he experienced, Rall knew that this was not the time to show the slightest hesitation in his commands.

"Very well, then," Rall concluded quickly, "then our opportunity lies in an attack back through Trenton to re-take possession of the town. From there, we will hold a solid position from which we can either attack in any direction, or successfully repel any attack by the enemy."

Rall knew that his statement smacked of gross overconfidence, and the looks on the faces of the officers around him clearly indicated they knew this as well. Even if they were to successfully recapture the town, they would still find themselves outmanned and outgunned. Nevertheless, a glimmer of hope was better than no hope at all.

Colonel Johann Rall faced his staff and drew his sword, pointing it toward the small group of buildings a short distance away. In a level, determined voice, he issued his order.

"Prepare to attack!"

***

The Hessians marched toward Trenton in perfect battle formation, even managing to keep in step. They were aided in this endeavor, somewhat oddly, by a small group of musicians who followed closely behind the infantry playing a rather sprightly Germanic tune.

While Colonel Rall had originally intended to lead his troops from the front of the formation, he had been convinced by his staff that such a location would almost certainly result in his immediate death at the hands of the rebel marksmen. Rall was forced to admit that, not only had these Americans proved to be excellent shots, but they also had not the slightest compunction in targeting the highest ranking enemy officers. Instead, Rall had chosen to be directly behind his men, still no more than a few yards from the leading edge of the attacking column.

At this point, the houses of Trenton were less than a hundred yards away, and Colonel Rall had seen very few enemy soldiers. He was beginning to wonder if the enemy had vacated the town in pursuit of some of the other Hessian units when a volley of musket fire exploded to his front. The flashes of the American muskets were clearly visible from the windows and doorways of the buildings, as well as from behind fences, walls, and any other structure that might provide protection.

Rall immediately noted that the reputation for marksmanship was well deserved, as quite a number of his men collapsed to the ground, victims of the horrible effects delivered by the massive musket balls. The Hessian officers began shouting at the men to close their ranks and maintain order, which was done with perfect precision. A second volley from the town had a similar effect on the men, but they seemed almost impervious to this one, as they had gotten their blood up and were beginning to move forward with greater speed and determination.

Colonel Rall, still astride his horse immediately behind the Hessian lines, shouted encouragement to his men.

"That's it, Hessians! Prepare to give them the bayonet! Drive them from behind those fences, out of the houses – this day is yours!"

At that moment, a deafening roar erupted to the right of the Hessian column, and the men furthest out on the right flank appeared to simply vanish. Riding quickly in that direction, Rall was horrified at what he saw. A dozen or more men – at least that was what they had been until just a moment ago – lay scattered on the frozen ground, their shattered bodies sprayed into the air, into the snow, onto their comrades marching close by.

A battery of American artillery had waited until the perfect moment to unleash its deadly cargo on the attacking Hessians. A moment later, a sizable force of American infantry located in the same position as the artillery delivered a devastating volley that claimed more victims.

While all of this was occurring on Rall's right flank, the enemy soldiers in the town now no more than fifty yards away continued to reap their deadly harvest from the Hessian front ranks. It was a bloodbath.

Colonel Rall realized that if he were to continue his attack, his entire force would be annihilated within a few minutes. Knowing it was his only option, yet still hesitating to give the command, Rall finally bellowed out to his men.

"Retreat! Officers, order the retreat back to the orchard!"

As his officers repeated their commander's orders, Rall rode back and forth along the lines, now pointing his sword in the opposite direction away from the death that awaited them in the town. Rall felt a sudden pain in his right thigh, and knew immediately that he had been wounded. Looking down, he could see a stream of bright red blood flowing from a hole in his uniform trousers. Well, he thought to himself, my men have certainly suffered far worse than that. If I ask them to continue this fight, then I must do the same.

As the Hessians made their urgent withdrawal back to the orchard, the air was alive with the zinging of enemy musket balls. All around, men continued to fall painfully to the ground, as they became the most recent successful targets of the Americans. Several other volleys of cannon fire did their damage as well, but not as badly as the first shots that had greeted the men with such a terrible surprise.

Colonel Rall continued to encourage his men, but he couldn't seem to shake a sudden fatigue that had crept into his body. Although he was fifty-six years old, a relatively advanced age considering the line of work he was in, he had always possessed vast reserves of energy, sometimes outworking and outfighting men half his age. For some reason, these reserves were nowhere to be found.

Colonel Rall arrived at the small orchard just a minute or two before his retreating army, intent on organizing a suitable defensive position. However, much to his dismay there was even more confusion here than within his retreating ranks. Men were milling about with no idea of what to do, and, to Rall's horror, that included the officers.

Rall rode back toward his retreating Hessians, urging them to make haste toward the orchard which offered some semblance of protection from the closely pursuing Americans. And close they were. Barely fifty yards away from the Hessians bringing up the rear of the retreat, Rall could see hundreds of enemy soldiers moving quickly but intently towards them.

If Rall was going to have any time to organize his men, he needed to discourage the Americans from their dogged pursuit. That meant a rearguard action needed to be executed by those Hessians closest to the enemy. Rall realized that he was the only one who recognized this, and therefore had to be the one to take direct responsibility for making that maneuver. To that end, he began to move his horse back in the direction of the enemy, intent on buying his men some much needed time.

Colonel Rall had gone no more than thirty or forty yards when he suddenly felt like he had been punched in the side, not once, but twice. The wind was knocked from his body, and he fell from his horse, toppling onto the snow-covered ground. Two Hessian soldiers close by rushed to their Commanding Officer, and carefully helped him to his feet.

"Back to your position, men," Rall ordered the two soldiers. "You must hold back the Americans until we are able to organize ourselves in the orchard."

Colonel Rall was surprised to see that his orders registered no effect on the two men, as they continued to support him.

"Did you not hear me?" Rall repeated. Back to your positions with your units. You must…"

As Rall's voice trailed off into the whipping December wind, he realized that he was speaking in little more than a whisper. These two men weren't disobeying his orders – they simply couldn't hear him.

Rall felt himself being dragged in the direction of a small building close by that he vaguely recalled being a Methodist church. Busting through the door of God's house most unceremoniously, the two Hessians gently laid their commander onto one of the wooden pews just inside the door.

The two men stepped back away from their commander, not sure of what to do next, and Rall got his first good look at these saviors. He could see that both men were virtually covered in blood, and he momentarily thought that he had been rescued by men who had suffered their own terrible wounds. But then the situation dawned on him – the men were covered with *his* blood.

Rall was cold, terribly cold – much more so than could be explained simply by the weather. And the earlier fatigue was now working its way deep into his bones. Perhaps it will be all right if I simply rest for a moment or two, he thought. Then my two bodyguards and I can rejoin the fight. Perhaps I can yet coordinate the men to defend themselves, and then launch a much needed counterattack.

He opened his mouth to explain his plans to the two men, but now there was even less than a whisper. Now, there was nothing.

General George Washington

Commanding General, Continental Army

Trenton, New Jersey

9:30 AM December 26, 1776

While the winter weather continued to fill the air with the sound of rushing wind and a mixture of rain and snow, the manmade sounds of battle began to decrease dramatically. What had been a cacophony of cannon and muskets just a few minutes before had deteriorated into a few pops of random musket fire at various spots in and around the town.

From his position just east of Trenton, General George Washington had observed the events of the last hour and a half with a mixture of anticipation and concern, as the poor visibility and numerous buildings had conspired to block his view of the battle. Any attempts he had made to move closer to the action had been adamantly discouraged by his staff, who insisted the best place for the Commanding General was a position from which he could receive reports and coordinate the overall disposition of the army. While Washington knew this to be sound advice, he nevertheless chafed at his inability to have a clear understanding of what was happening.

Reports from several enlisted and officer couriers had allowed him to patch together the events of the morning, each messenger delivering positive news that the Americans had caught the Hessians totally unprepared and were driving them back into small pockets of desperate resistance. From the sound of the battle, as well as occasional glimpses of the town through the mix of snow and smoke, Washington could tell that the outcome of the struggle had come down to the small orchard off to his right, and the southern part of Trenton off to his left.

However, it wasn't until the arrival of these two most recent officers that Washington allowed himself to truly believe what he had hoped for since the moment this attack had formulated itself in his mind.

***

"General Washington, I beg to report that the Hessians who retreated to the orchard to our north have laid down their arms and surrendered!"

The message was delivered by Major George Baylor, a member of Washington's staff who had been sent in that direction to determine the status of the situation. Baylor's disposition was one of pure joy and enthusiasm, and several men within earshot let out whoops of victory. However, they were quickly silenced by a stern look from their commander.

"Very well, Major," Washington replied calmly. "Do you have any new information with respect to the situation in the southern part of the town?"

Baylor, initially confused by the sober response of his commander, quickly regained his military bearing and responded to Washington's question.

"No sir, I have no word from that part of the field. But our most recent reports were very positive regarding General St.Clair's ability to continue driving the enemy backward."

Despite himself, Washington felt a strong irritation at the officer's remark. Of course, the man was simply repeating what everyone had heard, but the almost flippant response was not yet warranted at this point in the battle, at least in Washington's mind.

"I know what the *most recent reports* have indicated, Major," Washington replied coldly. "My question was, are you aware of any *new* information?"

Even as the words left his mouth, Washington knew that it was unfair to expect Baylor to know what was happening in an area of the battlefield that he had not visited. He quickly pushed his irritation aside, and addressed the man in a respectful matter-of-fact tone.

"Major Baylor, I very much appreciate your report of our success at the orchard. I am simply being cautious that we don't become too confident of the overall situation. We are, after all, facing a very well trained and capable army today."

"Of course, sir," Baylor stammered. "At your request, sir, I will immediately ride to the southern part of town and attempt to ascertain – "

Major Baylor was interrupted by the almost explosive arrival of Major James Wilkinson, another member of Washington's staff. Both Wilkinson and his horse were breathing heavily with what was obviously a recent journey that had been made with the greatest haste. Whatever information this man had was clearly of major significance. Washington felt a sudden tug at the pit of his stomach, preparing himself for the worst.

"General Washington, everything has collapsed in the southern part of town, sir!" Wilikinson stated breathlessly.

"Collapsed?" Washington asked, his worst fears suddenly being realized. "In what way?"

"The Hessians, sir! They have completely collapsed in that part of town, and have offered an unconditional surrender!"

This time, Washington allowed the men around him to erupt with a victory yell. God knew, if any army had ever deserved a celebration, it was these men now standing around him, and those amazing soldiers over there in the town that had made this moment a reality for all of them.

For his part, General Washington maintained his almost constant control of himself, at least outwardly. He offered not a shout of enthusiasm, nor a word of congratulations to anyone. But that was only because any attempt to speak would have been choked with such emotion that his men would have thought he had completely lost his

Douglas J. Shupinski

mind.

***

Almost an hour had passed since the fighting had ceased. The chaos that always followed a battle was beginning to sort itself out, as the Americans had finally begun to reorganize the many units that had become jumbled together over the last two or three hours. In addition, there were hundreds of Hessian prisoners that had been gathered into the center of town, having been relieved of their weapons and any other military possessions.

Washington was now waiting tensely for the final report of the day: American casualties.

Washington tried to convince himself that these casualties were necessary if victory was to be achieved. He rationalized that these men that had sacrificed their lives had done so in pursuit of a greater good that was worth dying for. While all of that may have been true, he could never avoid the feeling of profound sadness when he learned of the men that would no longer march into battle. Washington also knew that, were he to ever lose that sadness, he would have lost his humanity and should not be in command of an army.

General Sullivan came riding up, a piece of paper fluttering from his right hand as he arrived. Washington knew by the serious look on Sullivan's face that the paper he carried contained the numbers of casualties.

"General Washington, I wish to deliver the casualty report, sir," Sullivan said, extending the paper toward Washington.

"Read it to me," Washington ordered, closing his eyes and turning his head slightly to the side.

"Sir, I'm afraid I must report that Captain Washington and Lieutenant Monroe have both been wounded, although both are expected to recover. In addition, two privates were wounded as well."

"Please continue, General Sullivan."

A long pause hung in the air before Sullivan spoke again.

"There's nothing further to report, sir."

Washington opened his eyes and looked directly at Sullivan.

"How many dead?" Washington asked carefully.

A slight smile appeared on Sullivan's face, hardly the expression one would have expected when being asked such a grisly question. Sullivan spoke in a low voice, his own amazement clearly apparent.

"None, sir. None of our men were killed in the battle, sir."

Washington stared in disbelief at Sullivan for a few seconds, finally managing to speak.

"Are you telling me that this army suffered a total of four wounded men in the course of winning this battle?"

The slight smile on Sullivan's face was now a broad grin, as he nodded his head in affirmation.

"That's exactly what I'm telling you, General Washington."

Washington reached out and took the paper from Sullivan, looking at the numbers for himself.

"Dear God," he whispered. "It's a miracle!"

"If I may add to this miraculous result, sir," Sullivan continued, "I also have the preliminary numbers for the enemy. There are several dozen dead, nearly a hundred wounded, and at first count, approximately one thousand prisoners."

For the first time in weeks, Washington felt as if a heavy weight had been lifted from his chest. He had gambled with this army – with the lives of these men – and he had won. But never in his wildest dreams could he have ever hoped for such a result. For the second time this day he felt a welling of emotion that, for also the second time today, he quickly suppressed.

"Very well, General Sullivan. That is outstanding news, indeed. Please deliver my congratulations to the men."

"It would be my pleasure to do so, sir. But perhaps it would be more appropriate for you to address the men yourself, General."

Washington considered the offer briefly, but quickly dismissed it.

"Perhaps at some point in the near future I shall do just that, General Sullivan. However, right now we don't have that luxury. Major Baylor!"

Baylor moved immediately to Washington's side and saluted.

Douglas J. Shupinski

"At your service, sir," he stated simply.

"Major Baylor, issue orders to have my commanders report to me immediately. We must make immediate preparations to get the army back on the march."

Sullivan and Baylor looked at their commander, the surprise obvious on their faces.

"Of course, sir," Baylor responded. "I shall see to it right away. If I may inquire, sir – well, if I'm asked by the commanders…"

Major Baylor hesitated, not sure if he was about to breach some military protocol in questioning his Commanding General about his orders.

"If asked where we are marching to, Major?" Washington said, completing the question. "We are moving back to our camps in Pennsylvania."

The look of shock was obvious on the faces of the men around him. It was now Sullivan's turn to speak up.

"Sir, with all due respect, the men have been on the move for over twenty-four hours. Many of them have not slept nor eaten for much longer than that. In addition, sir – well, there is also the matter of having fought and won a major engagement against the enemy. Is it – well, sir, is it reasonable to expect them to move?"

Washington fully appreciated the gravity of the orders he was issuing. He knew his men were exhausted and were in desperate need of rest. But he also realized something else.

"General Sullivan, it is *reasonable* to assume that the sound of this battle may have attracted the attention of other enemy units in the area. If so, that information is now being passed on to General Howe as we speak. As a result, I will not rest – this army will not rest – until we have once again placed the Delaware River between us and the enemy."

The officers nodded their heads in unison, fully comprehending the situation.

"Now, Major Baylor, if you please. Deliver my instructions at once."

General George Washington

Commanding General, Continental Army

Assunpink Creek, New Jersey

3:00 PM December 30, 1776

As they assembled into what could only loosely be referred to as a formation, the soldiers of the American Continental Army looked as exhausted and miserable as they had ever looked. Not only was this day one of the coldest of the year, but these men had just completed yet another crossing of the Delaware River from the Pennsylvania side back to New Jersey. To many of the soldiers, and even some the officers, this crossing and re-crossing was beginning to become tiresome.

***

When General Washington had ordered the army to march from Trenton back to the Delaware River following their victory in order to place the river between the Americans and the British, the men had understood the reasoning. The order hadn't been popular, and it certainly hadn't been easy to execute, but there had been a certain logic to their General's actions. They had marched to the river, crossed in the

Douglas J. Shupinski

bitter cold of the day during which two more of their number froze to death, and finally collapsed at their camp in Pennsylvania.

But this most recent order to cross the Delaware River back into New Jersey had been extraordinarily unpopular for two reasons. First, unlike the crossing on Christmas night, this time the British were alert and ready, to say the least. Intelligence reports received by Washington had indicated that the British were embarrassed and outraged, and bent on revenge as soon as possible. It seemed to many of the Americans that this re-crossing back into New Jersey was giving the British the exact opportunity they were looking for. But even more significant than the readiness of the British was the lack of enthusiasm for the move: nearly every member of the Continental Army was due to be discharged from their agreed upon military service in just over 24 hours.

For a vast majority of the men, there had really been no consideration of re-enlistment, despite the fact that the offer to do so had been made repeatedly by their officers. In the minds of these men, they had done their part – many would say more than their part – and now it was time for others to step up and carry their share of the burden in making the thirteen colonies an independent country.

The problem for George Washington was that very few men had chosen to step up and fill these soon to be empty places. And those few replacements that were due to arrive in the coming weeks were completely inexperienced. Washington knew that if there was to be any chance of winning this war, it would be won by men who had the combat experience to face the British and Hessians on the field of battle, and not be intimidated.

***

The troops quickly quieted down as General Washington made his appearance at the front of the formation atop his seemingly ever-present horse. Despite the fact that most of these men were soon to be civilians, their respect and admiration for the man in front of them would never falter, regardless of their military status. The consensus among the men was that Washington had asked to speak to them in order to offer his thanks for their service, and wish them luck as they returned deservedly to their families and homes. Perhaps even a fond recounting of their time together would be offered by the Commanding General, although most doubted that such a speech would take place. While George Washington was well respected as a military leader, he had never been known as much of an orator. Such activities were usually left to the other generals, with Washington merely providing the key points for them to cover.

Washington couldn't help but become briefly choked with emotion as he surveyed what remained of his army. The men that stood before him had endured and accomplished what few armies in the history of the world had been capable of, but their appearance belied that fact. What was, by all measures, an army made up of some of the greatest soldiers that had ever carried a weapon into combat, it looked more like a gathering of desperate, forlorn men who had seen more horror and hardship than any man should have to witness in a hundred lifetimes. They were tired, they were cold, and they were hungry. And most of all, they deserved to go home.

It was for these reasons that George Washington was dreading this moment as he had never dreaded anything before in his life.

Thousands of breaths condensed in the bitterly cold morning air, as these magnificent men awaited the words of their General. When he spoke, Washington did so slowly and deliberately, wanting every word to land with impact and significance.

"Gentlemen, in the last few days you have accomplished a great victory. It was a victory that was against all odds, and it has completely changed the nature of this war. For the first time, victory and independence are realities to this army and to this country."

The men remained silent, long past the point of cheering in response to statements that they knew to be the absolute truth.

"But there is much more to be done," Washington continued. "While we have been victorious, this army must fight on, and it must fight on with a source of strength that will guarantee our ultimate success. That source of strength, gentlemen, is experience. It is experience gained through blood and pain and sacrifice. That source of strength – is you."

Almost to a man, the soldiers were dumbstruck by Washington's statement. What was he asking them? To remain as members of this army? To continue to give more blood and pain and sacrifice? They had done their part; it was time to go home.

"I realize that many of you may hesitate to remain with this army. I appreciate that you feel your commitment to this nation has been satisfied. It is for this reason that I offer you two incentives to consider: First, I am only asking that you remain with me for six more weeks. That period of time will allow me to recruit new soldiers, and will allow some time for you to teach them what you have learned. In addition, any man who agrees to stay for these six weeks will receive a bounty of ten dollars."

A brief murmur rippled through the ranks as the men reacted to Washington's offer. Ten dollars was the equivalent of several months of pay, and would certainly make for a nice start to their new civilian life. Even so, these men were beyond money being a true incentive: they were desperate for peace and quiet.

"Regimental commanders," Washington ordered, "take charge of your men and call forward those who choose to remain with the army."

Washington moved to the side of the formation, a harsh drum roll echoing into the still winter air, and the regimental commanders shouted out for every man to step forward who would remain a soldier. When the orders were completed, the drum roll ceased, and Washington gazed hopefully over the formation.

Not a single man had stepped forward.

Washington was incredulous. While he hadn't expected every man to choose to remain, even for the brief time expected and the bounty, he had at least expected a majority of the soldiers to rise to the occasion. Unable to contain himself, overcome with an emotion borne of desperation, Washington rode back to the front of the army and addressed them.

"Gentlemen, I know you are all anxious to return to your homes and families. But without freedom – without independence from a tyrant – what will you be returning *to*? You will never be the true master of your own destiny as long as we must carry the yoke of tyranny upon our backs."

The men, visibly uncomfortable, and many embarrassed, shifted from one foot to the other as the words of their Commanding General settled upon them. These men that still remained were patriots to their very core, and they believed very deeply in the Cause for which they had fought. Washington's words were hitting them in a place that was extremely special to all of them.

"We have come this far," Washington implored them, driving home his appeal. He paused and looked at the gathered soldiers. "We have come this far."

As Washington stared across the formation, each man swore that Washington was looking directly at *him*.

"Come with me just a bit farther," Washington stated quietly but forcefully, the men straining to hear his every word. "And we will create a Nation that will change the world."

Emotionally exhausted, Washington rode back to his position at the side of the formation, a silent order for the regimental commanders to again take charge. While the commanders stepped to the front of their respective units, not one of them shouted an order. None were necessary – everyone knew what was being asked.

The silence was profound as the desperate plea from their beloved Commanding General hung in the cold morning air. Finally, one man – a carpenter from Philadelphia – stepped forward, his head bent downward, gazing at the ground. He momentarily looked back at the man that had been standing next to him, a mute request to step forward as well. After a moment's hesitation, the second man stepped forward as well.

And then another. And another.

Soon, entire ranks were stepping forward proudly, knowing that what they were committing to was dangerous, and perhaps even reckless. But they also knew somehow, that it was the right thing to do.

***

Douglas J. Shupinski

After a few minutes, all who were willing to stay had made their intentions clear. And while not everyone made the same fateful decision, at least enough men chose to remain with Washington to give the army a fighting chance to continue the war.

Washington had experienced the ultimate in emotional highs and lows in just the last few minutes, and it had taken its toll. Even as the realization that he had retained much of his army began to sink in, the utter fatigue he felt was like a huge weight on his chest. It was all he could do to ride slowly back to the front of the formation, pull himself up tall and straight in his saddle, and render a heartfelt salute to the soldiers of the Continental Army.

The soldiers themselves possessed a bit more energy than their commander. Their cheering could be clearly heard by the British pickets scouting along the Delaware River just a short distance away.

Major General Charles Cornwallis

Division Commander, British Army

Road from Princeton to Trenton, New Jersey

8:30 AM January 2, 1777

Major General Charles Cornwallis considered himself to be the epitome of a professional soldier, and very few of his peers would disagree with that assessment. Along with such a lofty self-image came the belief that nothing came before one's duty to the army, and Cornwallis had accepted that burden since joining the British military nearly twenty years earlier.

All that being said, Cornwallis was still stinging at the fact that he had been so close to returning home to see his wife after so much time away from her. Her letters indicated that her health was not good, and he worried incessantly about her. The ship that Cornwallis was scheduled to take back to England had literally been hours away from sailing when he had received the urgent message from General Howe to return to his headquarters.

There had been not a moment's hesitation in his response, and the men around him marveled at the fact that he was seemingly unfazed at the sudden change of plans. But in his heart, Cornwallis had been crushed. During his return trip to Howe's headquarters, he had cursed his Commanding General under his breath over and over again. What in God's name could be so damn important that would warrant this cruel twist of fate?

Upon his arrival at Howe's headquarters and subsequent briefing on the events that had occurred in Trenton, the Americans became the newest focus of hatred for Cornwallis. How dare these no account, poor excuses for soldiers disregard the accepted protocols of warfare by attacking in the dead of winter – the day after Christmas, no less! Where was their sense of decency and honor?

The only silver lining to this dismal black cloud was the fact that Howe had given Cornwallis the responsibility for tracking down the Americans and making them pay for their transgressions. Cornwallis had been given command of 8,000 of the best British soldiers in North America to accomplish his task, and he had wasted no time in preparing them for their mission.

Departing from the small college town of Princeton, New Jersey, Cornwallis had elected to leave several brigades behind in order to serve as a rearguard, as well as to protect his supply lines. To accomplish this vital task, he had placed three brigades under the command of Colonel Charles Mawhood, an experienced and capable officer. Mawhood had specific orders to hold his position on January 2nd, and then bring two of the three brigades to join Cornwallis in Trenton on the 3rd. Mawhood's total force remaining at Princeton totaled about 1,500 men.

Happily, General George Washington and the Continental Army had decided to do their part in helping Cornwallis fulfill his military responsibility. As opposed to remaining on the Pennsylvania side of the Delaware River – which would have caused Cornwallis some serious logistical problems – the Americans had conveniently crossed the river back to the New Jersey side. Furthermore, reports indicated that Washington had chosen to place his army along the Assunpink Creek, with his back to the river. This meant that, once the British had successfully attacked across the Assunpink Creek and engaged the Americans in their defensive positions, there would be nowhere for the Americans to retreat. Washington and his men would be completely and totally defeated, and the war would be over.

Perhaps then, Cornwallis could finally return to England and see his wife.

***

"Major Jennings, how far have we traveled?" Cornwallis asked impatiently. It had been hours since his command had departed Princeton enroute to the Trenton area, and the progress had been frustratingly slow to say the least. The fact that the recent snow had turned to rain had created a quagmire through which his army was forced to navigate.

"About four miles, sir," Jennings replied. Major Marcus Jennings was the engineering officer that had been assigned to travel with Cornwallis' command. "The roads are a mess, General, and the cannon are having a difficult time making their way. The men aren't faring much better either, sir."

"I have eyes, Major," Cornwallis replied testily. "I'm just as able as you to *see* the problem. What I want to know is, what are you going to *do* about it?"

Major Jennings, who was a mere twenty-seven years old, looked at least five years younger than that, and his wide-eyed reaction to Cornwallis' outburst did little to bolster any confidence Cornwallis might have had in the young officer's ability to have a positive impact on the situation.

"Well, sir, perhaps if we were to wrap the axles of the cannon carts with – "

The major's nervous response was cut short by the distinctive crack of a Pennsylvania long rifle being fired from the direction of a tree line about 400 yards away. The long rifle was a weapon that the British and Hessians had quickly learned to fear, as it was capable of killing a man at nearly three times the distance of the Brown Bess musket carried by the British army. Add to the equation that this rifle was usually in the hands of an American that had excellent marksmanship skills, and the result was a nightmare for the British and Hessians.

Almost at the same instant that the crack was heard, a mounted

Hessian jager tumbled from his horse and hit the snow-covered ground with a dull thud. The soldier's body gave one violent spasm, and the man was dead. The ever-widening ring of dark crimson snow around the body was yet another grim testament to the accuracy of these Americans and their weapons.

"Deploy into line of battle!" Cornwallis shouted unnecessarily, as those exact orders had already been given by the commanders of each of the regiments. As always, the soldiers responded immediately to the commands they were given, and within a minute or two there was a line of battle facing in the general direction of the wood line from which the shot had been heard.

In addition, the lead company commander had organized a reinforced unit of skirmishers which he quickly pushed out toward the woods. The fifty or so men advanced cautiously, lest they become the next victim to the enemy sniping. However, after several minutes had passed and the skirmishers had reached and entered the tree line, it was obvious that the Americans had abandoned their position.

A major rode up to Cornwallis, rendering a brief salute before he delivered his report.

"Sir, I wish to report that there are no enemy soldiers in the woods to our right front. Some of the advance scouts seem to think that it might have been a single man, sir, perhaps not even an enemy soldier. It certainly wouldn't be the first time that one of the locals took a shot —"

"It is not a local, Major," Cornwallis interrupted impatiently. "Find me a local that has a weapon with that range, who can also use it with enough skill to kill a man with a single shot at almost 400 yards. No, that was an enemy soldier, probably one of their men from Pennsylvania — damn!"

Cornwallis would never make the statement out loud, but he would have given his right arm for a group of men in his own army that had the same marksmanship skills as these backcountry bumpkins.

"Very well, then. Let's get the army back on the road immediately," Cornwallis ordered to his staff. "And Major," he added to the officer that had just addressed him, "move your men out an additional three to four hundred yards. I have no desire to have to experience this same episode again."

***

However, despite Cornwallis' efforts to expand the distance of his scouts from the main body, this first encounter with the Americans was to actually be the least costly. Time after time, the British were forced to move from a column formation into a line of battle to face an enemy attack. The difference was, the closer his army got to Trenton, the more coordinated and violent these attacks became. What had started with a single shot became volleys of rifle fire that claimed dozens of British and Hessian victims. The result was that hours and hours passed before Cornwallis and his army had finally reached Trenton. Pushing through the town, still a cluttered mess from the recent battle, the British continued to make their way to their objective which was the Delaware River and, ultimately, the Continental Army.

What had started as sporadic shots being fired perhaps thirty or forty minutes apart had now become an almost constant crackling of musket and rifle fire coming from the direction of the advance units of the British force. Cornwallis had been forced to abandon the relative speed of a column movement, and had resigned himself to keeping his army in a line of battle. While such a formation was inherently more effective against attack, it also produced agonizingly slow forward progress. By this time, it was already late afternoon, and the sun was moving relentlessly toward the horizon.

A young lieutenant rode up to Cornwallis and his staff, clearly intent on delivering a message to the Commanding General.

"What is it, what is it?" Cornwallis nearly shouted, his patience having long been exhausted.

"Sir, Colonel Chalmers request that you ride forward in order to observe the situation first hand," the Lieutenant stated nervously.

The young officer had good reason to be nervous. Such a request was unusual, to say the least, as it was accepted protocol that generals remained at a safe distance from the fighting in order to be better able to control their troops – and stay alive. But whatever faults Charles Cornwallis may have had as a leader, cowardice was not one of them.

"Very well, Lieutenant," Cornwallis replied without hesitation. "Lead the way."

***

As Cornwallis moved briskly forward, a small rise in the ground separated him from the advance elements of his army, thus preventing him from seeing exactly what was up ahead. Accompanied by most of his staff, Cornwallis wisely slowed his advance as he made his way up the slight incline to its crest.

Upon reaching the top of the rise, Cornwallis was greeted by the sight of the entire American army – in all its ragged glory – facing him just a few hundred yards away. The only terrain feature that separated the British from their enemy was a small stream known by the locals as the Assunpink Creek.

"Well, now," remarked Cornwallis, "it appears we have located our enemy at last."

General George Washington

Commanding General, Continental Army

Assunpink Creek, New Jersey

3:00 P.M. January 2, 1777

From his position on the southern side of the Assunpink Creek, General George Washington was afforded an excellent view of the situation that was quickly unfolding. The good news was that Colonel Hand, in charge of a number of American units, had done a superb job of slowing the advance of the enemy, such that Washington had been able to deploy his men and artillery into positions that were favorable for a strong defense. The left flank of the Continental Army was anchored firmly on the Delaware River, while the right flank ended at Phillips Ford along the Assunpink Creek.

The bad news was that the Americans were still outnumbered in both men and cannon, and it appeared as if the British were about to launch a serious attack on their position. In addition, many of the Americans that had been conducting the successful delaying action on the opposite side of the creek were now attempting to make their way to the American side. However, the single wooden bridge that was being used by these men was simply too small to accommodate a speedy withdrawal. The result was that confusion, combined with just a

Douglas J. Shupinski

bit of panic, had begun to spread amongst these retreating soldiers.

"Major Baylor, if you please," Washington addressed one of his staff officers. Baylor responded by immediately positioning himself and his mount next to his commander, coming to stiff attention in his saddle.

"I should wish to position myself at the edge of that small bridge, and I would appreciate your company," Washington stated flatly.

Major Baylor was taken slightly aback by Washington's order, as were several of the other staff officers within earshot.

"At the edge of the bridge, sir?" Baylor responded, unable to hide the surprise in his voice. "General Washington, not only is that bridge well within the range of the enemy artillery, but in a minute it will also be within range of musket fire from the British advance units!"

"Major Baylor," Washington replied calmly, "of course I have every desire to escape from this engagement in one piece, as I'm sure you do as well. But we cannot place our own personal safety above the safety of those men attempting to cross that bridge."

The stunned silence of Washington's staff was ample evidence to demonstrate that everyone believed that their Commanding General had lost his mind.

"Gentlemen, please," Washington chided his staff gently. "I plan to remain there only briefly until all of our men have safely crossed to this side of the creek. Also, I trust you will all contribute to the safety of my men and me by providing a suitable cover of artillery fire during the next few – shall we say – rather interesting minutes?"

***

Just as expected, the enemy wasted no time in launching a major assault on the bridge. A large number of Hessians pressed toward the bridge as the last Americans made their way across, their guttural German curses floating across the creek.

True to form, Washington made no show of yelling encouragement to his retreating troops, but rather sat calmly astride his horse at the southern edge of the bridge. The soldiers, seeing the composure of their commander, assumed that this display of confidence meant that all was under control, and a level of discipline and order returned to their ranks. A number of American cannon had begun firing over the heads of the Americans in an attempt to cover their retreat. While this produced the desired effect of slowing down the oncoming British, it also caused more than a small amount of consternation on the part of the retreating Americans, as shells whistled over their heads with an uncomfortable proximity.

As promised, within a few minutes all of the Americans had safely made it to their side of the creek, and Washington returned to his position on the heights overlooking his position. While not a single man said a word to their commander, the collective sigh of relief that escaped Washington's staff upon his safe return spoke volumes.

The sound of battle had increased dramatically in the last few minutes, as hundreds of Hessian soldiers attempted to seize the initiative in a determined assault on the bridge. American artillery responded by concentrating their fire on the bridge, no longer restrained by the need to avoid their own men. Thousands of muskets joined in the battle, and the attacking Hessians suddenly found themselves in an untenable situation of their own.

The fire from the Americans was deadly accurate, and within minutes the bridge was littered with the bodies of dead and dying soldiers. Those Hessian soldiers that attempted to continue the assault were forced to slow down in order to make their way over and through the bloody forms of their comrades, and this served to make them even better targets for the blistering fire coming from their flanks.

The sickening thud of musket balls impacted the bodies of the troops still attempting to assault the bridge, as well as those that had long since lost the capacity to feel pain and suffering, could be clearly heard over the cracks of muskets and explosions of artillery. Drawing from a pool of courage that the Americans were forced to admire, the enemy continued to advance, until it became obvious that this attack had no chance of success. Finally, the Hessians began withdrawing quickly, but in good order back to their starting positions, leaving the mangled and bloody bodies of dozens of their fellow soldiers scattered on the bridge or floating lazily in the waters of the creek.

Douglas J. Shupinski

To no one's particular surprise, this initial assault was followed almost immediately by another, this one by British light infantry. However, the lack of creativity in the attack was fatal, as these soldiers attempted the same frontal assault on the bridge.

The result was similar and predictable. Most of the British soldiers never even made it onto the bridge, while those few that bravely pushed forward onto the rickety wooden structure were brutally cut down by the hail of bullets and shells that rained down upon them.

An eerie silence suddenly enveloped the battlefield, as the Americans ceased their firing as the enemy retired to a safe distance away. Gazing out upon their handiwork, more than a few men were sickened by what they saw. Literally hundreds of bodies lay strewn across the length of the bridge, floating in the creek and littered on the far bank of the creek. The attack had been ill-advised, and many Americans sent up a silent prayer that, at least on this day, they had not been on the receiving end of the slaughter.

**

From his position above, Washington had watched the full horrible spectacle, forcing himself to try and remain devoid of any emotion. This was war, and anyone who possessed glorious beliefs about its nature had only to witness this event to have such naïve impressions wiped away forever.

Cheers of exhausted victory finally erupted from the American lines up and down the Assunpink Creek, and even Washington's staff let out their own hollers of joy.

Washington, however, remained characteristically silent. He whispered his own thanks to God that his army had survived yet again, but warned himself in a voice that no one else could hear.

"This fight is far from over," he said quietly. "Tomorrow, they will come again."

Major General Charles Cornwallis

Division Commander, British Army

Assunpink Creek, New Jersey

4:30 P.M. January 2, 1777

Colonel William Erskine, Cornwallis' Quartermaster General, was sitting astride his horse just to the right of Cornwallis. Erskine, his eyes gleaming with anticipation, spoke up.

"Sir, this is a most opportune situation. We have the Americans trapped between our forces and the Delaware River. We must but attack again immediately, and the war will be over within the hour!"

"Attack? At this time of day? You must be mad, Colonel!" spouted Major General James Grant, the second in command to Cornwallis. "Our men have marched all day, under constant attack from Rebel sharpshooters during most of that time. It is nearly sunset already, which means our troops will be attacking over unfamiliar ground in the dark. Not to mention the fact that, well – "

General Grant's voice trailed off.

"Not to mention what fact?" General Cornwallis asked.

"Well, sir," Grant continued cautiously, "the fact that we have launched two attacks which have demonstrated the strength of the enemy's position. That is, sir, at least in my humble opinion – with all due respect."

"Oh, for God's sake, relax General Grant," Cornwallis said with exasperation. "I expect you to give me your opinions, as well as yours, Colonel Erskine. And while I understand the enthusiasm for an attack, I will choose not to do so."

"But General Cornwallis," Erskine pushed, "we have the opportunity – "

"We have the opportunity to make yet another frontal assault against a well-entrenched enemy with an army that is exhausted. I will not needlessly throw away the lives of my men in an attack that can be executed with much greater coordination and zeal in a few hours' time," Cornwallis stated firmly. "And while I appreciate the fact that our slippery General Washington has managed to weasel his way out of similar situations in the past, this is not such a situation."

Erskine, still clearly disagreeing with his Commanding General, clapped his mouth shut and stared at the ground.

"Don't worry, gentlemen," Cornwallis said, addressing his entire staff. "We've got the old fox now. We'll go over and bag him in the morning."

***

The morning of January 3rd dawned with the promise that the unusual warm spell had come to an end. The British soldiers, having spent most of the previous night huddled in their tents attempting to fend off the cold night air, were just now beginning to arise.

General Cornwallis, on the other hand, emerged from his tent feeling fresh and rested from a surprisingly good night's sleep. It was the slumber of a man who knows that he will be accomplishing something truly great when he awakes.

The first hint that the day was not to go as Cornwallis had planned came when he was greeted by Colonel Chalmers, one of his Brigade Commanders, whose face appeared white and drawn.

"Colonel," Cornwallis greeted the officer, concerned by the man's appearance, "you look as if you are feeling rather poorly. Did you not sleep well?"

"Yes, sir, unfortunately I did sleep well. However, it appears that not everyone passed a restful night," the Colonel replied ominously.

Cornwallis, never a man to be trifled with, replied with obvious annoyance.

"Colonel, say what's on your mind, man. I have neither the time nor the patience to attempt to unravel your comments."

Chalmers appeared unfazed by the obvious reproach from Cornwallis. Instead, without a word he invited Cornwallis to travel up the same incline he had traversed the previous day, which had given him such a fine view of the enemy on the other side of the creek.

In spite of his desire to remain calm and collected, Cornwallis could not help but to move with unusual briskness up the slope to the top of the rise, where several British soldiers were already standing and looking toward the American position.

Arriving at the crest, Cornwallis gazed across the Assunpink Creek, and immediately felt as if he had been punched in the midsection.

The morning mist was still rising lazily off of the small stream, slightly obscuring the American position. But there was no question of what was there − or rather, what was not there. Where there had previously been thousands of enemy troops and dozens of cannon the previous evening, now there was nothing but nearly burned out campfires and empty defensive positions. The American position was completely abandoned.

Cornwallis could feel his face turning bright red, both from his anger as well as the embarrassment of having been outfoxed yet again by General George Washington. His anger suddenly boiled over into an outburst that was heard by anyone within a hundred yards.

"For God's sake! How could we have let the entire American Army simply slip away? That is absolutely unfathomable to me! I want to immediately see the officer who was in charge of our forward units last night − now!"

As several officers quickly moved off to execute their commander's orders, most of Cornwallis' staff had arrived on the scene, experiencing the same shock at what they saw across the creek.

Turning to face these officers, Cornwallis posed what he expected to be a rhetorical question.

"If Washington and his army are not where they are supposed to be, then where in God's name have they gone?"

All heads turned to face the north, as Cornwallis received a most disturbing answer to his query. Clearly audible in the still, morning air, was the sound of distant cannon fire. And it was coming from the direction of Princeton.

General George Washington

Commanding General, Continental Army

The Quaker Bridge Road, New Jersey

7:30 AM January 3, 1777

The men were exhausted, having had no opportunity to sleep the previous night. Instead, they had been on the road since just before midnight, marching almost ten miles by this time. It was a journey that had not been without incident. At one point, the army had been forced to construct their own bridge, the existing structure not being strong enough to hold the enormous weight of the American artillery. On still other occasions, the darkness and unfamiliar roads had caused units to lose their way, eventually having to double back in order to rejoin their comrades. This had added unnecessary distance and time to an already difficult march.

Despite these things, the Continental Army was in surprisingly good spirits. After all, hadn't they just pulled another rabbit out of the proverbial hat, escaping from beneath the very noses of the British?

Their nighttime escape away from the Assunpink Creek position had been accomplished using simple but daring tactics. First, the soldiers were ordered to secure any items on their person that might cause any sound. This included weapons, canteens, ammunition

Douglas J. Shupinski

pouches, and personal effects. Next, the large wheels of the artillery pieces were wrapped in rags to prevent the recognizable sound of their squeaking. Finally, Washington had detailed approximately five hundred New Jersey militia to remain behind until the last possible minute. Their job had been to insure the fires located throughout the American position were maintained, as well as providing a certain amount of movement that would have been natural from a large encampment.

The Continental Army had ultimately been successful at deceiving their enemy. Just as they had done in their retreat from Long Island, they had utilized the overconfidence of the British to their own advantage. But unlike the Long Island situation, this was not simply a move to escape the enemy and possible annihilation: this was a move to strike at the British at a different location – a location that was ripe for the picking.

***

General George Washington had called one of his typical councils of war the previous evening, posing the question to his generals on whether they should remain at their position along the Assunpink Creek, or make a move against the depleted British position at Princeton.

The discussion had been heated and divided. While everyone appreciated their current precarious position, several individuals believed it was even more dangerous to attempt an escape. To do so would mean turning their entire army to the east, and marching across the face of the enemy. If the British were to be alerted to their intentions, it meant that an enemy attack would come against their flank at a point when the Continental Army was not only spread out, but in motion and in no position to adequately defend themselves.

On the other hand, roughly 1,500 British soldiers had been left virtually stranded at Princeton. Cornwallis was banking on the fact that he had the Continental Army trapped along the Assunpink Creek; therefore there was no need to worry about his Princeton position. If the Americans could give the slip to the British and make their way to Princeton unopposed, the Continental Army of over 6,000 men would have a significant advantage of both numbers and surprise.

The scales were tipped in favor of a move against Princeton by two factors. First, several members of a New Jersey militia unit were farmers from the local area, and had indicated an ability to successfully move the army along several little known roads that led away from the Assunpink Creek and in the direction of Princeton. Even more significantly, the Americans were the fortunate beneficiary of a spy that was located inside the British positions at Princeton. This brave individual had taken it upon himself to draft a document that detailed the locations of the British forces in and around the small college town, including artillery placements, troop locations, and avenues of approach that appeared to be unguarded.

For Washington, this treasure trove of information, and the opportunity it presented, was simply too good to pass up.

Consulting with the local farmers who were part of his militia, Washington decided the best route was to skirt the extreme left of the British defenses, first moving through the nearby village of Sandtown, and eventually placing the army moving north on the Post Road. This road, a well-traveled and therefore solid thoroughfare, would allow the Americans to maintain a relatively steady pace for most of the twelve mile journey to Princeton.

Once the army had gotten within about two miles of their final destination, Washington had drafted orders for his men to separate into two wings. One of these wings of approximately 1,100 soldiers under Major General Nathaniel Greene, would move off to the left and take up a position on the main road that connected Trenton and Princeton, known as the Post Road.

Greene's mission was two-fold: First, he had been ordered to destroy the bridge where the Post Road crossed over the Stony Creek, thereby affording him and his men an excellent opportunity to conduct a delaying action against Cornwallis' army, should they react quickly and make their way to rescue their comrades in Princeton. And second, this same road would most likely be the route that the British in and around Princeton would use to attempt an escape, once they realized that they were under attack by the entire Continental Army.

The second wing was placed under the command of Major General Sullivan, and consisted of the bulk of the Continental army, numbering nearly 5,000 men. This wing would advance along the Saw Mill Road, which led directly into the town of Princeton. It was this force that was responsible for carrying out the main attack against the British garrison known to be located within the town.

***

Washington had chosen to take up a position at the head of Sullivan's main column, such that he was able to observe the movements and position of most of that group. Unfortunately, he realized immediately that he would be unable to affect the actions of Greene's force, as they almost immediately disappeared from view behind a group of trees when they made their left turn toward the Post Road. While Washington had an initial uneasy feeling about this, he rationalized that the main fight would be here with Sullivan: Greene would be no more than a side show, if even that.

Of greater concern was the fact that the Continental Army was almost two hours behind schedule. To Washington's frustration, this was a virtual replay of his plans for the Trenton attack. The plan, in both cases, had been to make the attack just before dawn when the darkness and sleepiness of the enemy pickets would be in his favor. And now in both cases, the attack would be made in broad daylight, with the enemy fully prepared and alert for any situation.

Calm down, Washington thought to himself. After all, hadn't the Trenton attack worked beautifully? Despite the hardships of the march, the severity of the weather, and the reactions of the enemy, the Americans had won a stunning victory. And this day would see the same result. He had to keep telling himself that. Was his confidence to waiver to even the slightest degree, his men would see the change in his demeanor; and their demeanor would change to reflect that of their Commanding General.

***

Looking ahead, General Washington could see an officer on horseback riding at a full gallop directly towards him. What in the name of God? The army was still nearly two miles from Princeton. What could possibly be so urgent that this man felt the need to ride like a madman? Washington felt just a twinge of annoyance, knowing that the men needed to remain calm and focused right now. Clearly, an unnecessary display of drama would in no way contribute to the men's ability to do so.

Douglas J. Shupinski

Map #4: The Battle of Princeton

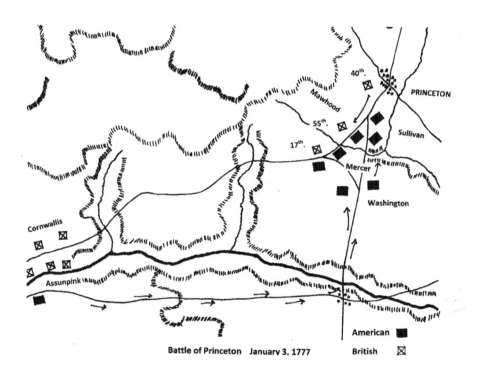

Battle of Princeton   January 3, 1777

American ▪
British ⊠

As the rider got closer, Washington could see that it was Major James Wilkinson, a staff officer assigned to one of the brigade commanders whose unit was located much further up the road. Arriving in a flurry of motion and barely controlled horse flesh, Major Wilkinson briskly saluted Washington.

"Sir, with General Sullivan's compliments, I beg to report that the British have been sighted!"

A mixture of alarm, excitement, and confusion washed over Washington, as he registered the man's report in his brain. Forcing himself to maintain an outward appearance of being calm, he responded to Wilkinson.

"Please elaborate, Major. When you say they have been sighted, where do you mean, and in what force?"

"Sir, I personally observed a force of at least five hundred enemy soldiers moving south out of Princeton along the Post Road," Wilkinson explained breathlessly. "And General Washington, several British cavalry scouts screening their movement clearly observed the rear of General Sullivan's column!"

Of course, Washington thought to himself, it made complete sense. General Cornwallis would likely have ordered reinforcements from Princeton to assist him in his attack on the American army where he believed they would be – along the Assunpink Creek. Washington was momentarily disgusted with himself. He had incorrectly assumed that the British troops in Princeton would simply remain in place, waiting for the eventual outcome of the battle further south. He had underestimated Cornwallis and his ability to bring his forces to bear at the most advantageous location. In outsmarting Cornwallis and escaping from Assunpink Creek, Washington had, in effect, outsmarted himself.

Washington was roused from his musings as Wilkinson continued to make his full report.

"Sir, after spotting General Sullivan's men the cavalry scouts made an immediate about face, and galloped back to the column of British

Douglas J. Shupinski

soldiers marching along the Post Road. I fear, sir that by now, the enemy knows of our presence."

"I have no doubt that you are correct, Major," Washington replied coldly. "The enemy is fully aware that we are advancing on him."

Pausing to consider the full ramifications of this news, Washington now addressed the most dangerous concern.

"The question is, Major, is General Greene aware of the situation?"

Washington realized that General Greene and his force of 1,100 men moving to the east, were almost certainly unaware that a sizable enemy force was about to come down directly upon them. And while Greene held the advantage in numbers, the element of surprise that the British would have could quite easily make up for that numerical superiority.

Major Wilkinson thought briefly before he responded.

"I would imagine that he is not, sir," Wilkinson replied. "I have been riding throughout the area, and General Greene's men have been moving through heavily wooded terrain. Most likely, sir, the British force would be screened from their view."

"Agreed, Major," Washington stated simply. "With all possible speed, you are to contact General Greene and make him aware of this development. And Major – "

Washington had stopped the man as he was about to dash off to carry out his orders.

"Sir?" Wilkinson asked.

"My orders to General Greene are to attack. Do you understand, Major? Attack the enemy!"

With just the hint of a smile and a crisp salute, Major Wilkinson galloped at breakneck speed off into the morning.

Lieutenant Colonel Charles Mawhood

Commanding Officer, 4ᵗʰ Brigade, British Army

Princeton, New Jersey

8:30 AM January 3, 1777

"What do you mean, you've spotted the enemy?" Lieutenant Colonel Charles Mawhood almost spat at the sergeant sitting in front of him astride his horse.

"Sir, the corporal and I," the young man stammered, nodding in the direction of a second frightened soldier, "were riding up along that ridge there, when we looked to our left, and there they were!"

Mawhood looked in the direction of the ridge being referred to by the man. It was less than a half mile away, to the left and rear of Mawhood's column.

Colonel Mawhood had received orders from General Cornwallis to leave a small force of men to fortify Princeton, and bring the rest of his command south to the Trenton area. Mawhood, whose 4ᵗʰ Brigade consisted of the 17ᵗʰ, 40ᵗʰ, and 55ᵗʰ regiments, had chosen to leave the 40ᵗʰ regiment in place within the town, departing just before daybreak with the 17ᵗʰ and 55ᵗʰ regiments moving south along the Princeton–Trenton road. Currently, the 17ᵗʰ regiment was riding in the lead, while Mawhood and the 55ᵗʰ regiment were a short distance behind.

Douglas F. Shupinski

"There *who* were, damn it?" Mawhood exclaimed, quickly losing his patience with this man. "Were they cavalry, were they militia? Who did you see?"

"No, sir, not cavalry. And not militia either, Colonel. These were Rebel infantry. Thousands of them!" the sergeant exclaimed, his eyes wide in amazement at what he had discovered. "They're marching directly toward Princeton, sir!"

Mawhood's eyes narrowed until they were mere slits in his face, peering menacingly at this man who had the temerity to deliver information that was almost certainly inaccurate. Charles Mawhood was no beginner at the business of war. He had served in the British military for nearly twenty five years, and had seen his share of combat both here in North America as well as back in Europe. It was this experience that convinced him that it simply wasn't possible for there to be thousands of enemy soldiers not more than a half a mile away.

Where could they have come from? The only sizable force of Americans was currently bottled up by General Cornwallis and the bulk of the army along the Assunpink Creek, which is exactly where Mawhood and his 700 men were headed. Had a second enemy force been anywhere in the area – even anywhere in New Jersey – the British would have known about it.

Unless, it dawned slowly on Mawhood, this wasn't a second enemy force, but the same one that was supposedly further south along the Assunpink Creek. Despite his combat experience, Mawhood felt a quick, cold shiver run up his spine.

Either way, Colonel Mawhood had no choice but to concentrate his command and turn it toward the enemy. No matter the size of the opposing force, his command was now strung out along the Post Road, and would be taken in the flank and the rear by any attack. This was not to mention the fact that Mawhood had posted just a single regiment in charge of Princeton. While he had no clear picture regarding the true size of this enemy force, he simply couldn't afford to take any chances.

"Captain Fitzpatrick, if you please," Mawhood ordered one of his officers. The man quickly appeared at his side.

"Captain, ride forward and instruct the lead regiment to conduct an about face and return to this position."

"Very well, sir," Fitzpatrick responded, and rode off to carry out his orders.

Mawhood turned to face Major Cornelius Cuyler, the commanding officer of the 55th regiment.

"Major Cuyler, you will move to the east and place two companies of your regiment along with your four guns on that small wooded rise just there," Mawhood stated briskly, pointing at a small hill covered by a group of trees. "From that position, you should be able to observe the entire area. The remainder of your regiment shall remain here under my command."

"Very well, sir, I'll see to it immediately," replied Cuyler.

"And Major," Mawhood continued, "I will need you to exercise appropriate discretion with respect to the employment of your men. From your position atop that knoll, you must determine whether you move your troops to reinforce the 42nd regiment within Princeton, or move to my aid here should an attack occur at this location. Is that clear?"

After just the slightest hesitation, Cuyler responded.

"Yes, sir, perfectly clear."

"Very well, then, Major. Make all speed in placing your troops as ordered."

Charles Mawhood had learned many years ago that while posting the necessary scouts to screen his army was valuable, the reports they delivered were notoriously inaccurate. Many of the men were young and inexperienced, and the heat of the moment often clouded their skills of observation.

"Captain Jennings," Mawhood ordered one of his staff officers riding next to him "if you please, send another scout in the direction of the reported enemy sighting."

"Yes, sir," Jennings responded.

"And Major," Mawhood stated, "insure you select your best man. I need a report that is both accurate and complete. Understand"

"I'll see to it, Colonel," Jennings assured his commander, and rode off to complete his assignment.

***

Douglas J. Shupinski

Within just a few minutes, Captain Jennings came riding up to Mawhood, accompanied by a middle aged sergeant on horseback as well. The look on both men's faces alerted Mawhood to the fact that the news they were delivering was not good. Jennings chose to ignore proper military protocol, which called for the senior officer to request a report. Instead, the young captain blurted out his news before he had even been properly acknowledged by Mawhood.

"Colonel, I beg your pardon, sir, but there are *two* enemy forces in our area!"

Mawhood forced himself to maintain his composure, aware that his staff and the surrounding troops of the 55th regiment had their eyes squarely on this unfolding scene.

"Explain yourself, Captain, and be specific," Mawhood ordered in a low, growling voice.

"Sir, there is definitely a large enemy force moving to our east along a road that leads to Princeton," Jennings stated slowly and deliberately, despite the fact that there was a noticeable quiver in his voice.

"Continue," Mawhood ordered, his eyes never leaving the young man's face.

"Sir, there is also another group of the enemy – not as large, sir – but a second unit located to our south. This second unit is moving directly towards us, sir!"

"Sergeant," Mawhood said, addressing the middle aged sergeant, "what would you estimate the size of these two forces to be?"

Unlike the young captain, this experienced soldier gave no indication of nervousness. This was a man that was no stranger to stressful situations such as this.

"Sir," the sergeant replied clearly and confidently, "I would estimate the size of the force moving along the road to be at least three to four thousand men. Perhaps more, as their column is stretched out and may include soldiers that are not visible."

"And the second group moving towards us?"

"A significantly smaller force, sir," replied the sergeant. "Probably not much more than two hundred men. But, sir, if I may?"

"Yes, yes, of course you may, sergeant, say what you have to say, man!" Mawhood ordered impatiently.

"Colonel, this second unit is only a few hundred yards away. They will be upon us almost immediately."

For the second time in the last few minutes, Charles Mawhood was compelled to draw upon his strength and experience in order to remain calm. Taking a deep breath, he shouted out his orders in a clear and deliberate manner, so that all of his officers would understand what they were to do in the next few crucial minutes.

"Light horse! You will move immediately to attack the smaller force of the enemy to our south. Move now!"

On that command, nearly a hundred mounted soldiers immediately rode off to confront the enemy.

"Major Watkins!" Mawhood continued, now addressing the commanding officer of the 17th regiment, "place your men, along with the companies of the 55th regiment, into line of battle and prepare to advance immediately behind the light horse!"

The British soldiers quickly formed themselves as ordered, and within two minutes had begun moving southward towards the enemy.

Meanwhile, the light horse quickly closed the distance between themselves and the enemy, sighting them suddenly when they had gotten a hundred yards or so away from them. The commander of the light horse, a young lieutenant barely twenty-five years old, issued the immediate order to let loose with a volley of musket fire.

Unfortunately, the relative disorganization caused by their dash to this location resulted in the volley being fired without sufficient time to take proper aim, and almost all of the bullets sailed harmlessly over the heads of the enemy.

But the main purpose of their mission had been accomplished. The Americans, momentarily shocked at the sudden arrival of an enemy force, stopped dead in their tracks, staring in open-mouthed surprise at the sight of their unexpected visitors. They had no way of knowing that this first sighting of their adversaries was only the beginning.

Brigadier General Hugh Mercer

Brigade Commander, Continental Army

Princeton, New Jersey

8:45 A.M. January 3, 1777

The sound of musket balls flying through the air in one's direction is rarely a pleasant sound. When it happens without ever having seen the men firing their muskets at you, it makes matters considerably worse.

General Hugh Mercer was leading a detachment of approximately 250 men, part of Sullivan's column that had been ordered to move off to the west while the remainder of the army continued toward Princeton. Mercer had been ordered by Sullivan to take the lead and move quickly toward the bridge that crossed the Stony Creek along the Post Road. Mercer had considered the possibility that he might encounter a small force of British soldiers when he approached the bridge. But he was nowhere near the bridge – where in God's name were these shots coming from?

***

Hugh Mercer was certainly no novice when it came to warfare. In fact, he was one of the few men who had had the opportunity to view it from two different perspectives.

Born in Scotland in 1726, young Hugh had chosen to educate himself in the practice of medicine, graduating as a doctor from the University of Aberdeen. After practicing his craft for several years in the civilian world, Mercer was drawn into the Jacobite Rebellion of 1745, serving as a surgeon's assistant in the service of the Jacobite army. Unfortunately, Mercer soon found himself on the wrong side of the battle lines, as the Jacobites were soundly defeated at the Battle of Culloden in 1746. As a result, Mercer was forced to flee his homeland, making his way to America and ultimately choosing to make Fredericksburg, Virginia his home.

The eruption of the French and Indian War between England and France soon drew Mercer back into the military, first as a doctor, but eventually as an infantry officer. Mercer quickly proved himself to be an extremely brave and capable combat officer, rising through the ranks to become a colonel, and receiving significant recognition for his exploits. It was also during this time period that Mercer became good friends with a young officer from Virginia named George Washington.

Hugh Mercer had long since proven his loyalty to the American cause. He had offered his services immediately upon the start of hostilities between Great Britain and the Colonies, and was always close to where the most dangerous action was taking place. Many of his subordinates believed too close.

***

"Company commanders!" Mercer shouted, seconds after the volley of musket balls had passed harmlessly over their heads, "form your men into a line of battle and prepare to advance on the enemy!"

Shouts from the officers resulted in a respectable line of battle formation within a minute or two, and the order to advance was immediately given. The ground they occupied – the property of a local farmer named William Clarke – was excellent for ease of movement of a body of troops, and the Americans quickly advanced, firing their weapons at the small force of cavalry ahead of them.

Douglas J. Shupinski

"Lieutenant!" Mercer called to one of his staff officers. "Inform Captain Neil that he is to place his two cannon on that small rise to our left. Tell him that he is to engage the enemy at the earliest opportunity."

"Very good, sir," the lieutenant replied, spurring his horse to deliver the message to the young artillery commander from New Jersey.

The British cavalry, realizing that they were no match for the numerically superior Americans coming directly towards them, immediately withdrew, firing a few defiant shots as they departed. Encouraged by their efforts, the Americans let out a cheer and continued advancing.

However, the cavalry had done their job. They had forced the Americans to stop and form their lines, giving their own infantry sufficient time to form their own line of defense. As Mercer's men continued forward, they found themselves facing a solid line of enemy infantry, reinforced by two cannon of their own.

Suddenly, the air was filled with deadly metal projectiles as the two forces fired furiously at one another. The Americans were compelled to halt their lines no more than forty yards from the British, exchanging volleys that started out as being poorly aimed, but eventually became deadly accurate. Soldiers on both sides suffered the terrible effects of the fight. Men doubled over in agony as a musket ball struck their body, or were hurled backwards by the tremendous force of a piece of canister from one of the artillery pieces.

Mercer was everywhere, shouting encouragement to his men, directing fire when he sensed a weak spot in the enemy line. Riding atop his large gray horse, he had an excellent view of the situation, in addition to being a visible display of confidence to his men.

"Aim low, gentlemen, aim low!" Mercer shouted, noting that most of the shots being fired toward his men were going over their heads. "Aim for the legs of those bastards!"

Almost without warning, a fierce growl emanated from the British line. Moving as one man in almost perfect unison, the enemy soldiers began advancing on the American position, bayonets leveled. Unfortunately, most of the Americans were armed with rifles, which caused two problems. First, their weapons took an inordinately long time to load as compared to a musket, and the short distance between themselves and the British would be closed very quickly. And second, it simply wasn't possible to fix a bayonet to the end of a rifle. These two facts put the Americans at a severe disadvantage in the hand to hand combat that was about to take place.

Captain John Fleming was the twenty-two year old commanding officer of the 1ˢᵗ Virginia Regiment, and the heir to a royal title and a significant fortune back in his home country of Scotland. Fleming stepped out in front of his men and shouted orders to dress their lines in preparation for the enemy attack. In that instant, a British musket ball struck Captain Fleming squarely in the chest, causing him to drop to his knees and clutch at the gaping wound to his body. The young man collapsed face forward onto the freezing ground, where he struggled to breath for several minutes before dying.

At that same time, another enemy musket ball struck the leg of General Mercer's horse, causing it to stumble and collapse to the ground. Mercer was able to leap away from the falling animal, and continued to shout orders and encouragement to his soldiers.

Colonel John Haslet had previously been the commanding officer of the 1ˢᵗ Delaware Regiment, a unit which had served admirably in several previous battles under his command. However, following the recent Battle of Trenton, almost all of the 1ˢᵗ Delaware had chosen to terminate their membership in the Continental Army as their enlistments expired. Colonel Haslet, at the enthusiastic behest of General Washington, had agreed to stay for one more fight before returning to his home in Delaware. As General Mercer rose to his feet after his fall from his horse, Haslet moved to his side.

"General Mercer, are you all right, sir?" Colonel Haslet inquired, genuine concern in his voice.

"Yes, yes, John, I'm fine," Mercer replied shaking his head to clear out the cobwebs caused by the fall. "However, I fear our line will not hold up to this assault. We must rally the men."

Looking around, it was apparent that the Americans were wavering. Some of the men had already started a headlong retreat in the direction of a nearby farmhouse, while others had begun a slower but steady movement in the same direction.

Colonel Haslet drew his sword from its scabbard, and raised it toward the sky.

"Americans! Form a line on me! Prepare to defend your freedom!"

A few scattered members of the command heeded the orders and began to move in the direction of Haslet, a growing sense of confidence in their actions. But this confidence was brutally shattered as Haslet was struck in the side of the head by a musket ball, the massive metal object causing a fountain of blood and brains to erupt from the man's skull.

Horrified at the sight of the fallen officer, the soldiers that had remained in place during the last few minutes began to panic, a reaction that was made worse by the British soldiers that were suddenly in and amongst the Americans, wielding their bayonets with ruthless efficiency.

General Mercer, momentarily stunned at having witnessed the violent death of his friend and subordinate, quickly gathered himself and attempted to take control of the situation. However, it was a situation that had deteriorated beyond the control of any one man. Despite his inability to rally his command, Mercer himself refused to give in to the panic. Slowly moving backwards, always facing the enemy, Mercer retreated until he was just a short distance from the nearby farmhouse.

It was at this point that Mercer took stock of his situation, and came to the rather uncomfortable realization that he was quite alone. Even worse was the fact that in virtually every direction he looked, he was faced with the sight of British soldiers quickly closing in on him. General Hugh Mercer was surrounded.

***

"Well, look what we 'ave here!" shouted one of the British soldiers as several of them began to cautiously circle Mercer. "I believe we may have cornered General Washington himself!"

"If this ain't General Washington," a sergeant mocked, "it sure as hell must be somebody else who thinks he's important! Now then, my raggedy Rebel friend," the sergeant continued, "give yourself up without a fight, and we'll see if we can resist the temptation to give you a nudge with these here bayonets."

A raucous laughter rose from the group of five or six British soldiers, but it was a laughter that lacked any humor. It was the sound of men who have crossed the line of being in control of their actions, and have fallen prey to the heat and violence of the battle. They had become nothing more than killing machines, and they were looking for any excuse to ply their deadly trade.

General Hugh Mercer, a man who cowered to no one, gave these men the excuse they were looking for. Raising his sword in defiance, Mercer glared at his enemies.

"Come and try, you red coated bastards," he hissed threw his clenched teeth. "I would be embarrassed to surrender to such a sorry excuse for soldiers."

With a roar of outrage, the group was suddenly upon him, some battering him with the butts of their muskets, while others attempted to drive their bayonets into his body. For a few seconds Mercer was able to parry away most of the blows, but quickly the lopsided numbers began to take their toll.

First one blow to the head from a musket butt, followed quickly by another, left Mercer stunned and defenseless, and he dropped helplessly to the ground. A combination of oncoming unconsciousness and blood flowing into his eyes caused his vision to blur, and the pain in his head was the worst he had ever experienced.

That was, at least, until the first bayonet was driven into his stomach. An explosion of agony burst through his midsection, which was followed by another explosion in his side, and then another. Mercer rolled over onto his stomach in a fruitless attempt to protect himself, but the attack only continued. What felt like two quick punches were delivered between his shoulder blades, but the searing pain that followed immediately afterward told him that these were two more bayonets entering his body.

Opening his eyes, Mercer caught a brief glimpse of the snow just inches from his face, his confused mind struggling to understand why it wasn't white, but a shocking crimson. This final view was quickly replaced by blackness, as unconsciousness mercifully overtook him.

Douglas J. Shupinski

Lieutenant Colonel Charles Mawhood

Commanding Officer, 4ᵗʰ Brigade, British Army

Princeton, New Jersey

8:50 A.M. January 3, 1777

Considering the situation had appeared dismal just a few minutes earlier, Colonel Mawhood was forced to admit that things had turned around quite nicely. Not only had his men responded quickly and calmly to the threats that had suddenly appeared, but they were actually driving the Americans back in almost complete confusion. It was this kind of performance in battle, Mawhood mused to himself, that got one promoted.

Riding forward nearly to the farthest point of the attack, Mawhood was somewhat shocked at the level of callous violence being displayed by his men. As he watched from atop his horse, he saw several of his soldiers drag a wounded Rebel officer out from underneath a cart, where the bleeding man had attempted to hide. Without even the slightest hesitation, the British soldiers proceeded to brutally drive their bayonets into the man's body, ceasing their barbaric assault only after they were satisfied that the man was quite dead.

In the center of a rather large field, Mawhood saw his men surround a high ranking enemy officer, and proceed to club and bayonet him until he too was apparently dead.

To the right of the British advance, Mawhood could see that the two American cannon had finally been silenced, after doing more than their share of damage to his men. Unfortunately, and inexplicably, several American artillerymen had actually been able to retreat with one of the cannon, despite the fact that dozens of British soldiers were swarming almost among them. The second cannon had been captured by Mawhood's men, the young Rebel officer that had been in command of the battery lying dead next to his gun, his body riddled with musket balls and bayonet wounds. As Mawhood watched, he was pleased to see that his men were in the process of turning the captured cannon around, pointing it in the direction of the retreating Americans.

Colonel Mawhood suddenly became aware of the fact that his men were scattered across the wide area of this local farm, their hectic advance having erased any semblance of coordination between units. This situation would make it more difficult for Mawhood to effectively continue his attack, and he decided to summon his aide, Captain Jennings, to begin the process of rectifying this situation. Looking around for the young officer, Mawhood was surprised to see the young man riding furiously in his direction, as if he had already anticipated Mawhood's orders.

As Jennings arrived by his side, Mawhood opened his mouth to issue the necessary orders. However, before he was able to utter a single word, he was shocked to be rudely preempted by Jennings.

"Colonel Mawhood, there are several hundred enemy soldiers coming from behind that slope there," Jennings stated breathlessly, pointing to a rise no more than a hundred yards to the north. "They will be in position to attack us within just a few minutes!"

Mawhood paused for a moment before responding.

"Are you sure it is only several hundred?" Mawhood asked.

"*Only* several hundred?" Jennings replied incredulously. "Sir, with all due respect, we only have several hundred men ourselves!"

"True enough, Captain, but we have several hundred professional British soldiers, and they have several hundred amateurs. The numbers may be even, Jennings, but the odds most certainly are not!"

Warming to the confidence being exuded by his commanding officer, Jennings' face broke into a wide smile.

"What are your orders, sir?" Jennings asked.

"Have all unit commanders assemble on my position and form into a line of battle," Mawhood commanded, his own devilish smile forming. "It's time to finish this attack on our American friends."

***

With their characteristic speed and efficiency, most of Mawhood's command was soon organized into a single force, having formed a line of battle approximately two hundred yards from the farmhouse that sat at the center of the battle.

While a few dozen enemy soldiers had maintained their positions and continued to fire annoying shots at the British, most of the Americans had already made a hasty retreat back up the rise in the direction of the farmhouse. Mawhood planned to take full advantage of this fact. If his men were able to generate enough panic and confusion, the retreating Americans would run straight into the ranks of the other enemy soldiers on the other side of the slope to his direct front. Mawhood knew from previous combat experience that nothing causes greater panic than existing panic.

"Company commanders!" Mawhood shouted above the sporadic firing, "prepare to advance on the enemy! We must drive them straight up and beyond the slope of that rise to our front!"

All eyes looked instinctively toward the objective, and with the shout of just a few brief commands, the powerful crimson line began moving forward.

As Mawhood had hoped, this coordinated attack had the almost immediate effect of causing the remaining enemy troops to turn and run back up the slope, realizing they were both outnumbered and outclassed. Just as fortuitously, as these retreating men reached the top of the rise, they met the oncoming American reinforcements advancing from the opposite direction.

The result was that the American reinforcements stopped dead in their tracks, their line wavering with uncertainty. It was obvious to Mawhood that these newly arrived enemy soldiers were novices, this fact demonstrated by their inability to maintain even the slightest level of discipline in the face of adversity.

Mawhood ordered his men to come to a temporary halt just long enough to aim and fire a volley into the enemy lines. This added effect further unnerved the Americans, and the lines of newly arriving troops began to break apart and join the retreat.

"Forward, men, forward!" Mawhood shouted, and a roar of approval came from the ranks of his men. Sweeping forward, their progress seemingly unstoppable, Mawhood once again experienced the deep exhilaration he always felt when he was part of winning a battle.

It was a perfect moment, forever captured in the memory of Lieutenant Colonel Charles Mawhood. He and his men were just a few yards away from victory and glory, and nothing could deny them their reward.

Waving his sword and encouraging his men forward, Mawhood was suddenly aware of the presence of an officer on horseback riding in and amongst the ranks of the Americans. He was shouting and cursing at his men, ordering them back into line. He was urging them to hold their positions and face the enemy coming at them up the slight rise.

And the Americans were beginning to listen.

General George Washington

Commanding General, Continental Army

Princeton, New Jersey

9:00 AM, January 3, 1777

After having ordered General Greene's column to attack the British, General Washington had chosen to remain at the head of General Sullivan's main column of nearly 6,000 soldiers. After all, thought Washington, Greene has 1,500 men and, according to the report he had received, the enemy force was no more than five hundred strong. The main objective remained the town of Princeton, and any enemy presence that was located there.

However, after hearing a few sporadic musket shots coming from the direction of General Greene's column, Washington began to doubt his assessment of the situation. When the deep-throated reports of cannon were added to the sounds of the battle, Washington knew a major engagement was occurring to his rear. Washington immediately turned his horse around to face the sound of the fight, and issued orders to Major Kessner, one of his nearby aides.

"Major, have Colonel Hand's Pennsylvanian's follow behind me, as well as the Virginia Continentals," Washington ordered, referring to two units that had been marching just behind him toward Princeton.

"Inform the respective commanding officers that they are to make all possible speed in the direction of the firing behind us. Is that clear, Major?"

Kessner, a completely competent albeit sometimes overly enthusiastic young officer, saluted his Commanding General and replied with complete confidence in his voice.

"Your orders are completely clear, General Washington," Kessner replied. "The Pennsylvanians and Virginians will be right on your heels, sir!"

Washington smiled slightly at the man's youthful exuberance, and shouted to his staff.

"Gentlemen, if you please! We have a battle to fight!"

Washington spurred his horse and galloped off to the southwest toward the growing din of the battle, a half dozen of his staff officers making every effort to keep up.

***

As Washington came over a slight rise in the ground, he was greeted by the sight of hundreds of American soldiers streaming back across an open field. Many of the men were limping noticeably, or had bloody bandages wrapped around various parts of their bodies. Following these men at a close distance was a dangerously solid line of British infantry, clearly intent on closing on and destroying the Rebels that had been foolish enough to tickle the proverbial tiger's tail.

Washington sighted Lieutenant Colonel John Cadwalader, the commanding officer of the Philadelphia Associators. The Associators were a militia unit from Philadelphia with a proud history, having been established by Benjamin Franklin in 1747. However, unless things were turned around quickly, today would definitely not contribute to the pride of that unit, as many of these Associators were part of the soldiers now retreating from the British assault. Cadwalader was clearly attempting to rally his men, shouting and cursing at them as they moved past.

"Colonel Cadwalader!" Washington called out. Cadwalader,

momentarily stunned at the sight of the Commanding General so close to the fight, quickly gathered himself and approached Washington.

"General Washington, with all due respect I would suggest that you remove yourself to a somewhat safer position, sir! As you can see, the enemy is but a few hundred yards behind us, and closing that distance rather quickly."

"Colonel, I appreciate your concern, but if it's all the same to you I prefer to stay where I am and do my part in winning this battle," Washington replied matter of factly. "Of course, I have no intention of doing so alone. As you can see, I have brought with me a number of individuals whom I believe will be of significant assistance."

Looking past Washington astride his horse, Cadwalader could see the Virginia Continentals and Hand's Pennsylvanians running at full speed in their direction. For the first time since the start of the fight, Cadwalader felt a sense of confidence at the sight of these veteran soldiers.

"Colonel Cadwalader, place yourself on the back side of that ridge," Washington ordered, referring to the rise that he himself had just crossed. "It appears as if your men, as well as several other units of our army, are heading for the safety of that rear slope. Rally as many troops as you can, and prepare to launch a counterattack against the enemy."

"Immediately, sir!" Cadwalader replied, snapping a hasty salute as he made a beeline for his designated position.

Washington realized that he was playing a dangerous game in which the British were not the only enemy. The other enemy was time. Unless Colonel Cadwalader was given a few minutes to rally the fleeing troops, the attacking British would simply roll right through them and turn Washington's Grand Plan into a rout. The problem was, Washington had virtually no troops with which to slow the assault of the enemy.

Despite this fact, the British appeared to have halted their advance for some inexplicable reason, although the volume on the battlefield had not decreased. Muskets continued to be fired, and cannon continued to roar. It was this last realization that caused Washington to look to his left toward a small rise about one hundred yards away. What he saw were two American cannon, completely alone on a vast open field, firing feverishly in the direction of the enemy advance.

The cannon were under the command of Captain John Moulder of the 2nd Company of the Philadelphia Associators, and they were performing in a manner that would have made Benjamin Franklin burst with pride. The two pieces were firing grapeshot – a shell consisting of dozens of small, lethal metal balls that acted like a giant shotgun – with such speed and accuracy that it had forced the British to not only come to a halt, but begin moving their lines to their left in order to get out of range of the American artillery.

This was the window of opportunity that Washington had been looking for. Turning and riding back to the ridge where he had ordered Colonel Cadwalader to organize his men, Washington was relieved to see that the colonel had done exactly that. In addition, the Virginia Continentals and Colonel Hand's Pennsylvanians had formed a line on the right side of the ridge, and were now being joined by the 350 soldiers made up of several New England units from New Hampshire, Rhode Island, and Massachusetts under the command of Colonel Daniel Hitchcock.

The table was set. Washington needed to coordinate the attacks of the newly arrived units on the right with the re-formed Philadelphia Associators on the left. If he was able to do so, the British would find themselves outflanked and outnumbered – a bad combination for any army.

First, Washington sent orders off to Colonels Hand and Hitchcock on the right to watch for the advance to their left. When that advance began, they were to immediately initiate their own attack. Second, Washington began issuing the necessary commands to organize the remnants of Mercer's and Cadwalader's commands here on the left, fully realizing that these men had just had a most unnerving experience.

These men that now surrounded Washington were not only

Douglas J. Shupinski

militia, but inexperienced militia. Most of them had never before been in a battle, and even the most basic understanding of military maneuvers was foreign to them. It was a desperate situation, which called for desperate measures.

"Pennsylvanians!" Washington shouted into the cold morning air, his breath billowing out as a cloud of steam, "Form your lines on me! Look at our numbers! The enemy is but a few, and now is the time to defeat them!"

A ragged shout of acknowledgement emanated from the scattered group, and the men began to organize themselves on either side of Washington. Within minutes, a somewhat solid line had been formed, and Washington prepared to issue his next set of commands. It was at this point that Colonel Cadwalader rode up next to Washington, demonstrating a most agitated demeanor.

"Colonel, I am impressed at your ability to rally these men," Washington complimented Cadwalader. "I would be most pleased to have you join me just now."

"Join you, sir?" Cadwalader almost gasped, his agitation heightened even more. "General Washington, surely you don't intend to lead the attack directly at the enemy? It is, sir, a most dangerous situation!"

Washington turned and faced Cadwalader, a look of mild confusion on his face.

"Dangerous, Colonel?" Washington asked. "Of course it is dangerous. And it is for that exact reason that I must lead these men. How can I possibly ask them to do something that I would not do myself?"

Turning in his saddle to face the militia surrounding him, Washington bellowed out the order to initiate the assault.

"Gentlemen, prepare to attack! But hold your fire until I give the order! Forward... march!"

With surprising confidence, the line lurched forward, dragged relentlessly by the iron will of the man in front of them. A moment later, the American line on the right side of the ridge began their movement forward as well, exactly as Washington had ordered. The result was an impressive, imposing force of several thousand men advancing on a front hundreds of yards wide. Most importantly, this frontage extended beyond both flanks of the British, placing them in a most precarious position.

***

On the American left, Washington continued to ride in front of the Pennsylvania militia, alternating his constant stream of orders between encouragements to keep moving forward, and telling the men to hold their fire. Looking to his front, Washington could see that the British had formed a battle line in preparation for firing a volley.

Judging the distance between the Americans and the enemy to be no more than thirty or forty yards, Washington located himself directly between the two battle lines and shouted out his next order.

"Halt! Prepare to fire — fire!"

At almost the exact moment, the two lines facing one another let loose with volleys of musket fire that shattered the air. Huge clouds of smoke billowed from the weapons, obscuring any ability of each side to view the effects of their respective volleys.

Within each line, however, the effects were as predictable and horrendous as they always were. Due to the relative inaccuracy of the muskets, even at this brutally short range, most of the men on each side escaped without harm. However, several unlucky men dropped to the ground in agony as the heavy metal balls found their mark.

A British private clutched desperately at his throat as a bullet turned his windpipe into a mangled mess. He survived for just a minute or so before the combination of a loss of blood and suffocation ended his life. The man next to him fared slightly better as his lower arm literally shattered from the impact of an American musket ball. If he was lucky enough to survive the likely infection that might result, he would only suffer the indignity of having one arm for the rest of his life.

Within the American lines, a young teenage boy who had been a carpenter's apprentice until just a few weeks ago, suddenly felt as if he had been punched in the stomach. Looking down in confusion and disbelief, he was horrified to see pieces of his intestine protruding from a gaping hole in his midsection. He dropped to the ground, curling into a fetal position in a worthless attempt to hold himself together. Within a minute or two he died, sobbing uncontrollably for his mother to come and tend to his wound.

Sitting astride his horse just off to the right of, and slightly behind the American line, Colonel Cadwalader was in the perfect position to watch as Washington placed himself directly in the line of fire. He looked on as Washington issued commands and, in the next instant, disappeared in the haze of smoke created by the opposing forces.

Cadwalader had feared this moment, even more than the possibility of his own death. He knew what Washington meant to this army and to this Cause, and to have him cut down at such a critical time was unthinkable. Refusing to witness the demise of his general, Cadwalader lowered his head and turned away from the scene.

As the crash of the volley died away, Cadwalader forced himself to look back between the opposing lines to the spot where Washington had been. Gradually, the smoke began to clear, but it was the sound of his voice that reached Cadwalader first.

"Reload men, reload!" Washington's voice boomed. "Prepare for your next volley! We will have our victory today!"

Staring in disbelief, Cadwalader saw that Washington was still sitting proudly astride his horse, without even an apparent scratch. Whether this fact was a testament either to the man's good fortune, or simply a poorly aimed volley by the British mattered not – General George Washington, it would appear, would live to fight another day.

***

The Commanding General of the Continental Army would not be the only one to fight another day. The Continental Army itself was on the verge of pulling off yet another surprise victory that would insure its existence, at least for the time being.

Washington continued to push the Pennsylvania militia inexorably forward, the men showed outstanding discipline and fighting spirit. They continued firing coordinated and well-aimed volleys into the ranks of the enemy, eventually forcing the British to retreat. While the British retired in good order — as they almost always did — they finally headed southwest across the Post Road bridge to relative safety. Regardless, they were out of the battle, leaving the remaining British troops in a completely untenable position.

On the right, the uncharacteristic numerical superiority enjoyed by the Americans was quickly beginning to take its toll on the enemy. The British made several valiant attempts to maintain their position, but it soon became apparent that these efforts would be useless. Colonels Hand and Hitchcock drove their men forward pressing on the left flank of the British, while the victorious men of the Pennsylvania militia soon added their numbers onto the right flank of the beleaguered enemy.

Seeing no other option, the commander of the nearly surrounded British troops ordered his men to retreat into the town of Princeton. While most made their escape northward through the town, some of them eventually found their way to the protection of Nassau Hall, one of the main buildings of Princeton College. However, what was initially seen as a stronghold quickly became a prison, as the building was surrounded by the pursuing Americans.

Several cannon of the Continental Army soon arrived on the scene and began pounding away at Nassau Hall and the British troops trapped inside. At first, the British knocked out several of the windows of the building and began peppering the Americans with musket fire. But a well-aimed cannon ball traveled through one of these windows and neatly decapitated a portrait of King George II that had been hung by local Tories on one of the walls of the main room. Many of the British soldiers considered this a foreboding omen, and it destroyed their resolve.

Within a few minutes, the British soldiers and their officers determined that playing the role of being fish in a barrel was the worst of their options, and several white handkerchiefs tied to muskets appeared through the windows of the building.

***

The Battle of Princeton was over. General George Washington had accomplished the amazing feat of slipping away from a numerically superior British force, marching sixteen miles north to Princeton, and surprising and defeating the British contingent that had been left there by General Charles Cornwallis as an ostensible reserve.

This marked the conclusion of ten of the most amazing days in the history of warfare. A ragtag group of citizen soldiers had outmaneuvered, outmarched, and outfought the most powerful army on earth, defeating them not once, but twice during that timeframe.

For his part, General George Washington knew that this in no way marked an end to the war. More victories, and more sacrifice would be required to bring about that desired conclusion. But at the very least, he appreciated the fact that these ten days would mark the emergence of the Continental Army as a viable force, and insured the continuing struggle for American independence.

General George Washington

Commanding General, Continental Army

Morristown, New Jersey

January 19, 1777

George Washington sat at a desk in the library of a large house he had appropriated as his headquarters near the center of the small town of Morristown, New Jersey. It was a setting that suited Washington — both the comfortable dwelling, as well as the surrounding area. Morristown was situated such that any enemy force that was determined to mount an attack against the Continental Army would be forced to make its way through a series of narrow passages formed by the surrounding mountainous terrain. It was a perfect defensive position, and its strength allowed both he and his army to breathe a welcome sigh of relief.

This respite for the Americans following weeks of marching and fighting had come none too soon. Just that morning, the Continental Army reached its lowest point in terms of experienced soldiers, as fewer than 1,000 veterans were reported present for duty. The remainder of Washington's exhausted force consisted of militia and new recruits.

That was the bad news. The good news was that the victories at Trenton and Princeton had created a modest groundswell of patriotism,

Douglas J. Shupinski

and while a few hundred new recruits began to straggle into the American camp, word was received that numerous other units were forming throughout the colonies, preparing themselves to join the army at Morristown in the coming months. Admittedly, the growth and preparation of the army would be slow, but at least the momentum was finally moving in the right direction.

Washington intended to fully capitalize on this momentum. First, he was insisting that all new recruits be enlisted for a term of three years, such that the constant shadow of terminating enlistments was removed for the foreseeable future. And second, regional allegiances would be at least somewhat decreased by the gradual elimination of unit identification by colony. In its place, units would be identified as simply being a part of the Continental Army.

***

A light knock on the door caused Washington to look up from the letter he had been writing to the Continental Congress. It was yet another in the seemingly endless series of correspondence that he dispatched almost daily, begging for additional supplies, money, and troops – none of which seemed to appear to the degree that he required. Despite the fact that he had issued orders not to be disturbed while he completed these distasteful duties, he was forced to acknowledge a wave of relief at being given an excuse to stop, if only for a few minutes.

"Enter," Washington ordered.

The door opened slowly, almost tentatively, and General Nathaniel Greene poked his head cautiously into the room.

"General Washington, I beg your pardon with my sincere apologies. Your staff informed me repeatedly of your orders to not be disturbed, but I must admit to having been most insistent."

Washington found himself unable to suppress a smile at Greene's characteristic candor, and he waved the man into the room.

"Please, General Greene," Washington said reassuringly, "I would truly be pleased to share your company just now. Please, have a seat."

Greene moved quickly across the room, despite the fact that he constantly displayed a noticeable limp. This physical limitation, to the surprise of many, had never had even the slightest effect on his ability to be present everywhere on the battlefield at the most critical times. Greene carefully lowered himself into the chair sitting opposite Washington.

Several awkward seconds passed as the two men looked at one another, one unsure of the nature of the visit, the other unsure as to how to best proceed. Finally, Washington broke the silence.

"To what do I owe the honor of your visit, General?"

Greene shifted uncomfortably in his chair, his eyes now looking down at his hat that he held in his lap. Looking up, his eyes blazed with emotion as he addressed his commander.

"Sir, I am painfully aware of the shortcomings of the past, as well as the missed opportunities that there have been. I fully appreciate the consequences that this army has experienced as a result."

At first, Washington assumed that Greene was referring to the army in general, but he quickly realized that Greene was speaking specifically about himself.

"General Greene," Washington replied carefully, "the things that we *all* have done in the past are just that – in the past. What is now of critical importance is how we perform in the future."

"Yes, sir!" Greene replied with enthusiasm, "that is true. That is exactly why I was so insistent on speaking with you now. I pride myself in my ability to learn from my mistakes, and I believe with all my heart that this is exactly the characteristic that will insure the ultimate victory of this army and of this country!"

Washington looked at Greene carefully, still unsure of the meaning of the man's words.

"What are you trying to say, General Greene?"

"General Washington, I have never believed in anything so completely as I believe in what this army is trying to accomplish. And I request the opportunity to remain a part of this army, in whatever capacity you deem appropriate. And if that means picking up a rifle and serving in the ranks – "

Douglas J. Shupinski

Greene paused, took a deep breath and looked at Washington before continuing.

"Then, sir, I promise that you would have found yourself a soldier whose loyalty and dedication would be beyond reproach."

Washington rose slowly from his chair and walked around the desk until he was standing next to Greene. Placing his hand on the young general's shoulder, he spoke with barely contained emotion.

"Nathaniel," Washington began, allowing himself the uncommon luxury of addressing one of his officers informally, "During this war, I have already had, and will continue to have, the honor of serving with some of the best soldiers in the world. What I need now, more than anything, are some of the best *leaders* in the world. And you, sir, have demonstrated every indication that you are such a leader."

Greene looked up at Washington, genuine gratitude in his eyes. He had arrived in this room unsure of his future with the army. Now he knew that not only was his future assured, but so was that of the army itself.

"Now, my insistent General," Washington said with a smile, "I must return to my work. And you to yours."

Greene rose from his chair, brought himself to rigid attention, and saluted Washington. Turning smartly on his heel, Greene strode confidently to the door and out of the room, his ubiquitous limp somehow having disappeared.

BLACK ROSE
writing™

CPSIA information can be obtained at www.ICGtesting.com
Printed in the USA
BVOW08s0924200916

462679BV00002B/2/P